John Lawrance studied Law at Queen Mary, London, before qualifying as a solicitor. He lives in Enfield with his wife and their Labrador called Victor. In his youth, he was on the ground-staff at Lord's as an M.C.C. Young Professional. A Spurs fan and season ticket holder, he enjoys watching matches with his son and daughter. At the age of seventy-one, *Hosting Andrew* is his first novel.

HOSTING ANDREW

JOHN LAWRANCE

The Book Guild Ltd

First published in Great Britain in 2022 by
The Book Guild Ltd
Unit E2 Airfield Business Park,
Harrison Road, Market Harborough,
Leicestershire. LE16 7UL
Tel: 0116 2792299
www.bookguild.co.uk
Email: info@bookguild.co.uk
Twitter: @bookguild

Typeset in 11pt Adobe Garamond Pro

Printed and bound in the UK by TJ Books LTD, Padstow, Cornwall

ISBN 978 1915122 711

British Library Cataloguing in Publication Data.
A catalogue record for this book is available from the British Library.

For Sally and my wonderful family.

"Memory is the scribe of the soul"
Aristotle

"I can't go back to yesterday because
I was a different person then"
Alice's Adventures in Wonderland
Lewis Carroll

CHAPTER 1

FRIDAY 17TH JULY

My name is Andrew Soulsby and I have been dead for eleven days.

I am on a balcony gazing down upon an expansive garden. Two gnarled cypress trees, tall and slender, could be pointing at a Mediterranean sky, and perfectly manicured lawns, bordered by a riot of mature shrubs, drift towards undulating country fields beyond the distant boundary hedge. It is difficult to comprehend that this is merely twelve miles from the centre of London.

Helen cooked my breakfast this morning: she thinks I am her husband. Burnt toast and curling, black rashers of bacon accompanying solid egg yolks suggest the kitchen as a place of endeavour may not be her spiritual home.

Since I returned from the hospital ten days ago, she has left me to fend for myself most of the time. I have been grateful because this ageing body is pumped with sexual libido. I struggle to control the urges as I must, for it is inconceivable that I should ever cheat on my wife. If I did, this would be a betrayal of our love and family, all we have built over the last twenty-two years.

1

Fortunately, there has been no embarrassment, no strong test to resist temptation. Helen and her husband appear to lead entirely independent lives. They have separate bedrooms within this palatial house, near the golf club in Hadley Wood, a wealthy North London suburb adjoining the Metropolitan Green Belt. By coincidence, it is only a few miles from my own home in Enfield, but there is a stark contrast between that modest Victorian semi with its small, neglected garden and this opulent, detached mansion. It is exemplified by the old, grey BMW 520 saloon, no doubt still languishing on the small drive at the front of my house, and the new Bentley Flying Spur, a gleaming metallic blue, parked outside on the sweeping carriage drive, in perfect harmony to complement the massive stone pillars at the grand entrance porch.

In the cavernous dressing room which adjoins one side of the bedroom behind me, adjacent to the en suite and whirlpool bathtub, I have found a fine black suit boasting smooth, red silk lining. The tailor's name and address are sewn within, Savile Row, and there is a silk black tie and designer black brogues. This afternoon I shall go to my own funeral service before I watch them bury me under six feet of London clay.

CHAPTER 2

ELEVEN DAYS EARLIER: MONDAY 6TH JULY

"Start counting down from twenty, please, Andrew."

What choice do I have as Joe Peng's masked face peers over my helpless body?

"Twenty, nineteen, eighteen, seventeen…" oblivion.

***

"It's all over, pet; your operation is done and all successful." The soft voice of a woman with a lilting Welsh accent is in my head, waking me from a blackness, devoid of dreams; and I become aware of how my existence had been turned off in an instant, like the flick of a switch extinguishing bright light.

I open my eyes to a nurse's smiling face and feel elation to be alive. Then I notice that my throat feels sore. I look round the room. It seems too small and the en suite is in the wrong place. The curtains

3

are pulled back, and through the reinforced window that reaches to the floor I can no longer see blocks of expensive flats, only the top of a tall tree against puffy white cloud.

"Where is my family: my wife Cathy, my son Geoff and daughter Lucy?" I say to the nurse. "They had promised to be waiting for me when I came round. And why have you brought me back to a different room?"

"It's not uncommon to be all confused after an anaesthetic," the nurse says, a frown of concern on her kindly face. "Your consultant, Ms Simms, has had to rush off, something urgent, but Mr Whicher – he was your anaesthetist – will be in to see you soon."

"I don't recognise those names. Has there been a terrible mistake? My surgeon was Peter Cheung. Please, nurse, fetch him immediately!"

She bites her bottom lip and says, in a faltering voice, "I'll go to fetch your wife," as she walks briskly from the room.

I am alone, bewildered and frightened. The door has been left open and I glimpse part of a corridor. I can hear constant chatter in the distance, probably from a nurses' station. Voices are raised intermittently and there is the occasional burst of laughter. As I am trying, unsuccessfully, to hear what they are talking about, my anticipation is raised by approaching footfall, but it passes my door and fades away. Where is Cathy? The pain in my throat is getting worse, and my heart pounds to escape its ribcage.

I am not sure how much time elapses before I hear the firm clunk of female heels, and a tall, glamorous woman, maybe in her late forties, appears in the doorway. She is staring at me, eyebrows raised, faint pink lipstick pouting in an accusing half-smile.

"Now, my darling, what's all this self-important fuss you're making? You've scared that lovely little nurse half to death."

She stands still, a willowy blonde, perfectly styled hair softly curling around her neck to frame a face which cannot disguise a few wrinkles but still conveys an impression of classical elegance. Slowly, she moves towards me, a languid, ageing beauty.

"Anyone would think you'd had major surgery, not just a few little snips in your throat to protect that pompous deep voice. They say your throat will probably be sore, but really, you are such a baby, my dear. What would all of your bigwig clients say if they could see you now?"

She speaks with what seems to be amused detachment rather than malice. Her plunging red dress looks expensive and highlights obvious breast implants. The letter 'H' is tattooed above a gold ankle chain and high-heeled red sandals. As she approaches, I am engulfed with the aroma of agent provocateur, the perfume Lucy often wears. Gold disc earrings the size of ten-pence coins dangle close to me as she bobs down quickly with an air kiss before drawing up straight at the side of my bed.

"They're quite happy with you – just keeping you in overnight to be on the safe side. I'll come back tomorrow morning to drive you home, but I'm leaving now; another rehearsal at the theatre, I'm afraid." She turns to go, then stops momentarily at the door to add, "Do be good, my love; you're not play-acting in court here, so no more attention-seeking and silly practical jokes about mix-ups with the nurse, poor little mite. I'm sure they'll give you more painkillers for your sore throat."

This woman, who acts as though I am her husband, sounds like a reproachful mother gently admonishing a mischievous child. I find myself mumbling, "But I don't understand… I don't know you, do I?" She is not listening, though, and with her posh voice still resonating inside my head, I watch her blow another air kiss and disappear.

Why wasn't she shocked to find another man presenting as her husband? A sudden image flashes into my mind: Joe Peng is at my side with Peter Cheung ready to drill into my skull, all of which means there has been no mix-up with patient records, no terrible mistake transposing the operations to be performed on two men.

So, what does it mean? Am I still under, experiencing a vivid and macabre dream as I drift away from the grip of the anaesthetic drugs? I screw my eyes shut, pinch my nose, then open my eyes to the same reality for confirmation of what, in honesty, I already knew: this is no dream. With a rising panic, I try to ease myself up in the bed, throwing back the sheet and blanket. It is more difficult than I expect – I feel so tired and heavy – and in the process I accidently pull off the probe attached to my middle finger, which sets off the continuous beep of an alarm. My legs and abdomen are still covered, but the top half of me is exposed, 'dressed' only in a short-sleeved and thin hospital gown.

I tear it away and examine, with incredulity, a broad chest sprouting tufts of coarse hair from copious fat, and then arms that are plump and flabby. Mottled brown freckles stain the skin with age. When I run a hand around my face, which should be oval and smooth, it is instead round and full, the texture blemished, the feel rough, even allowing for the afternoon shadow I would have expected.

In the hospital room with my family this morning, I had experienced a sense that an evil force was at work, that everything was not what it seemed, but I dismissed it as superstition and nerves, natural before a major operation on my brain. Now, I know it was real and prescient, that I should have spoken out, told my family and stopped it all happening. But it is too late. My breathing stutters, and as I stare down upon this chest, an invisible vice seems to ratchet it in a tight grip. I can smell sickly, damp perspiration all over the body I inhabit: it is an impossible conclusion, and yet the only one that is possible… because this is definitely not my body!

CHAPTER 3

The monotonous beeping of the alarm soon brought them running, first the Welsh nurse, quickly followed by someone else, a man I think, but after that my memory blanks. I must have slept for some time, but I am awake now, although still very sleepy. As I stare at the empty room and gaze through the window at a gathering bank of grey cloud, I feel remarkably calm despite everything that has happened. My mind wanders back three days to when I first met Peter Cheung, here at the Wellington Hospital in St John's Wood.

His room was bright and spacious on the first floor of the modern building housing the outpatient department, close to the main hospital on the Finchley Road and to Lord's cricket ground, where I had spent so many happy hours watching matches and enjoying good company. I remember sunlight cascading from a perfect blue sky through the large window behind Mr Cheung's desk, like a false harbinger of peace and serenity. Cathy squeezed my hand in support as we sat side by side, facing the eminent neurosurgeon and awaiting his verdict like prisoners in the dock.

He was a short man, not more than 5'6" tall, slightly overweight, but dressed with immaculate precision in a tailored, light blue suit.

We knew from our Google search that he was fifty-three years old, of Hong Kong Chinese origin and with a CV that attested to a stunning intellect. He peered at me over lightweight designer glasses on the tip of his nose, his chubby face confident and assured.

"I now have your MRI and PET CT scan results." The accent was an incongruous mix: the received pronunciation of an upper-class English gentleman, yet with more than a hint of Chinese vowels. His eyes fixed on mine. "Unfortunately, you have both pituitary and craniopharyngioma tumours. This accounts for your recent symptoms: the headaches, lethargy and difficulty in concentrating at work."

I have no direct recollection of the words that followed, just a blur really, a kindly voice echoing in my head in slow motion, but Cathy has recounted them to me so many times over the last three days in her reassuring and positive manner: "The good news is that we have identified the problem early and such tumours are often non-malignant. I am confident that I can excise both these growths in their entirety, but we need to act very quickly to maximise our chances of complete success."

I hung on to those words and Mr Cheung's confidence as I sat on the bed this morning in the plush, private room, naked save for a flimsy hospital gown. Yet I could not help feeling vulnerable and anxious. The black nurse who had taken my blood pressure five minutes earlier looked concerned and repeated the process, telling me to remain completely silent for the second reading. Then she hurried away, a forced smile on her face but no words.

"Do you think the operation will be delayed? I bet my blood pressure is sky-high," I said, looking to Cathy and our son and daughter for more reassurance.

"It'll all be fine, Andy; it's just normal nerves and tension." While Cathy's accent is not broad, my wife's flat vowels still betray Yorkshire roots and complement a dependable, loyal nature. "In no time you'll wake up with everything sorted. We'll all be here with you when you do."

She came to sit next to me on the bed and we embraced. I smelt Marc Jacobs 'Cucumber', her favourite perfume. She was wearing a white blouse and the gold drop pearl earrings I bought her in Brighton. "Don't worry, Andy, I'm going nowhere." She was being strong for me, but the strain and worry were obvious by the slight falter in her voice. "Mr Cheung told us you should be home in three or four days."

Her face was pale and drawn with the suspicion of swelling under her wide blue eyes, but if anything, that accentuated her charm. Short-cut brown hair mirrored her cute nose and pristine teeth. She has become a tad overweight in recent years for her 5'4" height, which has the effect of enhancing an ample cleavage, and to me she is the sexiest woman on the planet. I've been entranced by her beauty and in love with her since our bizarre first meeting twenty-two years ago when we were both trainee lawyers.

"A couple of weeks after you get home, we're all going to Provence," she said, and the words tumbled out quickly in a false and deluded excitement. "It's all been organised. I can easily get away from Chambers in August. Geoff and Lucy are home from uni. It's going to be a wonderful family holiday…"

It was a delightful thought, and for a few seconds the rich pleasure of anticipation trumped my fears; but I knew that I would need to return to my office quickly after the operation, before the growth of impatient files toppled from desk to floor and rivers of emails created a mindless electronic flood in my inbox. And that assumed, of course, I would have such a dubious privilege, that I would still be going anywhere, and then the dull ache of reality consumed me again.

"Mum has arranged it all for you," Geoff said, his voice a cheery manipulation and a semitone higher than his normal moderate pitch. "The locum's going to stay on for an extra month, so no need to worry on the work score. Every cloud, Dad; we can all have a lazy time together as a family while you recharge…" He trailed off, and I noticed him exchange a furtive, anxious glance with my daughter

Lucy. They were both sitting in cheap plastic chairs, positioned in separate corners of the room, facing the bed on which Cathy and I were sitting, next to the complex, high-tech monitoring equipment to which I expected to be hooked up on my return from theatre.

To a biased and proud father's eye they are both fine-looking young adults. Geoff, slightly taller than me at 5'9", is slim, handsome and athletic, with short-cut, dark brown hair. Lucy, petite and attractive with long, flowing blonde hair, is like her mother but with my fair colouring, and as she bit her bottom lip, I sensed the swell of emotion in her silence.

"I've already booked a villa in a little village not far from Avignon," Cathy said. "I'm so looking forward to it, Andy." Composure recovered, her voice was calm and confident, in contrast to the intensity with which she gripped my right hand. "We won't want the hassle of flying, so if I can't get late Eurostar tickets we'll drive down, but one way or another it's going to happen." There was that characteristic certainty and determination in tone that has reassured so many of her clients before trial.

I looked away from Cathy and stared, deep in thought, through the large window to my left. We were on the third floor. In the middle distance I saw blocks of expensive flats interspersed with established trees in full leaf, like overweight sentinels asleep on guard.

This was an unreal nightmare. One week earlier I had been a happy man living a routine life. True, I had been suffering from mild headaches for a few weeks and I was finding my solicitors' property practice stressful; but in honesty there was nothing unusual in that since the pressure of work was demanding in the high-volume, low-margin, small North London firm, 'Soulsby and Bright', that I ran with my business partner, Peter Bright.

I had almost not pursued the 'routine check-up' suggested by Matthew Campbell. I hardly knew him, a passing business acquaintance and a partner with Dorrell's, the prestigious City firm of solicitors. They were not a firm we would normally expect to encounter, but Matthew had been acting for the purchaser in what was for me a rare, heavyweight, commercial conveyancing matter: the sale of an hotel owned by Cathy's prosperous uncle in Leeds.

There had been a meeting and I was slightly nervous. He was a powerful, dominant man in his middle fifties, a hugely successful and renowned lawyer, but he had put me at ease quickly. I found him personable, quite charming, and he noticed and commented upon how tired I looked, which at first had seemed almost out of place at a business meeting; but he was that type of man, disarming really, a father figure full of wisdom, although only about ten years older than me. And so, I had opened up to him. I told him about the work pressures and the recent headaches.

As he had sat there dressed in an immaculate Savile Row suit with 'funky' blue glasses and balding, wispy white hair, offering to effect an introduction to the eminent Peter Cheung, his client and friend, it had seemed the obvious thing to gratefully accept. Cathy had been against it, but when Mr Cheung – because of the connection with Matthew Campbell – had offered to reduce his fees to comply with our BUPA policy limits, it had seemed to me an inevitable decision. However, not for one moment had I contemplated that he would diagnose anything serious, particularly since my GP had downplayed the symptoms and inferred I was one of the 'worried well' when he somewhat reluctantly provided the required referral letter.

And so there I was, this morning, in this hospital, about to undergo life-threatening brain surgery, and my family were stalking the elephant in the room, making plans for Provence a couple of weeks later.

"So, what do you think, Dad?" Geoff arched his back, leaning towards me, hands clasped together as he spoke. I realised that I should have reacted, responded to them. They had lovingly planned a family holiday, liaised with Peter Bright to do so and revealed this just before my surgery to emphasise to me, and perhaps themselves, the pretence that it would be a routine operation, that a swift, successful outcome was beyond doubt. Love often involves denial, and the love in that room had been overwhelming.

"It will be amazing." I paused. "Thank you. But just in case, you all know how much I love you, and there is substantial insurance in place. The pension policy funds will all become available. Cathy, you know where all the paperwork is—"

Lucy jumped out of her chair and rushed over to where her mother was sitting with me on the bed. She flung her arms around me. Her blue eyes were moist and red.

"Oh, Dad, Dad, please don't talk like that. You're gonna be okay." She lost control and sobbed. I put one arm around her and the other around Cathy, who was the dominant emotional strength in our family, but she merely rested her head on my chest to mask her tears. Geoff joined us then, like a sporting team's group hug.

I knew this was needed. Positivity is a virtue but not to the exclusion of realism and, certainly in my presence, the gravity of my condition had been denied. I said, "I expect I'll make a full recovery, hopefully as quickly as Mr Cheung predicts. But we must be realistic. It's a very serious operation and something might go wrong…"

Suddenly overcome with emotion, I could not continue, but Cathy, in control again, took over: "Andy, I just know it's going to be successful, call it female intuition." She laughed, and the mood lightened; the tears became natural, uninhibited. "It's incredible luck that it was diagnosed so early. Thank God for Peter Cheung. He's one of the world's best neurosurgeons and to him it will be a straightforward procedure."

We had been over this so many times during the last three days, but I knew Cathy was right. Given the circumstances I was very fortunate, and maybe I really would be in Provence in a few weeks.

The door opened. A short, stocky man appeared wearing a green smock over a blue gown, a plastic cover over his hair and a face mask pulled down under his chin so that he could speak with me. He walked purposefully to my side.

"Good morning, Mr Soulsby. I am Joe Peng, your neuro-anaesthetist today," and he took my hand, a firm double-shake. "Mr Cheung sends his apologies, but he is preparing and will speak with you shortly when you are taken to theatre."

He appeared to be Chinese, perhaps from Hong Kong like Cheung. His face was serious, just the glimmer of a half-smile. He ignored my family but eyed me up and down like the hangman surveying his quarry.

"Mr Cheung has explained the operation to you?" he said, formed as a question, but before I could respond he continued with details I would have preferred not to hear again. "This will be inter-cranial base of skull surgery, and it should be possible to remove your tumours by cutting holes of no more than three or four centimetres, even though they are quite large tumours." His face remained deadpan; he pervaded inscrutability.

"Do you think we should continue today if my blood pressure is too high?" Even as I said it, I realised how pathetic it sounded, and a hollow silence followed as if to emphasise my morose words.

Finally, he responded, the suspicion of a cold smile on his lips. "Your condition requires surgery to be carried out with the minimum of delay." He paused a moment, one eyebrow slightly raised. "There is nothing untoward in raised blood-pressure readings at this stage. I shall be monitoring this throughout, both when you have been anaesthetised and during the operation, which we expect will last at least three hours."

Then he looked at his notes and nobody spoke, a foreboding quiet like the deathly still at dawn in the trenches before the order to go over the top. At last, his monotone voice picked up. "Since you are clearly anxious, I will arrange for the nurse to give you a mild pre-med shortly to calm your nerves. However, you are slim, not overweight and in excellent general health. You have a good pedigree." He made it sound as though I was a prize specimen animal. "There is no reason why you should not make a good recovery from your surgery, and then we will know more after the laboratory analysis of your tumours."

I did not like this man. There was something in his manner, a lack of sincerity and human empathy. I could not explain the feeling since there was nothing in his words which was unexpected, and yet it disturbed me. He sent a shiver down my spine, and that was when I sensed, at some primeval level, something was very wrong.

He stood like a statue, staring at me with a fierce intensity, and raised his chin, directing his gaze above my eyes with an air of indifference as he told me: "Your care is safe in my hands, and safe with Mr Cheung. I have worked with him for many years. He is most eminent, a sound man."

It did not reassure me. I would have expected to be anxious and nervous at such a time, but I could not explain the chill that coursed my veins; an illogical fear, a deep sense of dread. It seemed, almost, that I was in another time and place, a dream world, yet with a hard edge of an unknown and sinister reality just a fraction from the grasp of my consciousness.

There was perspiration on my brow, the salty, bitter tang of sweat on my lips. Cathy remained silent, and so did Lucy and Geoff. I appeared to be alone in my premonition of evil. If only I had not ignored my gut instincts but acted decisively, put an end to it all, walked out of there and sought a second opinion on my condition, instead of convincing myself that such 'foolishness' was just superstitious hysteria, not helped by a medic with little personality and no bedside manner. It was a standing family joke that my fertile imagination precluded me from being a commercially successful conveyancing solicitor, the two being mutually exclusive.

As he went to leave there was for the first time a slight nod of acknowledgement to Cathy, although my son and daughter remained invisible to him. "The nurse will be in shortly with some calming medication," he said, glancing back at me, and I blamed my imagination again for the perception I had of malign intent behind his expressionless face.

"I will see you shortly in theatre," and with that he was gone.

CHAPTER 4

A few minutes after Joe Peng had left, the black nurse who had taken my blood pressure came in to give me a pre-med tablet. Then a porter arrived and the nurse accompanied him as he wheeled me along the wide, windowless corridor into a spacious lift. My empty stomach grumbled and sank, tingling into my bowels, as we began to descend suddenly. I was still fully conscious, neither drowsy nor relaxed.

I closed my eyes, lids creased hard, like a small child retreating under bedcovers to mask the stark reality of his monsters. We were moving; there were voices; a man was laughing. I had to look, and as I did so my trolley was pushed firmly through double doors with a no-entry sign and marked 'Operating Theatre 3', like some medieval tribute being taken to the altar of sacrifice.

To my surprise the room was smaller, more compact than the theatre of my imagination. Mr Cheung smiled at me and, somehow, he looked less imposing with surgical gown and smock, away from his vast consulting rooms and immaculate suits.

"Good morning, Mr Soulsby," he said. "We are going to transfer you to the operating table, and then you will find yourself back with family so very soon." His posh vowels with their Chinese edge resonated around the enclosed space which was flooded with artificial light by two large, round halogen lights suspended from the ceiling above the table. As they moved me to it from the trolley he continued in a matter-of-fact, business-like tone: "Before we connect up the monitors, I just need your signature to some paperwork. There is the formality of a consent form. My apologies for not dealing with this earlier, but I had a somewhat urgent matter to attend to first thing, and Joe also overlooked this when he saw you."

Joe Peng moved into view in his surgical scrubs and stood motionless next to Peter Cheung, an acolyte to the high priest. The blue mask he was wearing hid any expression, yet in my mind his piercing eyes were communicating an open and piteous contempt.

"We have already explained the procedures you are to undergo," said Cheung, and I noticed that he was holding a piece of paper and a pen in his hand. "There are risks since this is major surgery: a very slight chance of mortality, and, of course, the possibility of brain damage cannot be totally discounted."

When I think of this now it seems incredible that Peter Cheung stood at my side in theatre, requesting my signature to what might be a death warrant, as I waited on the operating table, ready for surgery. But the pre-med had kicked in, at last, and I felt only an aura of calm and fatalism envelope me with lethargy. So, I remained silent, and in truth what real choice would I have had at such a very late stage, even if I had still possessed my full senses?

And then, whether from embarrassment, vanity or a suspicion that he saw doubt in my drugged eyes, he said, "I am sorry to deal with this now, but it is just a legal formality as you should know. I have performed operations of this type on countless occasions with a phenomenal success rate compared to my peer group. You are in safe hands and we need to crack on."

He thrust the consent form in my hand, gave me a pen and directed where I must sign. It was clear he did not intend I should read it, and indeed he must have known I would have been incapable of doing so by then: it was as much as I could manage to sign it with a scrawl in a shaking hand.

Things moved along swiftly after that. I was connected to monitors and Joe Peng's monotone voice explained with apparent disinterest that these would show my heart rate, blood pressure and oxygen levels during the operation. He took my right hand; I looked away while he placed a drip into a vein, and for the first time I glimpsed four figures sitting quite still, high above us, watching behind the glass of a small viewing gallery.

And then Joe Peng was leaning over me, his masked face in mine, blocking out everything else as he said, "Start counting down from twenty, please, Andrew…"

CHAPTER 5

I am disembodied, looking down on Peter Cheung in surgical scrubs, waiting impatiently beside the operating table where my anaesthetised body lies prostrate, connected up to monitors that resemble the cockpit in a 747 jet plane.

Joe Peng wheels in a gurney carrying an unconscious patient whose face remains tantalisingly beyond my vision. A tall man, also in surgical scrubs, assists him, holding a drip which feeds drugs into a vein at the back of a large and lifeless hand. They park the gurney beside my body on the operating table, then quickly adjust the height to raise it level with me, side by side, like corpses in a morgue.

I can make out my mysterious partner is a large man, but still his face eludes me as they connect him to monitors matching my own and wrap a blood-pressure cuff around his arm above the right elbow. The three medics are talking. I cannot hear them, but I see Cheung's steely gaze fall upon the inert body beside me draped, like my own, in a thin surgical gown for modesty. I sense that he is smirking behind his mask, basking in a glow of sadistic pleasure.

Then Cheung moves towards me and, as the monitors beep to warn that my vital signs are fading, picks up the scalpel, gripping it between his dexterous fingers, before boldly making an incision into my brain.

***

"Back with us now, and feeling calmer, I hope," says the man who is peering down my throat. He is wearing a blue suit now, but surely this is the tall medic in scrubs I have just seen with Peter Cheung and Joe Peng. Without his mask a grey moustache is visible, which contrasts with his silky hair dyed black. The pretty Welsh nurse at his side looks worried. I must have drifted off to sleep again and been dreaming, a horrid nightmare, and yet this new doctor I have never seen before was taking an active role in my subconscious imagination.

His voice is familiar, a broad Lancastrian accent, and he is gazing at me, waiting for me to speak. All I can think to say is: "You sound just like 'Bumble', David Lloyd, the well-known cricket commentator." This inane comment comes in my new voice but slurred and slow, like a drunken man, and again I feel a dull ache of pain in my throat.

"I know." He smiles. "Folk tell me frequently. I don't even like cricket. It's a bore, too slow for me. You've 'ad a panic attack," he explains. "We sedated you and gave you more painkillers."

"Who are you?" I ask, attempting to raise my head from the pillow.

"Jeremy Whicher, your anaesthetist. We spoke this morning, before your operation. D'ya not remember?"

"No." What else can I say or explain to him?

"Do you recollect the nature of your surgery?"

"No, sorry." I know instinctively that I must keep my own counsel for the moment; if I try to explain, surely it will only bring disbelief and more drugs. First, I need to find out more.

He says, "Temporary memory loss is rare after anaesthesia, but it's been known to 'appen. We've been tinkering with anaesthetic drugs in that brain of yours, after all. But there's no need for undue concern. Most likely everything will come back to you very soon, certainly within the next few days." He nods to the nurse and she starts to connect me to a drip. I wonder why I have not already been hooked up to this but say nothing.

"It's a saline drip for your fluids while we keep you mildly sedated for a few hours. You've had a totally successful minor op and we've nipped out your vocal cord nodules. It'll be painful for a few days, but after that the hoarseness and pain in speech you were experiencing will be gone, and Ms Simms – she's top-notch, she is – 'as done a lovely, neat job on you, so there'll be no adverse effects on your voice."

He pauses and the nurse, at his request, leaves to retrieve some records. He regards me with a quizzical stare, the chatty, friendly manner evaporating like moisture in a hot, sticky sun, and he leans towards me, speaking in low and unsympathetic tones, a hint of menace in his voice: "No more grumbles about mistakes, please; pursue that nonsense and I can promise you psychiatrists with more drugs to dull your brain." Then he moves away and resumes his former brash but convivial manner as the nurse returns: "Penny Simms will want to see you in a couple of weeks to review your progress."

The nurse hands him notes on a clipboard. He smiles at her, the transformation back to Jekyll from Hyde complete, and carries on speaking to me: "She asked me to apologise because she was called away urgently, before you came round from the anaesthetic, so couldn't speak with you. She wanted me to stress that it's important you talk as little as possible over the next few days, rest the throat and vocal cords. You'll be able to skedaddle 'ome tomorrow morning, but, and here's the thing – I don't know if this is good news or not – we suggest you *do not* return to your office, or do anything that involves speaking much for a couple of weeks. Just ease back gently."

Then he looks down at his notes, frowning in concentration, and starts to take his leave, mumbling that he has another patient to attend to. However, at the open door he turns back to face me with a sickly smile and says, "I spoke with your wife earlier; quite a well-known actress, I believe. Ah... what's her name?" It sounds like an innocuous question posed as a friendly afterthought, the name which has momentarily slipped his memory, and yet I sense hidden mischief. Something in his body language suggests he knows I cannot answer and is taking sadistic pleasure in the moment, as though, just like the phantom in my dream, he is aware of my turmoil.

The nurse looks embarrassed.

"She would be upset if she knew that you hadn't remembered. Try a little harder," I tell him with barely suppressed aggression, and pleased with myself for this reply, as I take in that my 'wife' might be famous.

This appears to prompt his memory and he answers almost immediately: "I've got it! She played Carole Malone, the sexy young marriage-wrecker in that afternoon soap opera, some years ago. And isn't she playing at the National Theatre soon? She's a beautiful woman. You must be very proud." I believe he is still enjoying this, surprising me with information about the woman who thinks I am her husband. I remain silent. "Jenny will keep an eye on you tonight," he says, looking at the nurse. "Goodnight, then. I wish you a speedy recovery."

As he departs Jenny moves towards me in her smart, crisp uniform. The plump face regarding me with kindly eyes, and surely genuine concern, looks slightly odd for her small frame. She stands at my side checking the saline drip and I notice a delicate gold chain with a cross around her neck. She can't be part of this, and I am pleased she has the courage to wear the cross. Cathy would certainly approve.

My wife and I are both Christians, and in the early years of our marriage Cathy had tried hard to convert me to her Roman Catholic faith. Finally, she came to accept that I would not budge from my traditional C of E background, although I agreed our son and daughter should attend Catholic schools. It has been a source of regret to both of us that neither of them has grown up to pay more than lip service to either of our faiths.

Jenny speaks to me in a soft voice, like a mother to an ailing child: "I'm going to give you another sedative, a mild one this time. It will keep you nice and relaxed and help you to sleep." She gives me a tablet along with a plastic mug half filled with water to wash it down.

I decide it is safe to question her, probe a little into what might have happened. "Jenny – I hope you don't mind me using your Christian name." She smiles sweetly, clearly flattered by my courtesy. "I was wondering if you knew, or if not, you could check something out for me. I have a friend who was scheduled to have a serious operation at this hospital today. I know that, strictly, it's probably against the rules of patient confidentiality, but it would be reassuring to know if all went well for him and his lovely family – I know they were all in here with him this morning."

She is still smiling and answers me in a helpful voice. "What's your friend's name and do you know what type of operation he was due to have?"

"Andrew Soulsby," I say. "It was to remove two brain tumours."

"It was pretty serious then. That's another department, but I'll nip and check to see if I can find out anything for you."

She rushes away before insisting I take the sedative, which I have put on the bedside cabinet along with the mug, so I am confident she will return shortly. But when she does, a few minutes later, the smiling face has vanished to be replaced with the same worried expression which greeted me when I woke to find her alongside Jeremy Whicher.

"I've been told I must not give information about any patient," she says, apologetically, "It's strictly only to next of kin, I'm afraid. I'm so sorry. Now, you must take your pill," and she waits while I swallow it.

I fear the worst, since she was so keen to reassure me when she went to find out. And there was something in the changed tone of her voice, the awkwardness of her manner, that bodes ill for the body of Andrew Soulsby. I contemplate my slim frame, so healthy and unblemished by any excesses of life, with a sense of disbelief that it could have perished. I must know for sure, and see what face I present to the world, even if my brain – if it is my brain! – rebels against the very notion because, surely, none of this is remotely possible outside the pages of science fiction?

"Jenny," I ask before she leaves, "would you bring me a hand mirror, please? I want to look into my mouth and throat to see what's been done."

"I don't think that's such a good idea just yet."

"Please, Jenny." I must try to persuade her, and quickly, before the sedative kicks in. "I'm not going to become upset or agitated again. Mr Whicher has reassured me. My memory is beginning to return." I lie: how would I explain to her it has never left me, that I am really another man? "I would just like to view the evidence of Ms Simm's handiwork," I say. "Typical lawyer, you see."

"Oh, go on then, but it's to relax, please, and doze away after that; we need you ready for that lovely wife of yours when she's back to drive you home tomorrow. Quite a character, isn't she, very theatrical and ever so beautiful." I offer a small and silent prayer of thanks that she is going to humour me.

Jenny goes to find the mirror. As I wait, I wonder how many partners would behave like the glamorous actor: such a fleeting and peremptory visit, hardly suggesting any concern, let alone love and affection. I long for Cathy, and visualise her in my mind's eye, together with Lucy and Geoff, as the porter wheeled me away from them this morning: Cathy's kiss still wet on my lips, the confident smile for my benefit and her slim, black jeggings over curvaceous hips; Lucy, head bowed with long strands of blonde hair not quite hiding lips clenched together, and red, moist eyes; and dear Geoff, giving me a thumbs-up while shouting down the corridor, "Come on, you Spurs, Dad," and then reminding me again of that planned holiday. In doing so he had disrupted the calm serenity of the posh hospital and made the porter chuckle.

I shudder at the realisation that if my worst fears are confirmed, this may be the tragic and final memory of me for all three of them, the last time they will have seen me alive; and yet I will be able to see and speak with them… as another man.

Jenny has been very quick; she is back with her kindly smile to give me a small mirror. I put it up to my face for the confirmation of an impossible dream, the stuff of nightmares. The reflection staring back at me is not the distinguished man I remember meeting in his office less than two weeks ago, whose eyes had sparkled with confidence behind modern, blue specs. This face is unshaven, tired and dishevelled, the skin wrinkling and blemished, but still there can be no doubt – even without the glasses – that I am looking at the face of Matthew Campbell!

CHAPTER 6

The following morning is warm, if overcast, and Helen Campbell is driving me 'home' from the Wellington Hospital in her red 911 Carrera Cabriolet Porsche with a combination of carefree abandon and surprising skill in heavy traffic on the Finchley Road. The roar of the engine and rush of air in the open-top when she accelerates is exhilarating, although probably not an ideal prescription for my recovering throat.

"It might help you keep your little op in perspective, Matty, to know that some poor guy died under the knife in the Welly yesterday. He was a solicitor as well." Confirmation of my body's demise. I feel only numbness as her posh voice swirls around my head. "Some sort of brain tumours," she is saying, apparently unaware of any connection between us. "I heard the nurses talking about it. They were saying his wife and children were absolutely distraught, beside themselves with grief." She pauses and slows the Porsche, flashing to allow a waiting Nissan Micra into the rat run. "It all caused a real who-ha. It was awfully tragic." She turns to face me, and for just a moment her hazel eyes meet mine in what seems like a flash of accusation towards an unfeeling, selfish husband.

I steel myself. I am breathing and alive so there must be hope. I have no choice but to live Matthew's life and try to find out what has happened to both of us. "Poor man," I say. "And his poor family. So very unfair." Her expression suggests surprise at my obvious concern. "I think I knew him, vaguely: a local solicitor from Enfield. I had a matter on with him." For the first time, I have this woman's full attention and interest. "Actually," I tell her, "I recommended him to Peter Cheung for medical advice."

"Fuck. Some coincidence, Matty. And that slimy Cheung is supposed to be shit-hot as well."

I say, "I'll need to speak to his wife, to offer condolences."

"I'd be careful there just yet. I told you they were saying his wife was in a dreadful state. You could find out what went wrong from your friend, Cheung."

"Possibly, I must have a note of his private number or email address somewhere."

She looks at me askance. "Matty, your memory really is cocked up. I should think he is top of the contact list on your iPhone, the times you talk to him."

We fall silent as she drives and I consider this. It is good news since I should be able to speak with Cheung and arrange to meet him. Although I anticipate he will greet me as Matthew and put the death of Andrew Soulsby down to unforeseen complications, it will be useful to observe his demeanour and hear what he has to say.

I also need to speak with Penny Simms, the consultant who operated on what are now my vocal cords. She had been conveniently called away early, having just finished the procedure, with Matthew still anaesthetised in theatre. Perhaps I should bring forward the follow-up appointment to meet her; and, somehow, I must talk with my wife and children, however painful it will be meeting them as a stranger. I want to see my body, to confirm with absolute certainty its demise, and that probably means seeking Cathy's permission. However, tempting though it may be, I know that I must not reveal myself to them, or anyone else yet. If I do so, without having first discovered some facts that corroborate the truth of what I tell them, they will, surely, dismiss me as a madman, and I will likely suffer the mind fog of antipsychotic drugs when they certify me as insane.

Helen waits to filter into the stream of heavy traffic around Swiss Cottage. She looks gorgeous in tight denim jeans with a white tunic top. Her long fingers are curled around the sporty steering wheel displaying nails painted a delicate pale pink. As the column of vehicles with priority slows to a halt, a small Fiat blocks our way. The young girl driving it is alone, singing to music in her car, oblivious to us and her lack of courtesy.

Helen sighs, then smiles at me with raised eyebrows. "You must have this treatment regularly, my love. No rants from you at thoughtless drivers. How long do you think we can keep that memory at bay?"

I doubt Helen knows what has happened to me. She strikes me as entirely open and forthright; not a person who would be at ease with secrets.

The traffic remains heavy and we weave through the tapestry of vehicles from one bottleneck to another, like a pin ball on a bagatelle board stuttering to zero. I notice a battered Ford Fiesta making similar progress by different routes through the congestion, sometimes almost beside us in an adjoining lane, but generally a little distance behind. Its registration plates are illegible, caked in thick grime, and the driver is an elderly, gaunt man wearing dark glasses and a peaked baseball cap. He looks faintly bizarre. I mention it to Helen, but she is dismissive.

"London's full of oddballs. Nothing that strange about an old guy driving a rust bucket on this main road; don't get paranoid now as well as losing your memory, Matty. Perhaps it's a guilty conscience." She taps the screen in front of her and Queen's Fat Bottomed Girls plays through the speakers, volume high, and the conversation ceases. The Fiesta stays with us, though, never more than a few cars' distance away, which is surprising in the heavy traffic, but just as I am convincing myself he must be following us, it drives straight on as we turn off the A1000 in Monken Hadley, just past Barnet town centre.

I know this area well; it is only a few miles from my own home in Enfield, but when she pulls into the sweeping carriage drive of a palatial house in Beech Hill, near Hadley Wood Golf Club – a prosperous North London suburb adjoining the Metropolitan Green Belt – the contrast with my modest and rather neglected Victorian semi could not be starker. A new Bentley is parked in front of the massive stone pillars with steps to the impressive entrance porch. When Helen remarks that I should have parked it in 'one of the garages', I feel a momentary surge of excitement to think of this sumptuous car as belonging to me. But what riches in the world could compare to my love for Cathy and Geoff and Lucy? If only I was arriving home with them and looking at my old BMW 520 saloon, no doubt still parked on the drive at the front of my house.

When we go inside, she is amused, although patient with me, because I need directions to find the nearest loo, located within a marble shower room on the ground floor. Like everything about the house, it is stunning, larger than the average semi's master bedroom.

"Jean has stocked up with provisions so you won't go hungry. I doubt you'll feel up to getting out for a few days." I remain silent, and my lack of comprehension must be obvious because she sounds slightly irritated: "Jean: our housekeeper for the last ten years! Anyway, I'll be going out in an hour or so to meet Mark. I'll probably stay over. I suggest you explore, find your way around. It might jog your lost memory."

She leaves me alone, disappearing up an expansive, sweeping staircase where an ornate, crystal chandelier hangs from the ceiling above the central stairwell. It reminds me of the old Grand Hotel in Brighton. Cathy and I always spend our wedding anniversaries at the Grand, a custom that includes fish and chips with champagne on the Pier, and a visit to the Mock Turtle tea rooms for the large, puffy doughnuts she adores. I have to fight back tears accompanying the pang of nostalgia. Are these wonderful times never to be repeated, only memories of a happy family life to be cherished for ever in another man's shoes?

I am tired and exhausted, my throat still sore. I discover the kitchen and take a couple of the painkillers that the hospital provided on discharge, washing them down with a cup of warm tea. Then I heat up a packet of organic vegetable soup and sit to drink it on a bar stool at the marble-topped island, wondering at the size and style of the designer kitchen surrounding me.

I have regularly worked ten to twelve hours a day, often six days a week, and struggled to make a modest profit from my law firm; our family's reasonably good standard of living has, in no small part, been due to Cathy's part-time practice at the bar. How is it possible that Matthew Campbell has achieved such an opulent lifestyle, amassed so much apparent wealth, and at what cost to his health?

The hearty broth soup replenishes my aching limbs, helping to lift my mood, as the painkillers kick in to ease the discomfort in my throat. I find a leather, button-back armchair in a room lined with bookshelves and bound leather volumes, together with a large, carved mahogany desk in front of French doors to the gardens. My bulky frame feels so alien to me, so unhealthy, and I collapse it into the chair with a sigh; the smell of polish, wood and leather testifying to traditional wealth. Tomorrow, after a good night's sleep, I will make the short trip to my home in Enfield, driving that regal Bentley.

***

"I see you've found your study." I must have dozed off, but Helen is at my side, and her words wake me with a start from the comfort of sleep to a moment of disorientation, then the chilling recollection of my impossible new reality. "Sorry to wake you but I'm going out now. You should get to bed." She offers me a mobile phone. "I've charged it; you see I'm always thinking of you, Matty." She laughs, an ironic smile on her face.

"Thank you, Helen. It's good of you. Have a lovely time." She looks surprised, I think because I sound thoughtful and sincere.

There is the hint of concern in her voice when she tells me to speak to the consultant if my memory hasn't returned by tomorrow. She says, "It's weird," and then, as an afterthought: "Don't forget I gave you your specs – in that pocket," and she points to them. If only she knew the truth: my memory is perfectly clear, but it belongs to another man, not her husband. Somehow, I suspect the indifference she affects with Matthew masks a warm and affectionate woman; perhaps she has given up on a disinterested husband? I have to dismiss a fleeting temptation to confide in her now, to seek her sympathy and help, but it would be an indulgence that is far too risky.

I extract the specs, which I have found are essential for reading and close sight with my new eyes. These reading glasses are so much more powerful than those I had started to use about a year before the operation; I could forget and squint without them, but there would be no such luxury of oversight in future.

"Got them. Well done, Helen," I say.

"Okay. I must go. With your post-op memory lapse, you will have forgotten – although frankly, I doubt you'd have remembered anyway – it's the opening night for our new production of *Candida* tomorrow, so it'll be convenient for me to stay over at Mark's flat in town after dress rehearsal tonight." She hesitates, as if deciding whether or not to show concern, and then says, "I'd get to bed soon, Matty; you look all in. Don't forget to take your statins and blood pressure pills… in your bedside cabinet, my love," and with that she is gone.

I am regarded as almost eccentric by family and friends for shunning the dubious virtues of social media and only using my old basic mobile as a phone; although I did, reluctantly, begin to text recently. Yet it only takes me a few moments to master the logistics of Matthew's all-singing, all-dancing iPhone: it seems to come to me automatically, so easy and logical, just falling into place. I guess it is Matthew's brain powering his body, but it's impossible to comprehend because here I am: this is me, and my life with all my memories.

There are countless text messages. I delete the junk and glance at the social ones, all strangers to me. The invitation for golf when I feel up to it, from someone called Alex, suggests an ability to excel at a game I have never played, since I cannot envisage Matthew Campbell voluntarily partaking of any activity, leisure or business, unless his prowess would be admired and envied. Five texts are from the same person: the first, relating to work, comes from Dorrell's number and is signed 'Shivani'; the rest, from her personal phone, are signed, 'Shivi', and they are all short, anxious to speak with 'Matt', and end with 'xx'.

There are a few voice messages, most seemingly unimportant, social names that tie up with the texts. One is from 'Shivi': "Matt. It's me. How are you? Please do ring. You know how discreet I am, but I need to speak to you, to see you soon. I'll never let you down. Love you." The voice is soft and quiet, faintly beguiling with the hint of Indian tones not quite masked by a distinct North London accent.

The next voice is male and clashes in contrast, the brash, confident words, loud and harsh, resonating in my ear, quick-fire, no time to waste. No name is given – presumably he is too important and busy. It could be an ageing and posh city trader rather than the office colleague it obviously is, and as I repeat the message, I guess this is someone more senior than Matthew, perhaps Dorrell's managing partner?

"Matt. I see you've booked out a couple of weeks, but would be good to have you back asap. The Wilkinson Pharmaceutical case is blowing up, and a few more. Ken has Shivani in shackles – hold that thought, old man – nose to the grindstone-wise. Cold fish, that one; I doubt any mortal man is screwing her. Anyway, the department is struggling. Could do with your input soonest. I'll get them to

31

email you the latest garbage that's just been shit on us re Wilkinson discovery, and Further and Better Particulars required tout de suite. You can give them a bell. Hope you're not feeling too shagged out, matey." No doubt it is only the privilege of Matthew's rank that merits this final solicitation.

So, I have discovered Matthew may be involved in a clandestine affair with a work associate called 'Shivani', and that he is sorely missed in his office because of a panic over some big case. One thing I do know for sure: there is no way a provincial conveyancing solicitor can hope to provide any meaningful guidance to a city litigation practice under pressure, any more than a GP could advise a brain surgeon. Strangely, though, I feel no stress at the thought of having to face this eventually, just a rather detached feeling of curiosity.

However, the main reason I have checked the iPhone is to locate Peter Cheung, but there is no text or voice message from him, notwithstanding Helen's comments about how often Matthew speaks to him. And he is not top of the contact list. He is not on it.

CHAPTER 7

It takes me longer to recover than I thought it would. I had failed to appreciate that Matthew is older and less fit. The sickly, sore throat was persistent and only improved slowly, while the effect of the general anaesthetic has left me feeling tired and faint after the least exertion.

However, late on Friday morning, three days after leaving the hospital, I am sitting behind the steering wheel of the Bentley, admiring the gloss, walnut veneer and the smell of plush, cream leather, while I gaze at the complex touch screen panels and controls. But I am not overawed, because it is only a car, albeit a special one: I have been driving since the age of seventeen, so how difficult can it be? And, in truth, the heart within this body races; I experience a tingling of joy and excitement when I realise that to all the world, I am the lawful owner of this exquisite machine, the ultimate motor car.

When I start the engine, it is so quiet that I have to pump the accelerator pedal to check it is running, and a powerful roar leaves no doubt that it is raring to go. I select drive on the automatic transmission, press my foot on the pedal and lurch across the drive like a jack-in-the-box learner driver, crunching dry gravel and sending dust into the air. The delicacy of response and depth of power is amazing; the six-litre, twin turbo-charged engine on a tripwire, a lion ready to spring and like nothing I have ever driven before. It will require practice, a lightness of touch and timing to drive smoothly and with the serene authority this limousine demands.

I glance towards the house, embarrassed, hopeful that my incompetent handling of the Bentley has gone unobserved, but Helen, wearing a silk nightdress and no make-up, is looking out from an upstairs window. Her eyebrows are raised, lips stuck together like a schoolchild's picture of a glum clown: a beautiful woman with an ungainly frown, suggesting she cannot solve a simple puzzle.

Since I returned from hospital, she has left me to fend for myself most of the time. I have been grateful for this because even while I recover it has been obvious that this ageing body is pumped with sexual libido. I have struggled to control the urges, as I must, for it is inconceivable that I should ever cheat on my wife. If I did this it would be a betrayal of our love and family, all we have built over the last twenty-two years. It helps that Helen and Matthew have separate bedrooms and appear to lead entirely separate lives.

Helen has been out often, giving me ample opportunity to snoop around at a leisurely pace and familiarise myself with the house and its contents. But I cannot access emails or files on the laptop computer in the study which are all protected by passwords, nor open a couple of locked drawers in his desk. I have tried asking Helen, citing my 'memory loss', but to no avail: "Darling, since when did you confide in me about your business or finances? Unless something clicks pretty soon, you must talk to the medics."

I have also spoken to Penny Simms' secretary and brought forward the follow-up appointment, which is now arranged for this Monday afternoon at her Harley Street consulting rooms. This means I will only have to wait another three days before I can quiz her and, maybe, elicit some useful information about events surrounding the operations at the Wellington.

However, I have not been able to make contact with Peter Cheung or Joe Peng. According to their secretaries both of them are now on vacation and would not speak to me, anyway, without a GP referral. Helen said Cheung was Matthew's friend, and I know from my fateful meeting with Matthew that the brain surgeon is definitely his client, so I should be able to find his private contact details when I go to Dorrell's offices on Monday week, at the expiration of Matthew's scheduled sick leave. I have already decided against heeding the voicemail's plea urging me to return earlier; I will need to be fully recovered and have all of my wits about me for that.

As I come out of the drive, tentatively, and cruise slowly along Beech Hill, past the high hedges and wrought-iron gates protecting other mansions, for the first time I tense at the prospect of meeting Matthew's work colleagues. I know they are overstretched and anxious for me to assume control of complex litigation, of which they believe I have an intimate knowledge. And how to deal with Shivani? She has professed love in her texts, and there have been more of them, along with voicemails over the last three days, becoming ever more insistent. I have decided to ignore them all for now, along with the tome of documentation that has been couriered to me. I can't concentrate on it, and I will have to deal with these matters face to face when I arrive at Dorrell's offices. It should be easy enough to blame my lack of response on medical complications and a need for peace and quiet to facilitate full recovery. I also have the distinct impression that Matthew Campbell would be indifferent, even contemptuous of personal sensibilities in the workplace – save, presumably, for his furtive affair – and I doubt anyone would be inclined to risk speaking against his authority.

I am driving slowly through Green Belt countryside towards my home and family in Cheltenham Avenue, close to Enfield Town. A few cars race past, overtaking on straight sections of the winding, two-lane road. An old, silver Honda keeps a respectful distance; I had first noticed it behind me near the bottom of Beech Hill, at the junction with Cockfosters Road, and it is still there as I near the end of my short journey.

I think of that Fiesta, coming back from the hospital, but remember what Helen had said – 'don't get paranoid' – and so I dismiss the suspicion and dwell on the prospect of meeting my wife as a stranger. I am not sure how I will approach it, what I will say, but I must see her to try and establish that my own body – the physical manifestation of Andrew Soulsby – has perished beyond doubt and the powers of Peter Cheung to revive it.

I know others must be involved – surely Joe Peng and Jeremy Whicher – and that only I can attempt to find out what incredible medical knowledge they must have acquired, what they have done to Matthew and me… and why. For who else would give credence to such a fantasy?

CHAPTER 8

Cheltenham Avenue is a quiet residential street and comprises a hotchpotch of detached and semi-detached properties, a few of the original late Victorian and Edwardian houses quite large, others having been built in various shapes and sizes between the wars, with one or two incongruous additions screaming from the sixties. My home is No. 23, the Victorian semi that Cathy still adores, but my commitment to the house in which we brought up our children has become more ambivalent in recent years as the cost of maintaining it has drained our resources.

There are no parking restrictions and I pull in at the kerbside, stopping just short of the neighbouring pair of semis. Cathy's red Mini Cooper stands on our drive and the Vauxhall Corsa, shared by Lucy and Geoff when they are home from university, partially blocks the cutaway. There is no sign of my BMW which must be squashed in the garage normally used for storage.

With the air-conditioning disengaged, I open the car windows for fresh air, but it feels clammy and humid. Despite this, goosebumps prickle my arms and I listen to my rumbling stomach, knotted in stress. I am frozen in the comfort of the car's leather seat, contemplating the enormity of the emotional task awaiting me: to visit my grief-stricken family, yet only able to affect polite concern and offer formal condolences, remaining single-minded in the grotesque purpose of attempting to ascertain the whereabouts of my own dead body.

It is nearly 11am, but no signs of life disturb the empty street as gathering storm clouds devour the earlier hazy sunshine. A lone shaft of sun escapes the thickening gloom and dazzles multi-coloured reflections upon stained glass over the front door of No. 26, the tired Edwardian villa on the opposite side of the road. Curtains twitch in its front window, and Mr Shawcross, an elderly widower, peeks out surreptitiously at the presence of such a magnificent car in his once-grand street.

I close the car's windows as large blobs of rain assault the windscreen, a tentative sortie at first, quickly followed by an avalanche of water in a full-blown, violent attack, supported by a fork of lightning and rounds of thunder. It provides my excuse for further delay. As I sit in the car listening to rain battering the metal roof like machine-gun fire, I feel calmed by the security within; and my thoughts turn to that first meeting with Cathy all those years ago.

I had just finished law school and started my articles as a trainee with a firm of solicitors in my hometown of Barnet. I had been given conduct of a criminal legal aid case due to be heard in the local magistrates' court. My client was a young lad charged with the common law offence of 'lewd conduct and indecent exposure likely to cause offence to a female'. He had, so he maintained, forgotten to pull the curtains at his bedroom window after bathing, and his naked body had been seen by a young woman in the street.

The counsel I briefed had a better offer at the last minute and his chambers sent Miss Catherine Richards, a young pupil barrister, as a replacement. I see her again now in my mind's eye as I met her in the public foyer of the courthouse teeming with legal life at the sharp end: suited solicitors, pupil barristers and clerks; court ushers in black gowns; and the law's potential victims, nervously awaiting their fate. The determined and slim young woman with auburn, brown hair stood out from the crowd. She was smartly dressed, all black and crisp, with high heels and pencil skirt over hips and perfect bottom, the charm bracelet she still wears today jangling as she held out a hand to greet her future husband.

There was a sense of restless disinterest around the courtroom during Cathy's cross-examination of the sole prosecution witness: the justices looked bored, a court usher yawned and a buzz of whispered chattering came from the back rows. When she had finished, the chairman of the bench peered at the witness and asked his own question to a suddenly hushed court: "When you saw him naked in the window, was his penis erect?" Only then did it dawn on both of us novices that this was the only relevant question to establish innocence or guilt.

Since the witness 'could not recall', our client was acquitted forthwith. Afterwards, Cathy accepted my invitation to lunch at a local 'beefeater', where we celebrated our ill-deserved success, laughing about 'Dirty Dennis', the header we had both noticed was scrawled on a pocket folder police file. It was a memorable day which set in motion our future lives and destiny.

I can't hold back the tears of despair and self-pity for the loss of my family life, but fortunately my privacy is protected by the car's one-way mirrored glass. I let those tears flow unabashed, and although I hadn't counted on this, somehow, I think the release of pent-up emotion and stress helps me, finally, to focus again. Eventually, I compose myself, then use mineral water from the Bentley's mini bar to freshen up. I need to stay positive now, ready to offer Matthew Campbell's condolences to my family, and try to find out where my body is.

The storm passes and the rain gives way to bright sun. There is no longer any excuse for procrastination. I get out and flick the ignition key fob twice to lock the car, then walk purposefully towards my front door at No. 23. Beside the crumbling crazy-paving, overgrown, neglected shrubs glisten as drops of rainwater slowly evaporate in warmth from the sun.

The blinds at the windows are drawn and I stand under the porch in trepidation, like an ill-prepared actor on first night, waiting for curtain's up. There is only silence within, but I hear a cough and footfall behind me, the panting of an excited dog on a leash. I turn to see our lonely neighbour, Mr Shawcross, walking his handsome, young Dalmatian, and I almost call out by instinct, our usual social banter in a friendly greeting, but his curious eyes quickly drop from mine and act as a stark reminder: I am a total stranger to him.

As I press the bell and hear the familiar shrill ring echo through the house, a random thought pushes to the front of my mind: who is now in possession of my set of keys with the jovial insignia offering entry to the home dressing room at Lord's cricket ground?

CHAPTER 9

Walking away from my house towards the Bentley, I pass my business partner, Peter Bright, strolling along the pavement, heading in the opposite direction. His eyes are downcast, studiously contemplating the paving stones as though they hold the key to eternal life. I doubt he has ever met Matthew Campbell, so even if he did look up, it is unlikely there would be a flicker of recognition. Should I introduce myself as Matthew? I had spoken to Peter of our meeting at Dorrell's, so he knows of him, but I am too distraught to think clearly after the brief encounter with my grieving widow, and the moment passes.

I drive away slowly, past my house, and watch Cathy greeting Peter at our open front door. Her tears flow freely as they embrace and the charm bracelet falls loose on her wrist. Behind them in the hall, for the first time since the morning of my operation, I catch a glimpse of my son and daughter. Comfort from a family friend is normal, of course, but it dawns on me that suitors will not be slow to circle my attractive and intelligent widow of independent means, not least Peter, just through an acrimonious divorce. I have always suspected he has fancied her, like most men do. Cathy tells me not to be stupid, it's all in my imagination, and I know that our love has always been unconditional, a special bond between best friends and lovers.

The thought of her with another man makes me feel physically sick, and Peter will have every excuse to be in close contact with her over the coming months to help deal with my probate and the partnership succession at Soulsby and Bright. Cathy and I had sometimes joked that if one of us died, the survivor should be free to consider a 'second-rate substitute'. It hadn't seemed real, but now the idea fills me with selfish jealousy. Still, I am confident she will recoil in horror at the prospect of any new relationship or liaison for the foreseeable future, time enough, I hope, for me to convince her of the truth: although my body has perished, death has not parted us; I remain here for her and my family in the guise of Matthew Campbell.

I do not underestimate the task. It is clear from her reaction just a few minutes ago that even securing her consent to meet me will be difficult. After I had introduced myself, she had dismissed me from her front door swiftly, and it's obvious she blames Matthew Campbell for his fateful introduction to Peter Cheung: "My family are with me, and I have no wish to see you, or for your sympathy." Her Yorkshire accent sounded broad – it always did at moments of heightened emotion – and her face looked haggard with no make-up to conceal puffy eyes. How I'd longed to hold and comfort her, instead of only mumbling polite platitudes and vague offers of help which she clearly considered wholly inappropriate.

When I had turned to leave, I said, "I intend to show my respects at the funeral. I hope you don't mind, Mrs Soulsby," but she had already closed the door.

CHAPTER 10

MONDAY 13TH JULY

Arriving this afternoon at the outpatient department of the Wellington Hospital seemed surreal. I am in a consulting room just like the one I sat in ten days ago as Andrew Soulsby, accompanied by Cathy. Then, we were seeing Peter Cheung, but today I am alone, sitting opposite Penny Simms, who thinks she is speaking to Matthew Campbell.

She has already reassured me that my throat is healing nicely, ahead of expectations, and seems relieved when I lie to confirm that my memory is beginning to improve. "It's just one of those unforeseen things," she says, "a highly unusual complication, but not unknown. Fortunately, from what you tell me, it does appear to be resolving itself. The rest and calm for your throat is likely the perfect mind medicine as well. So, let's hold off referring you on this for now, but come back to me if it's not fully returned in another week."

A personable woman who wears a friendly smile, she looks quite young for a consultant, and I have already decided it is unlikely she is knowingly involved in any conspiracy against me. Yet she must have been used in some way, so as she scribbles a prescription for a further five-day course of antibiotics and more painkillers, I ask if she would sketch in some details about my treatment which I can't remember. When I suggest this might help to speed up the full recovery of my memory, she is keen to assist.

It transpires that Matthew's initial consultation about the pain he was experiencing in speech had been many months ago. The operation recommended by Penny Simms had not been pursued, and there had been no further contact with her until ten days ago – immediately after my consultation with Peter Cheung – when Matthew had suddenly requested the operation on an expedited basis for the following Monday, the day of my own operation. I gain the impression that he may have paid handsomely to smooth any rearrangements in her schedule to facilitate this. Apparently, the reason given for such urgency was the unexpected listing of an important case in the high court, which would come to trial within a couple of months, and he wanted his voice to be fully recovered and in pristine condition for the occasion.

"I understand you were called away urgently, just as my operation was completed?" I ask. This is delicate; if I imply any criticism she might clam up, so I try to probe diplomatically. "The stress you must have to cope with daily puts the worries of my professional life into perspective."

She bridles. The smile leaves her face and, putting down the biro, she says defensively, "It's quite normal to leave a patient immediately after the operation is complete. Your care was not compromised. You were in very safe hands with Jeremy Whicher."

"Of course. I wasn't suggesting otherwise. I'm well aware consultants often leave a patient in theatre before they come round. So many calls on your time. I fully understand." I had to raise this to see where it might lead, but it seems she is not going to reveal the nature of her emergency. Still, at least I have established she does not deny leaving me in theatre.

"Well, as I said, there was no danger to you whatsoever. My work was done, the operation routine and completely successful."

"Forgive me. No criticism was intended."

She relaxes, appearing to accept this, and leans across the desk to hand me my prescription.

"Not like poor Andrew Soulsby," I say. Her eyebrows rise at the mention of my name. "I'd met him recently; had a matter on with him at work. In fact, I recommended him to Peter Cheung, the neurosurgeon. He's a client of mine. I know him well. After what happened it makes me feel guilty, in some way responsible." I am likely breaking professional rules of client confidentiality to dig for more information, but what does that matter to me now?

"I can assure you there is nothing to reproach yourself about. Peter Cheung is a top brain surgeon, one of the very best. He would have done everything possible for your friend."

"I saw his wife on Friday. She is devastated," I say, taking a moment as my voice catches and I fight back the tears welling in my eyes. "I need to go to his funeral, pay my respects. I guess it will be after a post-mortem?"

I think she has been surprised at my reaction, the struggle to regain composure, and she answers me sympathetically: "I cannot discuss details of another case but, of course, everyone at the hospital is aware of the death that day, the same day as your operation. These things happen. You bear no responsibility." And then, in her attempt to reassure me, she all but confirms my suspicion of the tall anaesthetist's involvement. "Your friend had the very best treatment money could buy. In fact, our anaesthetist, Jeremy Whicher, is a friend and colleague of the neuro-anaesthetist who works with Peter Cheung. They are all so gifted, and leaders in their fields. They collaborate on research and write papers for the medical press."

A man's voice shouts through the open window from the street below, as if to highlight the significance of this revelation. We both ignore the foul language of the road-rage tirade and the screech of a vehicle accelerating into the distance, yet it prompts her to stand, the signal that it is time for me to leave.

"I might make an appointment to see Jeremy Whicher," I say as we both walk towards the door, "just to cover all bases about my memory loss. Perhaps the anaesthetic drugs—"

"I can't see how." She cuts me short with a shrug. "Patients generally don't see anaesthetists for follow-ups; and anyway, I think he's just gone on holiday so you'd have a long wait." She opens the door, beaming at me with a confident smile. "But as I said, I really don't think you have anything to worry about on that score now." She offers me a limp hand, and it really is time to go.

CHAPTER 11

I call on my business partner, Peter Bright, the following day since I know he will have spoken at length with Cathy. I want to find out what he knows; in particular, has a post-mortem been carried out to ascertain the official cause of my death, where does my body rest and has a date been set for my funeral yet? Then, there is a business proposition I want to put to him.

Our partnership agreement provides for two hundred and fifty thousand pounds to be paid for goodwill, which will now be due from Peter to the estate of Andrew Soulsby. The business pays life-insurance premiums on each of our lives for this sum, and so he will have no problem paying out Cathy – the sole beneficiary under my will – for my share of the partnership. However, there are bound to be practical difficulties in achieving continuity for clients and covering my work until he can find a suitable new partner. Perhaps that might be me?

Our offices are in Palmers Green, North London. We share the top floor of a drab, modern block with a firm of accountants and the administrative headquarters of a large retail furniture group, which also has a store comprising the whole of the ground and first floors. I use the intercom to gain entry, since it would arouse suspicion if I tap in the code originally set by me. When she answers, I ask, Kelly, our receptionist, if Matthew Campbell from Dorrell's might speak briefly with Peter Bright concerning a business matter. I am confident he will see me without appointment, out of curiosity if nothing else, and sure enough, after a slight delay, Kelly's friendly North London drawl directs me to turn left at the top of the communal stairs, then take the third door on the right, as she unlocks the entrance door.

It is my normal practice to jog up the wide, double staircase, but today I walk up more sedately to avoid this new, bulky frame becoming short of breath. I pick up a complimentary copy of *The Times* while I wait in the small reception area set aside within the general office. More allegations of cruelty and human rights abuses against the Chinese government make the headlines, but I find it impossible to concentrate on reading and the words convey no meaning to me.

Computers hum as Valerie and Joan tap their keyboards in diligent concentration. Kelly answers one call after another on the phone with her constantly cheery: "Hello, Soulsby & Bright, solicitors. How may I help you?" Partially shielded by a half-glass partition, in the far alcove, Tracey is almost hidden behind a pile of what look like my files. Between taking phone calls, she pores over papers while speaking into a hand-held dictating machine. I think that I had secretly hoped to find sad and miserable faces, a business obviously stumbling without my presence, but there is no evidence of this from the intense activity and usual colourful attire of the female staff.

A thin-faced little man with black hair and pot belly emerges from the adjacent conference room with a mug of coffee, scurrying into my private office, next to Peter's at the front of the building which overlooks the high street. He must be the locum. Before he closes the door, I make out my desk, creaking under the weight of papers and files. The fleeting sense of panic at the backlog of work, the apparent disorganisation, fades quickly into a feeling of relief, I cannot deny it, that this is no longer my watch or responsibility. It dawns on me how much I had hated the pressure and stress, the monotonous routine that had plagued my daily life for so many years.

Finally, Peter's office door opens, and his tall, lean frame droops shrug-shouldered as he stares at me with a curious half-smile. He is wearing his tired black suit, faded and shining in patches, along with the familiar blue silk tie, frayed around the edges. It strikes me, now more than ever, that he looks older than his forty-two years. As always, my eyes are drawn to the small gold stud in his ear, a tiny rebellion against the drab convention he represents.

"Mr Campbell?" He does not appear to recognise me from that close encounter outside my house last Friday. "I'm Peter Bright." He clasps my hand in a firm grip and beckons me into his office, closing the door behind us. "Please do take a seat… Sorry, I'll just move these," and he lifts a bundle of files from the straight-back chair he has indicated, putting them with a pile of law magazines stacked against the bookcase full of dusty legal tomes on the other side of the room. His office, as always, is a disorganised mess, like a charity-shop dumping ground.

The gold-framed photograph of his daughter as a young child has been moved from on top of the bookcase, where it had lived for many years, and is now perched, precariously, amongst more files and papers on his desk. He sits down, facing me, leaning back in the leather swivel chair behind the desk, holding a biro which he twiddles nervously just below his elongated chin. I know he must be horribly busy and anxious to get on, but in the silence, I hear the faint hum of the electric clock on the wall as he waits for me to speak.

"Thanks for seeing me without prior warning. I called in on the off-chance. I live just a few miles away, and I'm home for a couple of weeks recovering from a small operation." I hesitate, unsure for a moment how to continue. His impatience begins to show, a frown indicating an unwillingness to indulge in small talk or pleasantries, so I decide to get straight to the point. "The thing is, I feel a degree of responsibility for your business partner's sad death."

"I can't see how, unless you were assisting at his operation," he interjects caustically, the lingering West Country twang of his nasal tones betraying his roots, leaving an uneasy atmosphere in the room. This is not going well at all. Peter cannot do humour or sarcasm; it doesn't come naturally to his normally even-tempered nature, but, clearly, he is irritated and probably resentful of my presence.

"The fact remains," I press on, "he only saw Peter Cheung because of my recommendation; if it had all been left alone, perhaps he would have had more time with his family before the symptoms became worse. I want to help with anything I can do for his wife and family. Possibly—"

"Mr Campbell." Peter interrupts me again, his tone uncharacteristically authoritative. "I know you are a successful and wealthy man – Andrew spoke of you with admiration just before he died – but with respect, this is hardly your concern or business. I have known his wife and family for many years; I will be giving Cathy every support, dealing with the probate and financial affairs for her as my client and very close, dear friend. Partnership matters are all provided for, quite in order – everything is amicable." He is obviously stressed and his voice is becoming emotional and strident, a pitch higher.

"Cathy told me you called on her yesterday; I must have just missed you when I was there. The family are most distressed and, to be frank, this did not help; it's not really appropriate for a virtual stranger to knock on their door at such a time. I think it best if you leave them alone."

This is really unusual, Peter becoming animated; he is normally unflappable under pressure. I didn't expect this attitude from him. I must tread more carefully, and so I say, "I didn't intend to cause offence or add to the family's suffering, quite the reverse. Clearly, I've misjudged, acted impulsively. I'm sorry. I hope you will accept my apologies, Mr Bright, and convey them to Mrs Soulsby. Of course, I won't trouble her again, although I hope no further offence will be taken if I attend the funeral to pay my respects to Andrew. I'll keep in the background."

Peter puts down the biro and leans forward, his head in his hands, ruffling through his light brown hair before sitting back straight. "I'm sorry too, Matthew, if I may use your first name?" I mumble my consent, then keep quiet, allowing him to continue. "And please, do call me 'Peter'. I'm afraid I have been rude, quite over-the-top." He manages a strained smile, like a flustered shop assistant dealing with a challenging customer. "I'm sure you would be welcome at the funeral. It's fixed for 3pm this Friday at the North Enfield cemetery."

"Thank you. I shall keep a low profile, as I say, remain in the background."

"I'm sure you can understand it's a bad time; I've known Andy for more years than I care to remember. It was so sudden, a complete shock. He enjoyed such good health. We played club cricket together regularly." He was opening up and more at ease. I wonder, have I acquired Matthew's ability to charm friend and foe alike?

"Do you know yet, what went wrong during the operation?" I chance the question, and sure enough, Peter begins to assume his normal demeanour, happy to chat in that loquacious manner he has, as though now oblivious to the waiting files littering his office. I smile inside my head at how it used to so annoy me, that lack of direction and focus. "It was a dreadful tragedy," he is saying. "Turns out he was desperately sick with two large brain tumours. At least, thanks to you, he had a top brain surgeon doing everything to give him a chance, but he suffered a massive haemorrhage during his operation and couldn't be saved. Your man told Cathy that such risks are inevitable with surgery of that nature and he was just unlucky."

"Has the post-mortem evidence supported this?" I ask him.

"The coroner decided there was no need for further investigation."

So, there will be no evidence to dispute the accounts of Cheung and Peng. I say, "Surely it's surprising not to call for a post-mortem after a death during surgery?"

"I thought so, too, but the coroner discussed it with Cathy. He was very confident to accept the report from the surgeon and anaesthetist, both being such highly regarded medics, and since there were no suspicious circumstances, she was relieved to be able to get on with the funeral arrangements. I'm pleased she was at least spared the trauma of more messing around with poor Andrew's body. I'm not sure any of that would have sat well with her: she has strong religious beliefs, you know."

"That must provide some comfort to her. Do you know who the coroner is, Peter?"

"No. Does it matter?"

"No, just curious in case I might know him or her."

There would have been no reason, of course, for my family to harbour any suspicions that what had occurred was anything other than a terrible tragedy: a valiant but ultimately vain surgical attempt to cure a likely terminal condition by a world-renowned neurosurgeon and neuro-anaesthetist.

"Do you know who is handling the funeral? I'd like to send a charitable donation, or maybe a wreath?"

"Well… it's up to you, I suppose." Peter sounds dubious, but I just want to find out where my body is; I'm pretty sure Cathy would not put Geoff and Lucy through the trauma of having me in the house at any point before the funeral. And it works: he tells me the name of the funeral directors.

"This must all be very hard for you," I say. "Apart from the loss of a friend, I can see you are under a lot of strain here at the office with the sudden loss of your business partner."

"It's pretty chaotic, for sure," he says. "I've got a heavy caseload and Andy had a considerable amount on. He was neat and methodical, very conscientious, not a lot of flair, though; a bit slow. At least his work was faultless and up to date, although it's all getting behind now." He grimaces, a wistful smile of resignation. I must show no emotion but bristle within at this irony coming from the stereotype of a conventional, boring and predictable man; how could he possibly have thought of me in that way? "The support staff are good," he is still speaking, "but there's only so much they can do. There's a locum we took on to cover for Andy having his operation, but he causes more problems than he solves and I have to pay silly money for him to the agency. I'm afraid I'm chained to the office desk twenty-four seven for the foreseeable future." He snorts a funny little laugh.

As he lapses into silence, as if on cue, there is a knock at his door. Without waiting for a response, Tracey half-opens and drapes herself around it, announcing what is palpably a contrived and pre-arranged emergency concerning non-arrival of completion monies requiring his urgent attention. He stands, beginning to excuse himself, his tall, hunched frame as awkward with the manufactured subterfuge as the incongruous gold stud in his ear glinting in a shaft of sunlight from the window.

"Briefly, Peter, before I leave, I have a proposition that I would like you to consider," I say. "I want out from Dorrell's. I'm fed up with the high-powered work, all the pressure, stress and commuting. I'm wealthy but don't want to retire yet. I have a good knowledge of conveyancing; I've always kept my hand in with it, doing work for friends and family – sort of light relief from my commercial litigation practice." After I've said this, it strikes me that it sounds condescending, and I hold my breath it hasn't offended him. Fortunately, though, he tends to be in thrall of wealth and power and seems fine as I swiftly continue: "I could be your new partner; I wouldn't want much by way of profit share, just a way for me to wind down. I'm sure I could cope with Andrew's workload and, perhaps, get you out of this hole?" I must stick to my plan, suppress my anxieties at having to tackle the backlog of now-urgent matters.

"Good Lord!" he answers, then remains silent, dumbfounded. I resist the temptation to elaborate more. Eventually he says, "Are you really serious?"

"Of course, never more so."

He walks to the window and stares vacantly at the grim high street below with its down-market shops and the constant congestion of traffic, his completion emergency seemingly forgotten. "There's a lot to think about," he mutters, his eyes still fixed on the street scene through the window.

I say, "Okay. I'll leave it with you for a week, and then get back to you; see if you wish to take matters further. How's that?"

In truth, I have no idea of Matthew's true wealth and his position at Dorrell's. I don't know how quickly he could terminate his partnership, and whether it imposes any restrictions on him working as a conveyancing solicitor in Palmers Green. Even if it does, they might be legally unenforceable; anything can be achieved where there is sufficient will, but the first step is to ascertain if Peter wants this solution. And if he does, assuming I have not been able to find a way to speak with her properly in the meantime, I will then have ideal opportunities to meet his ex-partner's wife as the new partner and saviour of Soulsby & Bright.

CHAPTER 12

On leaving Peter yesterday, I walked ponderously down the communal flight of double stairs towards the street exit doors. Halfway down I noticed a mural of Formula One racing cars on the flat surface that drops at a right angle from the stairwell ceiling. Two of the accountants working in the building are enthusiasts and no doubt responsible for this display. It had not been there the last time I was at the office on the Saturday morning before my operation. I had popped in then to check the post, make a few notes on files for the locum and get my work up to date.

I remembered being late and rushing away that day, running down the stairs two at a time, hurrying to meet Cathy at Chase House Nursing Home, where we had arranged to visit my mother. Incredibly, that had been only ten days earlier, and the enormity of my life's transformation in such a short period from happy family man to living a stranger's life, divorced from everything and everyone I hold dear, suddenly overwhelmed me, like crashing into an invisible wall of despair. I felt nauseous and lightheaded, before a choking sensation as I held on to the handrail to steady myself, gasping and fighting for breath, my body sticky with sweat…

***

The next thing I remembered was sitting in the driver's seat of the Bentley on the sweeping drive at Matthew's house. I must have suffered some kind of fugue: a terrifying experience in which I lost all self-awareness and memory, for how long I don't know, but I had driven safely to the house in Beech Hill. It was as though my mind tripped a safety wire to sedate all self-awareness. When I came round, sitting in the car, my first thoughts were of my father, and my sister; and of Mum: I felt a strong need to see her, a yearning to talk with her.

Jane had been my only sibling. She was killed in a car crash shortly after her twenty-first birthday when I was fifteen. A part of my parents died with her on a cold, frosty December evening. Dad eventually found some relief from his pain with a belief in Spiritualism: Mum could never quite take that leap of faith. She was widowed fifteen years ago when Dad finally succumbed to lung cancer. Then, early this year, aged eighty, with a failing memory and no longer able to live safely at home alone, she was admitted to the BUPA nursing home.

I had cried in solitude when the sale of my childhood home completed this spring, organised and undertaken by me in what felt like abandonment of youth and cherished memories, but nearly £5,000 per month in fees brooks no sentiment. It was shortly after this that my headaches started and, initially, Cathy and I put them down to tension, to the anxiety and stress of coping with that challenging time; not least the harrowing task of clearing the possessions and keepsakes accumulated over fifty years. So many raw emotions resurfaced for the loss of Jane and my father, so many happy and nostalgic scenes from my past replayed.

By a benevolent irony of fate, Mum's illness has resurrected Jane for her in the form of my daughter. She had always doted on her only grand-daughter, and when she sees Lucy now through the kindly fog of fast-advancing dementia, she looks upon and speaks to her lost daughter, the family tragedy a merciful victim of her fragmenting memory.

Arriving today at Chase House Nursing Home, I half expect the blue Ford Focus that has been following my route at a respectful distance for some time to pull in behind me as I stop the Bentley in an almost-empty car park. It doesn't, of course, but I still feel compelled to walk back to the entrance and check out the residential street. There is no sign of it.

Since leaving hospital I have come to suspect that I am being observed and followed. Perhaps it is, as Helen first suggested, merely paranoia; a natural-enough reaction in my circumstances. I must try to fight the urge to look behind, always checking out the street for non-existent cars and imaginary pursuers. If I am not careful such obsessions might begin to cloud my mind and judgement, even risk my sanity. All my energy and efforts need to be focused on solving this mystery so that I can give myself a chance to prevail over whatever dark forces have targeted me.

When Cathy and I had last visited Mum on that Saturday afternoon eleven days ago, she failed to recognise either of us until prompted to do so. This had not happened before and marked a frightening new stage in her deterioration: it had been very distressing, and Cathy, normally so resolute, wept in the car driving home. I have decided to announce myself today as a family friend if challenged by staff, and to Mum I shall be Andrew, her son, who will regale her with his early childhood memories, most of which she still retains. Perversely, the tragedy of her condition will at least provide me the blissful luxury to converse as myself with Mum, an affirmation of my identity which has been denied to me since Joe Peng knocked me out with his anaesthetic drugs.

A gardener with long, greasy hair is hoeing weeds in the flower borders near the front door of the home with a distinct lack of enthusiasm. As I walk past him, I ignore what looks like a scowl of suspicion on his raised face but feel the glare of resentment spike my back. The reception is unattended, not uncommon in the early afternoon. Since I know the entry code, I don't ring the bell for attention but write up the visitor book using the name of Mum's elderly friend, then peruse it briefly and ascertain there have been no recent visitors. I had hoped that Cathy, Lucy or Geoff would have been in to see her, but on reflection I realise they must be too grief-stricken and consumed with grim arrangements to visit her. At least I am confident Cathy will ensure Mum is not burdened with another bereavement, that of her only surviving child. Although she would not retain the pain of such knowledge beyond a fleeting heartache of time, it would still be an unnecessary and profound sorrow.

As I pass through the home, the fading smell of cooked cabbage from lunch mingles with the pervading whiff of disinfectant. There is no obvious nursing presence, and I pause at the communal lounge to check if Mum is sitting in one of the armchairs which are all covered with protective vinyl. They circle the large room, like a wagon train at night in an old cowboy western. Mum is not there, but other pitiful faces with broken bodies and minds are either silent or mumbling and smiling vacantly. An obese woman is wheeling a tea trolley, and the cups she pours remain full, soon forgotten. A massive television flickers with unwatched images of daytime soaps.

Making my way to her room on the first floor, in the distance I hear a tormented female voice: "Nurse, where's my coat? I want to go home," and her cries continue on a loop. I feel an icy chill at the thought of having aged perhaps ten years in less than two weeks, as I silently mouth the prayer of all visitors here: please spare me such final ignominy. And I feel guilty, of course I do, that my loving, selfless mother should end her days this way. Chase House might be an upmarket nursing home, but there is no disguising the human misery that would not be countenanced for pet animals.

In the corridor I pass an Asian nurse I do not recognise from previous visits. She smiles at me sweetly as I near Mum's door, which is open. I pull it closed behind me, glad to have some privacy. It is a modest-sized room, recently decorated with fresh, bright paint, and the linoleum floor tiles sparkle with cleanliness. The car park below is visible from a large window, left open a crack to let in fresh air, but the central heating remains on to shroud us in stifling, dry heat.

Mum is dozing in an armchair beside her bed in a flimsy nightdress, a blanket around her ankles on the floor where it has fallen down. Her chin rests on her flat, bony chest, with hollow cheeks and deep wrinkles on her speckled and sallow skin evidencing a dramatic loss of weight. She has deteriorated even more since I last saw her. Tears well in my eyes to find her in this dreadful state: the dying embers of a proud, confident woman who had been the matriarch of our family. When I was a little boy, she always solved my problems and made it better; if only I could roll back the years, tell her what has happened and wait while she solves the puzzle to make it better for me now.

I pull over a hard-back chair from the other side of the room to sit on and take her frail, gnarled hand in mine. Slowly, her eyes open in a mist of confusion but, eventually, she appears to focus on me. A faint smile spreads across her face and the grip on my hand strengthens perceptibly, as she says in a faltering voice: "Hello, son; why are you here today?"

CHAPTER 13

FRIDAY 17TH JULY

For the first time since my arrival from the hospital ten days ago, Helen did not leave the house at the crack of dawn this morning. She joked with me at breakfast about her cooking – apparently the housekeeper has a day off. She seemed withdrawn and pensive, though; somehow less assured, less confident. Her hazel eyes lacked their usual sparkle, but it was difficult not to admire the glimpse of thigh and slender legs dangling from the stall next to mine at the breakfast bar.

"Is the play still going well?" I asked.

"Umm… not so bad, Matty." She forced a smile but was obviously distracted, her thoughts elsewhere.

"I'm sure you're a sensational Candida. I bet you pack in audiences to watch a beautiful actor in a classic role." Giving compliments always made me feel good, but this clearly surprised her from Matthew, and she laughed, shedding ten years, her weary face assuming a softer, natural beauty.

"That's a first: praise, and calling me an actor! It's only a limited run at the National Theatre, another five weeks, but we have almost sold out now." She paused, her eyes fixed on mine as I sipped lukewarm tea, then she said in a quieter voice, "What's happened to you, Matty? It's as though you're a totally different person since waking up from that little operation: kind, attentive and thoughtful. Your transformation from the brash, self-obsessed man with his veneer of false charm that I found myself married to is amazing."

"Those words are truer than you'd ever believe, Helen." I bit my tongue, again fighting the urge to share my solitary burden with her.

"I can't be doing cryptic wisdom, Matty; particularly this morning. What do you mean, my love? …What did the consultant woman say about this memory thing?" Her brow was furrowed with concern as she stretched out a hand to rest tender fingers on my shirt sleeve, and it dawned on me for the first time that she wore no wedding ring.

"I'm sorry, it's nothing really; just me reverting to type and being pompous." I put my cup of tea on the breakfast bar, withdrawing my arm from her touch as I did so, and tried to suppress the thrill coursing through Matthew's body. "What I meant was I've used the opportunity of my memory loss to turn over a new leaf." I laughed, a false, nervous little laugh.

"But what did she say about the memory?" She pursued her unanswered question. "I think it could be serious."

"She said not. Apparently, it can happen sometimes; a reaction, perhaps, to a build-up of stress and tension over the years. The anaesthetic acts as a catalyst." I found the lies came so easily, not like me at all. "She believes it will return gradually over the next few weeks with no need for any treatment." Which, to be fair, was pretty much what she had said.

Helen remained silent, but there was a frown of bemusement on her face since, clearly, the idea of Matthew Campbell succumbing to stress and tension did not sit easily with her. And I think she sensed I was lying, improvising Penny Simms' prognosis, but she couldn't work out why. Then she got up and began to clear the breakfast plates, clattering them together carelessly.

"You should know, Matty, that Mark and I have ended the affair." She was standing by the butler sink, staring vacantly out of the window at lumps of grey cloud being chased across blue sky on a strong breeze rattling through the garden trees. There was a wistful melancholy, yet resignation in her cut-glass voice. "To be brutally honest, darling, I've been dumped."

I wasn't sure how to react as she turned to face me, fighting to hold tears glistening on her eyes. Should I have comforted her, or been shocked, even outraged? I had no idea whether her husband knew or, if he did, whether he cared about this affair.

"I'm so sorry, Helen." I said what came naturally, what I felt, but unable to move, stuck in my seat.

She buried her face behind the lattice of her cupped hands for a moment, then lifted her head to stare at the ceiling with a frustrated sigh, showing the wrinkles not yet hidden by make-up. "God, Matty," she threw the words at me, "you don't remember, do you? Can you recall anything at all about our life together, our relationship?"

"No, I can't. The memory of my whole life is missing. I don't know how I am expected to behave… But, Helen, there is more to this… I just can't explain it to you yet."

I had said too much – I found it easy to open up to this woman – but fortunately she didn't appear to register those last words as she told me a little of her story. "I've been with Mark for the last couple of years. We met on tour; it was a wonderful time, those first few months around the country with my gorgeous leading man." Her eyes sparkled at the thought of her lover, but I don't think any malice or spite was intended towards her husband in the telling. "He appreciated me and my body. I knew it wouldn't last – he's only twenty-eight now – but I find that, unlike the others, I've grown very fond of him… not love, of course…" She took a moment to compose herself. "You've known, Matthew. It's all been open on my side, although you've always kept your own affairs secret." Her voice rose in a bitter spike, unable to mask her contempt. "I know your false charms have helped you screw anything with a pulse."

"For how long has there been no us?"

"We haven't slept in the same bed for more than ten years." She was glaring at me across the kitchen, her hazel eyes wide open, like fiery discs searing into Matthew's head, accusing and confronting past wounds and lost love. "I was besotted with you for years; your charm, that arrogant confidence. But finally, I saw through it all: the moment it clicked was when I spotted you in a fancy restaurant canoodling some gormless tart, and the spell broke; I confronted reality. For the first time I saw what must have been so obvious: the curtain rose and the spotlight shone down to reveal your grubby little soul to me."

There was such a depth of passion. It was confirmation that the nonchalance and disinterest had been affected and false, just as I'd suspected ever since she drove me back from the Wellington Hospital.

"You must hate me." I felt sorry for her and despised the man she thought I was. How could he have treated her in such a way?

"I did at first, and we've lived totally separate lives ever since. It's suited both of us to continue living under this same rather large roof and keep up the pretence of marriage, but our paths cross infrequently."

"Anything you may have done, any affairs trying to find happiness, it seems to me must have all been more than justified by Matthew's behaviour," I told her, hoping to convey how genuinely I felt this.

"You talk as if it wasn't you. It's been your behaviour. Just because you've lost your memory doesn't mean you're not responsible." But the fire and venom had gone, almost as quickly as it had flared up, to be replaced by words that sounded calm, a reflective sadness with that same hint of curious concern about me. "I'm sorry, Matty. Recounting all this rekindled the old hurt and briefly brought some of that buried emotion back to the surface... And I feel very fragile this morning."

In the silence that followed her eyes met mine across the room, and I felt her trying to fathom whether I was sincere. And so, I told her again: "I mean what I said, Helen. My conduct towards you seems to have been despicable."

"I'm confused," she said. "Are you for real, Mr Nice-guy Campbell? You see, I just can't get my head round this new persona since your operation. You're a better actor than me; you took me in for so many years, and I can't let you do that again... but you do appear to be different."

"I am different—" But before I said too much, what I would have regretted later, she interrupted me.

"No more words, Matty. I need to be on my own and have some time to think, my love." And I knew better than to say anything else to her as she strode purposely from the kitchen, but I was beginning to think I might be able to trust this woman, that she might have the instinct and imagination to believe the unbelievable.

CHAPTER 14

The thought of my funeral this afternoon fills me with dread, and yet I can't deny the singular buzz of morbid curiosity. I have left the balcony and I am sitting in a pink balloon backed chair, staring at the bed. My funeral attire is set out in readiness on the bedspread, which has an intricate braid design of golden swirls, like a maze to mirror the tumult in my mind. A silver case, embossed with the initials 'MC', lays open and full of slow poison on top of the bedside cabinet, and it takes a strong effort of will to resist the urge to smoke one of the cigarettes on offer. In a decisive moment, I get up and snap the case shut, then tuck it out of sight in a drawer. I am Andrew, for God's sake, not Matthew, and I don't smoke!

I walk to the French windows leading to the balcony and look beyond the garden towards the brook running through a distant valley where wisps of early morning mist still linger. The sun is gaining strength, though, burning bright warmth through the hazy sky. My head aches from thinking about this afternoon. I have played out so many scenarios: how I should act and respond to friends who will not recognise me; and then, even more harrowing, to watch the suffering of those I love. I understand the need to remain in the background and not draw attention to Matthew Campbell, whose connection to the deceased is nebulous. Every spin of tactics around my mind rests at the same conclusion: the objective, beyond morbid curiosity, is observation, hopefully to glean more information and clues.

I had finally galvanised myself to visit the funeral directors yesterday in the hope that, somehow, I might be able to see my body to be sure of its death. From the bustle of the high street, I had entered an eerily silent and sparsely furnished room where a green sofa clashed with the burgundy chaise-longue. I rang the bell beside a vase of white lilies on the teak counter, and a plump, middle-aged woman appeared whose fixed smile complemented her obsequious manner.

I am not sure if I was disappointed that my request to bid a final goodbye to a close friend brought a diplomatic but firm refusal: not without sanction from Mrs Soulsby. The enthusiastic assurance that the deceased reposed in their discreet Chapel of Rest next door dressed in his best suit, smiling serenely from a white satin bed, at peace in an impressive, mahogany coffin, brought a shiver and goose-bumps on my skin. Yet the trip had not been entirely wasted since it established Cathy had already viewed my body and, apparently, my business partner was due to visit later that day. So, I had what I needed: the certainty that it was my lifeless cadaver in the casket awaiting burial this afternoon.

I am still struggling to resist the pull of nicotine from where it calls within the drawer of the bedside cabinet. As a teenager I had a short-lived dalliance with smoking but soon tired of it, overcoming the peer pressure before addiction took hold. Since Matthew's body has released me from the compulsion to tear at my skin, which often became inflamed with flare-ups of eczema, I do not intend to succumb to his filthy habit. Resist it and I will at least not add to whatever damage has already been caused to the lungs and heart I now rely on.

I need some distraction, and picture again Helen at breakfast this morning: fragile and sad, her protective mask slipping to reveal kind tenderness; and then in a flash that intensity of fierce accusation and hurt. I see her willowy frame perched delicately upon the stool, the tattoo on her slim ankle, and the image brings with it a powerful erection which is impossible to resist.

It is not easy to manage this strange body. Certainly, there is delight in solving problems swiftly: the most difficult crosswords are easy; the veil of confusion lifted from technology. And yet there is despair to suffer aching muscles, creaking bones, to pop the statins and blood-pressure pills prescribed by a GP I do not know, and the yearning to smoke, of course, accompanied by shortness of breath after moderate exercise. And perhaps worst of all is my frustration at being quite unable to control such strong sexual arousal, which manifests itself involuntarily at the least provocation. Pleasuring myself had been just a distant adolescent memory, but now it is impossible to resist.

Hoping to lose this unwanted reaction to Helen, which makes me feel cheap and disloyal, I think of my distraught wife at our front door last Friday, one week ago today. It is as though my memory sees her through a magnifying glass, bringing every aspect of her features into sharp, vivid focus: those piercing, bloodshot blue eyes quite haunting; the agony so apparent from her tortured face; and the dismissive words to send me packing, all replayed in timeless and agonising slow motion. And then I am driving away again, and there she is crying in Peter's embrace.

For a few moments this distressing memory does the trick and calms Matthew's libido. But my mind is on fire and the image fades to be replaced by a new scene: Cathy by candlelight on Friday evening two weeks ago, sitting opposite me at a table for two in our favourite Palmers Green restaurant. She was wearing a blue dress with plunging neckline, and her short-cut auburn hair looked perfect following an afternoon away from Chambers at Toni and Guy's. Rouge lipstick and my favourite pearl earrings completed her jaw-dropping appearance. I had finished late at the office, trying to get straight before my enforced absence. She had suggested the romantic meal with a few glasses of wine, hoping we could forget about my impending surgery for just a few, sweet hours, although we both knew what remained unsaid: it might be our last evening out together.

The physical side of our relationship had been buffeted down the years as we pursued our respective careers while bringing up children, and, of course, the mundane routine of everyday life had taken its toll. Sex had become less frequent, maturing into the fulfilment of loyal friendship, the unquestioning commitment and deep affection of love. So, it had been unexpected when Cathy didn't drive straight home that night but risked the breathalyser to park up in a country lane. In a hidden access beside a field gate, while the ever-present M25 droned in the distance like an upset stomach, we had clambered over the gear change and squeezed into the back seat for the best sex I can remember in years.

If I am honest, I can't remember how long before that it was since we'd last had sex. It must have been many months. We had both been busy working, and to make matters worse over the last year, I had been living with the added stress of selling the family home and making all the arrangements for Mum. So that wonderful evening, Cathy's verve and desire was such a revelation and a comfort. It reaffirmed our youthful passion and the joy of lustful, spontaneous sex. I will never forget her words as we curled up afterwards, shoehorned together in a naked embrace: "So good, Soulsby." (I was always 'Andy' to her in everyday life, 'Andrew' being the rarity of frosty moods, but 'Soulsby' was reserved as the strange intimacy she used in moments when emotion was strong.) "I promise you much more sex like that. No more excuses that we're too knackered after work. I'm not going to leave you alone; I'll have you back renewed and raring to go after next week."

It had been over twenty-three years since we'd last had sex in a car; even then, before we were married with a place of our own, it had not been often. There had been more comfortable alternatives:

at my parents' house when they were out, at Cathy's flat in Camden when an accommodation was negotiated with her flatmates and at my late grandmother's empty terraced house on the less salubrious side of Enfield.

My roots are working-class and it had been a first in our family circle when I went to university and graduated to train as a solicitor. This had produced mixed reactions within the wider family, some petty jealousy and tensions, but my hardworking, thrifty parents were very proud, and so too my widowed grandmother who had appointed her trainee solicitor grandson to be sole executor of her will. After she had died, her little house was unoccupied for almost a year while probate was obtained and a sale eventually completed. During this time, I had the keys and did not rush to dispose of the furniture or clear the property; as Cathy and I joked at the time, legal ownership of Gran's property vested in me during the estate's administration.

It had been only a month after her death that I first met Cathy at the magistrates' court. It was not long before Gran's house became our secret hotbed of passion. Visits there were always late, under cover of darkness as though forbidden, and so they had assumed a deliciously naughty, almost illicit quality. Sadly, this felicitous arrangement came to an abrupt end after about six months when a neighbour had phoned to tell me he thought he might have heard noises in the empty house late at night. We were both too embarrassed to ever return!

These poignant memories of Cathy produce the inevitable reaction from the testosterone-fuelled monster I inhabit. I feel ashamed, yet unable to resist his base urges, as I slink naked into the shower to indulge the only relief available to me. When it is done, I cover his sagging flesh with a silk dressing gown and return to the balcony to find dark, grey clouds laced with purple menace brewing in the far west, teasing the prospect of rain for my funeral this afternoon. Wearing only this thin dressing gown, Andrew's slight frame would shiver in the morning's rising sun, but I feel refreshed from the shower and pleasantly warmed by Matthew's bulk.

Then the silly ringtone from Jack Bauer's *24* – evidence of Matthew's ego and an unsophisticated humour which is a rather surprising chink of immaturity in the serious City lawyer persona – calls from where the iPhone is nestled on top of a chest of drawers, beside his leather wallet. It rarely rings, and when it does, I always let it go to voicemail. Since I first checked it on the Tuesday Helen drove me here from the hospital, the only further texts and voicemails received have been from Shivani, providing conclusive proof of their secret affair. No doubt there will be another message from her when I check it again, imploring me, like the rest, to speak with her and arrange to meet.

I have still not responded to the file of papers delivered by courier last week from Matthew's office, since I have been unable to access his email account to do so. The papers relate to a multi-party action claiming damages for spinal cord and central nervous system injuries, resulting in a variety of outcomes, including paralysis, comas, amnesia and other brain damage, all caused, it is alleged, by a new anaesthetic drug manufactured by Wilkinson Pharmaceuticals, for whom Matthew's company, Dorrell's, are acting.

Surely this connection is not just a coincidence? Penny Simms told me Peter Cheung and Joe Peng collaborate in producing papers on medical research. What if they are linked to this company and there is more sinister, secret research? Yet one thing must be certain: Matthew Campbell would not be complicit in any conspiracy that left him a living shell, home to another man's consciousness.

Last night I tried to read the complete file in more detail, but my concentration strayed, always drawn like a magnet towards today's funeral and the terrible fate that awaits my own body within the bowels of North London clay. For a moment I contemplate trying again, but quickly dismiss the idea, convincing myself that it is prudent to wait and hopefully learn more at the funeral, before tackling all of these issues when I go to Dorrell's as Matthew on Monday morning.

I want to watch the TV preview of the second day's play in the fourth test match between England and Australia. It should be starting about now and might distract me for the next couple of hours until I have to get ready for the funeral. All I have to do is touch a button on the wall console and a large, flat-screen monitor will rise like a phoenix from the foot of the bed. But I don't move from the balcony. A herd of Friesian cattle are munching on lush pastures beyond the garden, while I am back inside Cathy's car, reliving with relish that invigorating sex with my wife.

CHAPTER 15

I hear a swift rap on the panelled mahogany of the bedroom door, and it opens on squealing hinges like the grating, high-pitched whine of a hungry cat. I feel irritated by this intrusion which breaks my reverie of that blissful evening with Cathy two weeks ago, jolting me back to confront my harsh reality. Reluctantly, I turn away from the balcony views and walk into the bedroom to find Helen's sardonic smile at the open door.

She is wearing blue jeans with black boots just below the knee, and the aroma of her perfume provides a sweet aftershock. "There's some post for you." Her face is now refreshed with pale lipstick and mascara glistening above her hazel eyes, and she enters with the languid chill I recall so vividly from the first time I saw her in the private hospital eleven days ago. With an air of casual disdain, she drops a small bundle of letters onto the bed, scattering them over the funeral clothes. "Mind games, Matty. I don't know why yet, but you're playing mind games with me." She throws an accusing glare, her fail-safe mask of nonchalant disinterest compromised by such evident contempt.

I cannot blame her. When she left me after breakfast this morning her confusion at my persona was as obvious and understandable as her distress for the end of her love affair. It seems that her deliberations have discounted the possibility of a reformed Matthew, imputing to his conduct only the base motives she has experienced from his past, and I see before me a woman determined to confront and defy the emotional turbulence in her world.

"That's not true, Helen, though I do totally understand why you would think so," I protest, sounding too reasonable, I expect.

She smirks, then glances at the black suit laid out on the bed, and asks, in a voice laced with reproach, "I presume you still propose to attend that poor man's funeral this afternoon?"

She is standing at the foot of the bed, struggling to quell simmering anger, a mauve jacket with black spots swaying open just below her denim hips, and it is impossible not to be physically attracted to her. How could Matthew have lived under the same roof for ten years and failed to repair his damage, to share his wife's bed? How could he have cheated on her in the first place, failed to cherish such a sensitive, kind nature screaming beneath the hurt and anger?

"I can't dismiss my involvement in events," I say. "He was obviously such a decent and hardworking family man. I only met him briefly, but I liked him; and the family's tragedy, what his wife and children must be going through… I just can't put it out of my mind. I need to pay my respects." I speak softly, my voice still slightly husky after the throat surgery, but I doubt that the posh, suave accent, like Helen's cut-glass intonation, will ever become familiar to my ear. There was a time when the younger me would have instinctively resented such refined and exaggerated speech, regarding it as an ostentatious manifestation of class and privilege: that was before the years of 'New Labour' governments taught me that while accents might sometimes change at the opera, nothing will trump the innate human desire for superiority. And now, by an unexplained, quite incredible irony of fate, in disillusioned maturity, I have acquired the lifestyle and characteristics I so despised in my youth.

"You know what I think, Matty: best left alone." Her manner is more conciliatory now, not so accusing, and the voice is softer. I can feel the mood change in this mercurial woman as she grapples with her emotions and confusion, like cotton wool entangled in her mind. "Still, the motives appear to be kind... thinking about other people's feelings for once. I hope you find what comfort you seek this afternoon, but do try to stay in the background, my love. No reverting to type; just stay with the New Man." Her laugh is hollow, yet I fancy it is not entirely cynical now.

"I will. Thanks, Helen." Then I hear myself saying, "You look much better now, quite lovely. It can't be easy for you... I mean, with Mark in the play... I presume he is?"

"It's just one of those things, darling. Sometimes I do think life conspires against me, but I will never let it beat me, Matty." The determination in her voice is impressive: the show – her life – must go on.

She walks, pensively, towards the bedroom door, boots and unbuttoned jacket clear notice of her intention to leave the house. I find myself wanting to delay her and blurt out, "Will you wait, Helen; I'd like to talk." She turns to face me again, flecks of blonde hair on her forehead, framed like a portrait in the open doorway with the sweep of wide landing and stairs behind her.

"The thing is your memory is blanked, okay?" she says, oblivious to what I have just asked as something significant dawns on her. "You say you can't remember me, your past life or behaviour, this house; and yet you do remember this poor guy – was his name Andrew? – that you hardly knew? In fact, you seem to be almost obsessed with him." She says this slowly, pondering the inconsistency as she tries in vain to fit my jigsaw puzzle together with missing pieces from two incompatible sets.

"It doesn't make sense, any more than your apparent personality transplant, my love." She becomes more animated. "I don't recognise this kind, considerate man who doesn't rush back to his office or want to see all his cronies. You've never behaved remotely like this, not even during the early years when I was under your spell... You do seem to be genuine, yet it doesn't all add up. If it's not play-acting – and God knows for what purpose that would be – I think, perhaps, that operation has skittled your brain more profoundly than a little temporary amnesia."

I pick up the fear masked in those last words: she is weighing my sanity. The events of recent days must have been traumatic for her. She has experienced the end of her love affair and the dramatic change of dynamic in the relationship of convenience with her husband: the accommodation, even familiarity, re-established with, no doubt, reluctant resignation over many years, shattered so quickly, like the shock of an unexpected illness.

"I'm not mad, Helen," I say. "I'm completely sane. Something dreadful, that I can't understand or explain yet, did happen to me in that hospital. It's connected to Andrew Soulsby, the solicitor who has died; that's why I want to talk with you and hope for your trust, even if on your past experience of me I don't deserve it."

I have spoken impulsively because it is now clear that to live in this house, ostensibly as Helen's husband, without eventually arousing overwhelming suspicion as to my sanity or motives is untenable. I may come to regret confiding in her, but what have I to lose really? And I am experiencing the most wonderful mood change. I feel such joy and relief at the prospect of sharing the onerous weight of my lonely ordeal; the chance to explain my tragedy and perhaps find a sympathetic ear to help make sense of the senseless, and discuss a plan of action.

I must trust my instinct that Helen is open-minded and capable of embracing the possibility of an unexplained, impossible truth, that she will not become a witness for my committal. Nevertheless, how I tell her requires thought; I must not rush headlong into disjointed, ill-prepared revelations while she stands before me on the cusp of her day and commitments.

Despite doubting my faith, I have often sought guidance over these last eleven days through solitary prayer, and the inspiration from this moment of decisiveness – the settled intention to reveal my identity to Helen as soon as possible – fills me with optimism. I am conscious that I have the advantage of Matthew's brain, so well versed in skills of advocacy, to ease my task. Perhaps my prayers really are heard and I am not alone?

Helen cuts a pitiful figure, confused and vulnerable, as she turns away from me momentarily, then sighs with the gnawing pain of indecision. Her right profile does not flatter and, but for the swell of silicone, this gaunt-looking woman could be someone else, much older, who appears faintly unbecoming in smart, young clothes. For once Matthew's libido is calmed, and as I watch her there is no hint of another man's lust to be contained, only a sense of hope that, even if only out of curiosity, she will agree to hear me.

She looks back, her eyes fixing mine with that aura of languid superiority. "Okay, Matty, but obviously not now. I must leave, and you have your funeral to attend." Such grim irony in her choice of words. "I shall probably stay over at the flat in town after tonight's performance; there's a matinee tomorrow as well as the evening show… I'll be here for Sunday?"

"It's a date." I try to hide from my voice the joy I feel at this small first step while supressing the broad smile aching to break over Matthew's wrinkled face.

Helen, graceful as ever, comes to join me. I feel self-conscious, still only wearing her husband's silk dressing gown, and with stubble on my face, unshaven since the morning of my visit to Mum's nursing home, two days ago. She pauses to reveal the hint of a fleeting smile, then kisses me on one cheek – lingering just a fraction too long to discount the possibility of affection – before making a swift retreat without words, the front door thundering shut a minute or so later as she leaves the house.

CHAPTER 16

This morning's mail, strewn like ugly pieces of giant, white confetti over the black clothes laid out on the bed, turns out to be junk only, although rather a larger daily dose than usual. As custodian of Matthew's post over the last eleven days, I have received a motley collection of literature, touting – with varying degrees of marketing sophistication – a multitudinous range of goods and services, including exciting financial opportunities, holidays of a lifetime, relaxing short breaks, a forest of fashion and the fastest good pasta or pizza in North London. Within this period only a dental inspection reminder, notice of AGM from Hadley Wood Golf Club and details of a forthcoming Ladies' Night from a masonic lodge, have escaped immediate recycling to remain, unanswered, within the letter rack on his study desk.

I am just leaving the bedroom to sacrifice today's ample offering in the recycle bin when I notice it. A sturdy, white envelope lying on the thick-piled, beige carpet, almost overlooked since it is partially obscured by the cascading skirts of golden swirls on the bedspread. It must have fallen there earlier, undetected.

I bend over to pick it up, an instinctive, sudden movement, what has always been normal for me with the knees flexing only slightly.

This swift manoeuvre rewards me with a piercing, sharp drill boring into my lower back. I sit on the bed for support, pushing the black suit to one side, and gently straighten my trunk, pulling shoulders apart. I hear creaking bones, like yelps of pain, but it quickly subsides into a dull ache which, I know from past experiences over these last eleven days, will persist for many hours. The sooner I can learn to accommodate this body's idiosyncrasies and not react for Andrew's physique, the sooner I will cease suffering the harsh lessons of sickening aches and pains, and also reduce the risks of causing more permanent damage.

The envelope is in my hand, good quality and watermarked, the words 'Hepplewhite-Brown' embossed in large print on its flap: this is important, certainly not a circular, and the name is familiar. I believe it is a large firm of Bristol solicitors. I find the gold-rimmed specs in the bedside cabinet and place them on the end of my nose. It is addressed to Matthew Paul Campbell, Esq., marked: 'Strictly Private and Confidential'. I open it with care to reveal two sheets of matching, quality white paper, folded twice, precisely into quarter-size, stapled together in the top left-hand corner. My own law practice could not have justified such expensive stationery and I wonder which wealthy client will ultimately be paying for this? As I smooth the sheets open to read the neatly typed paragraphs the chilling answer is soon apparent.

Dear Sir,

We act for Bradgate Financial plc who hold a Legal Charge secured over your freehold house in Beech Hill, Hadley Wood, Barnet, Hertfordshire, and your leasehold flat at Bedford Court, Covent Garden, WC2.

As you will be aware a Possession Order was granted against you in respect of both properties on 23rd March last at The Royal Courts of Justice in the Chancery Division of the High Court.

This was suspended following your payment of £100,000 at the Hearing towards the total mortgage arrears of £175,752, and further your agreement to make additional monthly payments of £5,000 towards the balance arrears and costs, along with the regular monthly instalment, currently £19,726.

We are instructed that you have failed to make those agreed payments in full over the last two months, and indeed we are informed by our client that to date no payments at all have been received for the current month, since both of your bank mandates have been declined. Our client cannot allow this serious situation to continue, and therefore no further forbearance will be granted, not least in view of the troubled history of this account.

Accordingly, we are instructed to enforce the Order for possession of both properties without further notice to you, unless you are able to make full payment, strictly within the next seven days, of the outstanding mortgage debt, interest and costs in the total sum of £4,085,724 as at the date hereof. Interest is accruing at the rate of £657.94 per day. Should this course of action become necessary further attendant legal costs and judicial expenses will also be incurred and strenuously sought against you.

We await to hear from you with the payment as a matter of urgency failing which you will shortly receive notices of eviction from the Sheriff's Office at the High Court Enforcement Department.

Yours faithfully,
Hepplewhite-Brown

My portly frame shudders. Outside, sunlight has faded into dull cloud cover and I think there are spots of rain in the cool breeze. The French doors are wide open to the balcony and, as the drapes rustle, I begin to feel chilly wearing only this silk dressing gown. I must get dressed, but first I slowly re-read the letter that is trembling between my chubby fingers, in order to fully digest all of the implications.

Helen has told me previously that she has no knowledge of her husband's financial affairs. Since the letter is addressed to Matthew alone, it appears she has no joint legal ownership of her matrimonial home, nor the London flat, from both of which she is shortly to suffer the shock of forcible ejection. Our forthcoming Sunday chat must be expanded: she has rights, and needs to take urgent legal advice, since unless complicated procedures have been fully, meticulously complied with, she may be able to successfully resist the bank's claim to remove her from this house, although probably not the flat.

Where is Matthew when the edifice of his character and reputation, no doubt a careful construct over a legal career spanning many years, begins to crumble? Has his consciousness somehow been lost with Andrew Soulsby's cadaver, which is awaiting imminent committal below six feet of cold, heavy clay? Last night I had that same macabre dream again, the one I had in the hospital, but the face of the man Peter Cheung was gloating over on the gurney next to my body was still obscured. It can't be real, can it, surely only a vivid dream? And yet I sense the other man hidden from my view must be Matthew.

And what of me, now Matthew to the world: where am I to live; who will care? Not Cathy, not Geoff nor Lucy, none of my friends at the cricket club, not Peter Bright nor my work colleagues. They will probably attend my funeral this afternoon, a few may notice me alone among the congregation in a remote pew, or standing solitary near the graveside, but my presence will meet with bland indifference at best, and a niggling rancour from some for the rich and ruthless city lawyer. Only Peter might wish to chat, self-interest trumping latent envy, should he be seriously considering my business proposition. And if he is, will he not change his mind on discovering the parlous state of his potential new partner's finances? Peter is a cautious man: his due diligence would be certain to reveal this.

The loss of my past is an almost impossible burden to bear: my soulmate – the love of my life – and my son and daughter, all condemned to live in ignorance of their doting husband and father; the loss of my fitness and health, so carefully nurtured, now trapped within this ageing body that has drunk life to the lees. And what of the scant consolation of wealth and power, to be held in awe with the hint of envy from colleagues; this too will likely soon be gone.

Does Matthew have any real friends to whom I could turn for support, perhaps for shelter when I am homeless? As if in answer to my question the ringtone from Jack Bauer's *24* fills my head again, and for the first time I seriously contemplate picking up the iPhone from where it rests on top of the chest of drawers and answering it. But the jingle stops before I gather confidence for another impulsive act this morning; and I am relieved. Stick to my plan: wait until after the funeral, then speak to Helen on Sunday and go to Dorrell's on Monday morning to see what unfolds.

Save for Shivani, there have been no follow-ups to unanswered texts, and no impromptu callers at the house, suggesting close friendships are unlikely. Matthew's secret lover would hardly risk coming here, but still her texts and voicemails continue, ever more desperate. It was almost certainly her again just now, yet I can't bring myself to look. I suspect both of this morning's calls, if I had answered them, would have revealed a live version of the sexy, beguiling voice recorded so many times on voicemail. While I can, eventually, explain and excuse to her my failure to respond – illness and temporary amnesia following my operation – I cannot contemplate continuing a sexual relationship, and in any event, her infatuation with an overweight, late middle-aged man is unlikely to survive disclosure of high court possession proceedings bringing, in their wake, loss of wealth and reputation.

As Matthew Campbell I have not really had to consider the availability of cash over these last eleven days. His wallet contained £520 in crisp £20 banknotes when Helen returned it to me as soon as we left the Wellington Hospital. Since then, I have broken into one note only, buying a few coffees and newspapers. The Bentley, despite my few excursions, has over half a tank of petrol left, and food, groceries, all household essentials, just appear, including cooked meals when required, courtesy of Jean, the demure and discrete housekeeper, who even picked up Penny Simms' prescription for me. There are also three credit cards in his wallet – a Platinum Barclaycard, a Mastercard and an American Express Gold – a Barclays bank card (I have not attempted to use any of these cards yet) and a rail travel pass, together with two condoms tucked deep within a zipped flap.

I have still not been able to access Matthew's email account nor any of his financial records. I assume his banking is online because there are no traces of any paper bank statements or correspondence. At some point after the weekend, I must gather his ID documents – I have already located his passport – and attend the local branch of Barclays in Barnet to get fresh codes and access his account. I should have done this before. But I do want to know now, before the funeral this afternoon, the validity of the bank and credit cards, and the extent of my cash liquidity.

***

I stand a respectful distance behind an old woman who is wearing a lilac-coloured mac and worried frown on a deeply furrowed face, her ancient frame cowered over the ATM. It has taken me less than five minutes to walk here from the house. We are outside the sub-post office in the parade of small shops adjacent to Hadley Wood Railway Station. She is flustered and muttering in a frustrated conversation with herself. I would like to help her but I know that would be considered inappropriate, a sad reflection on modern society. Her resolution, the determination to resist, to fight back against gathering frailty, is a brave response of will to life's final, harsh challenges. I hope she can keep her independence and be spared the indignities of Mum's final humiliation.

As I left Chase House Nursing Home on Wednesday, two days ago, I spoke to the Asian nurse I had seen earlier that day in the corridor near Mum's room. She was chatting to an even younger-looking colleague by the lift I was about to use but quickly abandoned her conversation, greeting me with a wide smile. It struck me she possessed glistening white teeth, marred only by a slight gap between the front two. She could see I was upset, fighting back tears, and her smile faded to one of concern as she reached a logical conclusion.

"You are Mrs Soulsby's son?"

For more than an hour I had been reliving childhood memories with my cherished mother. When I had last seen her with Cathy nearly two weeks before, she failed to recognise us until prompted, and so I had been confused by her instant recognition of 'Matthew' as her son. She spoke to me throughout the visit as 'Andy', without any prompt from me. Could her failing mind have miraculously developed a prescient sixth sense? In my confusion, in the emotion of the moment, I had answered the nurse truthfully, before quickly correcting myself with an embarrassed, false laugh: "I mean, *she* thought so, but I'm really only a neighbour – just shocked at how fast she has deteriorated…"

I remember the nurse's response which helped to dispel some of that confusion. "I see, yes. It's very sad for you, but good for her, I think? She can talk to whoever she wants to be with. She dreams of her son before you visit, perhaps? I am new here today but she must have a son she loves. This afternoon I was her dentist, and when the doctor saw her after lunch, she so happy; he was her husband." The tears would not be denied as I averted my face and hurried to the nearby lift without speaking. Once inside it, when the door closed, I cried alone, and prayed Mum's final release would come soon… I wonder what reason I shall find, explaining my presence as a total stranger at her funeral?

A fleck of rain on the breeze lands at the tip of my nose, followed by more spots dappling my cheek, moistening my hair. I focus again on the old woman in front of me, still struggling at her task, and I continue to wait patiently, at least three or four minutes longer, during which time the threatened rain dries up, although the fast-moving grey clouds remain ominous.

A young man in a cheap, navy suit that gaps from his collar, with designer stubble on his chin, stops beside me. He raises both eyebrows, sighing audibly with a groan of impatience, even as he joins my queue. Since I will need some time at the cash machine this might prove to be embarrassing.

At last, we hear the familiar beeping sound, and now there are banknotes in her hand. She leans upon the screen for support while counting each one laboriously and with shaking hands, then screws all of them into a small brown purse before clasping it tight shut. With some difficulty this is placed into a battered-looking wicker bag on the ground in front of her, which she picks up by gripping firmly on one of its long handles, and with her other hand she retrieves a walking stick propped against the wall. Finally hobbling away, a wizened face turns to smile sweetly at me, no doubt more in relief than apology for the delay, of which she seems entirely unaware.

I say to the impatient young man, "You seem to be in a rush. Please do go before me," and his surprise removes the scowl which becomes a stressed half-smile as he mumbles, "Oh, thanks. I'll be quick." And he is, leaving me alone in front of the ATM.

I know Matthew's pin number for the credit and bank cards. Helen had told me before she left, on that first evening after collecting me from the hospital. "I presume you've forgotten the pin numbers for your cards, Matty. I can't help with computer codes and passwords, but I know the pins. You use my birth year, less twenty-one; same number for all of the cards as well, that's unless you've changed them recently." Of course, she had had to 'remind' me of her birth year.

I try the credit cards. The pin does work for all three, revealing debit balances: £19,721.00 on the Platinum Barclaycard; £17,828.00 on the Mastercard; and £12,756.00 on the gold American Express. When I try to withdraw cash, each card declines, referring me to the provider, and so I know the credit limits have been reached on them. The same pin also works for the bank card, which reveals a staggering balance of £274,726.00, an accusing DR for debit also appearing after this mouth-watering figure. Needless to say, it is swallowed, and a spiteful message indicates the card has been cancelled due to 'unauthorised overdraft balance'.

CHAPTER 17

Traffic is light for a Friday and I make good time. The gold Rolex on my wrist confirms it is 2.08pm as I pull in to park between a white van and a red VW Golf, about fifty yards from the entrance to the cemetery. Mindful of Helen's advice to remain in the background, I have not used the on-site car park where family and friends will gather soon, although the gleaming new Bentley looks out of place in this residential street of spruced-up ex-council houses.

Raindrops speckle the windscreen, and it looks like no one else has arrived yet so I remain in the car, dreading the embarrassment to come of unspoken questions from my family and friends about the presence of a stranger amongst them. I stare at the granite stone wall bordering this municipal burial ground, all but overwhelmed by an unkempt, hawthorn hedge with prickly shoots thrusting, irrepressible, towards the heavens as testament to Life Everlasting. Only the indomitable steeple of the Victorian chapel is visible beyond.

The Wilkinson papers couriered to me from Dorrell's rest on the passenger seat. I had changed my mind, decided it would be sensible to try and read through them more carefully before going to

Matthew's office on Monday. Since I am early as anticipated, I take this opportunity to pick up the bulky ring binder and read more, trying hard to concentrate.

It seems the revolutionary new drug for use in general anaesthetics, developed and marketed by the company for whom Matthew acts, leaves patients alert and clear-headed immediately upon regaining consciousness after surgery, whilst simultaneously providing the required level of pain relief, thereby facilitating swifter recovery and hospital discharge. The plaintiffs' claims of serious, sometimes catastrophic, side effects are dismissed as groundless by a medley of experts for Wilkinson's. They will all testify at trial to a host of probable alternative explanations and maintain no credible or plausible causation has been established to link the plaintiffs' various individual outcomes to this new drug, which has been fully tested and approved by regulatory authorities in both the UK and the USA.

When I come to the minutiae of the Request for Further and Better Particulars of the Defence being pursued by the plaintiffs, what partial attention I have achieved before, evaporates like twilight into night. I check my watch again: 2.35pm, and a large Lexus slows as it passes me, driven by my best friend from school, Martin Walls. He is glancing at the dash; no doubt his sat-nav has announced he has reached his destination. Martin settled in Reading after university and we lost touch; I have not spoken with him for the best part of fifteen years. A pharmacist now, he must be thriving, driving this expensive car, a glamorous young woman at his side who is peering into the mirror behind the sun-flap, applying fresh lipstick. They disappear from view, through the gates, making for the chapel car park. Others drive by: members of the cricket club, staff from my office, other friends, many of whom I have also not seen in years.

It is time to join them, before the funeral cortege arrives with my family and the corpse that was my living body less than two weeks ago. I manoeuvre this large frame from the plush smell of new leather and walnut that infuses the interior of the Bentley, double-lock it safe and secure, then coax ponderous legs – cramped even in this grand car after the drive here and the waiting – gently along the uneven pavement, eventually easing away the aches and stiffness.

It is warm and humid but there are no longer rain spots in the light breeze, though the grey cloud cover still threatens. The aroma of sweet musk from a wild, rambling rose entwined amongst the hawthorn hedge above the old granite wall, flatters to deceive my mood on this sombre afternoon. I walk tentatively through the wrought-iron gates at the entrance to the cemetery, from which worn, dark-green paint is flaking away in rusty spots, like diseased pock marks on leprous skin. A council notice warns they will be closed at 9pm, and I fantasise about restless spirits waiting, impatient to roam free amongst the lonely graves at dusk, like toy soldiers come alive in a child's storybook.

A wide gravel path in front of me meanders in a circuitous route downhill, like a river cutting swathes through memorial stones and the patchwork of graves on either side; it flows towards the spiralling far boundary hedge, beyond which the clatter of a distant train echoes in defiant celebration of the living world. I make for the chapel, over on the right, following the tarmacked road to the car park. There are a few larger tombstones here, replete with cherubim and winged angels playing celestial music, guarding wealthy local dignitaries long since called to their Maker.

I slow almost to a halt on the road, unsure whether to approach my friends and acquaintances. They have gathered in small groups under the protection of an ancient cedar tree, whose highest branches spread like tentacles stretching to caress the chapel spire with their touch. There are so many people, all chatting quietly; I didn't realise I had been that popular, and I feel a perverse sense of pride. As I inch towards them, these familiar faces, many of them such an integral part of my life, exhibit no traces of recognition. I could be invisible but for a few furtive glances betraying curiosity as to the identity of this prosperous-looking stranger.

Eileen O'Connor is standing by the chapel doors with her diminutive husband, a stark contrast to her imposing frame. I first met her in the third form at secondary school when she was the new, young English teacher. Years later, at a rare school reunion, she promised to use me as the family solicitor, and I have acted for her, kept in touch, ever since. They are talking with my mother's elderly friends, a sweet couple I have known since childhood, but Eileen, whose naturally severe appearance has evolved a formidable scowl into retirement, turns from them to stare her uniquely intimidating frown of disapproval at this unknown usurper. I cannot walk over to speak with her, to explain; I can only ignore her and maintain a frustrated silence.

The sense of being followed and watched by unseen eyes every time I leave Matthew's house continues to plague me, although driving here this afternoon, preoccupied with so many discordant thoughts and emotions, there was temporary relief from what is surely a neurosis? But suddenly it is back again, the sense of an evil, brooding presence mocking my confusion, growing stronger as it stalks my uncertainty and feeds from my despair.

When I stirred this morning, it was there, waking with me to deaden hope and stifle the joy of daybreak. For the first time inside Matthew's house the eerie presence had left its psychic calling card, and my skin crawled in fear that the bedroom had somehow been violated while I slept. There was no definite evidence to support this, nothing obviously moved or missing that I could make out... except that the doors to the landing and bathroom were open. I'd had the impression they were both closed when I went to bed, but I could not be certain.

After I had thrown back the curtains to let the new day pour in, and heard the sounds of Helen moving around downstairs, the fear had faded and I saw it for childish nonsense again. When I remain positive it is contained. I can be rational then, understand it as perhaps an inevitable consequence of dealing with this nightmare. Who wouldn't be traumatised? It is so difficult to control the primitive, instinctive fear. And yet, I am determined not to let it take me under, to steal my sanity and my soul, the understanding of my true self. I keep telling myself: I am Andrew, whatever physical appearance I must present to the world.

I screw my eyes shut and take slow, deep breaths to calm the anxiety and exorcise my demons with logic, since there must be a sane explanation, however unlikely that seems now. Just like this morning, the fear subsides, releasing its grip, until the gentle, almost polite revving of a powerful car close behind makes me start and move aside to let it pass. A grey Aston Martin sweeps through driven by Peter Cheung, his small frame slouched low, half hidden behind the steering-wheel, and beside him, in the passenger seat, is Joe Peng.

I had not entertained the possibility they would turn up at the funeral: were they not both supposed to be away on holiday? And yet here they are to bury their patient. Both faces are deadpan, fixed straight in front with not a muscle moving to glance my way; no inkling of acknowledgement, let alone greeting from Cheung for Matthew Campbell, supposedly his solicitor and friend, as the car cruises away to park beyond the chapel in one of the last available spaces.

I move from the road and stand close to Martin Walls, who smiles nervously as I catch his furtive glance. The glamorous young woman is clinging to him with a morose expression on her face that somehow suits the occasion. He is keen to pass some words in polite conversation since few of the others here would be known to him.

"Sad day. Andy was a close friend from schooldays, but we'd not seen one another for years. How did you know him?"

"I was a business colleague... Matthew Campbell."

"Hello. Martin Walls. This is my fiancée, Fiona Riley," and we all shake hands politely.

It seems preposterous to listen to my old friend introduce himself to me as a stranger. I want to scream, "Martin, for God's sake, it's me, Andy. This is all a bizarre charade!" But, of course, it is my body they will be burying, so I swallow my scream and merely offer a weak smile.

We talk for a few minutes, killing time, Fiona managing to utter only a couple of words, although exchanging her former gloomy expression for a constant glazed smile fixed upon me: posh but dim, a cardboard trophy princess for Martin. I went to his wedding twenty years ago, and his wife had struck me then as charming and intelligent. I am surprised and sad that he has become such a different person from the friend I knew all those years ago; now so full of himself and self-centred as he gushes a multitude of unsolicited information to a stranger about his seemingly endless string of success stories.

My concentration wanders from his boring monologue, and I notice Peter Cheung and Joe Peng standing together, about thirty yards away at the edge of the car park, a discreet distance from all the other mourners. They are both staring at me intently, no hint of smiles, and are slow to avert their gaze when they know I am watching them. A sense of injustice swells into a rising tide of anger, seething with the sudden power of a tsunami: these two evil men must be responsible for my condition, yet flaunt their disinterest, almost contempt, for the torment they surely know I am suffering; shameless in their curiosity at my demeanour, and smug, no doubt, in the belief that their laboratory rat can never prove their guilt for an impossible crime.

Martin is waffling on, something about his role as Chairman of the Round Table in Reading, so immersed in his own conversation and importance that he does not seem to be aware, at first, when I cut across him curtly in mid-sentence: "I'm sorry; I have to go." Then I stride towards the two men, but with every step the weight of prying eyes from the mourners begins to temper my simmering rage, and Helen's entreaties to remain in the background replay in my head.

Peter Cheung looks dapper in his immaculate, dark navy suit, still wearing his designer reading glasses resting at the tip of his rather wide, snub nose. He takes a half step forward and thrusts a chubby hand at me, a false, tense smile fixed on his sallow face. Joe Peng, in an ill-fitting black suit that gapes from his stocky neck, remains inscrutable at his side, no trace of emotion, a brooding, sinister presence. I ignore the proffered hand, which is swiftly retracted as I stand before them, unable to find words, my initial anger transformed into an almost hypnotic trance of shock.

"Matthew; how are you?" The same confident, reassuring voice, soft and mellow with its Chinese burr, brings echoes of misery and false hope from my last days as Andrew Soulsby. And yet the spell of his former power and authority is broken by the tall, imposing frame I now inhabit looking down on random specks of rain christening his bald patch.

Speech finally comes to me, but not in violent recrimination, or even a demand for the urgent explanation that I crave; rather, I find myself talking quietly, with a pulsating heart almost drowning the sound of my words, conscious that the baritone pitch will likely make them strain to hear me.

"Why are you here? It's such a shock to see you. I've been trying to contact you but they said you were both away, impossible to reach—"

"We came home yesterday so that we could come to the funeral as a mark of respect for Andrew Soulsby and his charming family." If I had detected slight embarrassment, an initial awkwardness in Peter Cheung's manner, it has vanished now, and I can only revile at his audacity when he continues: "As, no doubt, are you, Matthew. You should not reproach yourself for recommending him to me for treatment. It was his only chance; he was a walking time bomb, poor man." He shares a fleeting glance with his accomplice, who maintains a chilling glaze of bland disinterest.

Before I can gather my thoughts to respond, Cheung is speaking again, his voice a notch louder to compensate for the gathering breeze: "Forgive me, Matthew. I have neglected to introduce my colleague. This is Joe Peng, a distinguished neuro-anaesthetist based at University College Hospital, London. We often collaborate and work together. Joe assisted me in trying to help poor Andrew Soulsby."

The false smile on his face widens, and Peng's upper lip puckers into a surly half-smile, but he does not make the mistake of extending his hand, instead shuffling a pace away to his left as though I am contagious. Cheung completes the bizarre pretence of introduction: "This is my illustrious solicitor, Matthew Campbell, who's fighting these ridiculous claims against our company. He's going to have them all thrown out of court with costs awarded to us for our unnecessary expenses and aggravation. He's the best man there is!" He says this with a flourish of false praise, before turning to address me again, moving closer and raising his eyes to mine, his mock earnest voice lowered to little more than a confidential whisper: "Your voice is sounding pretty good, Matthew. I understand you are due back to work on Monday, so I'll ring you then and fix up a meeting to discuss final preparations for the trial."

I feel a malign duplicity radiating from both of them, crawling over my skin and boring into my mind, like an invisible laser acting in spiteful jest. We all know they are playing with me – two cats pawing a desperate mouse. I say, "This is ridiculous. No one else is within earshot. There's no need for this game and your lies." Speech is coming to me more freely now, the swell of anger returning as I hear Matthew's sonorous tones rising loudly from me, culminating in a cracked, shrill pitch of despair: "What on God's Earth have you bastards done; and how; why me, for pity's sake?" I fight back the tears welling in my eyes since I must not give them the satisfaction of witnessing their victim crying like a child.

Spots of rain multiply on the freshening breeze, and although we stand apart from the other groups of mourners waiting for the chapel doors to open, heads still turn towards my violent outburst: curiosity from some amidst the prevailing frowns of silent censure, and I regret, at once, my lapse in control; such an indulgent mistake.

Bob Mullins, our cricket club chairman, has stopped chatting to a group of elderly social members, and the ferocity of his glare suggests the prelude to verbal admonition, but fortunately he returns to his conversation, no doubt to lament declining standards of behaviour and manners.

My tormentors exchange an incredulous stare, as though shocked and baffled in equal measure by my behaviour, before Cheung evinces mock concern and pity, replying to me in a voice dripping with condescension: "My dear chap, we haven't the slightest idea what you're talking about. I heard the rumour you have suffered from delusions and memory loss following your recent minor procedure." I screw my eyes tight shut, in frustration. "You must take care of yourself; don't rush back to work and stress. Shivani Kapoor seems to be on top of the case, most impressive; I'll talk with her next week. We need you to concentrate on becoming fit and well in mind, not full of wild accusations and manic ideas of persecution. It's most important that you overcome this soon, or it may result in most unfortunate outcomes."

"Why bother with this charade when no one else can hear?" I am in control, speaking quietly again, my heart pumping less frenetically. "And you've forgotten that we're friends, buddies, apparently... *Peter?*"

Peng has remained silent, a hint of disdain on his thin lips, and Cheung's expression becomes serious, affecting repressed anger as he replies, "Still such delusions... I'm sorry, I don't wish to be rude given your obvious distress, and it may be that you need professional help, but let me make this entirely clear: you are my solicitor and I respect your legal skills; I am the research director at Wilkinson's, where you are, of course, a non-executive director, so perhaps we might be described as business acquaintances; but friends, Matthew... I hardly think so?" His Chinese burr enhances the cold, crisp words that offer this scrap of further information about my new identity. "Now, if you will excuse us...?"

They walk briskly towards the chapel, and I realise the doors are open and most of the mourners have already gone inside. Only a few stragglers remain, perhaps delayed by the entertainment of an unseemly argument between three men they do not recognise. The last of them begin to file in, with Cheung and Peng close on their heels. I can hear a rustling of paper and mumbled, low voices as two young ushers standing just inside the vestibule hand them orders of service.

The arrival of the funeral cars, with Cathy, Geoff and Lucy, along with the coffin containing my mortal remains, must be imminent. I need to get inside quickly, and I almost slip on the moist grass as I rush towards the chapel entrance.

CHAPTER 18

My heart is thumping by the time I reach the vestibule, and a tall young man wearing a brown jumper – I think he is one of Cathy's second cousins – hands me an order of service. Everyone else is in the chapel, from where an organist hits odd notes off-key in a melancholy dirge.

The smiling face staring from the front cover chills my blood. It is a holiday snap of me taken by Cathy last year on the patio of our rented villa in Aix-en-Provence. The body now awaiting burial looked fit and well then with its slim frame and mop of fair hair, so little changed until the surgery just eleven days ago. Some believe they will be able to witness their own funeral in spirit from a realm of peace and understanding, but I am condemned to grieve a singular loss as I experience my family's tears and sorrow at first hand, trapped within the confines of a stranger's flesh and blood. I feel crushed by this stark confrontation with the true, awful purpose of today's events. I can't move, and the dead-weight of despair constricts my chest in pain; and suddenly I am lightheaded, faint, unsure if Matthew's legs can hold me where I stand.

"Here, let me help." The young usher takes hold of my arm. His eyes are kind, but he is anxious, unsure what to do. "You don't look well. Sit down over here." He has a broad Yorkshire accent, and guides me to a wooden bench, fixed under a cluttered church noticeboard in the vestibule. "This might help, Sir," and he produces a small bottle of mineral water from a sagging trouser pocket.

I thank him, touched by this kindness, and gulp the water down, splashing some around my face.

"Perhaps I should call an ambulance?" He is looking down at me, frowning with concern, a mobile phone now in his hand. Dreading the prospect of ambulances and hospital, I take slow, deep breaths to recover my composure and regain control. As the initial shock fades, I begin to feel a little better and the chest pain eases.

"No, no," I say, "there's absolutely no need for that. I sometimes have these panic attacks, but it's almost passed." I am thankful for the authority inherent in Matthew's voice, along with the seniority of age, to ensure an ambulance is not summoned. "I'm very grateful to you for your help, but I'm feeling much better. I'll just sit here quietly to recuperate for a while… You go on in, but thank you again."

"If you're quite sure?" he says, but I can see he is relieved, thankful not to be the catalyst for further drama today, and when I beckon him away with a smile, he hurries inside to take up his place, leaving the bottle of mineral water, now almost empty, on the bench at my side.

I need to rest here and hope the remaining tightness across my chest fades quickly. I can't risk joining the overflowing congregation I can see through the open chapel doors: there are so many people standing behind the bursting pews, cramped and huddled on either side of the nave. Tucked away in this alcove, sitting below the church notices, the light is dim and the view outside much restricted, but I can see clearly down the nave, highlighted by dappled reflections from the stained-glass windows at either side. The Reverend John Naughton is an imposing figure standing before the altar, resplendent in white surplice with mauve, braid ribbons and a prayer book clasped to his broad chest.

Only three months ago he was sitting before me, demure in my office alongside his wife's thunderous face, both poised to sign their new joint wills designed to thwart the taxman. Now he stands ready to comfort the bereaved and perform his ancient rituals as Guide to the Afterlife. I wonder what this man of God would advise if he knew that my spirit still resides in the body of Matthew Campbell?

The organ music comes to an abrupt halt, the last echoes whistling like a weary aftershock, to unmask the rumble of nervous anticipation: rustling paper, anxious coughs clearing throats and muted snippets of polite conversations, like a collective stomach rolling empty, whispering its discomfort while in thrall to the formal solemnity afforded by a Church of England funeral. At least Cathy will not be fazed by this; her own faith means she is used to even more pomp and circumstance.

In the dim light I squint briefly at the order of service and read with surprise that Peter Bright is giving the eulogy. Why has Cathy chosen him? We were not particularly close, rarely socialising beyond business functions and cricket-club socials. He must have pushed himself forward: I am convinced his motives are not merely altruistic.

Suddenly, Paul McCartney is singing one of my favourite ballads, his soothing melody on a Beatles CD reverberating around the chapel and beyond, to the margins of those decaying tombs; a personal message chosen by Cathy with such love, I am sure, imploring me to accept my fate, and to 'Let it Be'.

Out of sight, I hear car doors closing and catch Peter's West Country drawl shouting: "Steady; okay." An eerie silence follows. Then, four men in black suits walk past me carrying a mahogany coffin into the chapel, oblivious to my presence in the shadows. The brass handles look smooth, a fine lustre, sadly awaiting only earth and slow decay. I recognise Peter supporting the rear corner, so close to me. He is taller than the others, stooping slightly to compensate and keep the height even, his face contorted in a grim, red sheen. Two of the others must be funeral directors, but there is Geoff at the front, furthest from me, his face obscured from my view. He will be distraught but show few outward signs of grief. Thank God for my strong wife. Cathy will cope, know how to help and support him and Lucy as time goes by. Somehow, they must all survive until I can figure out a way to reveal I am still here for them.

Cathy and Lucy are following the coffin, a delicate veil hiding my wife's blue eyes. They will both approach the priest like condemned prisoners, bravely facing their executioner. Their arms are linked, hands clasped tight, clinging to each other for physical and emotional support. And so tantalisingly close to me as they pass by: I could almost reach out and touch them. Listening to my daughter sobbing while she rests a tear-stained face upon her mother's shoulder, the urge to do so, to comfort them and scream out the crazy truth, is compelling. But I am stunned into silence by this surreal spectacle, Matthew's limbs incapable of answering any call to movement, like a rabbit caught in headlights.

I know, of course, this is for the best, that it is essential I remain the silent stranger in this dingy alcove, and not add to my family's suffering by causing an ugly scene. That would be foolish, likely ruin any chance to be reunited with them, and provide only public confirmation that Matthew Campbell is mentally ill, bringing certain commitment to a psychiatric unit.

I watch two further undertakers in black coats, heads bowed low, walk past. They are a respectful distance behind my wife and daughter, and carry wreaths, beautiful arrangements woven together with white lilies amidst red roses: 'To Dad'; 'To a Wonderful Husband'. I taste the salty tang from tears streaming down my cheeks.

As the procession moves along the nave, I can see heads turn to reveal naked fear on the older faces at this stark reminder of mortality. The pallbearers pause before Reverend Naughton, who makes the sign of the Cross in an expansive and dramatic gesture, before they lower my body's elaborate coffin onto the brocade-draped bier, then turn, filtering into pews.

The priest calls on the congregation to stand, before intoning in his Suffolk burr: "I am the Resurrection and the Life saith the Lord..." Realising his oversight, one of the undertakers standing at the rear beside the heavy chapel doors has clunked them shut in a jolting echo, and the time-honoured words fade, too distant to decipher meaning. I toy with rising, turning the rusting, iron-ring handle to enter late and join those standing at the back. But I am still reeling and distressed, unsure how my surrogate body is dealing with this strain – the chest pain is much better, but I fear it could grip me again; perhaps it really is angina? And I am not sure how I would cope with faces turning in disapproval upon a stranger's late entrance, then the long wait on my feet through hymns and prayers, and Peter's inevitably long-winded eulogy. So, I remain seated on my solitary bench, wracked with uncertainty and indecision.

Should I leave now, walk away quietly and accept my fate as Matthew Campbell with so many questions unanswered? I think of Peter Cheung's false charm, picture Joe Peng's arrogant indifference, and vibrating through the oak doors comes a cacophony of raw voices, loosely tracing the discordant organ as they sing: 'Fight the Good Fight'.

It has always been one of my favourite hymns.

CHAPTER 19

The wind has dropped and it is no longer raining, but a humid calm threatens summer storms. The Reverend Naughton stands at the front of the open grave with his prayer book and a sombre frown of pensive reflection. Many of the mourners from the funeral service are not witnessing the internment. I am standing behind a clutch of those who have collected here to do so, and my new height allows me to see over them as I peer into the deep hole hewn from the bowels of the earth to expose sheer sides of smooth clay. This pit, swamped with discoloured, murky water, is about to receive the coffin: my body's final resting place.

A green tarpaulin has been thrown over the spoil heap at the far side of the grave in an attempt to ameliorate harsh reality, but when I glance over my shoulder, I can see two workman smoking, waiting under a fulsome sycamore – barely a discreet distance away – and close by is their JCB digger.

As I had listened to that rousing hymn echoing around me from my resting place in the vestibule, a surge of optimism banished the black dog of despair and galvanised me with renewed strength of purpose. I felt calm and the chest pains had disappeared, so when the congregation filed out from the chapel after the service, I followed the trail of mourners walking behind my coffin. It had been conveyed to this distant margin of the cemetery, at walking pace, by the hearse now parked on the track about fifty yards away, where the undertakers are preparing to hoist it upon broad shoulders for its final, brief journey.

While I wait, I find myself thinking of Helen and my decision to confide in her this Sunday, just a couple of days from now. Hopefully, I can gain her trust and her help to solve this mystery; whatever the state of their relationship, surely, she will want to know what has happened to her husband? Answers must lie with Peter Cheung – who somehow faded into thin air along with Joe Peng after the service today; I did not even glimpse them departing the chapel – and, of course, the pharmaceutical company, of which I now know both Cheung and Matthew are directors. On Monday I will learn more when I return to Dorrell's as their sorely missed litigation partner. I find myself speculating on whether Shivani is attractive and feel a buzz of excitement. Instantly, I regret this: it's not like me and horribly inappropriate, and I can only put it down, once again, to the distasteful, base instincts inherited with Matthew's body.

We are near to the railway down here and a local commuter train rattles by to break the silence, bringing my attention back to the terrible scene in front of me. The vicar's flowing white surplice over his black cassock skirts beneath, hangs as motionless as a sculptured statue in the deathly still. He peers at Cathy over the chasm between them; she looks so vulnerable and frail dressed in black at the foot of the grave, clasping Lucy and Geoff in a protective embrace. Behind them, Peter is standing with her elderly parents and her prosperous uncle. I never really liked her uncle; I hadn't wanted to act for him in the sale of his hotel: had I not done so, there would have been no fateful meeting with Matthew Campbell, no Peter Cheung and I would not be standing here, a stranger to my family, as we prepare to watch my body being committed to its grave.

Looking drawn and white, tears are seeping down Cathy's pale cheeks and I am sure she has lost weight. Hopefully, I can convince her soon that I am still here for her. I no longer harbour any delusions that as Matthew I can woo a grieving widow over months or even years. Why would she look twice at a portly, balding man in late middle age, especially one who will likely be bearing the yolk of financial distress?

As I look at my wife, I can't help thinking again of that great sex with her two weeks ago parked up in the Mini Cooper. I despise these thoughts and fight what feels like the craving of another man for an unfolding sexual fantasy, but it pushes to the front of my mind and will not be denied. It is disgusting amidst all this sorrow and distress, and yet while it lasts all my sadness and pain vanishes. My imagination is alone with Cathy in the long, yellowing grasses beyond the parked hearse, where I tear the demure black dress from her to reveal the smooth contours of her naked body…

The booming voice of Reverend Naughton releases me from this depravity as the pallbearers arrive with the coffin and gently lower it down, far below, on four sturdy, hessian straps into the grave. "Man, that is born of a woman hath but a short time to live, and is full of misery…" From my tall vantage, I stare in awe at the coffin, snug in the depths of thick clay, squelching up dirty water to ooze around the sides, like pus from a festering wound. "Our Lord Jesus Christ; who shall change our vile body that it may be like unto His glorious Body…" I smile grimly at the perverse irony: the change of my 'vile' body for this 'glorious' surrogate – Matthew Campbell, philanderer, adulterer and, my instinct tells me, a duplicitous lawyer.

"And now we shall sing that wonderful hymn, 'Abide with Me'. The words are printed on the last page of your order of service."

The vicar waits briefly on the rustling pages before launching his resonant, confident voice into song, drowning those few mumbled and choking voices raised in support. Emotion renders me mute, like many of the others, including my wife and children, who are huddled together, shell-shocked, their gazes drawn as magnets to the depths below them. When it is over women are weeping, men fixed with steely glazes.

The vicar speaks in softer tones. "We will now all pray; The Lord's Prayer… Our Father…" And we all mumble the final incantation together. The lead undertaker, a tall, burly man, moves forward from where he was standing with his colleagues. He is carrying a small platter on which there is a pile of dusty soil. With his gloved hand he scatters some onto the coffin, then offers this to Cathy, to Lucy and to Geoff, who all repeat the macabre custom in turn – the last act of love, the final goodbye as my body is returned to earth, 'ashes to ashes, dust to dust'.

Most of the mourners now start to peel away, moving slowly up the gentle incline on the wide tarmac path back to the cemetery car park. I stay with the few that remain, take my turn to throw dirt. Some pebbles clatter on the polished lid, sounding like hailstones peppering a skylight window. My stomach tingles to my bowels at the finality implicit in this ritual; there can be no denial as to the irrevocable loss of my precious body, the body that had so defined my life and personality.

Geoff has an arm around Lucy's waist to comfort her, a pained, vacant expression of disbelief on his face. She weeps openly, her head nestled against him. They have moved away a few yards, giving their mother space to say her final goodbye. She stands alone, close to the sharp precipice in front of her, black boots toying with the crumbling edge sending little shivers of loose brown soil helter-skelter below. Her sad eyes follow, cast down in hopeless resignation at her loss.

Peter Bright is staring at Cathy from where he waits near the path with her parents and her uncle. Something in his face, an almost proprietary concern, makes me act on impulse. I walk round to where she stands, adding to the squelching mud caked on Matthew's expensive black shoes and soiling the hems of his trousers.

"Mrs Soulsby… Cathy." I speak quietly, little more than a whisper. "Please be careful. You're very close to the edge." I yearn to put a protective arm around her but remain passive at her side. She makes no attempt to move or look at me, her eyes still fixed on the coffin below.

"Leave me alone. Just go away." The Yorkshire accent is broad, and there is a venom in her tone. It hurts me. She has never spoken to me like this: harsh and uncompromising; an angry response to a stranger.

"I'm so sorry," I murmur, wanting to say more but painfully aware that I must not do so, not now.

Peter is now engrossed talking to my in-laws and Cathy's overbearing uncle, but my son is looking directly at me with a searing contempt for what is, in his eyes, such a rude and inappropriate invasion of his mother's final moments with her husband's remains. I see much of myself twenty-five years ago in the anxious young man standing there with my beautiful daughter. He is about to intervene, but before he can do so I leave, scraping my shoes at the raised edging of the tarmac path before trudging wearily off towards the cemetery gates.

I have not gone far when I find Peter at my side, his hand on my shoulder.

"Matthew. May I have a few words before you leave?" He speaks quietly, and I turn to face his half-smile which fails to disguise the troubled expression. "I wanted to apologise again for being rude when you called at my offices on Tuesday. Not an easy time for me. Anyway," he sighs, waffling as usual, "we're all glad the funeral is over… It was thoughtful of you to come today. His family will appreciate it later when they come to terms with their loss and start thinking clearly. You just need to let the dust settle."

Not the most appropriate expression for the occasion. I manage a wry smile, but he remains oblivious to his gaffe and asks for my mobile number, the true reason, I suspect, for waylaying me. "I forgot to get it on Tuesday. It's not the time today, but I'd like to meet up and discuss your proposal. I'll ring you later to fix a meeting, if that's okay?"

I am uncertain whether I still wish to pursue this, and doubt Peter will when he surely discovers the state of Matthew's finances, but for now I keep my options open, replying, "Sure. I just need to check my number. My phone's been stolen. I picked up a new one yesterday; haven't memorised the new number yet."

I don't feel my usual embarrassment for a white lie. This one comes naturally, and I rummage in my wallet – an impressive, soft black leather Longchamp – to extract the scribbled note I had made when Helen told me. I really must commit it to memory.

An earnest glow suffuses Peter's face as he sidles very close, his long, thin chin angled askance. The gold stud in his ear-lobe glints conspiratorially. "This is delicate," he says, so quietly he is almost whispering. "The thing is… well…" His cheeks puff in an agony of pink embarrassment, but he labours on: "Andrew's wife – oh God, I mean Andrew's widow – took offence when you visited her house. She saw it as overfamiliar and inappropriate. I think I told you this when you called at my office. Obviously, she's very fragile at the moment. She considers you a stranger but involved in events leading to her husband's death… It makes her feel hostile. Of course, in time she'll come to understand you were trying to help, only being kind, but for now, well…" He falters again, searching for the right words to warn me off politely.

"I understand, Peter," I say; and I do. Cathy had never met Matthew, but I remember that when I had mentioned him, she bridled with what appeared to be an instinctive dislike, and then tried to dissuade me from pursuing his recommendation to seek a check-up with Peter Cheung. She believed he was interfering, meddling in our affairs, and events will now have reinforced her belief that she was right. If only I had listened to her, and to my instincts.

"Good," says Peter, at last coming to the point. "So, I hope you'll agree it's for the best if you don't come back to the wake at Southdown Cricket Club." He is clearly relieved to have got this off his chest, and my fixed smile encourages him to carry on: "If our business discussions are successful, I'll explain it all to her then; I'm sure she'll come round in time. Although I have the final say, of course," he can't resist boasting. "Insurance pays out Cathy's inherited share, and the business is mine."

"I see... So, I'll look forward to your call." I shake his hand, anxious to bring this encounter to an end. My head is throbbing and I need to escape and be alone.

"Thank you for coming." He seems to be enjoying the sense of importance, as though he is somehow in charge of events and the responsible party today, and it grieves me to admit that, in a sense, I suppose he is. "I do appreciate it, all your concern, and so will Cathy in the fullness of time." His brow creases, and he sighs with an alarmingly, wistful longing: "She's a beautiful and intelligent woman, you know."

Somehow, I keep smiling, masking my fury and frustration as I walk away up the gentle incline towards the cemetery gates. My heart is rattling like an ageing compressor by the time I reach them. Before I seek comfort from the waiting Bentley I can't resist looking back, and in the distance, I watch Peter comforting Cathy at the graveside, folding an arm around her waist while she buries her distraught face in his shoulder.

CHAPTER 20

I didn't want to go straight back to an empty house when I left the cemetery, so where else but the King's Head? As the pub fills with the swell of hungry punters, I pretend to read *The Guardian* in order to conceal my embarrassment at dining here, alone and sad, amidst rising decibels of noisy chatter from Friday evening's happy company.

Cathy and I have often driven to this popular gastropub in the Hertfordshire countryside. It is one of her favourites. I know the staff well, but nobody speaks with me this evening, beyond curt pleasantries whilst taking my order and bland entreaties to 'enjoy' when depositing food at my table. They do not recognise Matthew Campbell.

I had needed food to settle grumbling protests from an empty stomach – not fed since Helen's modest, early breakfast – and quell a slight feeling of faintness that was still about me. And to my shame, after just witnessing my own funeral, I had come away feeling ravenous. It seems nothing will supress Matthew's appetite, but I feel better now. My mixed grill – not my normal choice, but I couldn't resist it – has just been cleared away, and I have emptied a large glass of Malbec.

It was a decent meal. The food is as good as it gets without a proper chef in the kitchen. "Great ping food in a great atmosphere," Cathy always says. The copious portions invariably spill from the plates, a source of popularity for so many with bulging flab, like Matthew no doubt, who perceive value for money, while any passing angst is trumped by greed.

I have particularly enjoyed the wine, my first alcohol since the operation. It has revived the optimism I felt listening to 'Fight the Good Fight' on the vestibule bench. Glancing at *The Guardian*'s arts section, I am now sufficiently relaxed to start reading in earnest and spot a belated review of *Candida*. The National Theatre's show is, 'too dry… Helen Campbell's performance is disappointing, she makes a pleasant but uncharismatic Candida, lacking the repressed Victorian sexuality that Shaw intended to seethe throughout his play'. Poor Helen.

I should leave soon but dread returning to an empty house, so I decide to order another small glass of wine, enabling me to linger amongst the alcohol-induced bonhomie developing around me. I try to catch the attention of a waitress, but they are busy and well-practised to avoid eye contact, scurrying around, intent on other duties, other customers. A friendly young girl, Rosie, with a cheery, round face, has often served Cathy and me, but tonight she wears a pained expression as she hurries past my table, too harassed to attend the lonely stranger sitting in a corner alcove. I watch her dancing round crowded tables, her hands laden with dirty plates and cutlery.

"Do you want anything else, Sir?" I had not noticed Jenny's approach. She is the middle-aged partner of the manager, and I prepared wills for them earlier this year. But, of course, she does not see Andrew Soulsby. I guess she is hopeful I will ask for the bill and free up a table.

"Yes, thanks. One more small glass of the Malbec, please."

"Certainly." And away she goes to fetch it, not looking too pleased.

The wine tastes good, rich and smooth, it helps me think straight as I mull over an incredible day.

After the funeral I had sat in the parked car and not left for a couple of hours. I became engrossed reading more of the Wilkinson case papers. It was the thud of a child's tennis ball bouncing away from the windscreen, followed by screams of laughter, that had reminded me where I was, and of the advancing time. Children, and some not so young, were playing on a generous grass verge, which appeared to be a kind of communal front lawn for the yellow brick houses. My extended stay there, in a stationary Bentley, had become the subject of curiosity. And I needed to find a toilet soon, another problem I had noticed since inheriting Matthew's body.

But it was time well spent. I now have confirmation of the connection between the two anaesthetists, Joe Peng and Jeremy Whicher: they are both to be expert witnesses for Wilkinson's, the company of which Cheung and Matthew are directors. That is if the case ever gets to trial. Having read all of the medical reports and counsel's opinion, it seems to me the plaintiffs have grounds to be optimistic. Although I have no practical experience of civil litigation, I will be surprised if they do not receive a generous offer of settlement to limit exposure for further costs in a case I doubt Wilkinson's can defend successfully.

When I finally leave the country pub, night has descended and neither moon nor stars are visible. Although the car park is bathed in artificial neon, the narrow road leading from the exit disappears into a black void. There is still humid warmth promising the chance of summer storms, confirmed by a distant rumble of thunder just audible above the crunch of gravel under my shoes, as I find the Bentley surrounded but not quite boxed in by the evening crush of cars.

Even with the food, my second glass of wine might have taken me close to the legal limit, so I drive with extra care towards the outer reaches of the metropolis and my new home, the home under threat of imminent repossession.

The roads are quiet at this time and it does not take long. I cruise up Beech Hill. The alcohol's temporary lift has worn off and I fight back tears, while Mozart's famous symphony No. 40 in G minor reverberates within the car, courtesy of Classic FM. As I sweep past entrances to magnificent houses competing in opulence, I am tempted to carry on, beyond my destination, just keep driving into the night. But the falling petrol gauge is gathering momentum, less than a quarter tank remaining, and with no plastic money and less than £500 cash – which wouldn't sustain me for more than a few nights – what options do I have? Certainly not my own home and family, so, reluctantly, I turn in at Matthew's carriage driveway.

Security lighting comes on, portraying the imposing house as an eerie silhouette, stark against an invisible backdrop of garden and rolling fields, lost in the advancing night. The windows are like black eyes: I hadn't thought to leave any lights on when I left for the funeral, and Jean, the housekeeper, is not due back until tomorrow, Helen, unlikely to return before Sunday.

I stop the Bentley just short of the semi-circular stone steps that lead up to the entrance porch. The car's headlamps capture the marble pillars that support it in an oasis of brightness, like the unforgiving beam from a searchlight, and as the security lights click off, long shadows are cast between weak shafts of yellow light percolating through the front hedge from Victorian-style streetlamps.

I am reasonably confident that no one followed me back from the King's Head. (After such a dreadful day, I found it impossible to resist the urge to keep checking my rear mirror.) Through the windscreen, the house looks uninviting, almost sinister, as though it is warning me away. It fuels my anxiety and insecurity, and I remember how, as a nervous, young child I would be fixated on demons hiding in murky recesses of my solitary bedroom after dark.

But I cannot just sit here in the car for hours until the sun rises, or Jean arrives in the morning to hold my hand. And so, leaving the headlights on to guide my way, I take a golf club from the set in the boot, then move towards the steps. I start as a click, like gun fire supressed by a silencer, flashes the exterior lighting on again, surrounding the house in a moat of reassuring illumination.

As I struggle with the key to release the deadlock, I hear a vehicle going down Beech Hill, clambering slowly over speed bumps in the road. It has crawled by before I realise the key will not turn because the lock has not been engaged. I open the oak door with the Ingersoll and there are no warning beeps, no flashing red light on the burglar alarm console. It is not switched on. Surely, I had turned it on before double-locking the front door this afternoon when I left the house? I remember doing so, and checking all windows were shut tight, locked secure – quite a rigmarole in such a large property. I went through the whole ritual punctiliously – apart from Helen's bedroom, of course, which she always keeps locked.

The palm of my hand is greasy with sweat as I clench the golf club, then edge, tentatively, into the hall. The glow from the Bentley's headlamps outside does not extend far in here and I fumble to find the light switch, half expecting a malevolent shape to form out of the blackness, rise up and pounce upon me with murderous intent.

"Jean?" I shout loudly, without expecting a response, more a battle cry to deter imaginary intruders and bolster my sagging confidence.

At last, I locate and throw the switch. Everything appears normal, neat and tidy: a newspaper is perched precariously, folded but almost spilling off a dark, wooden tray proffered on the paws of a large, antique 'Bern Bear', intricately carved with a fine patina, his head lifted in a perpetual, fierce growl, warning off unwelcome guests. I remember putting the paper there just before I left for the funeral, intending to take it with me. But in my anxious state I went without it and had to stop at Tesco's this evening for another one, on my way to the King's Head.

I stand and listen. Of course, there is no reply from Jean, only the melodious, dull ticking of a grandfather clock emphasising the silence.

Perhaps Jean or Helen called in earlier, a brief, unexpected visit to collect something forgotten? But didn't Jean tell me yesterday she was going to Eastbourne today to visit her brother? And Helen's performance this evening at the National Theatre means she is unlikely to have come home. Even if one of them had, surely neither would have forgotten to secure the deadlock and turn on the burglar alarm when leaving? I wonder about an old gardener I've seen around occasionally, then remember Helen has told me he has no keys, no access to the house.

Something draws me to the dark, snarling bear, an ornate, almost Baroque figure, that now strikes me as curiously out of place within the contemporary opulence of Matthew's home. It is as though he is calling me, submitting the newspaper for my attention. And I know even before I have it in my hands, even these dull eyes without their reading glasses can make out clearly an edition of *The Times*; it is not *The Guardian* newspaper that I had purchased from the local shop this morning. Then, when I look more closely, I notice it is yesterday's edition, placed here in the exact spot I left mine earlier today.

Somebody has been in this house, maybe still is. But there are no obvious signs of forced entry, and Helen has told me that, apart from the two of us, the only other person who possesses a set of keys is Jean.

I toy with checking out all of the rooms. Maybe French windows at the rear have been breached, the study ransacked; who knows what Matthew might have hidden here, how many unsavoury creditors there are, how many enemies he has with scores to settle? I picture the rack of sharp, kitchen knives, a sinister figure in hiding, waiting patiently for the chance to exact revenge. He, or perhaps she, might be behind any door or curtain, poised to attack with a swift sudden thrust bringing death, obliteration for my soul and Matthew's body in one final moment of shocking terror.

During the nightmare of the last eleven days there have been occasions when despair has caused me to lose any care for my physical safety, and I have felt no desire to live as Matthew in such overwhelming emotional pain. And yet now I am frightened, I do care for this life, wherever it might lead, and I cannot contemplate venturing into every corner of this huge house to seek out evidence of intruders. Not for me the hero fashioned from indifference to life, nor the careless hero of fantasy fiction. I am surprised at how strong the life force feels, and my skin crawls with the cowardly fear of self-preservation as I flee the hall, a scared animal sensing danger from an unseen predator, instinct driving me to escape.

Seeking safety in the waiting Bentley and the comfort of its bright headlights, I reach the front door. I had left it wide open, but now it is pulled to, almost closed. When I open it and move outside onto the porch, there are no headlights, only darkness until the security lighting clicks on, revealing gentle rain descending upon an empty drive. The car has vanished with the speed and mystery of a conjuring trick. Except this is no sleight of hand. I had left the key fob in the car. It must have been stolen while I stood not forty yards away, spellbound in the hall, contemplating terrors within the house. I had heard nothing but the slow beat of the clock and the sighs of my own disbelief as a rustling newspaper had crumpled in my grasp.

My line of retreat is scuppered, and I fear another panic attack. I know that I must keep moving so that the security lights stay on, like a fire to keep the monsters at bay, monsters that lurk in my imagination within the black night surrounding the house. My heart thumps while I jog quickly, puffing my way across the driveway and front garden, praying the lights stay on.

It seems an eternity until I am finally on the pavement where I stop under a small streetlamp, ten yards or so down Beech Hill, away from the entrance to the drive. In the humid air, rain speckling on Matthew's black suit is almost a relief. The house has been left open and exposed, but I do not care; why should I? I feel safer here on public view, although at this late hour it is eerily quiet with no sign of any living soul in the prestigious street.

My heart rate slows down and my breathing becomes less laboured. I put on reading specs and extract the iPhone from an inside pocket of my black suit. My hands are still shaking and I tap the wrong numbers but get it right the second time. A calm voice asks me which emergency service I require.

CHAPTER 21

SUNDAY 19TH JULY

Friday night's storm had cleansed the air, but humidity is forecast to build again today. By 9am it is already warm under an azure sky. Beyond the close-trimmed lawn, the leaves of the orchards' fruit trees tremble on a whiff of breeze like the faltering hands of old age, and I can hear the looping melody of a song thrush as I wait for Helen to join me on the terrace.

She didn't arrive home until the early hours of this morning. I had slept only fitfully and so I heard her Porsche swirl to a crunching halt on the gravel, followed by the heavy thud of the front door slammed shut. I guess she may sleep in a while yet, so I'll just have to wait, perhaps browse *The Observer* I bought before breakfast from the local newsagents.

The remains of blackened crusts smeared with marmalade, and a discarded bowl of muesli soaking in milk, litter the small garden table where I am sitting under the shade of an apple-green parasol. Jean has already fussed around, chiding me for not asking her to fix breakfast. I assured her I want nothing else, just my own company until Helen joins me.

As I expected, Jean has confirmed she did not return to the house on Friday afternoon, but I will not bother to tell the police. They had appeared to lose all interest after discovering the vehicle repossession notice for the Bentley wedged within the brass letterbox. I had not noticed this when fleeing the house, and it had certainly not been served upon me personally, the due legal process required by law. The young police officer was dismissive of my complaints: "You'll have to consult a solicitor if you want to pursue that, Sir; it's a civil matter and not something we can help you with."

Checking the house and grounds had revealed nothing disturbed and no signs of a forcible entry. I had to confirm nothing was missing: how would I know otherwise? Both of the officers who had attended were clearly very sceptical of my contention that an intruder must have gained entry because the deadlock and alarm had been disengaged, and a newspaper on the Bern Bear was not the same one I had left there. Why, they had asked, would anyone conceivably wish to do that? Clearly, my agitated state had convinced them I was mistaken, perhaps drunk, and their only real interest was to breathalyse me since I had admitted to driving home. Thank God, the test result was negative, although it must have been a close-run thing.

I read the sports section, a report on a day of drama at Trent Bridge, but it is difficult to keep focus. I try to read it over a second time. A few weeks ago, I would have been passionately interested, and probably watched most of the test match on television. But still the newsprint jumbles into a blur of unseen words as my mind rewinds to that Saturday a couple of months ago, spent with my son at Lord's watching the first test match of the summer. Since he was five years old, this outing has become an annual pilgrimage for us, devouring sandwiches from the picnic prepared by Cathy, and this year drinking too much wine when prolonged rain had interrupted play. But it had not spoilt our day, far from it. We had found simple solutions to some of the world's intractable problems, recounted past games, laughed and daydreamed, spoken of Geoff's hopes for the future. And then, buying a fish-and-chip supper from Lord's food village at the end of the day.

Is that really only eight weeks ago? It is so painful to contemplate these lost pleasures of my family life.

"Matty!"

Helen's confident, plum voice commands the long terrace she enters through French doors from the study, and I turn to admire her leisurely approach in white leggings and designer trainers braided with gold. Rising from my chair, I can't deny feeling some sexual attraction, but mainly it is joy at the prospect of such cathartic relief, to literally lay bare my soul to this beautiful woman: my wife in the eyes of the law, yet to me, little more than a stranger. It is a massive gamble, and although a shadow of doubt momentarily crosses my mind, I have invested too much emotional capital in this decision not to proceed now.

I resume my seat and smile meekly as she sits down to face me, her back to the garden and panoramic views beyond.

"I have to say you look shit, my love," she says with a disarming frankness.

"I guess that's how I feel. It's been a tough couple of days." I fidget in my chair, anxious; where to start?

She removes a cigarette from the pack she has placed next to her on the table, along with a gold lighter which she flicks open to light up. The habit seems incongruous in the face of such classic beauty, still striking despite those hairline cracks wrinkling faintly on her forehead and stalking the corners of her mouth on close inspection. I am surprised she has not banished such minor imperfections by a regime of regular Botox.

She inhales the first draw slowly, sighing with satisfaction as she protrudes her bottom lip to waft rings of blue tobacco smoke around my nose, fuelling the manic craving I have inherited. It is all but physically painful to resist.

"This will help." She slides the packet and lighter across the table, her long, thin fingers briefly touching my extended arm.

I have to take Matthew's statins and blood-pressure pills and worry about the signs of angina, so I must continue to resist his tobacco addiction. It is not merely because his health is now my problem, but something even more important: I do not smoke because I abhor the habit, and I refuse to lose that strand of my own identity and self-respect.

"No thanks." I push the cigarettes away, although it takes a significant feat of will.

"Matthew Campbell not smoking?" She lets the question hang a moment, knotting her brow in a perplexed frown, an impish tease of disbelief in her voice.

"I don't smoke, never have," I reply truthfully.

Her wide, hazel eyes fix mine as she leans forward. "Okay, my new man. You have your wife's full attention. I'm intrigued... what's it all about, my love?"

I sigh. "It's so difficult to know where to begin."

Helen flicks away strands of blonde hair from her eyes, and her lips are tight shut in a pained expression that suggests more than curiosity: there is a genuine concern in her sober response. "Try at the beginning, Matty. We have all day."

She stares at me with a disarming intensity, and yet somehow her words and manner ease my tension. "You look so poorly," she says, resting her elbows on the table and cradling her chin in those elegant hands showing off pink nails. I notice a gold wedding band on her ring finger which has not been worn in my presence before. "It's weird to see you looking vulnerable and indecisive, Matty." Her breath brushes my face as she speaks. And then, with an air of vindication, she adds, "I told you not to go to that funeral."

"I had to go. You'll understand when you know what's happened to me..." I stop speaking because the kitchen doors onto the terrace open to reveal Jean carrying a tray of toast, croissants and coffee for Helen with an impeccable, almost uncanny, sense of timing.

"Thanks, Jean. You're a star." Helen's posh voice lingers in emphasis, loud and friendly.

"No problem, Mrs Campbell. Just call me if either of you need anything."

The housekeeper's expression is impenetrable, as blank as the City's sky on a rainy night, and she leaves us quickly, aware, I think, that she may have interrupted a very private conversation.

"So?" Helen's eyebrows are raised in expectation.

"Before I confide in you, Helen, there's something I need to know. Did you come home on Friday afternoon?"

"Friday? No. I had lunch with a couple of friends from the cast, which was rather jolly, actually, quite cheered me up. After that I stayed at the flat in Covent Garden until I left for the evening performance, which went pretty well, as it happens. So did yesterday's, particularly in the evening. Much better than I expected." She pauses, savours this for a moment, pleased to relive it. "But why should it matter to you if I had come back here?"

And so, I tell her about Friday evening: my conviction that an intruder had been in the house; the lack of interest from the police, who just went through the motions; and the Bentley, gone, snatched back by Premium Finance – I show her the notice itemising the instalment arrears, plus the total now due of £310,236 to reclaim the car.

The colour drains from her face: she is visibly shocked. "I don't understand, Matty. You're one of the main partners in a top City law firm, for Christ's sake, apart from whatever fingers you've got in other juicy pies. You leak money and wealth."

"There's much more," I confess, and then tell her the balances on Matthew's bank and credit cards, before producing the letter from Hepplewhite-Brown, solicitors. Her hungry eyes, wide open in dismay, scan it, devouring the neatly typed paragraphs. With a sharp intake of breath, she looks up at me, uttering a shrill cry: "Oh no, this just can't be right... Matty, tell me it's not true, a mistake?"

I remain silent as confirmation of the letter's apparent authenticity, the truth of her husband's financial malaise. Clearly, a little time is required to let these revelations sink in. Gripping the two stapled sheets of paper in trembling hands, she reads it again, more slowly, her lips moving, mumbling the contents to assist assimilation of this dreadful news, interspersed with gasps of consternation. She glares at me when she reaches that stellar figure of outstanding debt: £4,085,724. Hanging on this, she repeats the figure out loud, then the words *notice of eviction*, as the implications for her settled lifestyle dawn on her.

Finally, I reply, "I know it sounds crazy, but I'm going to explain why I am not responsible for any of this mess. In fact, I knew nothing about it until Friday." Her scowl is one of incredulity and disbelief. "But, first things first." I'm normally so diffident when it comes to offering unsolicited legal advice, but for some reason I just can't resist showing off. "I think you may have a defence to the possession claim for this house. You will need to consult a solicitor tomorrow as a matter of urgency." There is no doubting the authoritative ring that comes naturally as I employ Matthew's sonorous tones.

"But I don't own the house. It's in your sole name," she says in shock, I think, a small, quiet voice, not her usual form at all.

"It doesn't necessarily matter. It is quite complicated, but you might be able to argue 'proprietary estoppel'. Proceedings would have to be issued immediately against the bank with an injunction requested to stop them kicking you out while your case was heard. That's why you must see a lawyer tomorrow."

"Sounds like a nasty bowel complaint." Her wan complexion, the troubled frown, belies this hollow attempt at humour lacking in any conviction. "I have my own money and a little buy to let in Camden. I could live there a while if needs must – the current tenants are due to leave next month."

She stares through me, her blonde hair falling dishevelled as she links both hands behind her neck, squeezing facial muscles into a ball of anxiety.

"Jesus, Matty," she seethes now, her voice strident. "Where's all the money gone? How could you let things get to this state? …So now we have it," she declares bitterly, "the reason for this strange behaviour, your very convenient amnesia."

I can feel such anger in this accusation directed at an errant husband's perceived duplicity; she now believes that she has been duped again, there is no 'new man', just the same old Matthew, devious and cunning. Clearly, it was a mistake not to start at the beginning of my story as she had suggested; the task has become even more difficult, but I am still determined to tell her what has happened to Andrew Soulsby.

"No, Helen. I knew nothing about these debts when we last spoke on Friday morning. Please hear me out."

"I'm still listening," she says, but her face has glazed over, ice-cold with deep distrust.

"I am not your husband. I am Andrew Soulsby," I begin, speaking slowly, enforcing a calm upon myself, determined to convince her of my sincerity. "I first met Matthew Campbell about a month ago. We had a conference at his office to discuss a complex conveyancing transaction: the sale of an hotel in Leeds. He was acting for the buyer and I represented the seller, who was my wife's uncle. Matthew noticed I looked unwell. He was so helpful and charming that I opened up to him, told him I'd been sleeping badly and getting headaches, probably suffering from stress.

"He recommended Peter Cheung for a check-up, told me to mention his name, a 'special favour'. And it seemed silly not to take up the offer, especially since there would be no cost to me under my BUPA policy. Anyway, I did, never remotely expecting the diagnosis of large brain tumours. I'd always been so fit and healthy until the headaches had started a few weeks before. As you can imagine it was devastating news for all of us: for my wife, Cathy, and for Geoff and Lucy, my son and daughter."

"How old are they?" Helen asks dubiously, rather a random question. Yet her eyes are fixed on me in rapt attention, whether to humour a madman or giving serious credence to my tale, I cannot be sure yet.

I tell her they are both still at university, then continue: "I went into the Wellington Hospital three days later for major surgery. Cathy was there with Geoff and Lucy. We spoke of holidays, good things to come when I recovered, before they wheeled me down. I left them waiting in the private room.

"I remember it all vividly, seeing Cheung and Joe Peng, his anaesthetist, in theatre just before I went under, my last memory of life as Andrew Soulsby. Cheung told me I'd be with my family again so very soon. I can hear his exact words, his lies, in my head now, and there is an impression, a half-memory, of distant faces, perhaps some kind of viewing gallery for students.

"And suddenly there was nothing, a black void, maybe like death. When I came round, I had been taken back to a different room, no family waiting there, just a nurse who called me 'Matthew'. At first, I thought it might be a mix-up; had I been taken to the wrong room, maybe had the wrong operation? I was scared and pleaded to see my wife. When she came it was not Cathy, but you Helen, talking to me as your husband. I was speaking with a different voice, not mine; this new, deep voice, and posh like yours.

"It was then that I realised this was not just weird, temporary side effects from the anaesthetic drugs, and the sense of disbelief, the panic kicked in."

"This is crazy," she gasps, interrupting me. "Is it some kind of sick joke?" But her voice is soft, her manner calm; certainly not suggestive of a contemptuous dismissal.

"No, only this never-ending nightmare for me," I reply. "When you left me in that hospital room, I examined my body and found large limbs, blemished skin: it was not me, not Andrew Soulsby.

"I was still muddled, groggy from all of the drugs, but I knew it was real, impossible, yet no mad dream; and then a tall anaesthetist – not Joe Peng – was peering down at me. He was discussing my minor throat surgery: apparently it had gone as planned, and then it dawned on me why I had woken with a rasping, painful throat.

"I sensed he knew and was complicit in what had happened to me, in much the same way I'd had a premonition of something very wrong and evil that morning, just before the pre-med when I left my family, but too late to stop it all from going forward.

"Before they sedated me again, I managed to locate a hand mirror and saw the terrible confirmation as Matthew Campbell's unshaven face stared back at me through hollow, blue eyes."

I struggle to suppress tears that well up, clouding my vision with moisture, and pause as my words stumble in rising emotion. Helen exhales breath audibly, flopping back bolt upright in her chair; her mouth and eyes are open wide in awe.

"Jesus, what an incredible story!" Her voice is still soft, barely above a whisper, and her cigarette, now discarded and resting at the lip of a glass ashtray on the table, trails persistent smoke curling away like exhaust fumes spewing from a jet plane.

A tense silence is finally broken when Helen leans forward. "I can see you do believe what you tell me." She sounds like a mother humouring a frightened child. "But I think you must know yourself, deep down, that it can't be true… I fear you've had a serious breakdown, my love. All these financial traumas…" Her hand reaches across the table, the wedding ring glinting gold in the bright morning sun, then disappearing when those delicate fingers wrap around my hand. Perversely, I can't help wondering whether she has noticed that my nails are unkempt and too long. "You need professional help, Matty," she says emphatically, yet with kindness.

How to convince her I am entirely sane, that I am, indeed, Andrew Soulsby, and all that I have told her is true?

"Of course, it all sounds incredible, Helen." I speak slowly, with all the gravitas and authority I can muster. "Quite preposterous, I know. The stuff of science fiction. In your shoes I wouldn't believe it myself. And yet it is true. I don't know how or why, but it is true.

"I feigned memory loss, but the reality is that I have no knowledge of your husband, his life and friends, beyond what little I have learnt over the past thirteen days. I am Andrew, with his memories and experiences, all his desires, loves, passions and prejudices; his hopes and dreams. I miss my family, trapped in this stranger's body that I don't understand. It reacts so differently, often by instinct against my will. My own body has perished: I saw it buried on Friday afternoon when I threw dust on my coffin and witnessed my family grieving. That excruciating pain will never leave me.

"I dream of my wife every night, talk to Cathy in my head, think of her with every waking moment. I have tried to meet her, but she won't speak with me. Of course not, since to her I am Matthew, a stranger whose attentions and very presence is resented at a time of intensely personal suffering."

The sun is gathering strength, now higher in the sky, and I can no longer ignore the burning heat on the left side of my face. I get up to adjust the parasol, and Helen asks, "If this were true, what would you say has become of the real Matthew, my selfish, promiscuous husband?" I perceive no hint of sarcasm; this seems to be a genuine question.

"I don't know," I respond. "Perhaps a victim, like me. His spirit could be listening to us now; or expired within the rotting corpse of my body."

"If I suspend disbelief and accept your story, it's more likely he's stolen another's body, probably some virile, young man."

I smile as she picks up her cigarette and takes a long draw on it, blowing smoke rings high above her raised head before saying, as much a muse to herself as a question to me: "But why would you wait so long, until now, to tell?"

"Because it sounds preposterous, even manic. Who would have believed me? And I didn't know who to trust, who might be involved – I still don't, really – but I believe now that I can trust you, Helen.

"When you visited me at the hospital, do you remember what the nurse told you I'd said when I first came round from the anaesthetic?"

"Yes, yes I do."

"Well, had I carried on and blurted it all out then, I might have been drugged into oblivion. Jeremy Whicher, the anaesthetist, threatened as much when he was alone with me. I might even have been certified. Perhaps it would suit Cheung to have me locked up in a psychiatric hospital.

"You are an actor, a creative person. I'm counting on you being open-minded, receptive to all ideas and possibilities, to treat this seriously and give me the benefit of the doubt."

"Even so, Matty… or what should I call you now, Andrew? It's a huge ask, my love, a massive leap of faith."

"I know, of course I understand. I've found out—"

She interrupts me: "But what real proof can you show me? I mean, I'm looking at Matthew Campbell, large as life. How can you be someone else in there talking to me; how is that possible?" Her pained face is a portrait of bemusement.

"I have no answers yet, but it has happened and I have no choice: I must try to find out."

"Matthew could be a manipulative, cunning bastard." She shudders. "He knows I can be gullible; you could be messing with my mind."

"But why would he? There'd be no reason or motive for him to do so."

She remains silent and stubs the fag end of her cigarette in the ashtray. "I've found out," I continue, "that the anaesthetists who assisted with the operations – Joe Peng on me, and Jeremy Whicher on Matthew, in the same hospital on the same day – are closely connected with Cheung and Matthew through a drug company called Wilkinson's. There's ongoing litigation involving them that Matthew was handling… And somehow they avoided a post-mortem on my body!" I spit out these last words, undisguised desperation now.

"Are you sure, no post-mortem? I can check."

"Certain. I called on my business partner, Peter Bright, last Tuesday, as Matthew, of course, ostensibly to pay my respects and offer assistance. It was quite easy to fish for information. Apparently, it's up to the coroner to decide if further investigation is required. It seems Cheung's word, backed up by Joe Peng, was good enough, so my body was released for early burial."

"That must be very unusual with a death under the knife?" She frowns, pensive, then says apologetically, "Oh, I'm sorry," as she catches my involuntary wince at those graphic, harsh words describing the violent death of my body.

"Alex Grayling is a coroner and golf buddy of Matthew's who lives locally," she continues after a moment's delay. "He came here a few times with his chum Peter Cheung to see Matthew. I've never liked Cheung, smarmy bugger!" she exclaims with surprising venom. "Something about him makes my skin creep; can't quite put my finger on it, but I'd swear the man is not honest. Probably why he and Matthew always seemed to get on so well. I wouldn't trust him further than I could throw him, darling."

"He was at the funeral with Joe Peng. They tried to avoid me, and when I cornered them, Cheung denied any friendship, insisted we were merely professional acquaintances."

"What the fuck were they doing there? Bloody brass necks!"

Helen becomes animated, pushes her chair away to stand up and stares vacantly into the middle distance towards the fields beyond the garden. She has not touched her toast and croissants, nor the coffee. After a moment she turns, retrieves the packet of cigarettes and picks one out, then lights up again.

This ghastly body that imprisons me yearns to join her in nicotine heaven. Yet again I must fight to resist the craving, and also a desire that sweeps over me at the swell of her breasts when she bends down to replace the packet and lighter on the table.

Still standing, puffing at the cigarette, she eyes me closely. "He was lying to you because Matthew was definitely close to Cheung." She pauses before picking up another train of thought. "Why was he dealing with an hotel purchase? He's the senior litigation partner at Dorrell's, and he only ever dealt with court work. He loves the battles, the cut and thrust. The aggression and confrontation suit his temperament. When I was younger and foolish that attracted me; I called him my 'super-suer'."

She chuckles in wistful reflection for a moment, and I am encouraged that she is speaking of him in the third person. "He wouldn't know what to do with a property purchase," she maintains, arching an eyebrow. "Are you quite sure? I could easily check by speaking to one of the guys at Dorrell's."

"And if you could speak with Cathy, she'd also confirm; it's how the introduction to Cheung came about. We spoke of nothing else for days."

"Umm, Matthew has been totally immersed in that Wilkinson case for months," she muses. "He used to mutter about being on to something really big with amazing potential. I never gave it any thought because I'd lost interest in his life."

She comes to sit down again, pulls her chair closer, next to me.

"Oh God, I just don't know," she sighs earnestly. "I need time to think – why have you told me all this, my new man?"

"Because I've decided I can trust you and I had to confide in someone – I felt like my head was going to explode with the pressure of emotional isolation. Please help me, even if it's just being there to talk to. I'm absolutely sane; everything I've told you is completely true, and if only I can have the opportunity to speak with my wife in private, I'll prove it."

"Okay…" she says, slow and lazy, her mind planning. "How about we take the Porsche and go for a spin, perhaps a late Sunday lunch at a country pub – I'll pay?" She smiles. "I need to hear more, my love. But first I want to phone Jason about the house. He's a friend and a good lawyer; he'll know what to do."

As she reaches for my hand and leans close to me, I dare to hope she might eventually accept that what I have recounted is the terrifying truth, not the product of a deranged mind. Those wrinkles around the corners of her unmade mouth and eyes, the tell-tale signs of age creeping over her slender neck, do not detract from her beauty, which is enhanced by this tender gesture. For a brief moment I yearn to embrace her, and wonder if she would welcome this? But I could not trust where that might lead. It is a weakness to be resisted at all costs, as I think of Cathy, alone, grieving for me.

"Thank you." My voice almost breaks with emotion. I take a few seconds, control it, then stand slowly, gently releasing her hand from mine. "I would really like that, Helen. I'll change and shower while you ring your friend. See you down here in an hour or so?"

CHAPTER 22

MONDAY 20TH JULY

Alone in Matthew's spacious London office, I settle into a high-backed, leather swivel chair at his enormous mahogany desk, facing a chesterfield sofa and framed legal prints on the wall behind it. An expensive-looking traditional bookcase to my left is full of hardbound legal tomes that I doubt are ever read, and an open drinks cabinet reveals an abundant supply of liquor. Floor-to-ceiling reinforced glass behind me provides a panoramic backdrop with a stunning view when I turn round: below is the HMS *Belfast*, grey at anchor, while colourful small boats and working launches bustle past under Tower Bridge, and the indomitable Tower of London nestles beside the Thames, timeless amidst London's ever-evolving skyline.

A handwritten note marked 'For you to review' has been left on the desk beside neatly stacked piles of files bristling with clients' papers which, along with an open laptop displaying Dorrell's homepage, covers much of the inlaid red leather surface braided with a fancy gold-leaf design. This apparent calm order and silence seems false, almost contrived, and it is certainly an alien world to the frenetic activity that represented my working environment at Soulsby & Bright.

I experienced a powerful sense of déjà vu when I followed Shivani into this room about fifteen minutes ago. The reality of any new destination rarely, if ever, resembles the perception fashioned in advance by the imagination, yet this private office chimed an eerie chord, an overwhelming feeling of familiarity and recognition, of having been here before. Now the strange sensation surges again, even more intensely, like waves crashing back onto an empty beach searching for answers, as I peer into the flat screen of the laptop.

Could it be that today's visit has triggered memories submerged by the anaesthetic drugs, now gasping for air at the surface of my mind? But my only meeting with Matthew, little more than three weeks ago, was in a client conference room located in a separate suite, far removed from this office. A friendly young woman had escorted me there to meet him, and later, ushered me to the lift and exit when it was time to leave. I am certain that I never saw his personal space here.

There are a wealth of theories attempting to explain déjà vu but none are proven. However, such a widely experienced phenomenon cannot be in doubt. The human mind has evolved through countless millennia and plumbs unfathomable depths that defy understanding, presenting a subjective intrigue to every soul. Could it be that my unique circumstances have provided a catalyst, adding the clarity of premonition to whatever unknown forces conjure these singular powers from our minds?

Still, I must also not discount the possibility of a mundane answer for these episodes: the chance, perhaps, of subliminal prompts? After all, I was here at the firm's premises only a few weeks ago, and so I am well aware of its location and style. And, of course, I have been able to form a clear impression of Matthew and his tastes. This explanation would be logical, one of suggestion and coincidence rather than paranormal… And yet, the certainty of recognition is so intense?

This morning I had caught the 7.30am train. It was something of a culture shock, already packed with early morning commuters, but at least I avoided what would have been an even more disagreeable trip as the heat built towards midday – this heatwave shows no signs of ending. To think that I used to complain about congestion on my short car journey to work in Palmers Green.

Perspiration had bubbled on my skin – I felt it trickling down under my arms – as I left the throng at London Bridge Station to haul my overweight frame towards Dorrell's, arriving tense and apprehensive at the glass revolving doors leading into the ground-floor foyer at around 8.45am.

It seemed like only yesterday since I had been here as Andrew, gazing upon the intimidating swathe of empty floor space that dwarfs the distant reception desk, before being instructed to sit and wait on one of the three leather sofas which circle a low table splattered with reading material. This morning, a couple about to enter the lift on the far side had turned to look at me, along with the woman behind the desk staring over half-moon glasses, as the clunk of my black brogues under the high ceiling echoed to announce my arrival.

It dawned on me, approaching the tall, middle-aged receptionist, whose severe face cracked in recognition, that I had no idea where Matthew's office was within the fourth-floor litigation department, nor could I gain access to the lifts or the department without a personalised plastic pass. I could hardly ask for directions, and my chest muscles tightened in a raw panic, the culmination of rising tension since I had left the house early this morning. My heart was thumping, and the sudden surge in anxiety suggested a full bladder despite the surfeit of sweat enveloping my body. I froze to the spot, petrified.

And then, the next thing I remember, slouched again on one of those sofas, was meeting the gaze of a strikingly handsome, young Indian woman. Her slim bottom was perched close beside me, her body angled towards me. She was stunning: black pencil skirt rucked above dainty knees, and flowing, long, dark hair, cascading thick over slender shoulders. I think I knew immediately, but when she spoke, I was certain this was Shivani: the soft voice of Matthew's secret lover that I had listened to on the iPhone's recorded messages, its beguiling mix of North London and Indian overtones unmistakeable.

During this morning's commute, a plethora of chic summer clothes gracing women, young and old, had reminded me of Matthew's powerful libido. On one occasion, I was aroused to see a plain, middle-aged woman flirting with an unshaven, powerfully built young man. There was something slightly different about that feeling, almost as though the man was the focus of my attraction, and it had been mildly disorientating in a way I could not understand or explain.

Sitting close to Shivani, it was impossible not to feel attracted to her, and my panic and tension dissolved. "I've missed you, Matt," she purred, barely above a whisper. "I've missed your touch, missed you fucking me." No one else was near, least of all the po-faced receptionist. She had left her post to deal with a confused, elderly woman who had wandered in from the street, supported by a shopping bag on trolley wheels. "I'll stay late tonight, come to your office when everyone's gone." Shivani's wide, brown eyes were imploring. "Or we could go back to my flat, spend the night together. Please, Matt… why didn't you answer my calls?"

"It's complicated." This sounded lame, but I had no idea how to respond.

"Are you sure you're well enough to be here?" She inflected the last word a pitch higher, holding her head at a quizzical angle. "The receptionist said you looked strange, and you've lost your pass card. This is not so normal, Matt."

"It takes a while, recovering after an operation, and this heatwave, the train was so hot… But I'm fine now," I bumbled, sounding awkward and embarrassed; not at all Matthew's style, I'm sure.

"Okay," she said, with a finality suggesting that what I had told her was accepted at face value. Time to move on. And she did, shifting to face the entrance doors across the expansive foyer, her hand touching, lingering briefly on my knee as she did so. It was impossible to ignore, and I think even in my own body it would have been impossible not to be stimulated by her aching desire.

"We'd better go. I've got you another pass."

She stood in one swift, effortless movement, waiting while I eased out of the sofa rather more sedately. I took the plastic card she proffered, then followed her like some gross, overweight lapdog as she walked to the lifts. She was shorter than me, even with significant wedge heels, but her graceful steps and poise manifested presence and personality, an aura of importance, something far beyond mere physical attraction.

The wayward pensioner was gone, ejected without ceremony by the zealous receptionist whose prying eyes fixed upon us over her harsh specs when we stepped, alone, into the empty lift. Shivani pressed the button for the fourth floor and then pounced the instant that the doors slid together.

"Oh, Matt," she sighed, throwing thin arms around my neck. I could not repel the sudden onslaught as she pulled me close with surprising strength, crumpling the frills on her white blouse against my chest so that I felt her small breasts crush into me. She kissed me passionately, moving her tongue within my mouth, and my response was instinctive, impossible to prevent.

Her firm buttocks swayed with my touch, and I felt a breathless excitement, almost bringing me with a low moan in her throat as she slid a hand down to my crotch. Then it finished as suddenly as it had begun. The lift bell pinged and she pulled away in a flash, like a teenage tease, swiftly patting down skirt and blouse, tossing those long strands of thick, dark hair behind her shoulders, calm and composed when the doors glided apart to reveal a wide, vacant corridor.

It left me reeling, over almost before it began, but it had been electric, frenetic and spontaneous, in the blink of opportunity's eye and completely unexpected; ambushing me with no chance to consider and avoid temptation. I hadn't been able to control Matthew's body or resist, and in truth I had not wanted to resist any of it.

But I felt the sense of shame immediately. It was wrong and constituted a betrayal of the only woman I have ever loved: it is the only time I have kissed, held another woman like that, however fleeting it might have been, since meeting Cathy all those years ago. And poor Shivani; she is obviously besotted, but with Matthew, not me. In a way, simply presenting myself here amounts to deception.

I followed her flash of smiling white teeth from the lift, the wide eyes of mischief quickly evaporating into dull formality when she used the security pass to gain us access to the inner-sanctum of the department – strictly staff only. There were no hiding places within the open-plan pool of support staff: secretaries and paralegals rammed together like package tour sun-seekers on a crowded beach. Beyond were half partitioned cubby-holes shared two to a cell by ambitious trainees and associates, and then some individual, garret-like spaces for the senior associates. As Shivani led the way through, a few heads turned briefly to sneak a curious look, but nobody presumed to formally acknowledge the return of their senior litigation partner. I had the distinct impression of servile reserve, even fear: clearly, Matthew Campbell was a boss who should be approached with extreme caution, to be addressed only when spoken to, like staff below Victorian stairs.

At the far corner of the building, we reached a door marked 'Mr Matthew Campbell'. I knew I should leave it open to avoid further temptation – temptation that as Andrew I could have resisted – but the anticipation of her moist lips and slender body called me like a sad addict to crack cocaine. When she flung it open the door's hinges squeaked slightly as she walked in to stand beside this large desk, waiting for me with a business-like expression of curious detachment.

My resolve buckled and I quietly closed the door behind me. But when I looked beyond Shivani and gazed around, those first shockwaves of déjà vu rescued me from the moment of weakness. I stood, transfixed at the threshold, amazed to recognise everything I saw in there – it was all so familiar, and yet I knew that I had never seen it before. Why did I feel in my bones this was home, this was a part of me? Eventually, I paced slowly towards the wall of glass, aware of every detail of the stunning view as though it had formed the backdrop to my life for years. The feelings, those sensations, made no sense to me, and they still don't.

Perhaps she picked up on my confusion because when she spoke the lover was gone, and in her place was the efficient assistant solicitor. She had arranged an uninterrupted morning for me to peruse case files, catch up and 'ease back in and orientate'. She told me how time-consuming the Wilkinson case had become, with the trial date fixed for 20th September, only two months away. Apparently, there is a discovery dispute relating to whether or not a highly damaging email to me from the chief executive of Wilkinson's is privileged. If not, it could be used in evidence against us. Shivani directed me to the computer print-out of the contentious email on my desk. I sat down to read it.

Matthew,

Reference your email. Okay, I agree suggested response. Good approach, fingers crossed this is not another series of disastrous claims. I'm determined to root out fucking idiots who pushed these awful drugs when we have so much more important fish to fry – what a distraction.

Look to you for support at next week's board meeting. We'll catch up first at Peter's soiree this weekend.

Simon

"Can we keep that out?" I asked her. There was no reason I should care, but the natural curiosity honed by a lawyer's training had kicked in.

She raised an eyebrow. "You tell me, Matt... I think, yes – careless comments to send, but they follow instructions to you as company lawyer, not director, and sent to your email address at Dorrell's. Anyway, I've briefed Timothy Green QC for the hearing of the emergency application this Thursday. We've got a conference with him tomorrow in Chambers, Pump Court. I know he's really pleased you'll be back for input."

I heard my stomach rumble; how could I possibly blag wisdom and authority on this tomorrow? Perhaps a judicious relapse in my recovery would be called for.

And then, belatedly, the coincidence struck me: Timothy Green. I remembered his name from the case papers I had been reading last Friday, but at the mention of Pump Court I realised their counsel was from the same set of Chambers in the Temple as Cathy. I could not recall her mentioning his name, but then she practised criminal law, a quite different area of expertise, and their paths would not have crossed often, if at all, in such a large Chambers. Even so, I may have rubbed shoulders with Timothy Green since, over the years, I had been to a few of the Chamber's social functions with Cathy.

My mind raced over the immediate implications. Would Cathy have returned to work yet – she had booked a villa for our family holiday in France for next week, but I doubted she would go now – and, if so, how would I cope and react if I did go to Pump Court tomorrow and saw her?

"I'll come for you later, Matt?" Shivani's words had cut across my reverie, and the arched, black lines of her eyebrows, the slight pout of her lips on a deadpan face, were now suggestive and sensual again. Her eyes lingered upon me for a response, keen, no doubt, that I should confirm my desire for an evening of passion. I had to resist this woman, yet somehow use her to gain information without compromising further my fidelity to Cathy.

"You appear to have everything under control," I said, unsure of myself, trying to supress thoughts of her physical presence and those brief moments in the lift.

"I'm always in control." Her face was serious and tight-lipped. "Since you've been away, it's been down to me with a little help from the paralegals. Ken Brimley covering you is a joke; he's been relieved to let me take charge." Leaning in close to me so that her perfume infused my senses again, I felt the determination of Matthew's vulnerable body to resist her slowly wilting. She opened a desk drawer at my side, extracting a set of keys with a bright, pink fob. "Don't forget my flat keys." Her words pulsated in my head, echoing temptation as she dangled the keys in my face, before thrusting them into my trouser pocket, then slowly withdrawing her hand and manicured, blue nails. "Keep them safe," she mouthed softly into my ear. "Whenever you need to, just come to me. Whatever happens, I'll always be here for you, Matt."

There was no denying her vibrant sexuality, and her intelligence. Her knowledge and command of the Wilkinson case was obvious; here was a lawyer supremely confident in her own ability who had, I suspect, recognised from an early stage that her trump card with Matthew Campbell was the benefit of a slim figure and pert bottom oozing sensuality, and a soft voice that could not decide if it came from Hackney or Delhi but was all the more enticing for that.

But there had to be more to it. Surely her progress in the firm was assured by such obvious ability and talent, without any need for Matthew's help? Perhaps Matthew did sex rather well? An interesting thought, but more likely her attraction to him provided stark validation that wealth and power can be a mighty aphrodisiac, sufficient for a beautiful young woman, surely not much past thirty, to fall for an overweight, late middle-aged man whose wispy, white hair and blemished cheeks glare back at me every time I pass a mirror.

"I must go," Shivani said, easing away from me. "I have to get on with preparing the documentation for Friday's application. I've got the new associate and a trainee working fulltime on it, but it will still be a tight-run thing." Her gaze fell on the files stacked beside me and she smiled. "Have fun, Matt."

"Thanks. I'll try." I was relieved but surprised that she hadn't asked me to take over, or even help with this urgent case. She was at the door when I remembered, just in time. "Peter Cheung… I should speak with him, but I've misplaced his contact details. Would you be so kind as to look them out before you leave?"

"Okay. Why so formal, Matt; this is me, Shivi? And you're always talking to Peter Cheung; you must know his number. Anyway, it's bound to be keyed into your phone's memory, surely? …This is not like you at all."

"I'm sorry. I don't know; this op, it's knocked me for six."

"You're sounding like my father, always with the cricket terms… As it happens, I do need to speak with Peter. He's been away but due back today. You can imagine how awkward it's been, not having the research director of Wilkinson's around to consult with on the case. I seem to remember you needed to talk with him almost daily just before your leave… So, I'll put him through to you then, when I get back to my desk?" Her late inflection formed a question, and I nodded to confirm.

There was no smile, only a troubled expression as she left, gently closing the door behind her. Those parting words rang a bell, surely? The talk of her father and cricket. And her accent, of course, the memory came to me, the coincidence quite striking.

I had met Matthew's lover before, a chance encounter at the Starbucks in Palmers Green about a couple of months ago on a dull Saturday afternoon. I had been at my office capturing quiet time – no phones or unannounced clients – to work on drafting leases for a new flat development we were handling. Mid-afternoon, I popped into the coffee shop for a break. It was crowded with weary shoppers, and I had been lucky to secure one of the comfy, leather armchairs at a window table.

My cappuccino was all but drained when I glanced up from the *I* newspaper I'd bought at the till, to see a young woman in jeans and burgundy sweatshirt scanning the shop in an attempt to find a vacant seat. She held a large cup of coffee in one hand and a plastic bag emblazoned with the name of a local dress shop linked over her other arm. She saw me looking at her and so I averted my eyes back to the newspaper but glanced up again when she spoke, a quiet voice right next to me.

"Is this taken?" Her eyes indicated the other empty armchair at my table.

"No, please do sit down," I said, feeling a tad awkward, my personal space breached, but quite reasonably so in the busy shop.

She sat down, placing the store bag at her side. Taking a sip from her coffee, she placed the cup on the small table between us. I remember thinking she was attractive, and there is no doubt in my mind when I recall this now that it was Shivani. I had felt awkward and said, "In fact, I'm about to leave."

"Please don't go on my account. It's nice to have someone to chat with for a change." She smiled nonchalantly, reaching for the cup and taking another sip of coffee.

I recall wondering if that was a 'come-on', and so, just in case, I replied quite firmly, "No, really, it's fine. I want to get home in time to watch some cricket on *Sky* before close of play this evening." In fact, I was going back to work but thought that sounded better, and I certainly had no interest in chatting up other women, no matter how good they might look.

I remembered that's when she'd said it, as I got up to leave. "You're sounding like my father," she'd laughed, "he cannot bear to be separated from his beloved cricket. My mother says it rules his life." It was the same confident voice with that strong Indian accent breaking through, like her parting words to me just a few moments ago.

The coincidence was explained when I pulled the key fob from my trouser pocket. I read the address written neatly on the small tab under plastic: 32 Fountain Road, Palmers Green, N13. Somehow, I would have expected her to have a more upmarket home than a flat near to my firm in Palmers Green.

***

Before trawling through the files left out for me to review, I decide to check the emails on Matthew's computer to see whether they reveal more information on Peter Cheung and the extent of any friendship between them. The account name and password are noted, along with other information and instructions, on an aide-memoir prepared by Matthew to assist Shivani during his absence. Fortunately, she has left it beside the files on my desk.

I click the mouse, log in and a blank page dismays me. No emails, and I cannot seem to access those recently deleted, nor traffic over previous months. This is frustrating, but presumably Matthew's absence was well advertised and Shivani dealt with what electronic post he did receive, probably sending it on to her own office email address to do so. Just a pity that she, or someone, has permanently deleted his records, perhaps for security reasons.

I am about to close the site when an email pops in from the managing partner: stephenbrinkworthdorrells@hotmail.co.uk. I open it and read. The style is instantly recognisable; it must have been Stephen Brinkworth who recorded that brash voicemail message I had listened to, almost two weeks ago, the day I returned from the hospital.

Thank Christ you're back, at last. Shivani has been a legend. Watch your back – she's going far.

I guess it's manic – I know Ken's skiving today on a management training course of all things – but we need to talk. I can't find any interim billing or money on account for Wilkinson; the case should be a cash cow! Don't prove me wrong, allowing you to run it, Matt, notwithstanding your directorship. Should I have let you persuade me? Talk to me, matey. Pop up and see me after 3.00pm. Okay?

I take off my specs for a moment, put them on the desk and rub my eyes as though for inspiration. How to respond; more to the point, how will I even find his office? The senior litigation partner at Dorrell's can hardly ask any member of staff as to the whereabouts of the managing partner!

It's all too much; my mind is on overload and can't seem to keep focus. It drifts back to Sunday with Helen. This cheers me up because things had gone pretty well. A good lunch and company. She has a keen sense of humour; we had spoken much about nothing, a few more personal details, rather like a first date. During the evening we had watched TV together and it felt strangely homely, a relief to largely ignore the momentous events I had recounted at breakfast.

I think she may decide to believe me; she wants more time but promised to talk with me later this week. Of course, she may report me to the medics as suffering from a total nervous breakdown, rather than try to broker the meeting with Cathy that I requested. Having made my choice to confide in her, though, I can now only wait and see.

Perhaps I should start to look at these files Shivani has left out for me to review? Without any conviction, I pull one from the top of the pile, but before I can open it, I hear raised voices, a 'kerfuffle' outside; the door rattles on its hinges before bursting open. Two men march in, the taller one carrying a smart, black briefcase, followed by a smaller woman. They stand in front of my desk, facing me like a military detail firing squad, with bland faces devoid of emotion, the men flanking the lone woman.

She is middle-aged and her deportment conveys an air of authority despite her meagre frame. The navy business suit she wears, skirt hem comfortably below the knee, is smart without suggesting ostentation. Her thin, unattractive face is punctuated by a pinched nose pointing a piercing, silent stare at me. In slow motion she reaches for her inside breast pocket, withdraws a folded, black wallet which she opens flat and proffers for my inspection, arm held out straight in a flourish before me. I reposition the reading specs at the end of my nose.

As she speaks with an unusually low voice in a robotic, sombre monotone, my heart sighs in a flutter and my bowels roll loose at the glint of a silver crown above the official Royal insignia, resplendent in stark contrast to the photograph of her glum face on the other side of the warrant card. "I am Detective Chief Inspector Doyle from the National Crime Agency. These are my colleagues, Detective Sergeant Hancock and Detective Constable Mitchell." She indicates each officer by a brief nod in their direction. They pull up chairs and sit down, uninvited, still facing me across the desk.

Surprisingly, the DS is much the younger man: tall and slim, he is neatly groomed, wearing a black suit and a striking, blue silk tie. The contrast with the wide girth and slipshod appearance of his older but junior partner could hardly be more dramatic. He is balding, the rambling, white moustache covering his upper lip somehow complementing his cheap, shiny brown suit sailing at a distressed distance from his thick neck.

I stare into the woman's unflinching face, expressionless and cold with no trace of emotion or humanity, and when I open my mouth to speak no words come. She lifts her head slightly, one eyebrow arched high to match the inflection in tone as she asks, "You are Matthew Campbell?"

"You can't barge in here unannounced like this." I find my tongue. "What do you want?" My words tremble with nerves, not the deep purr of confident authority intended.

"Just answer the question, please. I need to confirm your identity." Her hollow voice, the deadpan persona, does not change, and her two companions remain motionless, sitting beside her like silent zombies. A sense of repressed hostility charges the electric atmosphere, as though I am an alleged paedophile in the dock awaiting his jury's verdict; how heinous is the crime to be levelled against this man in whose shadow I now live?

It crosses my mind, momentarily, to tell the truth, blurt out that I am Andrew Soulsby, victim of some unfathomable conspiracy, that I am not responsible for any of Matthew Campbell's transgressions. But her harsh, grey eyes still fix me like a gimlet, predicting the disbelief and derision, the dire consequences that would inevitably follow if I did so.

"It's complicated. I guess for your purposes, I am now Matthew Campbell."

Her forehead crinkles in a frown. "This is not difficult. I need formal confirmation, not smart-arse semantics." Her voice rises in exasperation, the hostile tone unmistakable, as she almost shouts at me, "It's a simple enough question for a two-year-old. Confirm your name."

"Yes, okay. It is Matthew Campbell."

She makes no reply, only glancing sideways at the young officer, who acts on cue, producing a document from the briefcase now nestling on his lap. He pushes it across the desk towards me and says, in a low, bitter-crisp voice, "We have warrants to search these offices, your house in Beech Hill, Hadley Wood, and your flat in Bedford Court, Covent Garden. A team will begin here shortly and other police officers are attending at the residential addresses now. They will take whatever action is necessary to gain entry."

Before I can begin to compose myself or collect any thoughts for response, the detective chief inspector, whose eyes have never left mine, is talking again: "Matthew Campbell, I am arresting you on suspicion of money-laundering, theft and false accounting. You do not have to say anything, but it may harm your defence if you fail to mention when questioned something which you may later rely on in court. Anything you do say, may be given in evidence."

After she falls silent, I am not sure how much time passes before I become aware of three curious faces honed upon me, waiting with trained eyes to assess my reaction. They sit like statues, by their silence seeking to coax an incriminating reply.

It is only for the last three days, since the episode outside the chapel on Friday, that I have been taking Matthew's statins and blood-pressure pills. They had reminded me to take them when I left the hospital two weeks ago, but it is hardly surprising those strictures were initially forgotten. It may be that failure which contributes to my heart racing again, pounding beneath the grip of tension squeezing across my chest-bone. Struggling for breath, I make a conscious effort to breathe deeply and slowly. My throat is hurting; it seems almost as bad as in those first few days after the operation, and my mouth feels dry, my lips sore and chapped.

They are still staring at me, Matthew's accusers – how long without speaking now? – and I fancy a corner of the woman's upper lip is raised, sneering in sadistic gratification at my obvious discomfort. I have to speak, say something, and I think of what Cathy always advises. The words form in my mind… I will tell them that I have no comment until I have seen my solicitor and taken advice. But instead of this, still trembling with shock and fear, I find myself mumbling in a low voice, "I'm an honest man. The only crime I'm involved in has been committed against me."

This prompts an immediate reaction from all three of them, released simultaneously from patient stalking of their prey while they waited on my first move.

"That's original," she snorts, laughing cynically. The sergeant, head down, records my comment in a notebook. The burly constable pushes his chair back noiselessly on the thick carpet, standing up to reveal lines of creasing to the thin material of his suit. He moves smartly around the desk, surprisingly nimble for his weighty frame, stopping at my shoulder.

"Stand up, please, Sir." It is the first time he has spoken and, though formal, he is polite, no hint of rancour. He takes a pair of handcuffs from a trouser pocket. "Hands behind your back, please," he says, and I comply meekly.

As he clasps them shut with a metallic clunk, I venture a weak protest: "Surely this is not necessary. I'm hardly going to run away."

"Standard procedure, Sir," says my captor, but I know from Cathy this is used as a symbolic ritual to emphasise their power and authority, to reinforce my ignominy and shame, the better to intimidate me, crush my will prior to the formal questioning that will doubtless follow soon.

"I must ask you to come with us now," he says, like a fictional detective at the denouement of an Agatha Christie murder mystery. This only serves to heighten the sense of disbelief, the dream-like quality that pervades my existence now, carried along by a fate that does not answer to logic or the known laws of nature. Every night when I toss on my pillow, I pray to sleep and wake the next morning in my own bed in Cheltenham Avenue, this whole terrifying experience consigned to a distant nightmare by whatever dark powers created it. But only in the dreams of a troubled sleep that sometimes follows does Andrew Soulsby experience a temporary renaissance, and it is still within the body of Matthew Campbell that I wake each morning.

He places a hand between my shoulder blades, pressing firmly, and says, "Come on, Sir, time to go."

I look up at their harsh faces, all devoid of any kindness or humanity, and cringe with embarrassment as my tummy rolls loudly and my bladder urges relief. "I'm sorry, but I need to use the bathroom," I venture, like a nervous schoolchild.

DCI Doyle frowns her contempt at this weakness, and my humiliation is complete.

CHAPTER 23

Fidgeting on a thin mattress and squinting through heavy eyes that cannot find release in sleep, the walls of the police cell shift closer to confine me as the gloomy light from a night bulb plays tricks with my senses. I bury my face into the flimsy pillow, trying to forget all those questions from DCI Doyle this afternoon that I couldn't answer, but there is no escape for my mind which replays the day constantly, particularly the humiliation of my arrest this morning: struggling to pee at the urinal while Detective Constable Mitchell hovered in close attendance, waiting to re-cuff me; the gawping, incredulous faces at Dorrell's, staring in disbelief as I was led away in those handcuffs; and the silent journey in the rear of an unmarked police car enjoined to that bulky policeman, the acrid whiff of his body odour making me want to gag.

Fortunately, the screech of a siren had hastened our journey to Holborn Police Station, where I was processed by a custody sergeant with a broad Scottish accent. My pockets were emptied and all possessions confiscated; they even asked for my shoelaces and I had to scramble about, breathless, on my knees, fumbling to comply.

The sergeant had handed the iPhone back to me briefly so that I could make my one permitted call. The only person I could think to ring was Helen. I should have been allowed a private conversation, I'm sure, but they had watched me, my captors – DCI Doyle, DS Hancock and DC Mitchell – beside the uniformed Scotsman whose silver tunic buttons glinted in the glare of artificial light in the basement custody suite, like beacons of false hope in Hell. As my unsteady hands held the iPhone, found her saved number and willed her to pick up, their silence mocked me: grim, unforgiving faces, savouring the fall from grace and lost reputation of a city lawyer leaving a garbled voicemail message.

When another uniformed officer had led me away towards the cells, his firm hand resting on my shoulder, I stopped, turning back to shout in desperation, echoing down the corridor: "I forgot… to tell Helen in my phone message, the most important thing; I need a criminal law solicitor. Shouldn't you have advised me about that, offered me a duty solicitor? Please," I pleaded, "I need to ring her again."

Not a soul had stirred, no one looked up; it was as if I did not exist, until the young constable tugged my arm. "This way, please, Sir." There was a hint of sympathy in his manner, perhaps because of my age, the professional dress or my cultured voice which was almost as foreign to me as this place had he known it. Still, it was reassuring to be addressed again, even briefly, in a semi-civilised manner. "I'll mention it to Sergeant Willett," he had said, "but I think there's already been a call about you. Someone's on the way."

I remember standing motionless, numb with shock, in this small space devoid of natural light as the heavy door slammed shut behind me with a harsh, metallic thud, then the sound of the lock turning, clunking tight and secure, keys on a ring jangling away with footsteps receding into a hollow distance. Eventually, I had sat on this thin mattress which rests on a concrete slab against the wall of cold, hard bricks, the 'bed' I am now trying to sleep on. Tears had welled, trickling slowly in a confused maze at my cheeks, my sinuses soon swollen and blocked, my eyes a heat of stinging pain. I sobbed, almost silent in my distress. But I did not care, even finding solace of a kind in my self-pity: the terrible injustice of what had become of me, the appalling pain being ratcheted up to scale new heights of misery.

Lost in that wretched state, I did not hear movement and voices outside before the sudden, harsh sound of keys turning and locks disengaged made me jerk my head up as the cell door was flung wide open, revealing the embarrassment of my tear-stained face to the custody sergeant. He strode inside, towering above the short, stocky man following him.

"This is your solicitor," said Sergeant Willett, who frowned down upon me with an amused disdain, then addressed himself to the stranger, smirking as he joked in his broad Glaswegian dialect: "Shout through the slat in yon door when you're done, then maybe we'll let ye out… Okay, my man?" He chuckled, not waiting for any answer, and bid a hasty retreat, the door clunking shut and locked again behind him.

Through blotchy, red eyes I watched the man announced as my solicitor approach me, then thrust out his hand in a confident gesture of greeting. "My name is Michael Shapiro, sole principal of Shapiro & Company." A friendly smile swathed his face. "I'm here to help you."

He spoke quietly with a distinct Jewish accent. A deep voice. At least sixty years old, I thought, and I noticed the bald patch at his crown when easing myself from the bed to stand and take his hand. It was surrounded by hair dyed black, untidy, straggling whiskers and a grey beard – quite a strange contrast to his immaculate, navy-blue suit and silver-grey tie.

"I'm sorry," I mouthed, falteringly, embarrassed at my appearance.

Kindly eyes had surveyed me from above the round, black-rimmed spectacles on the end of his nose as he carefully placed his briefcase on the bed. "I know it's not a good time or place for you now," he said, "but things will get better for you, Andrew." Those eyes, searching and bright, continued to hold my attention like a magnet, and for a brief moment I wondered if I may have misheard or imagined this. But no, it had been clear and certain, no mistake: he had called me 'Andrew', and his intense expression told me he knew the impact this would have upon me and that he was keen to observe my reaction.

Like a telephone ringing in the small hours, this had roused me, the self-pity forgotten: a stranger aware of my real identity; maybe he knew what had happened to me? A thousand questions raced within my mind but on my lips, there was only a gasp of shock.

His wrinkled face had cracked a slow smile. "Why don't you sit down again?" he said, and so I settled on the small bed, my thoughts still scrambling, stunned into temporary silence. He was peering down at me, very close, and when he spoke again it was slow and reassuring, like an elderly uncle with wise advice in time of trouble. "I do know you claim to be Andrew Soulsby, and I believe you." He paused to let this sink in, his gaze still intense upon me. "But since his death certificate has been issued, and there was a funeral on Friday, it's hardly a defence we can disclose." There was no hint of sarcasm or malice, just a statement of fact. "We'll stick with the amnesia line for now," he continued. "No memory of before your operation, so you can't answer any relevant questions or give any other information or comment."

He had turned away from me then, pacing around slowly within the few square metres of the cell as he spoke. "Let me explain to you how things stand now... I've spoken, briefly, with Detective Chief Inspector Doyle. She's a nasty piece of work, but I have the measure of her." His calm voice exuded confidence and a quiet certainty of purpose. "The alleged offences are serious, and Campbell is guilty. However, I doubt they have sufficient evidence to lay charges yet. They will question you this afternoon, then try again tomorrow morning when they've had a preliminary examination of the computers and papers being seized now from his business office and properties. But it will take weeks, if not months, for them to sift through all of it, and you cannot be held for more than twenty-four hours unless they charge you or get an extension from the superintendent, which I doubt will be granted. So, I anticipate getting you police bail – your release – tomorrow, which is a good start, Andrew, yes?"

He had looked directly at me again, that piercing gaze below his bushy eyebrows willing my positive response. But only now, alone in my cell this evening, have I appreciated the importance of his words. I am desperate to regain my liberty, to be released from this concrete and brick tomb in the bowels of the police station. Yet the only thing I could focus on then was that this man knew I was Andrew. All those questions racing within my mind, as they still do now: how could he know, and why was he here; who had done this to me, and how was it possible; and why me?

Apart from a young nurse and my garbled words to her in the clearing mists of my anaesthetic, the only person I had confided in was Helen, the previous day. I doubted she would have disrespected my trust so quickly, and, anyway, she was seeking help from a solicitor called Jason. Michael Shapiro had told me he was a sole practitioner, and so surely not connected to Jason? In any event, the timing did not add up. She could not have organised the rapid appearance of a lawyer, let alone fully brief and convince him of an incredible claim, since the hurried message I had left on her mobile little more than an hour before his arrival. And then there was the young constable's words as he led me to the cells: someone, he had indicated, had already called about me and was on the way.

"Who are you, really; who sent you?" I had finally loaded my swirling thoughts into words that shot out like bullets from a machine gun. "How do you know I am Andrew; it can't be Helen, so you must be involved with Peter Cheung and Joe Peng; you must be part of the conspiracy. How did they do it, and why me; please, have some pity; tell me what you know?"

I ended up shouting, and before he answered we were interrupted by the sound of a fist thumping against the steel door, then a heavy clunk as the viewing slat opened. A strong voice bellowed from outside, "Is everything alright in there, Mr Shapiro?" My heart raced even faster, fearing that my words had been overheard. I imagined them being recounted to colleagues for ribald amusement – the posh City lawyer who had lost the plot – or worse, reported to superiors.

"Yes, all is well, thank you, Officer. Please leave us alone." Michael's calm reassurance worked, the slat closed with a bang and we listened in silence, waiting, as heavy footsteps echoed into the distance.

I loosened my collar and felt perspiration at the nape of my neck. Trembling, I buried my face in my hands to cover the shame of my appearance, no longer able to look at the man who might have so many answers.

I must have cut a forlorn figure as he came to sit next to me. He moved his briefcase from the bed onto the floor and then placed his large hand firmly upon my shoulder. It had seemed slightly inappropriate yet oddly helpful, the soothing influence of tactile human contact. But more than that it made me aware of the need to regain my composure and pride, behave as a professional person in the face of adversity and in the presence of an elderly man I had only just met.

"Try to calm down, relax a little, Andrew," he had said to me, his gentle tones coaxing serenity in the midst of my chaos. "I will never lie to you. I am, truly, Mike Shapiro, a jobbing, criminal law solicitor." As he said this, I remember thinking, quite randomly, that I could never view this apparently avuncular man as 'Mike', as a mate. "I'm good at what I do, really good, just as you're a good conveyancer." His eyes twinkled; just how much did he know about me? "But property law is cotton wool to me, and I suspect it's the same for you with criminal law. That's why I'm here," he smiled, squeezing his hand on my shoulder, "to help – on your side. Okay?" I remained silent but thought that sounded condescending. I wondered if he knew my real wife was a criminal law barrister, and if he'd heard of her? "I said only that I believe your claim to be Andrew Soulsby. There's no time now for all the details. Certainly not here. We must prioritise on the questioning that's going to follow. They're anxious to start and will only give us a short time for this consultation; in fact, they might arrive to take you up at any moment, so we need to address this – get it done."

"At least tell me who sent you here? I've only confided in Matthew's wife, and it can't be her." His hang-dog face frowned, full of kindly regret, but he made no response. "Well, I can't pay your fees," I groaned. "I've no access to my own money and I've found only massive debts for Matthew. Perhaps I qualify for legal aid?"

"Please, Andrew, leave it for now. Trust me – okay? My fees are not a problem. The important thing is that I'm here for you, sent by those with your interests at heart." His rumpled face, crinkling around the unkempt beard, had viewed me with a compelling candour that invited trust. "Remember, stick with your first lie, the one that was instinctive for self-preservation: you can remember nothing – total, not selective, amnesia; everything before your operation has gone. Make no other comments, offer no opinions or views. They will try to intimidate and provoke you, so just try to stay focused." And then he added, without any hint of irony, "I'll be there for support – to stop any bullying or duplicity."

With this he had reached for the briefcase at his feet, getting up smartly, his movement surprisingly agile for a man of his build and age, while I remained seated. He glanced towards the small sink beside the toilet in the back corner, stark in its lack of privacy from the cell door's peephole. "Now, I suggest you wash your face, tidy up before the interview and questioning. I'll make sure you have ten minutes alone before they come for you." He paused, before adding with a grim expression conveying determination and resolve, "Do not let them beat you down, Andy. Remember, stay sharp and focused." So, now it was 'Andy'.

He had turned, then, bellowing from directly behind the cell door to the custody suite outside, a thunderous roar that made me start and brought a speedy response as the door creaked open, and he was gone. I prayed this man was truly my friend, not my enemy.

CHAPTER 24

TUESDAY 21ST JULY

She looks up, focusing somewhere above my head, and speaks in an exaggerated voice: "Interview with Matthew Campbell recommenced at 10am on Tuesday 21st July at Holborn Police Station. Present are the suspect, his solicitor Michael Shapiro, Detective Sergeant Hancock and myself, Detective Chief Inspector Doyle.

"Okay." She focuses on me, throwing a watery smile that oozes insincerity. "I must remind you that you're still under caution, Matthew. Let's try once more; a last chance for you to provide answers that may help in your defence." She pauses briefly, to glance at notes on a legal pad. The subtle change of tactics is transparent: her tone has mellowed since yesterday, the repressed hostility replaced with mock concern for my welfare.

We are in the same small room as yesterday afternoon. There are no windows and it feels uncomfortably warm. The faded cream walls are chipped and dirty with scuff marks near the floor where they meet worn, grey carpet tiles. The detective chief inspector and her dapper sergeant are sitting on the other side of a desk, facing me and my new friend, Michael, who is scowling at them across the expanse of cheap wood. She looks up at me, the same false smile on her thin lips. "You've had the night to sleep on things, mull over the implications if you fail to co-operate—"

"Sleep, in that cell last night?" I interrupt her, my voice fluttering hoarse with tiredness and anxiety. "I hardly think so."

My solicitor fidgets in his chair, clearing his throat as he leans forward to interject, "Detective Chief Inspector, you know very well that my client is *not* failing to co-operate." Michael's voice resonates within the confined space, the Jewish accent more pronounced when he is provoked to stray from his normal, calm demeanour. "On the contrary, he has been distressed and frightened for over two weeks, since 6th July, when he emerged from the anaesthetic following his operation and found that his total memory had been wiped blank by an episode of amnesia. This is the reason why he cannot answer your questions or provide any information. If, hopefully when, his memory is restored, he will be only too willing to answer questions and provide what information and assistance he can."

A nerve twitches in her cheek, the upper lip curling with a venom her drab voice conceals from the tape. "Thank you, Mr Shapiro, but please save your speeches for the court. I'm trying to conduct an interview with your client." At her side DS Hancock remains motionless, no hint of expression, like a mummified sphinx.

But Michael is not finished yet. "My comments, Detective Chief Inspector, were made for the benefit of the tape, to reiterate, for the record, what has already been explained yesterday. Given the circumstances, I fail to grasp the point of this further interview, but if you must put your questions to my client yet again, when he is not in a position to answer them, may we please get on without any more inappropriate threats."

She fixes him with a surly stare, her body taut, bridled with suppressed fury at this admonition, this clear slight to her authority and integrity. I wonder, when the tape is replayed, if it will begin to convey this sour atmosphere, the undercurrent of bitterness, almost loathing, between this woman and my solicitor?

"I was not… I would *never* make threats. I was merely clarifying your client's position as we see it, doing my job. It is a matter for Mr Campbell as to whether or not he feels able to respond to further questions this morning." Her voice now conveys a weary resignation at what she perceives will be my continuing and obdurate failure to respond, to offer them any explanations or comments. "He has received your advice about this. It's up to him. We just wish to provide him with one more opportunity."

She has been staring at Michael but now regards me accusingly down that pinched nose, and any pretence of contriving a false partiality for my interests has vanished as she says, "As your solicitor will have told you, the tapes of these interviews may be given in evidence and replayed to your jury. Do you understand this, Matthew?"

"Yes."

She pauses for a moment, glancing at papers spread out on the desk beside her legal pad. "We've seized your computers and records," she continues eventually, "from your properties and your office. We're liaising with the Solicitors Regulation Authority, and forensic accountants are pouring through everything with a fine toothcomb to uncover all transgressions, however minor or technical. But it's only the serious stuff, some of which we touched on yesterday, that I'm going to be concerned with this morning, and we have some further facts now which may jog your memory. Let's hope they do, so we can help to ease your distress." She can't suppress a slight smirk. "Please stop me if any memories do resurface. I'll be happy to break for you to obtain Mr Shapiro's advice before you answer."

I press the small of my back firmly against the upright chair support, shoot a nervous, sideways glance to Michael, who is frowning at me over his spectacles, a look that reminds me of my coached, stock answer: *"Unfortunately, I am unable to answer or comment due to my amnesia."*

"I'd like to start this morning by reminding you of your words immediately after arrest and caution yesterday." She makes a show, looking down to read slowly from her notes: "'I'm an honest man. The only crime I'm involved in has been committed against me.'" She pauses for a moment, wrinkling her nose in fake bemusement. "That's a very strange thing to say. I'm wondering what you meant: what the crime is and how you know you're an honest man when you have no memories beyond three weeks ago... Care to elaborate?"

I try to suppress a sense of panic when I realise our prepared answer cannot be employed, and my brain shuffles possible alternatives, desperately seeking a suitable explanation. I resist my natural urge, conditioned by upbringing and habit, to seek the temporary satisfaction of telling the truth, explaining what I really did mean and demanding a full investigation into the circumstances of Andrew Soulsby's death. But the promise of mental units and antipsychotic drugs screams in warning from the pragmatic chief inspector's accusing eyes; a future of indefinite detention, perhaps the ideal solution for those ranged against me? I glance at Michael for inspiration, but he remains impassive, a curious uncertainty suggested by his quizzical expression. Is this man truly here to help me?

The hum of a fluorescent light tube on the ceiling swells the hanging silence into a bubble of tension that compels me to burst it with words, although I remain unsure of what to say, until at last I blurt out, "No, I don't really know. I was, I am, frightened and confused. I mean, I know, instinctively, that I'm an honest man. I'm sure of that. It's a crime that I'm here accused of serious wrongdoing. I just know that can't be me." I steal a furtive look towards Michael again, and his lips have cracked slightly to imply: 'well done, good answer'.

DCI Doyle frowns. "Umm, we'll leave that for now," she says, extracting a sheet of paper from the file in front of her and sliding it across the desk towards me. "Please examine this carefully." I pick it up, put reading specs on the end of my nose and read the list of ten companies with variable but massive sums of money recorded as passing from each one of them to an off-shore company registered in the Isle of Man.

"Recognise this?"

"Yes. You showed it to me in our last interview, yesterday."

"Good. I wanted to check if you were able to remember it," she says caustically, turning to share the moment with her colleague.

"My client has already explained his amnesia relates to before his operation just over two weeks ago, not since that event," Michael's voice booms. "It is a serious, worrying condition, Detective Chief Inspector. Your sarcasm does you no favours."

She ignores him, her attention focusing exclusively upon me. "The chief cashier at Dorrell's recently picked up on a pattern of electronic bank payments, ten over a short period, and amounting, in total, to over twenty million pounds sterling. They were made from funds held on behalf of those ten private UK companies and credited to the off-shore company registered in a tax haven. He reported this suspicious activity to his money-laundering partner who made full disclosure to us. The report records that her initial investigations revealed you act for all ten companies, Matthew, and that you authorised those payments. Is this correct?"

"Unfortunately, I am unable to answer or comment due to my amnesia." My reply sounds hollow, false, like a duplicitous politician under pressure, evading the truth.

She turns to one side, bending down to reach for a briefcase nestled under the desk near her feet, and extracts ten pocket files which she passes to me. "These are paper files, one for each company. Please read through them. Take your time. You will find your initials, 'MC', as references on the few papers in each file. It may help to jog your memory."

There had been no mention in my interview yesterday as to the source of police information and the reason for their investigation, nor any sight of these files. I anticipate this was withheld until today in an attempt to intimidate and wrong-foot me into making prejudicial admissions.

"It won't take long." DS Hancock utters his first words this morning, and his expression is a study in disbelief. "You'll find only a couple of email print-outs in each one, along with identical, copy fee invoices, all for one thousand pounds plus VAT." His stare lingers in my face, and I avoid it by studying the papers in front of me.

Over recent years I have been to a number of professional development training courses on money-laundering with my business partner, Peter Bright, and so it is clear to me immediately that this smells like a massive money-laundering exercise. The responsible partner at Dorrell's would have committed a criminal offence, punishable by imprisonment, had she not reported such suspicious circumstances to the National Crime Agency. She would also have been guilty of a further serious crime, along with the chief cashier, if either of them had breathed a word about this to anyone else, including the other partners and staff at the firm.

After a few minutes I close the last file, looking up to find both of the police officers staring at me, no doubt keen to gauge any change in demeanour, perhaps some slight movement in my facial muscles, or any other signs that might validate their belief in my guilt, and banish any remote, lingering doubts they may harbour.

"Now, Matthew, please remind me," says DCI Doyle, "of the words recorded on each copy fee invoice, the same narrative description on all ten, of the work you billed for each company."

Michael leans forward, placing his arm on the desk towards me, cautioning that I should not respond. "My client can confirm neither his conduct of, nor involvement in these cases," he growls, then snaps at DCI Doyle: "He has lost his memory."

She ignores him and, still looking directly at me, says, "We've established you'd like to co-operate, Matthew, if only you could, so please, just humour me by reading aloud for the tape the wording on the fee notes."

I pull out a copy fee invoice from one of the files, then read out, "Professional charges for services rendered."

"That's all?" she asks.

"Yes," I respond, adding, "It's a normal form of wording." Michael frowns at me. I should not have volunteered the comment.

"I see; so, it's the form of words you would use on your bills, then?"

I reply in haste, before Michael can intervene: "I didn't say that, but it is commonly used."

"Okay." She smiles, the same sickly smirk, like a hyena circling its prey. "I assume you have no recollection of these companies, nor of the money transfers exceeding twenty million pounds in total?"

"No, I do not. I can tell you nothing about them." I relish this variation from my scripted response, speaking with the earnest conviction of an honest man.

"And yet you know the normal form of wording for some legal bills, so presumably you remember that you are a lawyer?" Her upper lip crinkles into a leer for just a moment, enjoying my discomfort.

"Well, yes," I mumble, uncertainly. "I do recall being a solicitor, but not who I am. It was my first day at that office when you arrested me. I was trying to familiarise myself with files, but I remembered nothing." Michael catches my eye, his glare insistent that I should say no more, stick to the script.

"Umm... Humour me some more," she muses. "Although you maintain you know nothing of these matters, in your opinion as a solicitor, do you agree they appear to be sham files – no real legal work done – just companies being allowed the facility of your firm's client bank account to pass huge sums of money to another company in a tax haven; highly suspicious, almost certainly money-laundering and a clear breach of your professional rules?"

I agree, of course, but it would be foolish to admit this, and I begin to waffle: "Well, there could be entirely innocent explanations—"

As I try to come up with suitable scenarios, Michael rides to my rescue. "My client cannot be asked to speculate. How much longer will this last, Detective Chief Inspector? My client's position is clear. This is a waste of everyone's valuable time."

She shoots him a withering stare, meeting his frown in a grim moment that crystalises their mutual loathing. "I'll be the judge of that, Mr Shapiro. It's my call; you're just the lawyer with a very vested interest. I decide here. I decide what to ask the accused." She almost shouts this at him.

DS Hancock clears his throat, throwing an anxious glance at his boss, daring to imply she should regain her composure, as Michael replies in measured tones, "And I decide whether to advise my client to answer."

She ignores this, letting the moment pass, and turns back to confront me, her voice reverting to its dull, even keel. "I have something else for you to examine, Matthew, that we didn't have a chance to deal with in our first interview yesterday afternoon. Perhaps this might kindle your memory."

Her face is submerged as once more she delves down into her briefcase below the desk. Grey roots are showing below the short-cut, dark hair at the crown of her head, and then she bobs up, producing three sheets of paper stapled together in one corner. Like a croupier dealing at the blackjack table, she skims them across the desk to me. "Look at the client's name in the top heading and the accounting entries," she says, planting her elbows on the desk and cradling her chin in cupped hands, while fixing me with those unforgiving eyes. "Do you recognise this, Matthew?"

So far as I can tell it is a print-out of a client's ledger account with Dorrell's, comprising a confusing spread of figures recorded in what appears to be, but is clearly not, a haphazard manner. Receipts and payments are denoted by meaningless abbreviations or codes, with a running balance which always remains a six-figure sum. However, it records a zero-closed balance near the foot of the third page. Although a part-time bookkeeper is employed to write up the accounts at Soulsby & Bright, Peter and I had always been able to readily understand and interpret our basic system. But I cannot begin to decipher this sophisticated and complex solicitors' accounting package.

She shifts her position, sitting upright and reaching for a biro beside her notebook, tapping it impatiently on the thick writing pad, her gaze still firmly upon me. "Any memories stirring yet from the hidden depths of a great legal mind?" And then a tone of weary disbelief trumps the sarcasm. "Do you, at least, know what you're looking at?"

"Unfortunately," I recite, "I am unable to answer or comment due to my amnesia."

She lets my anaemic words hang in a hideous silence, finally punctuated by my rolling stomach. Michael clears his throat, and I dread to think what is coming next as she exchanges a fleeting, smug grin with her colleague.

"At our request," she says at last, "the senior cashier and the money-laundering partner did some poking around, discretely, without alerting anyone else at your firm. What you are looking at is the account record of an elderly, private client who instructed you to act for her, following the death of her husband a little over five years ago, to deal with the probate and administration of his substantial estate. Unusually, and contrary to your firm's policy, this work was not passed to the probate section but retained by you personally.

"There had been very few entries, hardly any activity on this account over the last three years, despite a substantial credit balance of £825,000 which was retained in a separate deposit account. That is until three weeks ago when it was closed suddenly, and the total balance sent by cheque to..." She pauses, glancing at her notes, then continues: "Miriam Pryor, at an address in Manchester, despite the will providing that your elderly client was her late husband's sole beneficiary. We've been unable to find any trace of a Miriam Pryor at that address in Manchester, and we're still trying to locate the missing money, since an account in her name at a local bank was closed immediately after the cheque cleared and the balance had been withdrawn… Any comments or recollections on this, Matthew?"

As the extent of Matthew Campbell's duplicity unfolds to accuse me, I have a crazy thought: could he have planned all this to escape his nemesis? They are waiting on my inevitable response, and while I reiterate the standard line – "Unfortunately, I am unable to answer or comment due to my amnesia" – I realise that such a thought is not credible at any level. What escape for him in the death of his soul, leaving me alive in his body to be punished for crimes I can neither remember nor defend? It is a fantasy that makes no sense.

She carries on, obviously determined to let me know they are unravelling the secrets of 'my' crimes. "The file shows you hold an old-style enduring power of attorney for your client dating back many years. Alice Nicholson appointed you to be her sole attorney, and this should have been registered with the Public Guardianship Office because she is now suffering from dementia in a council residential home. It has not been registered, so there has been no supervision of its use. Your firm have no record she was ever advised to make a will, and the home fees are publicly funded. Enquiries are ongoing, but I can't imagine anyone at the home or council knew of her undistributed inheritance. We already know she has no children, no visitors, and to date we've been unable to trace any other relatives.

"I find it difficult to think of a legitimate explanation for any of this, and if you cannot provide one it's not looking good for you, is it?" I assume this as a rhetorical question and remain grimly silent.

"You must see, it reeks of fraud and theft," and with that she rests her slight frame against the chair back, a cue for DS Hancock to pipe up, only the second time he has spoken during this morning's interview.

"All your partners at Dorrell's have now been informed of this investigation, Matthew, and they will also be enjoying an unexpected visit this morning from the Solicitors Regulation Authority; in fact," he breaks for a couple of seconds to glance at his wristwatch, "they should just be arriving as we speak." His tone is harsh, although lacking the spiteful edge of his boss; no good cop, bad cop routine here. "Is there more shit to hit the fan yet, Matthew?"

"Unfortunately, I am unable to answer or comment due to my amnesia."

The tall detective sergeant lifts his chin high, running a finger under the knot of his blue tie to loosen it slightly at the collar. It is warm; Michael's jacket was discarded, draped over the back of his chair, when he first entered this stuffy room, but DS Hancock's black suit jacket remains on, despite the tiny beads of perspiration glistening from his brow. Both he and DCI Doyle are still wearing the same clothes they had on when they burst into my office yesterday. Perhaps the pervading whiff of body odour, like bad eggs, is not entirely my creation; I wonder, have they returned to their homes and showered since then?

"We do know there is more," he says, a hint of Essex in his voice, as his boss pushes two further sheets of paper across the desk to rest in front of me. "When the Nicholson ledger was checked in more detail, an expenses claim was noticed. A little over three years ago you obtained reimbursement for first-class return air fares to New York with accommodation for seven nights at the Four Seasons Hotel in Manhattan. Apparently, you had to meet a fund manager there to…" – he pauses to consult and read from his notes – "'*discuss issues relating to substantial investments held by the deceased*'."

He looks up, his face in mine, cracking a knowing smile. "Your firm's chief cashier has admitted that your claims for expenses have rarely been scrutinised properly, always taken at face value owing to your seniority and importance to the company as – I quote him – 'a prodigious fee-earner'. Pretty handy position, eh? Seems they've all been shit-scared of you, Matthew.

"Anyway, it must have been some complicated and prolonged discussion that justified such a trip, at no expense spared to your client. Memorable as well. Any recollections?" His eyebrows are raised to prompt my inevitable response.

"Unfortunately, I am unable to answer or comment due to my amnesia."

"Well, perhaps this is one memory that can never be recovered, Matthew," he says with a gleam of satisfaction in his tired eyes, enjoying the moment, "because maybe it's a memory that doesn't belong to you, or is just entirely false?"

"What!" I shout, my heart thumping in shock. Might they know something of the truth? But their expressions of surprise at my reaction appear genuine, dampening any such expectations. But what did he mean, though?

"So," he says, "are we wrong then; do you remember something now?" My reticence teases him to encourage me. "It's clear from your reaction this means something to you. It can only help you if you tell us; tell the truth... Look at the copies of the flight tickets and hotel invoice again."

I glance down, re-read the staggering totals as he asks: over twelve thousand pounds to fly to New York and back, nearly nine thousand pounds to stay in a hotel there for just seven nights. The sight of these figures briefly ignites my youthful flame of socialism: how can such decadent luxury be justified in a world where millions starve; and, what hope where many who attend conferences to address such poverty and injustice, or lecture on the dire consequences of global warming, likely avail themselves of these facilities on a regular basis, financed from aid or charitable funds?

"The thing is, Matthew," he is speaking again, "does it surprise you to know the hotel have been unable to trace your booking, and British Airways' records indicate the flight ticket was issued to someone else?" So, that's what he meant, that Matthew had likely falsified it all and not travelled to New York himself, merely pocketed the inflated expenses claimed.

For a moment I remain mute, too shocked and disgusted with all of these revelations to speak; how much more remains to be divulged of Matthew's behaviour and lifestyle, his apparently cavalier approach to honesty, loyalty and the rule of law which his profession, my profession, is pledged to uphold?

All eyes remain on me, the detectives, no doubt, hoping against all odds for a change of heart, even more unlikely, an admission of guilt; and the silence is broken by my stomach grumbling yet again, long and loudly at its lack of solid food since I was arrested – only a 'dinner' of cheap ham, congealed egg with a few chips and a meagre, fried breakfast that made me heave this morning – and so I utter the same, meaningless words in dead-bat response: "Unfortunately, I am unable to answer or comment due to my amnesia." Both detectives exchange a brief glance of tight-lipped frustration.

"Very well then," he says,; "but you should be in no doubt this looks bad for you, and our enquiries are continuing. Dorrell's will be looking now into all of your expenses claimed over the last five years, carrying out a thorough review… Watch this space, Matthew."

They are ominous words of warning, and perversely, in my heart, I agree their stance: the determination to pursue, rigorously, this vile man who appears to represent everything I despise. But staring at the righteous zeal in their expressions, the contemptuous indignation that bubbles upon the flat surface of their even-toned voices, there is emphatic confirmation, if ever such were needed, that it is me, only me, who should fear the retribution they seek.

Detective Chief Inspector Doyle runs a hand over the back of her short hair, then leans forward to take up the baton: "You see, you really are doing yourself no favours here. We know you have massive debts, cars and properties being repossessed. We've accessed your personal bank account records and discovered the withdrawal of one million pounds almost a year ago, since when no further credits have been received, leaving the balance to wither into serious overdraft.

"It is obvious big things are afoot, Mr Campbell" – the random use of my surname, a formality that surely taunts her disrespect – "and enquiries are continuing. We have already uncovered plenty, though not yet where all the money has gone. We *will* find out, so why not come clean now, gain credit with the court for co-operation and a guilty plea? No one will take 'I can't remember' seriously. It will just antagonise the judge by wasting time and costs, adding years to your sentence."

At this point Michael's broad frame slouches forward. He splays his arms across the desk, thumping his fists down, almost shouting: "Enough, Detective Chief Inspector," but then, more calmly: "My client's position remains clear: he has no memory of events before his recent operation, and I'm advising him to make no comment to *any* further questions." He glances at me, eyebrows raised to ensure my understanding and compliance, then, facing my inquisitors: "It seems to me that all you have here is speculation and suspicion, some vague circumstantial stuff but no hard evidence against my client that might hold up in court; indeed, no certain evidence that crimes have been committed, so—"

"Perhaps not yet, Mr Shapiro," she interrupts him, "but rest assured, we will get all the evidence we need."

He checks his wristwatch in an exaggerated gesture, dismissive of her comment. "I make the time 11am. According to the custody record, which I checked earlier, my client was booked in at 11.15am yesterday. I assume you have completed your searches and seizure of assets under the warrants, which means you must either charge Mr Campbell or release him within the next fifteen minutes, officers." These words are quietly spoken, but there is unmistakeable menace, an air of power and authority, as he glares, grim-faced at both of them, like a drill sergeant-major demanding compliance.

The detective chief inspector's expression is sullen, not chastened. "We were finished for now, anyway," she says in a clipped voice. "For the tape, interview terminated at 11.01am." Her chair scrapes the floor as she pushes it behind her to stand, her unrecorded voice, spiteful and determined, speaking down to where I still cower in the chair.

"Our investigations have only just begun, Matthew," she says. "I'm going to find out everything. Believe me, I'm here to haunt you until I get full proof. I'm sure your solicitor," she glances contemptuously at Michael, "will suggest an expert quack for hire who, at a price, can confirm he's been inside your head and found it empty of a past. But I'm very sure, in the long run, with the case I shall build, that's going to help me convict you; convince a jury of dishonesty, your guilt, send you to prison for a very long time." She pauses, squinting her grey eyes almost shut, as if she cannot bear to look at me whilst confirming my temporary reprieve. "In the meantime, you'll be released on police bail to report here again in one month. The custody sergeant will explain the conditions of your bail, and if you breach them, I promise you will be back in that cell; your feet won't touch the ground… Make the most of your month, Matthew," and she turns, flouncing from the interview room without another word or glance at anyone.

For a moment nobody moves or speaks until Michael begins to gather his papers, sprawled before him on the desk, then deposits them into his battered, old briefcase. DS Hancock stands up and says to me, "Okay, let's take you down to sort out bail."

Ignoring him, I look over at Michael and sense in his bland expression that his thoughts are now elsewhere – the geniality and kindness exhibited towards me yesterday has disappeared, like sunlight on a crisp winter's evening. "There is so much I need to discuss with you," I say, and he appears genuinely troubled for a moment before turning to DS Hancock and muttering, "Would you give us a few minutes alone, please?"

The detective grimaces, clearly irritated, before responding impatiently: "Not long then, I'm busy. You can organise meetings when you like, out of here," and with that he leaves the room reluctantly, mumbling, "I'll wait outside for a couple of minutes," before pulling the door closed.

Michael turns in his chair to face me, his broad back bending in a low arc, hands resting on his knees as he leans close to converse in little more than a conspiratorial whisper. "Not here, not now. I'm due in Tottenham Magistrates' Court at 1.00pm, and you need to sleep."

I reply in the same hushed tone, "But there's so much I want to know; about you being here; everything. My mind is on fire."

He waits before responding, his lips puckered together, obviously contemplating his next words with care, although I doubt this man ever speaks injudiciously. "We'll talk properly later, but rest easy, your welfare is in hand." He becomes more animated but still quietly spoken lest unseen ears are listening. "All bail conditions and the financial guarantee they will require have been taken care of. You'll need to give the house in Beech Hill as your permanent address and go back there when they release you.

"I've made enquiries. The lovely Helen Campbell is bound to be granted an interim injunction by the family court later this week, allowing her to remain in residence for the time being. After that the proceedings will last for months, so even with the possession order against Matthew you should be able to stay as her guest, provided you maintain a low profile and continue to keep her onside; it seems you've done a good job on her to date... That's all you need to know for now." He takes a frayed, leather wallet from his inside jacket pocket and extracts a twenty-pound note. "Here's something to cover fares, in case you need it."

"I have cash and an Oyster card in my wallet. I'll get that back with my iPhone, surely?"

"Well, keep it, just in case," he says.

It feels like an eternity since I was incarcerated, and yet it is only twenty-four hours. Suddenly, the prospect of no more interrogation, and not having to return to that tiny, claustrophobic cell – however fleeting my liberty proves to be – fills me with a profound sense of relief, almost elation. However perverse it might seem, optimism floods my senses, like a healing tsunami of hope, buoying the belief that Helen, unlike Michael Shapiro, is untainted by the conspiracy against me and can be trusted to help. She will surely convince Cathy to meet me, to hear me out?

My pragmatic wife does not suffer fools gladly; her 'brass-tacks', working-class upbringing in Yorkshire has blended a unique nature with a loyal heart that will be shocked and outraged by my claims. I understand that and anticipate her derision and scorn at first, but hope, eventually, to convince her with knowledge of so many intimacies, so many memories that only I could know. Then my beautiful Cathy, and my son and daughter, can be released from the pain of bereavement. With this comfort I should survive whatever fate has in store for me: their belief and support will fortify me against any number of unjust years in prison, the opprobrium of friends and colleagues never known, and a fleeting media storm that will quickly fade in search of fresh sensations, whether true or contrived.

"Wait, please." In a flash it strikes me. "How do you know about the house and Helen's plans? Who did send you?" I shout after him, pleading for answers as he starts to leave.

"Ssh!" He presses a finger to his lips. "I said not now," he mouths at me in a whisper. "Go to the house. I'll be in touch."

As he flings open the door, bundling out, DS Hancock's stern face reappears, beckoning me to follow him.

CHAPTER 25

I am naked astride a terrified woman on a double bed. We are in a dull room, but bright sunlight searches beyond heavy, mauve curtains. Her face is shrouded in the gloom, like a media image preserving anonymity, but I can just make out moist tears, streaks of mascara and smudged lipstick, like a tragic clown's face hiding in the shadows of a macabre circus.

My hands grip her wrists in a tight vice, pressing each one on either side of her body with harsh brutality, deep into the fabric of the black, silk quilt beneath us. A crushed dress in disarray around her hips is torn, revealing breasts and red marks on the skin where a bra has been pushed up, roughly, under her chin. Her head shakes in denial beside an ornate, brass headboard, and whimpering sobs protest that she has changed her mind and does not want this. The stench of alcohol pervades her stale breath, and I have an uncanny sense of a loving husband, children and hidden eyes that plead no more, for their sake, please, no more.

I know it is wrong. A moment of sanity brings this clarity of thought. My mind and conscience urge me to pull back at the last before it is too late, heed her desperate appeals and atone for my shameful behaviour. But it is as though another person controls my actions: I am a spectator watching from above, a perverted voyeur, as he forces himself into her without mercy in a frenzy of rabid excitement, her body throughout the ordeal limp and unresponsive, like a ragdoll with an obscured face I can only imagine must convey despair and misery.

Eventually, when I finally roll off her and gaze down at my body in disgust, it is not my own slight frame that I see, of course, but Matthew's satiated broad torso and stomach paunch. I feel disorientated and confused, wondering who this woman might be and where I am. The image of the room and the broken ragdoll beside me begin to fade and warp into my own bedroom at Cheltenham Avenue. There are the familiar chintz curtains, the Victorian dressing table, the soft touch of Cathy's warm body asleep in my embrace.

And then I am torn from her in a sudden flash of violence. I shudder at the thunderous bang of what seems to be a single gunshot, after which I wake with a jolt, and what had seemed so real dissolves into the fantasy of dreams. For a fleeting moment, I still expect that reassuring bedroom in Cheltenham Avenue and my old life. Instead, I am slouched on a sofa, my neck creaking with pain as I sit up straight to scan strange shapes and furniture through bleary eyes. Then I focus on Helen in a blue summer dress, watching me from across a vast room, and it is the sight of her that brings me back to my new reality, here in Matthew's house.

Following my release this morning, I had caught the train, arriving back at about 1.30pm. Jean greeted me, a new dynamic to her perception of our relative social status apparent in her voice and manner: fear replaced by confidence and familiarity, even a hint of superiority as she abandoned her usual respectful reserve and talked to me like a solicitous friend.

Apparently, she had spoken with Helen and was aware of my spectacular fall from grace. Of course, she fully understood we must let her go due to 'the financial difficulties', and she would take no heed of the scandal, believing implicitly in my innocence. Her lack of sincerity was obvious as she hoped 'things all come right for you, Matthew', the first time I had heard her use my Christian name. Her regret to be leaving this Friday was probably genuine, 'after all the happy years I've spent with you both', but there was no denying the gleam in her eyes; she may or may not still believe in Matthew, but the thrill of sharing this hot gossip had probably already begun.

I look from Helen to a mug of cold tea on the low coffee table. Beside it a plate of untouched sandwiches is curling at the crusts like frayed lips. I remember Jean putting them down, nothing more. I must have fallen asleep, overcome by fatigue and sheer exhaustion, before experiencing that vivid nightmare which felt so real and menacing. I sense the unfortunate woman and her trauma are not merely the myth of dreams; if I had seen her face, would I have known her? And yet this feels like a stranger's hidden shame, the replay of a dark, secret memory that surely must belong in Matthew's mind, not mine?

I concentrate on Helen, hoping to dispel the nausea gathering at the pit of my stomach. A kindly smile forms at the corners of her mouth as she reacts to my long, steady gaze. It works. The sight of her, the elegant beauty of her bearing – such a curious bedfellow to an uncomplicated, forthright manner – and the bright sunlight that floods into the room when she moves to pull back heavy curtains at the front windows, calms me and helps the dream escape from my mind.

I check Matthew's gold Rolex – 2.40pm – then notice the crumpled jacket and tie that I must have thrown down on the carpet before I dozed off, like shreds of an abandoned second skin. I realise that I need to shower. I have not had a change of clothes since leaving the house early yesterday morning, and I am conscious of perspiration under my shirt.

"I think I must have disturbed you when I came in just now," Helen says, sauntering towards me, and I wonder whether the languid movement exuding such irresistible charm, is simply her natural style or an affectation contrived to prickle male skin? The posh, velvet drawl of her voice seems so familiar, almost reassuring. "Banged the front door hard shut, I'm afraid – my usual trick… How are you?" So, the 'gunshot' that punctured my dream was her heavy hand at the door. She does not wait for my response. "One hell of a bloody shock for you, my love… I got your text message. Thought I'd pop back to look in on you before I leave for tonight's performance." I had texted her earlier, outside Holborn Police Station, to confirm my release and let her know I was on my way to the house.

"I must have dozed off. I couldn't sleep last night in the police cell. I need to shower and change."

"I can imagine. It must have been absolutely crap for you, darling. I didn't pick up your voicemail from the police station yesterday until the evening, too late for me to do anything. I knew something bad had happened, though, because I'd called at the flat in the morning, before going on to a meeting at Jason's offices – about the house. That's when the police arrived with their search warrant. At least they were quick and efficient, left everything as they found it, and, to be honest, they were rather sweet and apologetic, although they wouldn't explain what it was all about."

"It must have been difficult. I'm sorry, Helen. I take it that you have nothing to do with Michael Shapiro?" I ask.

Her lower lip protrudes as she pulls a face. "Who's he?"

"My solicitor, apparently."

"Tell me more," she says, settling into a nearby armchair resplendent with patches of variegated bright fabrics. There is an eagerness in her voice, a glow of interest writ large on her avid expression, that confirms my optimism just before I left the police station this morning: although she has not confirmed it in words yet, I am almost certain Helen is going to help me.

I explain the events of the last thirty hours and my encounters with the mysterious Michael Shapiro. Clearly engrossed, she is quick to offer an opinion: "Well, obviously he was sent by Dorrell's; must have been, my love." She has stopped calling me 'Matty' but is still uncomfortable with 'Andrew', I guess, and uncertain in her own mind what is now appropriate. "You should speak to thingy, the top man there." She struggles to recollect his name.

"Stephen Brinkworth?" I say, guessing she means the managing partner. I wonder if he knew from the start about the secret investigation by the National Crime Agency? DCI Doyle told me the senior partner had been informed, but in these large firms the senior partner and managing partner are often not the same person. And yet those messages he had obviously sent, anxious for my return to the office, the query on accounts yesterday morning, suggests he may have known. One thing is for sure, the power of my memory has improved significantly in this body: I am amazed that I have remembered his name after a brief reading of that last email before the police raid, the only one he had deigned to attach his name to.

"That's the one," exclaims Helen. "He's been here to dinner, more than once. You've smoked and drunk with him in the drawing room. You know him well… I mean, Matthew does." I am delighted she corrects herself since it's further confirmation she is beginning to accept the possibility that I have told her the truth.

"I'm not so sure," I muse. "The thing is, I'm not allowed to speak with anyone at Dorrell's; it's one of the strict conditions of my police bail. And it might prove difficult, anyway. There's an associate solicitor called 'Shivani'." I tell Helen about Matthew's secret lover: the early voicemails; how she came on to me yesterday; and the further text messages that have come in today, still desperate for me to visit her flat.

"Will you go?" she asks, and I wonder if there is a whiff of jealousy? After all, it must be hard for her not to see me as a reformed Matthew, the man she had once loved.

"Of course not. The police would like nothing more than carting me away to prison for breaking bail – they're probably watching me."

It has dawned on me since my arrest that the occasions during the last couple of weeks when I have sensed being followed may not have been wholly paranoid after all. "And anyway," I protest, "I don't need more complications. All I want is Cathy; I have to convince her somehow that it's Andy in here." I hold a clenched fist against my chest, my voice almost breaking with emotion. But she stares through me, not really listening, her thoughts still focused on my revelation of Matthew's latest lover.

"It doesn't surprise me. There's always someone," she says. Unless I'm mistaken, though, she is talking with me as a confidant, a friend, utterly separate and distinct from her husband, the man we are talking about.

I can wait no longer; I must know. "So, Helen, have you decided yet: will you help me to fix a meeting with my wife?"

The direct question recaptures her full attention; there is a smug glow of satisfaction on her face as those hazel eyes open wide and her pink lips form a rich smile. "I *am* going to help you. In fact, I met your wife this morning. I told her about the profound changes I've observed since you returned from hospital, and your revelations to me on Sunday; I told her everything you claim, and how it seems to chime eerily with some of my husband's curious behaviour over recent months."

When she pauses, I hear myself asking her in a shaking voice what reaction she received, not sure I can bear the answer and yet desperate to know at the same time. She makes me wait, delving into the tan handbag at her side to extract a cigarette from the packet before lighting up. "Not for you?" She gestures to me. I would love one but nod to decline, impatient for her response. Finally, she answers, "She believes you're more likely evil, the manipulative, scheming heir to Prince Machiavelli, than just an innocent suffering from mental illness. But it's definitely one or the other for her."

My head droops. Perhaps it is inevitable that my dreams and brittle plans are to be crushed.

"Well, what can you expect?" Helen says. "This is an intelligent woman grieving her husband's death; how would she react when a stranger tells her such a tale? It's understandable that she was contemptuous and dismissive at first; offended to listen to what she considered rubbish, spouted with her dead husband centre-stage."

"Of course," I lament, self-pity building to find false comfort in numbed senses, a mindless resignation to the will of fate. "Cathy has always had a well-developed sense of justice and she doesn't suffer fools gladly. It was inappropriate; she was bound to be outraged. I'm sorry; it was unfair of me to ask you to speak with her... It's just that I thought, just now, from your body language... I dared to hope."

"O ye of little faith, darling," she preens. "Let me finish. I don't give up easily. I talked her round. Do not ask me how, my love, but eventually she agreed to meet you at her home – your home?" she queries with a smile. "Provided that I come as well; she insisted on that, said it was a deal-breaker. She's a plucky woman, though, already throwing herself into work, but she is free this Thursday morning. So, you will have your chance then, to convince her – and me – of the impossible."

CHAPTER 26

THURSDAY 23RD JULY

I know when the Porsche roars into Cheltenham Avenue this morning that the outcome of events today will be pivotal for my future. I utter my first words since we clambered into the sports car: "It's No. 23, just coming up on your left; you need to slow down, Helen." She responds dramatically, veering sharply to the kerb, then screeching to an abrupt halt directly across the front drive to my old home in a manoeuvre that locks my seat belt with a sudden jolt.

I put on Matthew's gold-rimmed reading specs and check my wristwatch. It would be easier to leave them as a fixture on the end of my nose, but not today, not when I'm about to meet my wife. The face on the Rolex shows 9.58am precisely. The four-mile journey has taken a mere four breath-taking minutes with scant regard for speed restrictions or my blood pressure – a worry in this body – enabling us to reach our destination a couple of minutes early.

My grey BMW is parked on the drive, mud caked around the rims and splattered above the wheel arches. It looks neglected, like the rambling shrubs in the front garden, now overrun by coarse grasses and thrusting weeds. There is no sign of Cathy's Mini Cooper, nor my son's and daughter's Corsa, although the garage doors are closed.

We both walk tentatively towards the front door, treading on more weeds pushing through cracks in the crumbling crazy-paving like pox marks of disease. Birds singing are oblivious to my racing heart, a gut knotted with tension and my hands clenched in a tight fist: this has to work!

A cool breeze chases cumulus clouds across a blue sky. Helen, whose slender arms are exposed in a short-sleeved blouse, feels the chill, suppressing a shiver as we wait together under the entrance porch which protrudes like a peaked cap above the door. She still looks elegant in casual jeans. I had dithered when she finally appeared this morning, at last ready to leave the house, unsure then if my choice of a blue linen suit from Matthew's wardrobe was too formal, but time had been short and it was too late to change my mind.

Standing at the threshold of my old home, neither of us dares to ring the bell, stilled momentarily by a shared apprehension of what is to follow. I glance to my left where the house juts in an 'L' shape, throwing the front half of the lounge towards the street, but any view within, through the side window, is blocked by a fully extended cream blind. However, looking beyond Helen to our right, the curtains to the study bay window are drawn back and, despite falling in heavy shade from the adjoining semi's overgrown privet hedge, I can see inside. There are the old armchairs, the battered piano beside my treasured writing bureau with my books and papers just as I had left them, waiting for me in a room becalmed and abandoned like the *Mary Celeste*.

I am still staring at my ghosts when Helen finally pushes the button on the door, holding it too long, I think, to produce a harsh, long ring that clashes with the expectant silence. Cathy is sure to have heard our robust arrival in the Porsche and will have been waiting on the bell, wondering why the subsequent delay. And, sure enough, it is not long before we hear the jingle of her charm bracelet accompanying approaching footsteps.

She doesn't speak when the front door swings open, but the sophisticated aroma of her familiar perfume reaches out to cajole my senses. She stands, motionless, her wide eyes locking on mine with a lingering stare that seems to convey not merely anxiety and hurt but a surprising depth of anger for the man she thinks I am.

My mouth opens to recite well-rehearsed words, but my tongue is gripped in a vice by her cold face – the one normally reserved for hostile witnesses – and the startling sight of the red summer dress she had bought while we were on holiday in France last summer. I had admired it so much at the time, but not once have I seen her wearing it since then. She looks gorgeous, but I am not sure whether to draw any conclusions of hope from her choice of attire: could it be some kind of test to see if I recognise it?

Helen's rounded, confident vowels soon boom out to capture Cathy's attention. "So good of you to agree to this meeting, my dear." As my wife's gaze shifts from me, that faint spark of optimism fades at the sight of her lips creasing in a thin smile, eyes filled with pity, suggesting a reluctant indulgence afforded to a notable actor, an allowance made for a gullible, artistic temperament. "In the circumstances, maybe I should skip introductions?" Helen laughs nervously, her attempt at humour to diffuse the tension falling as flat as the vowels in Cathy's voice when she responds.

"I'm sorry… This is difficult, isn't it? I'm still not convinced I should have agreed to meet you." She glares at me whilst saying this, another piercing stare, but her sexy voice still sends the old thrill of desire to my thumping heart as she moves aside, murmuring, "Okay, you'd better come in."

Helen steps smartly past her into the hall, the heels of her brown leather sandals clunking on the laminate floor. I follow after Helen, whose jeans expose both ankles, displaying a thin, gold chain on one and her 'H' tattoo on the other. It strikes me that I am the centre of attention of two beautiful and exceptional women, each one of them yet neither of them my wife. I smile, unable to avoid fantasising about the potential – surely Matthew's gross instincts? – but feel my anxiety slip away as a strange feeling of confidence surges through me. It is time to take control, time to emulate the personable charm and authority of my host body.

When I hear Cathy shut the front door quietly behind me, I walk towards the lounge, past Helen, who is waiting politely in the hall. Left of the stairs rising beyond her, the hall spins round into a small square from which there is access to lounge, cloakroom and kitchen-diner. I push the lounge door open and proceed through, choosing to sit down in my favourite leather armchair beside the Victorian fireplace.

So many happy hours have been spent here with my family: relaxed evenings watching TV; reading; helping with homework; talking; laughing and occasionally crying – the trivia of life that seemed so important at the time. We have watched our children evolve from infants to young adults in this house, and so now I refuse to be chaperoned around it as a stranger.

"You've made yourself at home, I see." Cathy's sharp tones as she enters the lounge, closely followed by Helen, make no secret of her disapproval; no doubt she has already checked out the arrogance attributed to Matthew within the higher echelons of the legal world. "Please, Helen," she says loudly, an exaggerated invitation for Helen to sit down, emphasising my indiscretion. They both settle to face me from either end of our large sofa and, at last, I have my chance.

"Thank you for meeting with me, Cathy." Matthew's assured and personable manner comes naturally. I know it will call for exceptional skills to persuade my barrister wife she is in the presence of her husband, but I have a wealth of information to use, facts only Andrew can know. "You know why I'm here," I say, enjoying the sudden feeling of self-belief, so unusual for me but helped, I think, by the sound of this rich, deep voice. "I did not intend to be rude or cause offence, only to prove my knowledge of the house and choose to sit in my favourite armchair; Matthew Campbell never visited here, so how could he have known?"

"That's pathetic; anyone might have guessed. I'm sure you're pretty good at dressing up arrogance and deceit as virtue. So, I expect much better than that before I'll award any marks for effort." I have witnessed her use sarcasm in court, sometimes to discredit police evidence or perhaps an expert's credibility, but I know this is no ploy from Cathy; her bitterness, the sincerity of emotion is all too genuine. But still, I now feel confident in my ability to pull this off.

"It sounds mad, impossible, but this is me, your husband Andy, trapped in Matthew Campbell's body. I will convince you because there's a million things, facts only I could know."

"I've agreed to meet you briefly, purely as a favour to your wife, but frankly, your allegations are insane, preposterous nonsense… I suppose they suit your current predicament in an outrageous yet hopeless kind of way."

"But it's the truth, however crazy it may sound. I know it will take far more than identifying my favourite chair in the lounge or recognising that dress. It's the one I liked so much when you bought it on our holiday in Provence last summer, from that tiny shop next to the ice-cream parlour in L'Isle-Sur-La-Sorgue. I remember we went in after an alfresco lunch at a little restaurant by the river, only intending to browse and take a short break from the oppressive heat on our walk back to the self-catering villa. I can't recall ever seeing you wear it since, until now."

In this moment I see the certainty of her belief in my dishonesty, her contempt for my perceived lies falter in a brief second of doubt. A muscle twitches near her cheekbone, and a fleeting shadow over her face casts a transitory expression of puzzlement, like a candle flickering on a passing breeze. She recovers the appearance of composure quickly, though, her belief that I am a fraud apparently unaffected, but I know my words have shaken her despite the assured manner in which she responds: "Andy must have spoken with you. He was always inclined to be too open and trusting – you coaxed some personal information from him… Well done!"

Helen looks askance at Cathy, asking her, "Why would he do that, and how likely is it that your husband would discuss such minor, very personal details, my dear?"

"Who knows? Maybe there's another answer, but there is always a logical explanation."

"I feel your last kiss on my lips now," I tell Cathy, pressing on, "see your positive, brave smile in the hospital room when the porter wheeled me away from you; poor Lucy's tears…" They both remain silent as my voice catches with emotion for just a second, before I continue: "You were wearing black jeggings, similar to Helen's jeans." I glance to where Helen is sitting, legs crossed, in the opposite corner of the sofa. "I remember you all standing together at the door, Geoff giving a thumbs-up and shouting after me down that wide corridor, his loud voice reminding me of the holiday you'd booked for us all: it was to be my convalescence in Provence."

Helen uncrosses her legs, fidgeting as she turns to Cathy and says, "Is this all accurate?"

"Almost too exactly." Cathy's words, the ironic delivery, still suggest cynicism, but her face has become pale, her growing doubts difficult to mask.

"But how could he possibly know all this, unless…" Helen's posh voice trails away and, in this moment, I know she, at least, is convinced, having decided to accept the impossible truth which cannot be explained by logic, or reason, or any of the known laws of the natural universe.

"He must have spoken with the porter or nurse who took Andy down." There is no conviction in Cathy's voice, though; all her certainty and repressed anger has gone as she gazes down at our worn, green carpet and avoids looking at either Helen or me.

"You can't begin to imagine what I've endured since then, coming round from the anaesthetic in an unfamiliar room; a stranger" – I smile forlornly towards Helen – "presenting as my wife; and discovering the terrible truth that my body had perished, somehow leaving me in the form of Matthew Campbell. Just imagine it, in the blink of an eye to have lost my life and family, to be ten years older, fat, unfit and craving tobacco; needing statins and blood-pressure pills… You know how I tried to speak with you, Cathy, but of course I had to be careful. Then at my funeral, seeing your grief, and Geoff and Lucy…"

My words again catch in mid-flow, and I pause to regain composure. No one speaks. Helen's face looks pained; Cathy sits motionless, a blank expression suggesting disorientation, shock. A lone ambulance siren calls faintly from a distant street.

"I am Andy and there's so much I can say to convince you, Cathy. Not only mundane and domestic things like this fireplace – the time we spent sourcing an original Victorian surround, and we finally bought it from that weird little place off the Southend Road, not long after Lucy was born – but intimate, really personal stuff; you can grill me on anything you wish."

I glance towards Helen, who is quick to understand. "I should leave now," she says, "or at least wait in another room to give you privacy? Whatever you prefer, Cathy."

My wife ignores her, no doubt still dwelling on our son and daughter and the profound effect my revelations will have on them. "I don't want you speaking to Lucy or Geoff," she tells me. "Promise me that, before this goes any further."

"Of course, I understand. For them to hear the truth right now might do untold damage. I know how amazing you are, Cathy, the perfect mum helping them to cope, and I'll go along with whatever you think is best. But there's one thing I would be grateful for, and that's to know how they're managing so far: I worry in case Geoff is bottling up his emotions; and I suspect Lucy might not want to return to university next term?" I am genuinely worried, but I also know it will do no harm to show a father's understanding of his son's and his daughter's respective personalities.

I don't actually expect a response, doubting she will talk to me about them yet, at least not until I have definitely convinced her the overweight man sitting in her lounge, wearing a designer suit and expensive glasses, really is her husband. But she surprises me, speaking freely, as though to share her news and information about them is to unburden herself from pent-up worries, a kind of therapeutic relief. And her tone, her manner, has changed. It is now less defensive and confrontational, more like my Cathy.

I learn that both of them had been numb with the shock at first, in a dazed denial, finding it inconceivable they would never see 'Dad' again, but healthy tears flowed eventually, and they are now talking to their friends, beginning to confront and deal with their grief. After a little less than three weeks they have, apparently, come to terms with the reality that their father has gone. Whilst I am my own living proof this is not true, nevertheless, I can appreciate Cathy's determination that no inkling of my claims should mess with their heads and hearts at this stage, since – even if they eventually come to believe me – the man they recognise as Dad has certainly perished, his flesh and bones left to decay and rot within the coffin buried at the cemetery last Friday.

Cathy tells me that after the funeral they went to stay with Stan and Janet in Leeds. They get on well with Cathy's parents and are still there. I am able to chip in a few extended family names, some obscure reminiscences relating to her Yorkshire clan, and although she says nothing, I sense in her expression and manner further progress has been made.

The holiday in Provence has not been cancelled; they feel it might do them all some good, and Stan and Janet are going to join them since there will be plenty of room at the rented villa. They'll travel by rail with their grandchildren, direct from Leeds, this coming Saturday, the day after tomorrow. The plan is for Cathy to get the Eurostar down later, next Tuesday, because she has a criminal trial fixed for hearing tomorrow which is scheduled to last a couple of days.

Helen remains quiet throughout this discourse, her face a study in wonder at Cathy's gradual acceptance of a miracle unfolding before her eyes. The muffled melody of chimes from next door's grandfather clock striking 11am interrupts a brief silence, and prompts her to persist with that unanswered offer: "So what do you say, Cathy; shall I give you both some privacy now; maybe I can wait in another room?"

I stare at Cathy, anxiously waiting on her response, since I want to be alone with my wife to reveal intimate details of our relationship. These should have an even more profound effect, finally convincing her that she is definitely with her husband. And if it works, who knows what might follow here, now? That is why I am praying she will tell Helen to go, leave the house, and a frisson of anticipation will not be denied, shivering through my blood.

"You have a performance this evening?" Cathy asks Helen, her eyebrows raised quizzically.

My heart sinks, momentarily, at Helen's reassuring response: "I have plenty of time, my dear."

"No. I think you should go now. Leave us alone; I'm okay... really."

I struggle to conceal my delight that Cathy appears content for her to leave, not merely wait in the dining room. She smiles at Helen, a serene, confident smile as she rises from the sofa decisively, and Helen gets up immediately, anxious to follow her prompt. I stand too, and Helen touches my shoulder affectionately as she passes me, following Cathy, who has already moved into the hall.

Helen speaks to me in whispered tones: "I'm staying at the Covent Garden flat tonight and tomorrow, making the most of it, and I must finish packing up before the keys have to be returned to the bank's agents next week." She delves into her handbag to find a set of keys with a blue tag which she hands to me. "Take this set of spare keys for the flat. I took them from Matty when he started to break our unwritten understanding that I'd have sole use of it. Try to meet me either before 6pm today or tomorrow morning. I need to know how this pans out between you." The lounge door is open and from where Cathy stands waiting in the hall, I think she can hear, as

Helen continues: "I think that you are telling the truth, Andy, and I'll do whatever I can to help, but we must be careful." Her hazel eyes gleam with a sparkle of excitement, like precious stones in a jeweller's window. "Something evil has happened; the people out there who are responsible must be ruthless, and very dangerous."

CHAPTER 27

Left alone with my wife, I am determined to overwhelm her with a litany of personal facts, intimacies and trifling remembrances that nobody else can possibly be aware of. The fluke of chance or luck will be discounted by providing detailed recollections in such numbers so as to establish beyond doubt my true identity and ensure her acceptance of the incredible truth.

I had brooded over what to include and made a list yesterday in order to be fully prepared. Once I had sat down in Matthew's study and swivelled the leather armchair to peer across the garden through the French doors, I relaxed, and my thoughts flowed in a sudden deluge, an endless supply bobbing to the surface of my mind in a heated rush, a few almost lost as I scribbled, with frantic enthusiasm, to save them on a notepad.

I am surprised at how easily I managed to commit such a long list to memory, ready to fluently rattle off the evidence this morning. I know the importance of presenting an assured manner, conveying confidence without any suggestion of a faltering mind, ensuring there is no inkling of the hesitation that comes with duplicity. And I pull it off perfectly, as though a guardian angel sits at my shoulder, guaranteeing the quality of my speech and the sincerity of my words. Cathy perches on the lip of the sofa, gently swaying forward with her fingertips touching together in a 'V' shape on her lap. On more than one occasion her jaw drops as though about to interrupt, but she remains silent, enthralled, with eyes open wide as I speak.

There is the annual ritual of our wedding anniversary in Brighton with champagne and fish and chips on the pier, followed by doughnuts at the Mock Turtle Tea Rooms; our first meeting and 'Dirty Dennis'; young love and embarrassment in my late grandma's cottage; details of intimacies parked up a few weeks ago and her promise of so much more sex like that. And it goes on: shared memories of our son and daughter (first words, favourite toys and books, their schooldays, and our trips to their universities – I remember it all); our holiday experiences over the years; so many trips to the theatre which I also recall with surprising clarity; the silly argument with a young police constable who insisted on searching us over twenty years ago…

Eventually, my monologue recounting so many snippets of our life together exhausted, I slump back in the armchair. It seems less comfortable supporting Matthew's heavy frame; for the first time I am aware of sagging leather and springs creaking under his weight.

I study Cathy anxiously. Have I done enough to convince her? She remains silent, not moving from her tense pose at the edge of the sofa, as still as an artist's model. Her eyes are glazed with a film of moisture, and her wedding ring glistens yellow in a shaft of light from the table lamp, a beacon of hope in the dull room. Finally, she says in a soft voice, "How can I believe this; and yet how can I not after what you've just told me?" As her lips move, I imagine kissing her and feeling the smooth, sticky tang of her lipstick.

I remain silent, while insistent barking from the young Dalmatian across the street, desperate for his midday walk, calls faintly, like a warning siren beyond the double glazing.

"Come and sit next to me, Soulsby." She lays an outstretched hand on the sofa's leather cushion beside her and I need no second bidding. And she has called me 'Soulsby', the name reserved for moments of affection! Settling next to her in that short dress with its low neckline, I have to drag my gaze to the mantelshelf to avoid staring at her cleavage.

"Do you remember where she came from?" Cathy asks, following my eyes to the Dresden ornament, a dainty ballerina whose spreading tutu is formed with four descending layers of delicate china lace.

"It's a miracle she's never been damaged over the years. We bought her from the china shop in Cockfosters just before it closed, must be over twenty years ago, shortly after we got married. All that dithering about whether to buy." I laugh. "I remember she cost us over two hundred and fifty pounds back then."

"So many men have no interest, would never remember these things, but I know you always have." Is she acknowledging me as her husband? "But one more thing, to reassure me. I'm really surprised you didn't mention your first meeting with my mum and dad. You haven't forgotten that?"

"Of course not; I'm not sure why I didn't think to include it." I smile at the recollection, before recounting the time, not long after we had first met, that I decided to visit her, unannounced, shortly after she had gone home to see her family in Leeds. Cathy was out when I arrived, but having introduced myself as 'Andy', her mother directed me upstairs to the small backroom and a malfunctioning computer. There were some awkward moments and words until it became clear I was Cathy's new boyfriend from London, not the new computer repair man called Andy they were expecting. After that they had made me very welcome, raising no objections that I slept in their only daughter's bedroom, and the incident had lived on to become a running family joke.

When I finish speaking, she leans towards me, her hand seeking mine, squeezing it tightly. I know then, before she utters another word, that it is this happy memory which has sealed the deal for her. "I have to accept you now as my Andy," the confirmation soon comes, "although we buried your body last week." She falters, a pained expression creasing her face as the full implications of what it has meant for me hits home. "I'm so sorry, Andy." The use of my name seems to come naturally now. "It must have been horrendous for you." She slides even closer, her thigh nudging mine, and rests her other hand on my knee. "We'll find out who is responsible and what's happened, for sure; however sinister it might be, we'll find the answers together." Her face is very close, and I am both elated and so aroused it becomes difficult to retain focus and control.

Whenever I have dared to hope for this moment over the last seventeen days, I have imagined celebrations on a grand scale: spontaneous tears of joy, ecstatic laughter and passionate embraces for the husband returned from the grave, reunited with his incredulous wife. But events rarely trace imagination, and Cathy's reactions are clearly subdued by the continuing reality of Matthew Campbell's face staring at her. For my part, I refuse to let his body's strong sex drive – such intensity of response to physical attraction – spoil my joy: to regain the love and friendship of my wife, to once again experience her affection. And I must admit to also feeling pride, not like me, really, but it feels great, such satisfaction to know that I have managed to convince two beautiful, intelligent women of an incredible, fantastic truth.

"Thank God I have you back, Cathy," I say, my voice barely above a whisper, and she squeezes my hand again. "You've always joked about my vivid imagination. After what's happened to me the limits of what's possible are extended beyond reason." She neither moves nor responds, save for the hint of a sigh that tells me she understands. And yet still I lack the confidence to take her in my arms, lest I ruin everything by exhibiting a depth of passion she will not recognise as her Andy. "Cheung must be central to it all," I tell her. "But why me, why our family?"

She shrugs, rising from the sofa swiftly, releasing her hand from mine. Striding purposefully towards the drawn blinds, she says,

"Time to stop hiding away as if we have a guilty secret. We're going to figure this out." Pulling on the cords, she reveals a clear view through the window of a large clump of grey cloud above the houses on the opposite side of the street. For the first time I hear the soft chatter of raindrops on the glass with a spreading contagion of spots.

Turning to face me, my pragmatic wife speaks with her customary resolve and determination: "So, what do we know, and what are we going to do? ...You're right, it must be about Cheung, working with others, no doubt."

"I tried to contact him, without success, before the funeral, and then he was there at the chapel with the anaesthetist... I'm not sure how much Helen's told you?"

She comes over to sit beside me again, deep in thought, perching on the edge of the sofa at an angle to face me, and her bare knees brush against the fabric of my trouser leg.

"Helen believes you, it's clear," she says, the husky, flat Yorkshire vowels that I adore even more pronounced, "and she hates Peter Cheung, thinks he's a slimeball. She told me about Matthew's connections with him, and with the coroner who is a golf buddy. There was a story about her husband's drunken boasts that he is involved in research with them and close to a momentous breakthrough; something she thought crazy at the time about 'a scientific coup representing a change in what it means to be human'."

"I didn't know about that; she hadn't told me," I exclaim, interrupting her, as a chill shiver courses my veins. But whatever has happened to me, surely my future is now laced with traces of optimism? My wife and Helen are going to help me. They both believe in me, believe in my sanity and agree with me that foul play by Peter Cheung and his cronies is the only possible answer.

"It all seems to fit," Cathy says. "We must try to find out how many are involved with Cheung, exactly what they did to you and that shit Matthew, and the medical implications for you, going forward."

"And why they picked on me; on our family?" I can scarcely

believe this conversation is really happening; Cathy is back, sharing my pain and planning for me, in control of our destiny as ever.

"I know," she says, easing towards me, tantalisingly close; and then in a firm voice that brooks no debate: "But the one thing we must accept, Andy, however hard it is for both of us: your body is gone, forever. There's no going back from that. We have to move on, progress from here, and one way or another make this work."

The influence of Matthew's body explains the strong urge I feel to make the first move for once and finally embrace her, or even just clasp her hand in mine. But I still resist the impulse, determined not to put a foot wrong, and merely answer, "I agree. I can ask for no more." Then I tell her all I know about the Wilkinson case, the police investigations of Matthew, my arrest – including the emergence of my mysterious counsel Michael Shapiro – and also about Matthew's lover, 'Shivani'. I let her listen to the last saved voicemail on my phone and she winces when she hears it.

"His wife is right about him," she says, "far worse, probably, than she suspected." Her words are hard, almost bitter. Being Catholic with a strong moral code, the extent of her disapproval is no surprise. Although Helen may have hinted to her about the state of her marriage, Cathy is still disgusted to hear how this dishonest man has cheated on his lovely wife.

"What has the vile creature done to you, my dear husband?" I let the outburst of emotion against the amoral man whose body I have inherited pass, but surely that can't be right? Why would Matthew be complicit in the death of his soul, his sense of self? It takes Cathy a moment before she continues: "We know what we're dealing with, Andy: Matthew was dissolute, selfish, corrupt and probably going bankrupt, which means you're not going to be short of enemies!" Her lips crack a tight smile, but she is deadly serious as she slides her hand across the few inches between us on the sofa, tapping her fingertips lightly on my thigh before telling me, "Make sure to keep your hands off that young woman."

"You must know, Cathy," I gush, "it's always been you; I've never wanted anyone else. Over the last couple of weeks, I could have slept with Shivani but I haven't. I've never experienced anything like the strength of responses in Matthew's body before. I'll be truthful, resisting temptation has been very tough, but even trapped in another man's life I would never betray you, Cathy." My final words falter, and I feel tears prickling my eyes.

She lifts my chin and kisses me, at last a tender kiss that lingers on my lips before she pulls away. "We're going to sort this out. We have our memories to share… And I do fancy you still, even in Matthew's well-nourished body." She giggles, drawing her fingers in tiny circles, the lightest of touches upon my knee. "It could be fun, Soulsby."

Matthew's body urges me to grab her, tear the clothes from her body and take her now. It takes all my willpower to resist, maintain my own character, act as I always would and should, but I can't help my emotions spilling into words, articulating crazy hopes and dreams. "I can divorce Helen," I gasp, clasping her dancing fingers in a tight squeeze. "We can get married – again! Just imagine the amazing secret we would share at our second wedding. If I'm convicted of Matthew Campbell's crimes, we could apply for permission to marry in prison. And the kids, perhaps—"

"I don't want them to know any of this; certainly not yet," she interrupts, easing her hand from my grip. "It's so complicated. For now, I must deal with this magistrates' court trial fixed for tomorrow and Monday: a juvenile of fifteen accused of arson on flimsy evidence. I must focus on that, Andy. His liberty, potentially his whole future, is at stake." I wonder if I have lost the moment as she reverts to pragmatic considerations and, typically for my wife, the needs of others, her voice assuming business-like confidence: "After that I must join Lucy and Geoff with Mum and Dad in France."

"Perhaps I could come as well, maybe stay at one of the small hotels in the town – we could meet in secret?" As I say this, I know it is a hopeless wish, not really a genuine suggestion.

"You're on bail, Andy. Don't the police have your passport? Anyway, it wouldn't be practical; far too dangerous."

"I know," I sigh. There is no justification for despondency after the distance travelled today, far exceeding realistic expectations, yet I feel sadness and frustration that I cannot holiday with my family, confide with all of them and plan together for our new future.

"I'll try to do some research in Chambers at the weekend on Peter Cheung and Joe Peng." Cathy is planning with phlegmatic assurance. "I'll also do some digging on Matthew Campbell's finances to see if I can uncover anything else."

"There's also Jeremy Whicher," I offer, "another anaesthetist I think might be involved with them." I tell her about his behaviour, his words when he had been alone with me, and also his connection to Peng.

"And we mustn't forget the mysterious Michael Shapiro," she ponders. "Something is just not right about him. I need to check him out thoroughly and, apart from anything else, ensure you get the best legal representation."

"Could you speak to Timothy Green? Perhaps find out some background from him? As lead counsel in the Wilkinson case, he must have spent considerable time with Matthew and Cheung. It's a bonus he's in your Chambers."

"Good idea," but she sounds distracted; and then a silence settles in our old house while we both muse on the incredible nature of what we are discussing.

I look at the pine bookcase nestling within the alcove beside the chimney breast. It is cluttered in disarray with worn paperbacks and battered, hardbound volumes, like the spent passions of desire. Our surreal conversation seems to chime with the print of Frans Francken's *Allegory of Man's Choice Between Virtue and Vice* hanging on the wall above it. I inherited the hideous, dated painting with its gold-leaf frame years ago from a severe great-aunt, and somehow its retention has become a charm to banish evil, to promote good fortune – a silly superstition, but we have never been able to throw it out.

Cathy notices me staring at it. "Still looking down to challenge and accuse us." The almost reverential calm of her hushed words soothes the silence.

"My great-aunt Hilda," I say, unable to resist the temptation to gloss a cause already won. "We should throw it out, Cathy. It's finally brought us evil, not good fortune." She grimaces at the stark memory of Hilda and her strident lectures on the impending moral doom of society.

"You'll need to remain at the Hadley Wood house for now." Cathy has reverted to practicalities. "For the sake of appearances, you understand, and in case plans change and the family pitch up here tomorrow before they catch the Eurostar to Avignon on Saturday. I doubt they will, but I don't want to take any chances."

Leaving me pondering this on the sofa, she jumps up again with sudden purpose, stepping to the low sideboard against the far wall, and takes a set of keys from the drawer. I recognise the BMW fob. Handing them to me, she says, "Take your car when you leave today, Andy." Cathy's mind spins like a carousel at the fair, scattering words in haste: "It's got a full tank, and you need wheels – Helen told me what happened to the posh Bentley. I reinsured the car in my name after the funeral, but with my permission it's legal for Matthew to drive it... And that's another thing: distasteful as it may be, I will need to call you 'Matthew' in public."

"Okay," I say, "that's sensible."

"I think you should visit Helen later today, at her flat. Did I hear her say before 6pm?" I nod to confirm. "She'll be expecting you, and we're going to need all the help we can get. Come here on Sunday and I'll let you know the results of my research. We can discuss how to proceed after that." She is in charge, the barrister explaining to her instructing solicitor what must be done, her voice commanding and resolute, yet reassuring at the same time. As an afterthought she adds, "Just ring before you arrive to check the coast is clear."

And then, after only a brief pause, she changes the mood in an instant, her voice soft and sexy as she holds out both hands to pull me from the sofa. "Now, Soulsby, we have time to catch up properly before you need to leave." As I fall into her arms, she raises her face to mine, whispering, "What was that promise about much more sex for you?"

CHAPTER 28

The barriers at Leicester Square tube station are busy and I have to wait a few moments. It is 4.55pm. Early commuters spill from the streets above in an anxious rush, darting for the escalators and their subterranean trains home, like frantic shoppers let loose in the New Year sales. As I battle towards sunlight, struggling up concrete steps against the descending hordes, I am so thankful I have never had to endure the daily grind of working in the city: the frenetic pace and tiresome routine; the polluting soot, dust and crush travelling like rats in a crowded sewer.

Beads of perspiration trickle under my arms and around the collar of my suit as I reach the summit and the heady swell of London: pavements thronged with pedestrians striding purposefully; black cabs dicing cars, red buses and lorries on roads gurgling traffic despite the congestion charge; and crash helmets on revving motorbikes, along with a few brave cyclists. Hoots of frustration are vented as they all attempt to dash short distances when lights order the charge, like infantry at the front fighting over every inch.

A youngster, about the same age as Geoff, is offering free newspapers to commuters. Tall and slim with a gold stud in his right ear, he grins at my broad smile as I take a paper. I find myself hoping he is a student earning extra cash, not struggling with only this dead-end job. Somehow, the concern I feel for him is not quite paternal. It is something new for me, and if I am honest the sensation is not unlike attraction.

I dismiss such thoughts as a momentary aberration and look at the front page which makes for sombre reading – political intrigue and hypocrisy, needless deaths and human frailty – so I glance briefly at the sports pages. Geoff will be pleased that Spurs have signed an expensive Brazilian striker, and I wonder who might use a dead man's season ticket to watch the home matches with him this season? If I have my liberty when the first game is played, could I contemplate sitting next to my son if I am still a stranger to him?

But nothing can diminish my exuberance today as I fold the paper under my arm and walk away with a spring in my step, down Charing Cross Road towards Cecil Court so I can cut through Mays Court, behind the London Coliseum, into Bedford Court to find Helen's flat. The fixed smile on my face cracks a few of the worried frowns passing me in the street. Like an eager child, I am full of enthusiasm to share my news with Helen, the only person who will understand my joy.

Just before reaching Bedford Court, I pause to check Matthew's iPhone. I want answers from Michael Shapiro, who has not contacted me since my release on Tuesday morning. I discovered yesterday – Wednesday – that his office is in South Tottenham. A receptionist had fobbed off my calls, so I decided to catch the train, presenting myself there in the afternoon, and found he works from two modest rooms on the third storey above seedy shops in the High Road. But he was out, allegedly in court and not expected back that day. A plump, elderly Jewish woman was the sole occupant of Shapiro & Company's premises, but she seemed to have understood the gravity of my request for her boss to phone me today.

But when I look, he has still not called. In fact, with the exception of Shivani, nobody has rung or texted since my arrest on

Monday. The hand-delivered letter received from Dorrell's yesterday morning, suspending Matthew, cancelling his mandates to draw against company profits and authority to touch clients' money, does not appear to have diminished his lover's ardour; if anything, it has fanned the flames of her infatuation.

I picked up on one of her calls yesterday, not long after getting home from Shapiro's office. She was tearful, desperate to see me, and said that she could help me deal with any police charges. I was able to establish Shivani was not responsible for my representation at the police station: she had never heard of Michael Shapiro. Then I had tried to let her down gently, hoping to stem the flow of texts and messages. I emphasised the grave risks they posed to her career and liberty – as well as my own – since my bail conditions precluded contact with partners and staff at Dorrell's, not to mention the risk of breaching draconian money-laundering regulations. And I needed time alone, I suggested to her, 'to get my head round everything'.

However, it is now apparent these efforts were to no avail as I grip the mobile to my left ear in a tight embrace and listen to the recording of her sensuous voice, like a private peep show of words on a busy public street: "Hi, Matt. It's Shivi. I know what you said, about wanting space, but you're just being kind and selfless, only thinking of me. We can be careful, though, discreet as always, except now you must come to my flat. I'll get back by 7.30pm Friday evening. Bring a bottle and pizza. Please come and stay the night. It's been so long and I'm so horny for you, Matt. I need you."

Unwelcome memories stir Matthew's body: that sexy clinch in the lift on Monday, her tongue in my mouth, my hands squeezing her buttocks. I struggle to supress the surge of desire. It could not be more inappropriate following the wonderful outcome of my meeting with Cathy earlier today. Before, in my own body, I would never have given her a second thought – indeed, I hadn't at the crowded Starbucks in Palmers Green a couple of months ago – but now it is difficult to suppress these urges; at times it's almost as though

Matthew's thoughts and reasoning are trying to infect my mind. Slowly, though, I calm the heart racing in false anticipation of a young woman who is certainly the last thing I need.

As I puff smartly across Bedfordbury, I jump at the impatient tooting of a black cab shooting off with a new fare, then saunter into Bedford Court, and once again all my thoughts rest solely upon Cathy, upon our new life in an uncertain future.

CHAPTER 29

The entrance to the Bedford Court flats is not obvious. As I amble round trying to find it, I feel self-conscious and awkward, anxious that I might attract unwanted attention. I glance up at the CCTV spies in the sky, scattered like confetti on high buildings to left and right, and feel them peering down, sneering at my uncertainty, bridled with suspicion at the motives of the large man in an expensive, blue linen suit. A couple enter the thin alley from Bedford Street and approach me. She is smiling at him, hanging on his words, and he throws a brief, wary glance my way as they pass by towards Mays Lane and the Coliseum.

Perhaps the entrance is shielded in a blind corner to my right, behind a large BMW and a black Audi parked carelessly? As I walk diffidently towards the cars, a workman from a nearby construction site stops to lean against the alley wall and smoke a cigarette. He stares at me below his yellow hard hat and I look away, expecting a firm hand on my shoulder at any moment, a harsh voice of accusation demanding explanation: exactly what am I up to here, loitering with dubious intent in close proximity to desirable vehicles and expensive flats? But I feel only the gentle breeze around my shoulders and neck, while a group of tourists who have just walked through the alley pore over a street map.

It turns out my guess is correct. Numbers are marked on a keypad beside the intercom. I press the button for Helen's flat, which produces a grating ringtone. Bending slightly, I hold my ear close, waiting for her velvet tones to bubble up in static from deep inside this grey building. But I hear only a distant crackle echoing the silence. And when I try again there is still no response.

Helen had asked to meet here either before 6pm today, or tomorrow morning. According to Matthew's Rolex it is now precisely 5.14pm; she should be in, and I am looking forward to sharing my news with the only person who will understand. I turn to face the cul-de-sac. The workman and the group of tourists are gone; only the CCTV monitors remain, and the incongruous screech of seagulls, far from home, echoes around the Square.

Perhaps the intercom is faulty, but Helen gave me a set of flat keys so I guess I have her implicit consent to go in. I just need the code. I turn back to the entrance, determined that I will speak with her tonight, and it comes to me in a flash, the certainty, almost like the return of a lost memory, that it is Matthew's birth year, which I feel sure is 1964.

It may be a lucky guess, or possibly Helen had mentioned it to me, but, sure enough, when I tap it in, the heavy door clicks open obediently to reveal a spacious foyer dominated by an unoccupied reception counter. A digital blackboard stands just inside the door and indicates her flat is on the third floor. There are two lifts beyond thick-piled, brown carpet, and a staircase that turns sharply after one long flight.

The door closes behind me automatically in a gentle movement that is not quite silent. There is no sign of life as I make for the lifts and stand in front of them. They look small, like the police cell, and my skin prickles with distaste at the raw memory. I glance towards the stairs, but they fade into a steep and uncertain future distance.

While the old me would have bounded up them in double time, I catch my apprehension and reach out a finger to call the lift. But at that very instant, before I touch the silver button, a strong voice booms behind my head and my heart leaps in shock.

"Mr Campbell – is that you, Sir?" I spin round to encounter an elderly black man beaming at me, just a few feet away. His baldness shines a rich patina in the bright, artificial light, like a polished gemstone, and his thick-set, sturdy frame is immaculately dressed in a smart, navy suit with a grey tie knotted perfectly. "I thought it was," he says, thrusting a large hand towards me which I dutifully shake. "Long time, no see. How are you?" He speaks with perfect, slow diction and retains his firm grip, like an old friend, sounding genuinely interested and pleased to see me.

"Good, thank you; and you?"

It is as though I have said something wrong, even insulting. He stares at me with a puzzled frown, letting his hand fall from mine. "If you'll forgive me, Sir, but that does not sound like you at all."

"I'm sorry… I don't understand." I smile nervously, but his piercing eyes remain fixed on mine, increasing my sense of unease, not helped by the lack of windows and deathly quiet in this foyer. Surely there should be some evidence of residents or visitors to the many flats here, not merely this stranger? "I can't think how I might have offended you," I blurt out. I wonder, might this man be connected, however tenuously, to the conspiracy? His appearance just now was so sudden and dramatic, as if he had purposely set out to shock me; and what am I to make of his curious reaction to a mundane pleasantry – what other response would have been appropriate?

Slowly, his frown creases into a broad smile, followed by words at a leisurely pace: "I'm not offended, Mr Campbell. It's been such a long time, you don't remember, do you, Sir?" He studies my blank expression, then continues: "Whenever I saw you, asked how you were, it was always the same response, without fail, Sir. 'Ben,' you would say, 'I'm still growing old disgracefully.'" Then his thick voice shrinks to little more than a whisper, and I smell his pungent aftershave as he shifts even closer, his tone intimate. "And I remember the twinkle in your eye every time you asked me if you could count on my discretion… But you are on your own tonight, Sir?" he chuckles.

"I'm visiting my wife," I explain, venturing a tight smile, keen to terminate this awkward conversation as soon as possible without causing offence or raising any further suspicion. I have grasped now that Ben must be the concierge with whom Matthew has at some time in the past considered it expedient to strike up a friendly accommodation. I guess my fears of his possible complicity, of any sinister motives, are probably misplaced.

His bright eyes open wide. "Your wife!" he exclaims, unable to conceal surprise but quickly regaining his composure. "I'm sorry, Mr Campbell; all of that was a long time ago…" He sighs to suggest a fond reminiscence, his words hanging in abeyance. Just as I contemplate turning to the lifts, bidding him a swift goodbye, he continues: "I often bump into Mrs Campbell now. Such a beautiful lady. I haven't noticed her today, but I have been sneaking away to my office to catch up on the test match. That's why I nearly missed you, Sir." He exhales a throaty laugh.

As Andrew it would have been my passion to keep up to date with the cricket, but I had forgotten another test started today, hard on the heels of the last one. "Did we win the toss?" Damn, it slipped out; I couldn't resist enquiring, extending the conversation.

"We did," he responds with enthusiasm. "And doing well – over two hundred runs for only one wicket…" He stops abruptly, the zeal with which he speaks melting into a broad grin. "Always the perfect gentleman, Mr Campbell, to show interest; but you hate cricket, find it dull and boring. Don't I remember you telling me that rugby is your passion, rugby and golf; isn't that right, Sir?" Do I detect a mocking edge in his plush diction now; has his voice lost its uncomplicated, friendly tone? He does not wait for my response. "I'm impressed you are aware it is the first day's play."

It is so difficult to remain constant and positive in mood, to inhabit the real world, when my life has imploded into a vortex of paranormal intrigue, like a fantasy land in which I fear that nothing is what it seems to be. I believe I have sensed a subtle change in his manner: slow, precise words still but slightly higher in pitch; and his eyebrows are arched, perhaps in knowing and scornful accusation?

Anxiety descends into panic, and mundane incidents from outside, just moments ago, assume the possibility of sinister meaning to nourish fear: the countless CCTV monitors spying on me; the lingering smile of the workman whose eyes had seemed to scan my soul; those 'tourists' in the street feigning their disinterest in me; and now this huge man, powerfully built with strong muscular arms, who crept up on me so stealthily. Time is suspended, awareness of my surroundings lost, like the experience after leaving Peter Bright last week – could it be a kind of protective shield for my battered mind? – but on this occasion it is brief and the fugue is broken by loud words ringing in my ears.

"Mr Campbell, Sir, are you alright?" I see his worn face frowning in confusion, his wide eyes staring into mine, so close, invading my personal space, and his large hand rests firmly on the top of my shoulder. "You don't look so good." I remain silent. "Come and sit down over here." He removes the hand from my shoulder, indicating a couple of plastic chairs behind the reception counter.

"No. Thank you, I'm okay." I find my voice and it sounds decisive as I edge away from his imposing presence. I notice the highly polished shoes on his large feet; he really is the kind of man you want to be on your side.

"Well, if you're sure. You seemed to just blank out, and your face is still very white. At least let me fetch you a glass of water?"

"No, honestly, I'm fine now."

And I am composed. The mania that stalks me like a prowling wolf has passed for the moment; I begin to think clearly, logically again. Fresh realisation of today's joy, of regaining Cathy, chases off my demons. How foolish to suspect passers-by in the Square, and this kindly man whose quiet voice and anxious face conveys what is surely genuine concern.

"I'm sorry, Ben," I say confidently. "I had a heavy night – you know how it is?" I grin, Matthew's poise and charm coming easily to me now, and he smiles wryly.

"What are you like, Mr Campbell?" He laughs, appearing to understand and sympathise, feeling kinship with me as he believes I suffer for yielding to the temptations of excess last night.

"My wife will be waiting and I want to take a rest in our flat now. Good to see you again, Ben. Enjoy the cricket!"

I summon the lift and the door slides open almost immediately. That Scottish custody sergeant, his warped humour and jangling keys, flashes in my mind, and stepping inside the lift becomes strangely disconcerting. I have never suffered from claustrophobia before, and yet my heart quickens at the prospect of confinement in this small, solitary space. I swivel round, expecting to catch a parting glimpse of the concierge before the door clicks shut, but no one is there. He moves so quickly and silently for such a big man.

I press the button on the control panel requesting the third floor and when the ascent begins with a jolt, I have already screwed my eyes tight shut to escape memories of that stark prison cell in this tomb-like metal box. I count out loud to help me cope, and on ten it slows with a shudder, crawling on by inches to a final stop.

I need to get out, but when I open my eyes, the door remains closed, spiking my panic again. Has the lift failed, perhaps been tampered with? The air conditioning does not function in here and it is hot: I can feel beads of perspiration dripping from my armpits as I stare at the red emergency alarm on the consul. I hold my thumb over it; after a count of five I will... But with a weary grumble, after four more limping seconds, the door finally eases open. It was merely slow to respond. I rush out to escape into the calm relief of a wide corridor with worn carpet and distant windows at either end.

The entrance to the flat is very close and the sturdy door is made of panelled oak with bold, brass numbers screwed on to a facia plate. I am uncomfortable with using the keys to enter unannounced, but there is no individual bell, knocker or letterbox, reliance being placed solely on those outside the main entrance.

I dither, uncertain what to do until it dawns on me to ring her mobile. I have the number programmed into Matthew's iPhone; why on earth did I not think of this earlier when I couldn't make the intercom work? I find the saved number and tap the screen, but it just cuts straight to the recorded mantra informing me she is unavailable and suggesting I should 'Please try later'.

There is nothing for it but to go in. I release the deadlock, then turn the latch key, rapping a fist strenuously on the door and shouting loudly as I enter: "Hello, Helen. It's me, Andy." I close the door gently behind me and marvel at how sweet it feels to openly use my own name again.

I am standing on exposed, polished floorboards in a good-sized hall. Open double doors at the far end lend a glimpse of daring red carpet and a large, wall-mounted TV. It is toasty warm, and the furious sound of cascading water suggests a power shower in use behind the closed door of one of the rooms leading from the hall; the reason, no doubt, why Helen had not answered the intercom, or her phone just now.

Suddenly, the tumultuous noise ceases, and Luciano Pavarotti is singing 'Nessun dorma'. It's coming from the room with the red carpet, perhaps Alexa or Google on repeat, a CD left running, or maybe the radio on Classic FM. A firm clunk, much closer, indicates a shower cubicle opening and I boom out quickly, in Matthew's base tones: "Hello, Helen. It's Andy. I've used the keys you gave me." I want to announce I am here; spare her the shock and embarrassment of stumbling upon me when she exits the bathroom.

I am not sure if she has heard me as the tenor's voice reaches its crescendo, but when it fades, her rolling consonants echo loudly in response: "Darling, I thought my luck had changed." She laughs, and I am relieved, so pleased to be certain that she is here. "I'd rather given up on seeing you again today." Her voice sounds quite shrill when raised. "Didn't I tell you I have to leave for the theatre by 6pm at the latest?" I apologise; I must have misunderstood her this morning. "Would you wait in the living room? My clothes are in the bedroom, so I need you to vacate the hall, please."

I hesitate momentarily, ashamed as I contemplate seeing Helen naked, but quickly suppress this body's gross instincts and pass through the double doors into a surprisingly modest living room where the summer movement from Vivaldi's *Four Seasons* is now playing. A radio is perched on top of one of the many cardboard packing boxes that are scattered at untidy angles, like dodgems at a fair ground. None have been taped closed yet, though some appear almost full while others are still empty. Ornaments remain displayed in a cabinet along the far wall and some books languish on shelving near the window.

The dishevelled scene suggests scant regard for order, in marked contrast to the sense of style, the meticulous attention to detail, so apparent at the Beech Hill house. Clearly, Helen has much last-minute packing to finish before she must hand back the keys next week.

Near to a dining table and chairs, a sofa marooned in a sea of clutter crouches under the window. I move aside papers and a few more books to clear a space, then settle down to wait for her. The Classic FM presenter confirms the Footsie has finished thirty points up today as the bathroom and bedroom doors slam shut in quick succession, followed by muffled sounds of movement: drawers and wardrobes open and close intermittently; the dull thud of hasty footsteps over carpet; and then the high-pitched hum of a hairdryer.

Time passes slowly, like a child's wait for Christmas, and that excitement of anticipation to share my news begins to pall into anticlimax as a Mozart piano concerto plays on the radio. It is approaching 6pm when she will need to leave.

At last, she appears, looking vulnerable and lonely, drifting gracefully towards me through the confusion of this crowded room. She is wearing blue jeans, and two pink bobbles dangle together at the front of her white blouse. "Sorry for the wait, my love." Her loud, posh voice overwhelms Mozart's gentle music. "I had to prepare my public face." All traces of wrinkles have been erased from the face which highlights that immaculate, blonde hair and the delicate beauty of her pink lips.

She flicks off the radio, and I stand up when she reaches me to place those lips firmly on my cheek. They linger for a moment before she draws away, raising her eyebrows and indicating the room with an expansive hand gesture. "What a state." She laughs. "And I know I must finish packing up by Monday of next week."

"I have news." I blurt it out. "Cathy and I are together… She believes me." My voice catches with emotion, and I think, for a split second, Helen looks disappointed: it must be the shock. She moves to hug me, affectionately, the first time I have felt her body against mine. I notice the smell of her perfume and need to pull away from her embrace smartly to avoid embarrassment, since it is impossible to control the reactions of Matthew's body. How is it that he cheated on her and hankered after other women?

"Congratulations, Andy," she gasps, no hint of a smile in her deadly serious expression. "To have convinced your wife is immense, and it dispels any lingering doubts I may have felt. And have I told you? Jason confirmed what you advised me: I can fight the bank on the house but I have to leave here. Matthew would have had no idea about that." She stares beyond me, out of the window. "This is really momentous for all of us… My God, what on earth have Matthew and his cronies done; what has been created?" It is as though the long fuse lit when I confided in her on Sunday has finally burnt through to ignite the moment of complete certainty, scorching her mind with the magnitude of this knowledge and its astonishing implications.

"There's so much to tell you, Helen. I beg you not to view me as a freak. We're counting on your help."

"Of course, Andy. We're all in this together, you, me and Cathy. I'm sorry, it just hit me, the sheer enormity of it all." She glances at her wristwatch, and when she speaks again her mind is settled. "I must do my performance tonight. I'll walk to Leicester Square Station with you now and we can talk briefly on the way. I can get the tube to Embankment from there, and you can go back to the house. I'll get away as soon as I can after the play and we'll talk properly when I get home, however late it is. Okay?"

"Okay. Sounds good, Helen." For a brief moment her reaction had unsettled me, but I now know this momentous day will end well and I feel a glow of satisfaction, both that her engagement and enthusiasm are confirmed, and to remember my elation earlier today: holding Cathy in my arms and feeling her happiness as we experienced such intimacy; and the novelty and excitement of sex in Matthew's body, which turned out to be amazing for both of us.

"Come on. Let's go," Helen urges, and I follow as she weaves swiftly around the boxes and clutter, through the hall, then pauses for a second at the front door before turning back and darting into her bedroom, mumbling absently, "I just need to fetch my handbag and jacket."

I look through the open door, then freeze at the mirror image of my recent, vivid nightmare. The black, silk quilt on the same large bed, the same heavy curtains but now pulled open to let in late afternoon sunshine which licks the room clean with daylight. What can only be the vile product of my imagination is stark reality here, before my eyes!

Helen's slender frame is draped across the quilt as she leans over to retrieve her scattered jacket and bag, discarded near the brass headboard from my dream. I shudder at the intensity of the scene replaying in my mind: the anonymous woman's face, obscured yet clearly contorted in misery beneath me, on this bed, in this room;

the pungent smell of alcohol on her breath, with me again now, so real; and the rape that follows, making me want to gag in revulsion and disgust.

"Andy, are you alright?" Helen is at my side, her hand extending to rest gently on my sleeve. "You look like you've seen a ghost."

"An impossible memory I can't really explain has just surfaced." I spin away from the bedroom and my dream, anxious to banish the revolting secret that cannot possibly belong in my mind.

"Do you need a glass of water?" I shake my head to decline. "I can't begin to imagine how difficult, how absolutely impossible, this must all be for you," she sympathises, gripping my arm and affecting a false cheeriness. "But you need to buck up, my love; be positive. This has been a stellar day for you. I want an outline of your wonderful news, to know what Cathy thinks, as we walk to Leicester Square tube. Then we can talk more and make plans when I get home late tonight... But now, we really must go."

CHAPTER 30

I have a good journey to Cockfosters after Helen leaves me underground at Leicester Square. I grab a quick coffee and toasty at the café near the station, before retrieving my BMW parked nearby – how good it feels to have it back – and returning to the house in Hadley Wood.

I arrive at about 7.30pm to discover that Jean, the housekeeper, has already left. She was not due to go until tomorrow – Friday – but when I check her small attic room it has been cleared: the single wardrobe door yawns empty, and the modest laminate chest beside it reveals four barren drawers peeking open, devoid of contents, like a crime scene. The house is lifeless and silent save for the melodic ticking of the grandfather clock in the hall. She must have departed in haste, since, yet again, neither the deadlock on the front door nor the alarm system have been engaged.

When she had found out this morning of Helen's original intention to stay over at the London flat tonight, she had lavished praise on her in an effusive display with hugs and tears that was so out of character it appeared false, a tearful goodbye in such marked contrast to the muted, stiff smile reserved for me. I had assumed at the time that our farewell would take place tomorrow morning, but perhaps she always intended to depart early and had no inclination to offer even spurious good wishes to the man I suspect she has always secretly despised. And who can blame her?

Suddenly, a chill of discomfort grips me. Probably, Jean has just been careless with security before her departure, but the same fears that plagued me when I returned from the funeral last Friday evening pepper my skin in goosebumps. Suppose I am not alone in this rambling house? There are so many places to skulk unnoticed. I swallow in a hard gulp and walk purposefully down two flights of stairs, then into the kitchen, where I grab the chef's knife from a block on one of the granite worktops.

I clutch the blade for comfort, waving it before me like an invincible shield, giving me courage to check every room and every space, all of the windows and external doors. I even drag a heavy chair onto the cellar trapdoor and deposit some tomes from the bookcase in the study on it for extra weight. No way am I going down there!

But everything is fine; no indications of forced entry or tampering. The house is secure. I feel foolish and thankful, at least, that nobody has witnessed my unmanly caution; behaviour that would be unbecoming even in a nervous child.

I look down at the gleaming, wide blade in my hand and, before sliding it back in the kitchen block, shudder at the reflection of Matthew's face staring at me, the steely gaze quivering with the tremor of my tight grip. I doubt that I will ever fully reconcile myself with this hideous reality, and it takes a moment, coaxing my mind to think positively, to remember again this day's momentous advances: convincing Cathy this is me, her Andy; making plans as husband and wife once more; touching her, kissing, and our naked bodies consummating such passionate desire only a few short hours ago.

It's a sweet image, and I have to pinch myself to remember it is true as I wander from the kitchen into the hall. All of the internal doors are solid mahogany, and while checking the house I had ensured with obsessive care that they were shut, as though this might somehow enhance my safety. Still, the prospect of all these empty spaces in expansive rooms seems unappealing, and so I decide to settle for the evening in a small room that is tucked away, almost like an afterthought, at the far corner of the house, where its only window faces the front garden beyond the sweep of the carriage drive.

On entering my chosen retreat – just for the added peace of mind (although I know it is ridiculous, almost 'OCD') – I wedge an upright chair under the brass handle of the door, after having closed it swiftly behind me. When I step across a Persian rug, the oak floorboards beneath creak like old timbers groaning on an ancient galleon, and a muffled chime from the grandfather clock in the hall strikes once to record the quarter-hour – 8.15pm. I pause at the window to admire the mature, golden haze of the summer's evening: perfectly coiffured shrubs and plants drifting towards a dense, laurel hedge shielding the show-case garden from the quiet street beyond. I press my face against the pane to glimpse where garden border laps the end of the dusty, gravel drive, way off to the left, and I can just make out the rear of my BMW where it is parked outside the garage block at the far side of the house.

It is a peaceful scene, all quiet as it should be. I begin to relax, to forget Jean's singular departure, and sit in a comfy armchair facing a small TV in the corner. I intend to finally watch some of the cricket highlights on Sky since Helen will not be home for a few hours, but I have forgotten to pick up the remote resting on a shelf within the TV stand. I decide to wait a few moments, enjoy the evening sun's warmth magnified through the glass of the window. It is stuffy in here and I should open the top window flap, but I can't bring myself to do so. And then the day's scrambled thoughts jostle for attention in my mind but slowly fade as I drift away into slumber.

I wake with a start and sharp pain cramping the calf in my right leg. I pull myself up, breathless, from the chair, another disconcerting dream still vivid in my mind. I was the child standing in a lean-to style conservatory, while a thin woman with grey hair and a severe face harangued me about my school report. A bald man lounging in an armchair nearby was reading a newspaper, oblivious to my humiliation. The clear image remains as I press all my weight onto an outstretched leg, and the cramp eases. In the dream I had pleaded in a timid voice, "Mother, please, I'm so sorry, but all the others are 'A's." She became incandescent with rage at my protest. Only perfect would do. I was sent to my room until a suitable punishment could be devised for such a lazy boy; such a disappointment, a failure with only a B for music.

It makes no sense. I don't recognise the horrible woman – the opposite of my dear mum – or the disinterested man; I don't recognise the conservatory we were all in. Yet something nags at me, suggesting a realism not consistent with just a weird dream; and it is disturbing in the same way as the horrible premonition of the bedroom in Helen's flat. Could these be fragments of Matthew's memories, the dying embers of another man's soul?

I shudder at the thought. But then, fully awake, this begins to seem ridiculous; surely these are merely disjointed, crazy dreams formed by the subconscious from an over-active imagination, the uncanny resemblance to Helen's bedroom just a strange coincidence? I must take back control of my mind and let nothing spoil this amazing day: the felicitous culmination of my hopes after waking to face such horror in that hospital bed nearly two and a half weeks ago.

Daylight has faded now and I peer into the gloom that casts an invisible shroud over the room's unfamiliar contents, lurking like sinister chameleons in the dark. I stumble towards where I believe a light switch should be, crashing my knee on the upturned chair against the door. Nobody answers my curse at the sharp pain, screamed full volume like a raging warrior, as I locate the switch and flood the room in welcome light.

Helen calls this her 'snug little hideaway', where she escapes for solitude to learn her lines. Nothing has changed. It remains cluttered with the same odd furniture: the sprawling armchair where I had been dozing; a couple of others with mismatched soft coverings that clash, like fingernails scratching down a blackboard; a little occasional table with a glass top beside a battered old sideboard of hideous dark wood; and the modest flat-screen TV perched on its plastic stand. It is all so different from the grandeur in the rest of the house.

I approach the window which throws back Matthew's imposing reflection from the black void through the glass. As I press his face against the pane, I see vague contours of hidden trees above looming shapes, shrubs and bushes guarding blind depths where the dense hedge must lurk. It looks spooky, so still and quiet, no hint of any sound penetrating the double glazing.

I imagine Cathy, alone like me, poring over a tome of papers, studying them conscientiously for tomorrow's case as she struggles to put aside her personal life and today's incredible events. In my mind's eye, I see her standing before the magistrates' court tomorrow in a smart business suit, heels and navy tights, commanding her stage with such power and authority. I thrill at the prospect of pulling her close, the touch and smell of her body when we can be together again on Sunday.

Just before I left her to see Helen this afternoon, she had explained the extent of her workload. I accepted that, barring emergencies, there should be no contact between us until Sunday, giving her time alone to prioritise her case. She has always needed seclusion around the time of a court hearing, but it is so much to ask, not even to speak until then. What harm in one brief call?

The impulse is irresistible, so I pull the iPhone from my pocket, punching in her number. There is no ringtone, though, only a recorded message: the number is unavailable, please try later. I feel deeply disappointed, as if there has been a purposeful rejection. I know this is silly, of course, like a sulking child. Her phone is probably turned off, either for an early night or while she continues to work late, preparing her case. But still, I can't help feeling it.

I reach for the cord and draw the set of heavy, blue curtains closed. In the silence I listen to the faint wheeze of my breath and once more the dull chime – this time twice for the half-hour – from the grandfather clock. Moving away from the window, the thought of unknown enemies and hidden dangers in this vast house returns, and I need some distraction to settle my nerves again. I pick up the remote from the stand in the corner, but before I can turn on the TV, the mobile's shrill ringtone startles me (the first time I have heard it since before my arrest on Monday). I don't recognise the number but still flip it open to take the call, relieved at the prospect of comfort from hearing a human voice.

"Hello?" I mouth cautiously, reluctant to announce 'Matthew Campbell', even with his voice and his phone.

"Ah, Mr Campbell? ...Matthew?" He corrects himself. There is no mistaking Peter Bright's hesitant style with its West Country burr.

"Yes, it is me, Peter. How are you?" I am grateful to speak with anybody, even my old business partner, especially since I now know his designs on my wife are doomed to certain failure. Perhaps it is because of this that he no longer rankles me. In fact, how can I blame him for his good taste, for trying? I smile. Although he doesn't know it yet, the poor guy will have to console himself with replacing me only as the opening batsman for our local cricket team!

He laughs nervously. "I'm impressed you recognise me... Is this a convenient time?" It is typical of Peter to be ill at ease and lack confidence. But I guess why he has phoned: news of my arrest will have made the national papers, and so it is pretty obvious he is steeling himself to tell me that he would prefer not to pursue my 'business offer'. I wonder how long he has been worrying about making this call? He has principle, though; so many would have simply ignored me, but he has promised to give an answer to my proposals and he always stands by his word.

"Certainly, it is," I say. Why don't I tell him straightaway that I understand he cannot take up my offer after what has happened? It's not my way to be unkind, but something holds me back and all I say is, "It's good to hear from you."

"Well." He pauses, trying to find the right words. "First an apology, for the delay in getting back to you. As you can imagine there's been so much to consider, so much happening."

He doesn't come to the point, end his discomfort quickly, but that's Peter, always long-winded. Yet still I don't end his embarrassment, tell him that my circumstances have changed and I no longer want to be his new business partner. I have Cathy back now and, even if Matthew is declared bankrupt, she can provide: there is my significant private pension she has inherited following my death, and as she reminded me before I left her today, her practice at the bar is generating decent money at long last. But I let him continue; for some strange reason I find myself almost enjoying him squirm, amused to hear his waffled excuses.

"The thing is, since we last spoke there's been a letter from a young solicitor. He's looking for a position to make a career in property-based work with a local firm. Sounds very keen…" I know we have always binned speculative job requests, printed standard-form letters enclosing imaginative CVs from 'no-hopers', as Peter calls them. He would never consider one seriously.

I should be ashamed of continuing to relish his self-inflicted ordeal, and yet I remain silent when he falters, before continuing: "Obviously, he is not in your league, Matthew, and it goes without saying," he fawns. "I mean, all things being equal, I'd be thrilled to accept your offer, no choice to be made there…" Then he lowers his voice, as if he might be overheard. "But it's just the matter of these nasty allegations." At last, he has come to the point. "You see, after the news reports, I'm afraid everyone is talking. Lots of nonsense, most of it; all false or wildly exaggerated, I'm sure. Still, if you joined my firm after what's happened, well, I wonder how we could ensure it didn't make matters worse for me. So, you see…" He pauses again, dithering how to deliver his final coup de grâce.

"Say no more Peter, I understand." At last, I end the poor man's misery. "It's been such a shock for me – more than you would ever believe – and of course it changes everything."

"I'm so glad you understand." I feel his relief as he gushes: "In different circumstances it could have worked so well. As it is, I've decided to keep the locum on for a few more months, and maybe to give this newly qualified youngster a chance as well. It will be expensive, but I'll just have to grin and bear it." He laughs. I smile to myself, knowing he will be receiving an insurance payment under the partnership policy to pay two hundred and fifty thousand pounds to Cathy in full consideration of my interest. All future profits will now belong to him, along with the goodwill I have built for us over many years. He has every reason to laugh.

"How is Andrew's wife? It must be very difficult for you. Presumably she is entitled to payment for her late husband's share in the business? I just hope you had adequate insurance to avoid difficult negotiations." I just couldn't resist that.

He bridles, giving him the backbone to terminate our conversation swiftly. "With respect, I'm not sure that's any of your business. Cathy is my close friend. My only concern is for her welfare. I hope things work out for you, Matthew. I wish you well. Goodbye then," and the line goes dead before I can respond.

CHAPTER 31

Imagined horrors stalk this dark house. The vast gardens clinging to it, shrouded in the night, had unravelled long-forgotten childhood terrors. But my short telephone conversation with Peter Bright has allayed those fears and I feel calm again, if not entirely relaxed. I wonder how long Helen will be? Hopefully she will not be too tired; I so want to talk with her tonight as she suggested, rather than wait on the morning.

There had been scant opportunity to speak and consider plans on leaving her flat earlier this evening as we rushed through the busy streets of the West End towards Leicester Square Tube Station. At the entrance, I had accepted another free newspaper proffered by the same young man I had seen when I arrived. He smiled warmly at me and I felt curious pleasure, almost pride, that he should recognise me. No words were exchanged, but it was difficult, uncomfortable, to descend as Helen linked her arm in mine to navigate the throng on the heaving stairs.

Every day brings fresh confirmation of Matthew's rampant sexuality. He appears to contemplate sex at every conceivable opportunity, an obsession way beyond my appreciation of attractive women. His body responds independently, almost in spite of my mind and thoughts, and it is impossible to control. Whether it had been Helen or the paper boy who was responsible for arousing Matthew's body earlier this evening, I do not know; it may have been both of them, probably it was. I feel disgusted by him and his apparent attraction to a boy who couldn't have been more than twenty. I am totally straight, monogamous and loyal to Cathy, yet trapped within this body which I now suspect may have been a sexual predator of men as well as women.

Having alighted from the escalator, Helen had turned to face me at the parting of our ways between the Piccadilly and Northern lines. Fellow travellers swarmed around us, flowing fast and furious towards their packed trains. It was then that I had finally blurted it out, my wonderful news, shouting to make myself heard above a young woman busking – coins scattered in the case at her feet – her violin resonating Mozart atmospherically with the natural acoustics down there.

"We made love, Helen. Cathy and I; we made love."

Matthew's base tones had echoed those words around the deep, cavernous space in powerful harmony with the classical violinist, a real-life opera as the frantic crowds rushed by, oblivious to us, trapped in the tunnels of small lives like blind moles beneath the earth. Only Helen had heard. Her face froze for a split second before contriving a broad smile to disguise her pain. I should have been more sensitive, remembered that she had once loved the man who stood before her.

"I'm so pleased for you, darling," she exclaimed, fingering the sleeve of my jacket affectionately. "You've really convinced two women of the impossible."

"Helen, I'm sorry. That was thoughtless. Too much information."

"No, it's fine. I was indifferent to Matty at the last. But I like you, Andrew Soulsby. And I am pleased for you…" Almost reluctantly, she had withdrawn her hand from my arm. "I must go. I'm already late… Until tonight then, Andy?" Her thin eyebrows arched as she turned away, and I watched her long, blonde hair and willowy frame melt into the crowd of commuters; a haunting image I shall never forget.

As the manic screech of a fox barking beyond the double glazing jolts me, I take comfort from the chair wedged at the door. I glance at Matthew's Rolex. 11.30pm. Helen is late.

The urge to smoke a cigarette hits me. I imagine the smoke wafting over my tongue, the relaxing hit of nicotine. It is so weird to crave tobacco, something I experimented with in my teens, and remember finding it revolting. How is it possible for me to have inherited Matthew's addiction, this powerful feeling and sensation, completely at odds with my past experience?

It helps that the unopened packet of cigarettes is in the drawer beside my bed upstairs, since I would not relish the prospect of leaving my safe space until Helen arrives. For distraction, I press the remote to find Sky Sports. Perhaps I might still catch the test match highlights. But the screen flashes the inevitable message I should have foreseen: 'disconnected; please refer to service provider'. No doubt the monthly subscriptions to Sky stopped being paid some time ago.

I switch to the BBC's news channel on Freeview, and a story is running about an evil gang of moped robbers using acid and knives. Then my eye catches an item rolling across the display at the bottom of the screen: 'Commuter disruption this evening in London following closure of Northern Line after incident at Leicester Square'. There is no further information, but this might explain why Helen is late; it could have disrupted her journey home. I must be patient; after all, her performance would not have finished until after 10pm.

I try her number on my phone but it goes straight to voicemail. This is reassuring; if she is underground there would be no signal. I sigh; more waiting, but I cannot concentrate on the news. I flip through other Freeview channels and settle on a traffic-cops in action repeat. The lurid display of real-life police exploits battling crime begins to capture my interest, but then the light bulbs ping and die with the screen, leaving me blind in the pitch black.

It takes a few anxious seconds before I realise there must have been a power cut. Even though my eyes adjust to the dark quickly, as before, I can make out no more than murky outlines of shapes littering the room, like ghostly tombs in a mausoleum. I try to remain calm and tell myself that I am quite secure and safe in Helen's 'snug little hideaway'. I need to open the curtains. Although there is only a sliver of moon tonight, with starlight it should help, unless the storm clouds threatened earlier have rolled in.

I get out of the chair to feel my way, gingerly, towards where the window should be. Finding the drapes, I haul them back to reveal silver light from the heavens unhindered by clouds. And I can see the garden more clearly too, without the glare of electric light inside the room.

That's when I see it. My heart shudders momentarily before racing in panic as the security lights click on to reveal a police patrol car pulling into the drive. I press my face hard against the glass, peering to the left. It stops at the entrance steps leading up to the fancy porch. I move away from the window, hoping they have not already seen my startled face. I cannot bring myself to look again, to confirm what I dread: the sight of DCI Doyle, or Hancock, or Mitchell, even all three of them, here to haul me away in the night to permanent custody, having gathered more evidence, conclusive evidence screaming for Matthew's incarceration. Where is the enigmatic Michael Shapiro and his softly spoken reassurance now?

For one crazy moment, like the fictional fugitive Richard Kimball, I think of flight, escape through the rear French windows and into the night, over the garden, across the invisible fields and woods and nocturnal wildlife beyond, towards Hertfordshire. But in truth the thought scares me almost as much as prison cells: what unknown snares and dangers would await this unfit, overweight man; and the inevitability of ultimate capture would bring further ignominy, proof of guilt from my own hand. So, I stay in the dark little room, frozen like a terrified rabbit in the glare of his executioner's floodlights, awaiting the next instalment of my fate and the crowning glory to what was nearly such a perfect day.

I anticipate loud shouting as the front door is battered down; will they be able to breach such sturdy oak? I am not expecting the ping that brings back the light, nor the recorded sounds of blues and twos bursting into sudden life on the TV where cops chasing robbers are again in full view. The mains power is restored, and with it comes my expected summons, but in a surprisingly modest, civilised fashion. The bell rings once, its deep chimes echoing in gravitas through the house, followed swiftly by two polite raps on the heavy knocker against its brass keep.

There is no alternative but to face this, so I remove my improvised barricade, leaving the door to the room open for borrowed light while I tread heavy steps across the dark hall towards the front door. My legs tremble with weakness, a combination of nerves and exhaustion at this late hour – I have eaten only the light snack at the Cockfosters café since Jean's full English this morning, which seems so long ago. I stub my toes on the scrolled feet of the Bern Bear's round base as I reach across to flick on the switches, flooding both the porch outside and the house downstairs with comforting light. Stripped of its mysterious, black mask it all looks so innocent, so familiar without shadows and secrets; the hall positively sparkles in the crystal hues of the cascading chandelier.

I had dead-locked the door as soon as I came in this evening and left my keys on the wooden tray proffered up on the outstretched paws of the roaring bear. I retrieve them, reconciled to opening up, and slightly surprised at the patience being exhibited on the front porch. Swinging the door open, I am face to face with a young, female police officer, and just behind her stands a tall, male officer, also young and in uniform. They are patrol cops, and there is no sign of DCI Doyle or her colleagues.

"Good evening, Sir," she says politely. "Are you Mr Matthew Campbell?" Her manner is tense, her voice rather high-pitched and whiny. When I confirm that I am Matthew Campbell, she casts an anxious glance at her partner, before continuing: "May we come in for a moment, please?" This polite caution, the uncertainty, is hardly the demeanour of late-night raids and arrests, for which, surely, at least one of the detectives would be in attendance? DCI Doyle would be enthused at the prospect of re-arresting me.

It is approaching midnight, and my initial relief that I might not be bound for a police cell again sours quickly into suspicion and a sense of vulnerability as I stare at these uniformed strangers hovering on the doorstep. Their unease is infectious while they wait in tense silence – their radios strangely mute – on my invitation to cross the threshold of a substantial, lonely house. My imagination is on overload and, for a fleeting moment, a stupid, childish thought hits me: the prospect of spending eternity as an evil vampire in the form of Matthew Campbell.

The male lurking behind the tight smile of the whining female is not only tall but broad, an imposing physical presence that would be capable of overpowering me in an instant if he chose to. My skin crawls, not at the fiction of vampires – although I am still struggling to get that chilling image out of my mind – but at the thought this couple might be masquerading as police officers in some elaborate ploy connected with the conspiracy against me, or perhaps they are simply intent on aggravated burglary?

"I need to see your warrant card," I stammer finally, although if their purpose is sinister, it is hard to envisage this helping, with the entrance gaping wide behind me. She is quick to extract the card, though, from her inside tunic pocket. And it looks authentic, like the one DCI Doyle had shown me a few days earlier. While I am checking it, her colleague's radio crackles into life, spouting inaudible words as he turns away, but I hear him reply briefly: "Not yet. We're attending now in Beech Hill," and he turns it off.

I begin to feel reassured these are genuine police officers as I gaze past them to the patrol car parked on the drive and illuminated in the security lights. It certainly looks the real deal. After all, I know the paranoia that plagues me flares suspicion and fear at the slightest pretext. So, if they are genuine but not here to detain me, what on earth do they want at such an hour?

"Okay," I say rather curtly, Matthew's superior manner returning with my confidence. "Why do you ask to enter my house? (It feels bizarre to call Matthew's over-mortgaged pile *my house*.) Exactly why are you here, and what do you want with me?" I sound self-important and rude. This is not me at all. I don't know where he has come from, this pompous lawyer. I have never been that, and I feel embarrassed immediately the words are out, but know I can't take them back now.

I guess this is the prompt for her to tell me on the doorstep: "Your wife has been involved in an accident, Mr Campbell. I'm very sorry to inform you" – she hesitates for a split second, but I know in that moment the inevitability of what is to follow – "she is dead, Sir."

It is such a shock, so sudden and apparently random. How can this be true? I expect her home soon; there is so much to plan and do, so much unfinished business. And she is, she was, so full of life; elegant, kind and talented. A woman still searching for love. Although I have known her for less than three weeks, I feel numb with disbelief. And I feel regret – beyond what I would have expected – when I realise that I never held her in my arms, never held her close in an embrace of affection; and now, apparently, it is too late – she is gone forever.

I remember how she had left me late this afternoon, fading away into the faceless crowd underground, and I had sensed something between us then. I haven't admitted it to myself until now because it seemed disloyal to Cathy and, of course, I would never betray her. But still, there had been something.

"Are you alright, Mr Campbell?" The young woman has her hand on my arm. "Is there somewhere we can sit down?"

I lead them across the marble floor of the hall, and I notice both of them look askance at the dark, gothic bear, while trying not to gawp at the opulence of ostentatious wealth, the massive chandelier showcasing the grand sweep of the central staircase, as they tread, gingerly, in my wake towards the drawing room. We all settle into comfortable armchairs. She asks me, kindly, in her whiny voice, if I would like a cup of sweet tea. I prefer a shot of brandy from the cocktail cabinet, and the burly young constable, who has yet to utter a single word to me, silently obliges.

"Helen… dead?" I muse, sipping from the brandy glass he locates and fills with Courvoisier cognac – far too much. He remains standing, still mute, clearly feeling awkward and out of place, longing to go.

"I'm really sorry, Sir," and she does appear to be genuinely upset. What a horrible task: to be the purveyor of such terrible news.

I ask her, "How did it happen, and when; how long ago?"

"She fell under a train at Leicester Square station this evening, just after 6pm." At last, the man speaks; perhaps he is responsible for the grisly details? His face is suitably downcast, not quite meeting my eyes, like a lawyer confronted by his client in the cells after the shock of a harsh prison sentence.

"How was that possible? I need to know the details." I recall she had been in a rush, running tight on time for her performance, and there was no doubt she had been affected by my thoughtless revelation as she left me. Could I bear some responsibility for this tragedy?

"The platform was packed solid," he replies, and his cockney accent strikes me. "There'll 'ave to be a full investigation, but CCTV footage looks like it's not suicide, or foul play, just a terrible accident. We believe someone had a heart attack, and stumbled, pushin' her on to the track right when the train approached. She was standing too close to the line… But then people do," he offers philosophically.

Something doesn't feel right. Effectively, she has been bundled onto a live line at the precise moment a train enters the station, and the suggested explanation is a random heart attack suffered by the person standing behind her in the packed mêlée. The odds against this happening are minuscule. Furthermore, is it just a coincidence that this occurred so soon after I revealed my true identity and she had promised to help me? She was an acknowledged actor, known to the public and not without influence. And to have happened on such a momentous day, after Cathy had also been convinced and reunited with me; surely this stretches the bounds of coincidence beyond credulity? I find it impossible to believe she was just in the wrong place at the wrong time, a victim of capricious fate.

"Is this heart attack victim dead?" I ask coldly.

"Err… dunno, Mr Campbell, we don't 'ave all the facts yet," he responds, his tone now matter-of-fact. "It was only a few hours ago. The priority was to tell you as soon as possible, Sir. We'll need a formal identification." His colleague throws him a sharp, sideways glance, and he finishes apologetically, "But course that can wait 'til later; maybe tomorrow?"

The female officer is still perched on the chair next to me and asks if I have anyone to call who can be with me tonight, but I assure her I will be fine alone.

And then I hustle them to leave. It is 12.30am Friday morning, and I have to ring Cathy. Whether or not I manage to speak with her first, I intend to drive to my real home immediately, regardless of the hour and what we had arranged earlier. Everything has changed now. I sense we are both in real danger.

CHAPTER 32

TWO YEARS LATER

There is a hold-all bag on my back and a film of sweat on my brow as I hurry towards you, struggling to carry a suitcase along the path that leads to the visitors' car park at Ford open prison. Yesterday, I was riding a tractor-mower over the lawn beside this path – one of my favourite activities in the gardening section I had been assigned to during my time here – and I can still smell the freshly cut grass this morning in the pleasant warmth of the early sun.

It is difficult for me to describe to you my mood in these first, magical moments of freedom – euphoric, I guess, sums it up best. Only when your own liberty has been removed can you truly understand the sheer joy of release: that sense of abandon, no longer obliged to comply with petty rules, no longer in constant fear of unwitting transgression. To be observed and regulated at all times is so incredibly stifling, even in the relatively relaxed environment of an open prison. Think of when you were a schoolchild – the delight of walking through school gates having broken up for the long summer holiday. Multiply that pleasure by twenty plus. It feels something like that.

And yet it could have been so much worse for me. I have been lucky, treated well, but I must never tell you the truth, the reason why. Even if you failed to believe me you would still not be safe. Michael Shapiro made that entirely clear when the deal was cut two years ago: not a word of it to you, nor to Lucy and Geoff, not a word to any living soul, at any time, under any circumstances. I believe your lives depend on that; I know how ruthless and powerful they are, never to be crossed.

You were in the public gallery, one long year ago today, when that gnarled old judge's harsh face peered down at me from behind his high bench and delivered the sentence. I cringed with shame and fear in the dock as his hectoring voice lambasted me for monstrous breaches of trust, for my greed and despicable deceit. The public humiliation felt like a noose slowly choking the last dregs of life from my battered reputation.

I still hear your shrill cry of anguish, like a tortured seagull's wail, high above the gasps of shock around you when the sentence was handed down, and burly hands held and cuffed me. He gave me credit for pleading guilty, but it did not feel like it. You will go to prison for five years, he said, on each of the three counts on the indictment: money-laundering, false accounting and theft, the terms to run concurrently.

I was numb with disbelief when I looked up to catch your tear-stained face. As they bundled me down below to prepare for an unknown journey in a black maria, I caught a glimpse of smug satisfaction on the prim face of Detective Chief Inspector Doyle, sitting demurely behind the prosecuting QC, almost anonymous within the ranks of CPS support staff.

When I reached the holding cell below the dock, Michael Shapiro had arrived quickly, keen to calm and reassure me. Despite the 'nominal' sentence – purely theatre to frighten the children and pander to the mob's bloodlust, he had joked – I would be out on parole in one year, and I would go straight to Ford open prison (no nasty stay at a local closed prison for assessment) where I would be granted full privileges immediately. There would be day release for a trip into nearby Arundel once a week, a town whose every street is now etched in memories I can be certain that I truly own, and a 'cushy' job pottering around in the gardens. He had made it sound like a lazy year, full board in a holiday camp. But it turned out to be nothing like that, and had it not been for the special treatment and the thought of you waiting for me, I cannot imagine how I would have survived in this place, either physically or mentally.

Of course, I must never tell you any of this, never the truth of what they did and how I have been forced to adapt to a new reality. To lack this knowledge should guarantee your safety, and the safety of Lucy and Geoff. I secured this undertaking from them before agreeing to their terms two years ago. Failure to agree then, trying to convince others of the truth, would have meant a best outcome facing derision, drugs and permanent incarceration in a mental facility.

Whilst I would never overplay a modest hand, I am beginning to appreciate my importance to them, and I am not surprised they have kept their word – so far. But it is your support that has been crucial for my survival in here, both in the year on bail waiting for the trial (it seems so long since we last made love that evening before I was sentenced) and your regular visits to Ford after I was sent down: twice every month, without fail, and always on the few extra occasions that were allowed, despite the long journey from North London, despite your heavy caseload of demanding clients.

Ever-thoughtful, you dressed so demurely for me during those visits, never wearing a hint of make-up, only loose, shapeless clothing, matronly and drab, like a nun on vacation, as Wesley Butcher, my friendly warder and minder, would joke with me good-naturedly. Yet still I have lusted after you, fantasising your sexy presence with me every day, every night: working in the gardens, in my single bed during the small hours, and especially early in the mornings when I was alone in the showers, coming at every opportunity as you screamed with pleasure in the heat of my imagination.

If only the overnight visit in Arundel you tried so hard to secure had been granted, but in the eyes of the law we are neither married nor yet in a long-term relationship, so the request was doomed to failure. And you were steadfast in refusing to meet on daytrips, anxious to avoid circumstances that would risk temptation and rule-breaking, lest my parole date should be jeopardised. If only I had been able to explain to you why my release today was virtually assured.

As I reach the edge of the car park, I know that my frustration is about to be lanced. I know it will be you waiting in the small, silver Peugeot parked neatly, alone in the far corner of this almost-empty space, too early yet for visitors here. It is the first time I have seen your new car which is waiting to whisk us both away towards the challenges of our new, uncertain future. It's a perfect match for your confidence and feisty femininity.

I move closer, within thirty yards, before a chance look in your mirror reveals my reflection. I enjoy the short, white summer dress moulded to your body, the dangling earrings and the delicious flash of thigh as the driver's door swings open wide and you slide quickly from within, rushing to meet me. I put down my case to catch you in my arms and we kiss passionately in a clinch that I hope will last forever. We want each other, desperate to fulfil the promise of a year's pent-up desire: my body is quaking with a yearning and excitement for you, my heart crashing with such an intensity that I fear it will burst like the crumbling walls of a breached dam. But it is you who pulls away, gasping in a breathless whisper at my ear, "I checked in at the Oaks last night. It's close. We need to be there, now!"

I know the hotel. It's very posh, set well back from the road into Arundel, within its own substantial grounds. I've seen it from the window of the bus on my day-release trips into town, gazing towards it with a melancholy resignation. I think it once would have been a wealthy local magnate's Victorian pile, now converted and extended, so that it survives, indomitable, to command the surrounding countryside: the grand gatekeeper to a traditional English town. The sign at the roadside indicates four stars and three of those AA red rosettes for food. It must be very expensive, the kind of establishment Matthew would have been familiar with but only ever a rare treat for Andrew. And forbidden fruit to an ex-convict and a bankrupt. Or so I had thought.

I grab the case from where it rests beside my feet. It contains all the possessions I have in the world now, if you include the few bits in the bag strapped to my back, and they both fit with ease into your car's small boot.

Life in prison has steeled me to the trauma of perpetual scrutiny and observation, but as you pump the accelerator, speeding too fast down the long, open drive towards the public road, I feel no sensation of being watched by hidden eyes, despite the inevitable CCTV record that must exist of most, if not all activity on Her Majesty's land. Perhaps no one does care about me here anymore, and since the events of the night when Helen died – of which you must remain ignorant – I am aware there is no longer need for them to watch me constantly. They had promised it would stop, and although I did not entirely believe them, it had been reassuring to discover the sense of being followed and spied upon was no delusion, at least not every time; it had been real often enough.

At the end of the drive, you take the left turn, sharply, and roar up to seventy on the quiet, straight road. Today, I must banish the memories of that night; so often they are replayed in my mind on a constant loop, as if to re-analyse those momentous events and my part in them might somehow change the past and my fate, perhaps erase the terrible truths I learnt.

In my past life, I would have picked at the stodgy, bland prison fare and saved the trifling sums earned in the prison, together with the money you sent me, so that I could spend it all on healthy food in Arundel, not waste it, as I have, on burgers, chocolate and crisps. But Matthew lacks culinary discrimination, and I have been unable to resist gorging on whatever food has been available. Despite moderate exercise in the prison gardens, the weight gain is apparent, and now I am squashed into the confines of the front passenger seat. This Peugeot is so small. I guess this is something I will have to get used to; the best I can hope for to borrow your car occasionally, or at least to be the grateful passenger. It is a far cry from the BMWs taken for granted over the years, let alone the joy of my brief encounter with the sumptuous Bentley Flying Spur.

As if reading my mind and somehow aware of all the facts you must never know, you ease off the accelerator, and your tender hand wanders from the steering wheel, squeezing my knee affectionately. Then, reclaiming both hands, you swing us right, off the road, and we bounce over speed bumps that pepper the long drive up towards the impressive country-house hotel. We pass manicured lawns punctured with majestic trees in full leaf, and a naked-cherubim pluming celestial water into a large, ornamental lake from its central plinth. Gravel crunches in a spray of dust as we sweep around an island bordered by shrubs in front of the imposing main doors. A graceful weeping willow drapes its skirts full onto the sparse grass below, and you brake the car to a shuddering halt in one of the empty parking spaces on the far side.

A lone, young woman behind the reception desk is wearing a blue suit with a nametag I cannot decipher from across the entrance lobby. Her dark hair is tied back in a ponytail, and as you breeze past her towards the lift, she returns your friendly smile with a cautious, "Good morning." I lag behind, burdened with the bag on my back and carrying the heavy case. She glares at me with a suspicious frown.

"Do you need help with your luggage, Sir?" Although the words are polite, their tone accuses the ageing man she sees, the alleged husband you informed her last night would arrive today after a fictional business conference in the town. But it is only 10.30am, the prison is close, and my white linen shirt and chinos do not fit her profile.

"How kind," I say as you pause to wait for me beside the lift. I am passing close to her now and my eyes manage to focus on the nametag, despite the absence of reading specs. "But I'm perfectly fine, thank you, Janice. My doctor would approve; he's always telling me to take more exercise." I emit a little chuckle for her, and I see you smile. "Helps to keep me fighting fit," I joke.

Matthew's habit of peddling insincere charm to gain favour and influence comes so naturally with his deep, cultured voice. In the harsh realism of prison life there is scant room for pretence, nor the worship of appearances and celebrity; a wholly different pecking order holds sway, and my dulcet tones had often raised hackles, met with coarse and ribald banter, producing sour resentment of the class and privilege it epitomised to most of the inmates. But in the shallow comforts of the country-house hotel it represents a passport to acceptability. Janice is suitably impressed, her bridled reserve dissolving into polite laughter and a kindly, broad smile of confident respect, as if my posh accent and easy manner has cast a wizard's spell upon her.

"I'm sure you're fit, Sir; if only all our guests were like you." The charming hostess now, almost flirting with me. Your smile has vanished, and I sense irritation revealed on your crinkling forehead. "Would you like me to make a dinner reservation for you tonight?" The question is directed to me alone; you are forgotten, her large, wide eyes fixed on mine.

"We'll decide later; we may want room service." You throw these curt words at her across the lobby in a shrill voice before I can respond, and you do not notice the surreptitious smile of apology I give her, a brief glance between us, as I follow you into the lift. My initial pang of guilt at this concealed disloyalty is more than compensated by Janice's coy blush as the lift door clicks shut.

It's harmless, my feelings for you quite unaffected, yet for me it is a new joy, this natural ability to attract women. The moment is quickly forgotten when you reveal, at the end of a short corridor on the second floor, not the decent double room I had been expecting but a sumptuous suite that must have cost you a fortune to hire for two nights.

We walk in and I drop my case in the lounge, pulling the bag from my back to rest beside it, where they both sink into the deep pile of a lush, green carpet. I want you so much, and hardly notice the soft comfort and grand furnishings which surround me. I follow, eagerly, as you lead me into the bedroom, dominated by its king-sized bed covered with a purple quilt. The massive Art Deco Tiffany pendant light hanging from the ceiling adds a touch of period elegance, if not decadence, and, somehow, a hint of depravity.

"What do you think?" you whisper seductively, standing at the casement window which overlooks an impressive garden at the rear of the hotel. "Do you approve of my choice for your first taste of freedom?"

"It's amazing, like you," I reply, my heart pounding in anticipation. I have been waiting a year for this moment. I pull you close and we are kissing, your breasts pressed against me, my hands on your waist feeling the thin fabric of your tight dress.

"Not yet." Your voice is breathless as you pull away. "I have another surprise." You kick off your sandals. "I promise you'll be pleased." You laugh, rushing away from me towards the bathroom, your bottom swaying in a tantalising enticement. I glimpse lingerie – black lace and tiny, red bows – draped over the corner of a white bath, before the door shuts firmly behind you and I hear the lock turn.

I recall your penchant for sexy underwear, your own pleasure heightened to painstakingly don so much of so little, to then be discarded so soon in the heat of lust. I must wait a little longer for you to perfect your appearance: clipping stockings to suspenders, adjusting a black thong below a camisole. What are a few more minutes, if not to savour the joy of anticipation after my year of frustration and angst?

You must never know of the struggle I have endured in prison to maintain my sexuality, to control urges and feelings alien to my history, to the background and experience of the life that I know. I have had to become adept at manipulating events and circumstances to reduce risks of novel temptation, always using you, my love, as a last resort: imagining your lips on mine, the touch of your soft, smooth skin, to ensure it was you who sustained every erection I failed to suppress, and you who provided the muted pleasure of the secret, solitary relief that would eventually follow.

The lower half of the old sash window has been left open and it rattles intermittently in a gentle breeze, like the rumble of a distant train. I gaze over the garden, where a huge and ancient cedar tree spreads sedately, morbidly obese, at the centre of a parched lawn. On the far side, a wide border in a riot of bright summer colours nestles beneath an old wall of crumbling bricks, and beyond, patchwork farmland stretches like a picture postcard towards the horizon. I am struck by the similarities to the wonderful views I enjoyed for almost three weeks from the bedroom in Matthew's house, and it dawns on me I will probably never see them, or that huge bedroom, ever again.

It takes me back to that haunting night two years ago when I learnt Helen had died, and the full truth of what they had done – the extent of their evil – was revealed to me in the small hours of the following morning. The endemic fear still haunts me; it is with me again, and I shudder at the chill coursing through my body.

I pull a packet of cigarettes and matches from my trouser pocket and light one up to dull the memories of those dark hours. As I exhale the smoke through the open window, I feel the tension ease. I know I had promised to resist the craving while I was inside, but the damned things are so easy to come by in prison, and it proved too much to resist what has come to feel so natural to me.

You have pestered me to write a prison diary, thought that it might help me to cope. You know how I have tried, but the words wouldn't come, at least not until now, the day of my release, with events I want to record and celebrate. But it must end here, for I can never show you this; not if there is to be any chance of a future for us, not if I care for your safety.

It is essential for you to remain in ignorance of what I discovered during those dark hours.

THOSE
DARK
HOURS

CHAPTER 33

The tall policeman lost no time in pulling the front door open, then moved out onto the porch steps. "I'll leave these with you, Mr Campbell: some details of services many people find helpful," the female officer said before joining him. At last, the oak door could be slammed shut, and it was such a relief to be alone so that I could gather my thoughts.

I discarded her leaflets – about Samaritans and Counsellors for the bereaved – with the pile of unopened post resting in the antique bear's wooden tray. Pulling the iPhone from my trouser pocket, I rang Cathy's number again, but just like earlier in the evening it went straight to voicemail. I checked Matthew's Rolex: two minutes past one in the morning. Maybe still preparing her case for later today or, more likely, she had gone to bed. Yet it was essential I speak with her urgently, and so I had to risk driving to Cheltenham Avenue, despite the slug of brandy downed when the two police constables were with me.

A spare set of keys to our home would be in the key access box. I had arranged to have this fitted on the flank wall of the house about five years ago after we accidentally locked ourselves out – we'd had to pay a locksmith three hundred and fifty pounds for an emergency call-out – so if I couldn't raise Cathy when I got there, I should still be able to gain entry. I doubted she had changed the security code since I had left home for my operation eighteen days ago. We had never bothered to alter our original choice: why should we, since only our immediate family knew the number?

Pumping adrenalin banished my earlier tiredness as I grabbed the car keys from the rack near the front door, then rushed out to my BMW. Matthew's body must have a high tolerance to alcohol because I felt no ill effects from the brandy as my mind raced over sinister possibilities.

How could anyone have known yet that Helen had been persuaded I was Andrew Soulsby and that she was determined to help me? Just who might she have confided in since last Sunday when I first told her? I had no idea, but the more I thought about it, the more convinced I became that someone did know, and this was the reason why she must have been murdered.

Clearly others were in cohorts with Peter Cheung and Joe Peng. Obviously, Jeremy Whicher and Michael Shapiro, maybe more? Whoever was responsible, I doubted they would have expected my claims to be taken seriously should I be foolhardy enough to risk confiding my secrets. Matthew's imminent fall from grace – which I suspected they had prior knowledge of – would only strengthen an impression that the poor man had lost his mind. How shocked they must have been to discover Helen did believe me. I feared it was her resolve to assist in uncovering the truth that had proved to be the deciding and fatal factor in their deliberations, the reason why I now had to live with her death on my conscience. Had I not involved her, spoken with her so eloquently and persuasively, she might still be alive.

And what of my prospects now that they knew I was capable of convincing someone to take my claims seriously? But the risks to me had to be kept in perspective: it was unlikely they would have let me survive the operation only to kill me later. Hopefully, there were compelling reasons why they needed me alive as Matthew Campbell.

My urgent priority, though, was Cathy, and I reasoned she was safe for the time being because there was no way they could have known yet that she believed me: little more than fourteen hours ago she had despised me as Matthew Campbell, and since leaving her to work on her case at home, I had told no one but Helen, only moments before her alleged freak accident. If or when they did find out, though, Cathy would be in danger, so I could not afford to take chances. She had to be told of Helen's death immediately, before any chance remarks or enquiries made to the wrong person raised suspicions; no one must be aware of any interest shown by her in the Wilkinson case, or in Matthew Campbell and Peter Cheung. We would have to re-think our whole strategy and be very careful.

Dry gravel crunched under the spinning wheels of my car raising a dust bowl, floating in the haze of security lights like a sinister cloud of gas, as I swung the BMW out of the front entrance at speed, intent on warning Cathy. I tore down a deserted Beech Hill in boy-racer mode and reached the end of the street in seconds, braking hard at the last moment before pumping the accelerator violently, shooting erratically to the right at the junction with the Cockfosters Road. I just managed to squeeze in front of an advancing juggernaut's flashing headlights and blaring horn, before veering off sharp left up Ferney Hill, towards North Enfield.

I knew the vagaries of twists and turns on this narrow, unlit road, and sped into the night, following the path of main-beam headlamps, weaving between farm fields on my left and the dense trees of Trent Park skirting the right-hand side. So much had happened to reshape my emerging new life since I had made this same journey as a passenger in Helen's Porsche – could it really be only yesterday morning, a mere fifteen hours earlier? I had experienced such a rollercoaster of highs and lows in that brief time, fresh hopes and dark fears juggling with my memory and sense of self.

Within a couple of minutes, I reached streetlights and the darkness receded. I ignored a 30mph speed-restriction sign flashing the command to slow down. The road was empty and I knew there was still some distance before the mini-roundabout junction with the Enfield Ridgeway. And besides, a terrible thought began to gnaw inside my head: if Helen and I had been followed on this same journey yesterday morning, their suspicions might already have been aroused, especially given the length of time I had remained alone with Cathy after Helen left. There was no time to lose.

I pressed my foot down to retain speed as the road widened up an incline lined by large 1930s semis facing smart detached villas on the other side of the street. A manky fox trotted along the pavement, flashing beady, feral eyes, before dashing down a front garden and disappearing into the shadows.

I heard the sudden wail of a siren approaching rapidly. The rear-view mirror revealed no warning lights, just empty tarmac behind me fading into the night. But it was getting louder, more insistent. I was near the junction, slowing down, when I saw a police car fly past in a hail of screeching noise and flashing blue, right in front of me, skirting across the small roundabout – just a circular blob of white paint – heading along the Ridgeway towards Enfield Town.

I turned right in its wake, reluctantly tempering my speed so that it was soon far off, almost at the end of a long section of straight road past Chase Farm Hospital, getting close to my own destination. And then, in a moment of dread, my worst fear materialised when the patrol car's brake lights came on, shining like red dwarf stars in the distance. In an instant it disappeared to the left, out of sight, like the fox I had just seen, into the maze of residential streets where Cheltenham Avenue was buried. Was it answering a call from No. 23? I struggled to push this terrifying thought away, the implications too awful to contemplate, and attempted to reassure myself that there were many other dwellings with potential disasters or false alarms in the same direction.

My pulse was racing when I pulled into Cheltenham Avenue less than a minute later, desperate not to find the patrol car but somehow resigned, I think, to the crushing blow of that dreadful sight: the same heavily marked Ford Mondeo straddled across the cutaway to my garage drive, behind a couple of other police vehicles at the kerb outside our house.

Our home glowed like a beacon in the row of sleeping houses, blazing lights burning bright behind closed curtains. As I drove past slowly, I saw a canopy erected over the front door, where a lone police officer glanced towards me from her solitary post, guarding the house. With horror, I saw fluttering blue and white tape across the entire frontage marked, ominously: 'POLICE LINE DO NOT CROSS', and beyond, Cathy's red Mini was parked in front of open garage doors. Surely, they had been closed, her car securely within, when I had left not long after 4pm yesterday?

My stomach churned and a wave of nausea made me gag, leaving the taste of sickly bile on my tongue. I felt lightheaded as I eased into a vacant space, further down, on the other side of the street. Slow, deep breaths helped me regain composure and focus. It was possible she had survived; after all, the police must have been called, and Cathy was nothing if not a shrewd, resourceful woman who could look after herself. She always kept a mace spray in her bag for self-defence; perhaps she was recovering in hospital from an attack and providing detectives with details of her assailant?

I understood the risks of waiting there, even more of asking them what had happened. I knew further suspicion might fall on me since I had no legitimate reason to enquire, but I had to know immediately, whatever the consequences. I could not leave clinging to tenuous hopes. And if it turned out for the worse, my dreams of a life reunited with Cathy dashed, then what did my safety or my liberty really matter?

It felt cool, almost chill in the night air when I walked tentatively towards the house. I heard Mr Shawcross's dog bark, spooked by my presence, and looked up to see his curtain twitch. If only I could ask him, or any of those other secret eyes likely watching me – fascinated by the police activity – just what they had seen tonight.

The police officer's gaze fixed my approach, curious as to what this respectable-looking, middle-aged guy in a blue linen suit was up to at this time of night. And my mind was racing with each step I took. Should I cross the tape or remain behind it and shout at her from a distance? How should I address her to have any chance of finding out what had happened to Cathy?

I reached the pedestrian gate, which was open, and stopped on the path where the tape cut across the garden. My heart pounded as I returned her stare with a weak smile, and my chest tightened – despite Matthew's statins and blood-pressure pills which I had, at last, started to take conscientiously. We were facing each other down, eyes locked in a silent stand-off, neither of us sure what to say. I opened my mouth to speak, began to mutter something indistinct, but her voice piped strongly, overpowering mine.

"I'm not sure what you're doing here, Sir, but it's not a show; there's nothing to see. This is a police investigation on private property, so unless you have official business, I must ask you to move along… Now, please, Sir." She was not aggressive, but her voice carried an air of authority.

Before I could answer, the front door behind her swung open to reveal a tall, lean man with hunched shoulders, clutching a small briefcase. His head was down, partially shielded by her ample frame, but as he advanced along the battered crazy-paving towards me, I recognised the unmistakable, lumbering gait of Peter Bright. Shortly before reaching me, he must have sensed my presence – a looming figure caught in shadow at the end of the path – because he raised his head, an expression of surprise on his sombre face that matched my own astonishment to see him there, standing frozen to the spot in front of me.

"Matthew Campbell!" That distinctive, long chin seemed to droop down in caricature towards his feet, while his jaw gaped open with incredulity. "What in God's name might you be doing here?" The burr to his accent seemed so pronounced, reeking of his West Country roots, while the tone of his voice accused me of impropriety by virtue of my presence.

"I was out late visiting friends who live just round the corner and saw a police car drive into Cheltenham Avenue on my way home. I was concerned because I remembered this is the street where Cathy Soulsby lives." Normally so honest, quite unable to improvise, I don't know how I did it. I had answered him with fake confidence, the first words that had leapt into my head, while I pondered just why he was in my house with the police at such an hour. "But what's happened, Peter? Why are you here?" I asked him.

"Gentlemen, will you please leave now?" The female officer was insistent, and Peter stooped under the tape to join me, but we stayed on the pavement outside the front gate.

"It's a dreadful business," he whispered, right in my face; I felt his breath on my cheek and eased away from him slightly. He seemed anxious to talk and had obviously swallowed the explanation for my presence at face value. "I'd been working late at the office, and I needed Cathy to sign some probate papers I'd prepared. When I last spoke to her on the phone earlier this evening, she said she would be working into the small hours and was happy for me to pop around on my way home, whatever the time.

"The front door was wide open when I got here. There was no sign of forced entry but everything was in darkness... I found her in the lounge." His voice caught with emotion and his big blue eyes reminded me of a forlorn golden retriever, as he pushed strands of brown hair from his forehead, struggling to regain composure.

"Is she alright?" I stammered, but I knew the answer before he responded.

"She's dead, Matthew. She was slumped on the sofa. At first, I thought she was sleeping, until I moved closer. Her eyes looked like they were staring at me, wide open, and her mouth as if she was trying to tell me something." He broke off again, distraught to recall the image, and then blew his nose like a fog-horn into the large, white handkerchief he had pulled from his pocket. "I'd known her for so many years and there she was, so still and lifeless – unbelievable!"

The night air chilled my skin through the lightweight suit, and soon I was trembling, thinking of Geoff and Lucy, who had lost both parents in less than three weeks. I wondered if they had been told yet and winced at the searing emotional pain that wracked me when I imagined their suffering. It was so cruel that I could not be with them to share our grief, to console and comfort each other.

If only I had gone straight home to Cathy, ignored her caution and sense of duty, taken charge for once, then I might have been there to save her, instead of cowering in Matthew's empty house. What a weight of guilt I had to live with for as long as they intended to let me survive, the deaths of two innocent women on my hands: Cathy, the love of my life and mother to my children; and Helen, a talented, beautiful woman in her prime.

"Is she still inside, Peter? If only I could see her?" I heard my own voice echoing inside my head like a drumbeat. Before he could respond, I asked, "Had she been attacked?"

"They wouldn't let you in." He glanced towards the guard at the front door, whose suspicious eyes were still pinned on us. "I'm not sure why you'd want to see her – there was no sign of an attack, but it wasn't a pleasant sight. You sound rather ghoulish, Matthew."

"No, I'm sorry. It's just that I have some experience of coroner's court work, and I might have been able to help." Again, the lies seemed to flow effortlessly, made to order without any prior thought or planning, and, somehow, I was keeping my cool, remaining outwardly composed, behaviour that I expected Matthew Campbell would be proud of.

"Well, it's official police business," he said, looking at me askance. "They told me nothing has been disturbed, no sign of intruders or a break-in."

"Apart from the front door left wide open. Pretty suspicious, I'd say." I wondered if they had checked the key safe on the flank wall, whether the key inside was missing?

"I agree. After I phoned 999, the first car was fairly quick. Quite a few more have come and gone since then.

"There was a sealed envelope propped on the mantelshelf, addressed to Geoff and Lucy – that's her children – and an empty box of sleeping pills on the carpet beside the sofa. I've told them she would never have taken her own life, but I think they do believe it is suicide – the grieving widow and so on. At least they're being very thorough. A SOCO team is carrying out a full forensic investigation of house and garden. They've just told me I can leave, although I have to provide fingerprints and a DNA sample… for elimination," he was quick to add.

Peter paused, looking over his shoulder towards the front door again where the grim-faced officer still had us both under close scrutiny, like a predator eyeing its prey before the kill.

I said to him, "Wasn't she a Catholic? And with two youngsters at university, do they not realise the idea of suicide is preposterous?" If only they could have all known how happy Cathy was when I had left her about nine hours ago.

"I've told the police all that. You seem to know a lot about them?"

"Not really, I just picked up a few things the one time I met Andrew – we got on well."

At that moment, the thumping of leather shoes on concrete alerted us to the wide girth of the female officer bustling along the path, like an old-fashioned matron bearing down on tardy nurses, the stretch marks creasing over her snug, blue tunic. She reached us in a few strides, her frowning face burning red.

"I've asked you more than once, and I'm not going to say it again. If you don't want to be arrested for obstruction, leave now."

We exchanged a brief glance, and I think we both realised it might be best to avoid antagonising her with pompous declarations by lawyers that there was no obstruction, and our presence on the public path was lawful. There were no more words between us then, just a token nod of the head from Peter before he left, and I began to walk off, slowly, in the opposite direction, towards my parked car, as a sense of despair at the enormity of what had happened began to close around me.

"Just a minute." Her raised voice growled at my back like a stalking bear, and it pulled me up with a start. I turned round to face her. "I want a note of your name and address, and an explanation as to what you're doing here?" Her tone was now both aggressive and confrontational.

I no longer had any plan of action or sense of purpose, and I was wondering whether my tormentors would ever reveal themselves, maybe offer answers and explain what they expected of me. For now, though, I had to deal with this officious woman, then return to Matthew's house – what other choice was there? Somehow, I managed to retain my composure, despite everything: Cathy and Helen murdered, surely, and all my dreams of resurrecting family life cruelly dashed.

The police officer's insistent eyebrows were raised, impatient for my response, and, despite my sorrow, it was strange that I warmed to the task with perverse enjoyment, lying without compunction, exhibiting a natural ease that should have been so foreign to my nature. I spun the same yarn that had persuaded Peter, and although I knew he would confirm me as Matthew Campbell if she checked, I still gave a fictitious name and the address of my childhood home in Barnet. Her eyes squinted over me as though they were a lie detector scanning for the truth hidden in my soul before she drew notepad and biro from her tunic pocket to methodically record my false details.

I prayed she would not run a check on my car, no doubt still registered at DVLC to Andrew Soulsby. If she did, there would be questions about ownership and insurance I could not answer. As she wrote, I cast a nervous glance over my shoulder to where it was parked, fortunately some distance away and not near a streetlight, so the registration plates were not visible. When the notepad was tucked away, she threw a withering glare and severe words to dismiss me. "Well, this is not a spectator sport for nosey rubbernecks. I think you should know better. That's it. Off you go, now."

Her acerbic tone stung my pride, her parting words still ringing in my ears as I unlocked the BMW and began the now-familiar and forlorn drive back to the empty, silent expanses of the vast house in Beech Hill.

CHAPTER 34

Alone in my car, a sense of anguish again stalked the composure I had fashioned so quickly for the benefit of Peter Bright and that suspicious, female police officer. Perhaps for the last time, I drove down Cheltenham Avenue, creeping along at a snail's pace in order to savour so many precious memories. Eventually speeding up, the familiar touch of my BMW in the local streets, the sights and feel of home so mundane and normal, suggested nothing had changed, as though the last few weeks had been only a figment of my imagination.

But there was no denying the chubby hands of another man gripping the steering wheel in front of me, and I felt the weight of that despair pounding like a heavy stone in my head. The protective shield my mind had constructed finally shattered as I drove along Hadley Road, skirting the dense woods of Trent Park, where red-eyed foxes prowled and rabbits hunkered deep under tree roots. My arms, my whole body began to shake violently, even my newly healed throat was aching once more, as I sobbed with distress for Cathy; for Helen too; and for myself: such an innocent victim of evil.

I became aware of the car swerving violently across the empty road. Fortunately, I managed to regain control just in time and stopped in a lay-by. It was so still and quiet, the solitude almost overwhelming in this lonely spot, with only a wisp of moon and a dusting of faint stars in the polluted night sky. Although my tears were subsiding, I craved company, a sympathetic ear to provide some solace, but I had no friends now, at least none known to me and certainly no one I dared to confide in.

My head ached with tension – far worse than the headaches that had sent me to Peter Cheung – as my mind churned thoughts, shuffling them to find a better hand, but the deal remained hopeless: Cathy dead, and Helen; no money beyond the few pounds remaining in Matthew's wallet, only massive debts; perhaps a couple of hundred miles left for travel in this car before the petrol ran out; and a lonely house waiting – even the new gardener, engaged so recently by Helen, now gone – soon to be snatched away by bailiffs enforcing the bank's possession order. The thought of being penniless and sleeping rough put the prospect of prison into sharp perspective.

Just as my misery seemed complete, it hit me, an epiphany moment, the solution to my short-term problems: Shivani; and the glow of joy at the prospect of pure, hedonistic pleasure and enjoyment cleansed my muddled head; it made me feel alive. She had given me her keys just before my arrest on Monday. Her words then were suddenly ringing in my ears: "Whenever you need to, just come to me… whatever happens, I'll always be here for you." And that voicemail, how could I have forgotten it, pleading with me to go to her flat at 7.30pm on Friday, and it was already the early hours of Friday morning. I felt such a frisson of sexual excitement remembering how she had pounced on me in the lift at Dorrell's four days ago, and found myself fantasising about her, imagining the sight of her naked body, the touch of her smooth skin.

It was such a dramatic mood change – the death of Cathy discounted by shallow thoughts of physical pleasure. Suddenly, all I could think of was Shivani, her incessant texts and voicemails, all desperate for me. Perhaps she was naked in her bed now and dreaming of me? I knew in that moment: of course, I would take up her offer to stay, live there as her Matthew, let her keep me, if necessary, and have fun for so long as it lasted, until something better came along or my tormentors showed their hand and put a stop to it.

This was so unlike me, and a part of me knew it was wrong. I had been devoted to Cathy; where was my grief – so debilitating just moments before – and my conscience, such an essential part of my personality? But I didn't care. The thought of Shivani had suddenly made me see clearly, in a new, positive light. I had no ties now, and it dawned on me as pointless to feel sentimental commitment to a memory. I felt good, as though I was reborn and enthused with a new sense of conviction to embrace Matthew's life, to live for the day. If charged and convicted of another man's crimes, I would display repentance to mitigate the sentence. And then a strangely selfish thought caressed my senses with a further thrill of excitement: surely Matthew would have stashed his fortune away from creditors, and his doting lover might help me to find it?

It was a novel sensation for me, to be decisive, and I could hardly believe that I had been in such a state just a few minutes ago. Determined to take control of my new life, I pulled the iPhone from my pocket to ring Shivani, intending to tell her that I wanted her very much and I was on my way to her...

But the phone rang in my hand before I could make the call. The ringtone of Jack Bauer's *24* no longer seemed silly and immature; it was just fun, after all. As I flipped the screen with my index finger, I fully expected to hear Shivani's soft, sexy tones – who else had rung me over these last weeks? My anticipation was crushed, though, by a familiar voice rudely disabusing the fanciful notion I had entertained as the phone rang, of some mystical, telepathic connection between Shivani and me.

"Hello, Andrew." Michael Shapiro, there was no doubt. "We should meet and talk now. The time has come for you to have answers... What do you say?"

"You!" I gasped in shock, momentarily disoriented to hear the deceptively kind voice. "I've been trying to contact you since Tuesday; but why now, why call me, finally, in the middle of the night, and this night of all nights?"

But I understood the reason, even as I asked the question: he must have known that Helen and Cathy had been killed, perhaps even that I was parked up here. I looked around, out of the car windows and into the rear mirror. Nothing; no movement or sounds. It was deathly quiet, the dense, black woods sleeping, the road empty; no signs of any life. I glanced down to check what I already knew: that my car was securely locked, the key still in the ignition, ready for a swift escape.

The phone was pressed tightly against my left ear, and I could hear the fat man's breath, singing like a bellows, while he waited, patiently, on my further response, ignoring my question to him. There seemed little doubt he was one of those who controlled my fate, and, at last, he wanted to meet and talk with me, only hours after they had surely murdered Helen and Cathy. Yet Michael Shapiro seemed an unlikely hitman. Maybe my instinct that they wanted me alive as Matthew Campbell was right.

"Okay," I told him. "I'm listening. Tell me everything you know…"

"I'm waiting for you in Matthew's study. I know you're on your way. Come now, quickly, and I will explain everything."

I'm sure I had locked up and engaged the alarm before I left the house, so how could he have gained entry without using force? In the silent seconds while he waited on my confirmation, I scanned my options like a cornered dog. It could be a trap to lure me there – that instinct they wanted me alive just self-delusion – and for a moment I contemplated flight, speeding off into the night towards Shivani. Yet that risked putting an innocent young woman in danger. And it was true: I needed the promised answers so badly. I tried to think logically. I did believe they wanted me alive. After all, if it was the plan to kill me tonight, surely, they would have done it earlier this evening when I was alone in the house?

"It's safe." He read the doubts in my silence, my faux bon-homme, speaking in his friendly, avuncular manner. "I'm alone. Those I speak for wish you no more physical harm. To be honest, Andrew, if they did you would be dead already," he said, confirming my own conclusion.

"You're a disgrace, masquerading as a trusted solicitor yet involved in conspiracy and murder. I presume you've killed Cathy and Helen?"

"Just come to the house; join me in the study. Please. I assure you, Andrew, that nobody else is here." His voice was so calm, so reasonable, and I knew then that I had to risk going there in the hope of finding the truth.

CHAPTER 35

Delightful thoughts of Shivani added a bravado to my steps from the car towards the house. Most of the lights in the downstairs rooms at the front had been turned on, providing false encouragement and reassurance as I climbed the porch stairs and found the front door ajar. I went in without hesitation, instinctively closing it with a firm clunk behind me to announce my calling card.

The hall echoed silent and empty under the tread of my heavy shoes on the tiled floor. There was no voice of encouragement or welcome, but when I entered the study Michael Shapiro was alone as promised, sitting in a large swivel chair behind the mahogany desk, his broad back against the invisible expanses of night beyond the French doors to the garden. The curtains were not pulled closed, and I imagined unseen eyes watching me from outside.

Tuesday morning's crisp business suit had been discarded for casual dress; regular jeans and a brown sweater looking slightly tight on his bulky frame. He said nothing, making no attempt to get up or shake my hand as I approached the desk, and his unkempt, grey beard, those straggling whiskers, reminded me of an untidy garden gone to seed. The craggy face which met my gaze held it steady with a smile that spoke of regret and sorrow, and I had to remind myself that this man was my foe, the kind manner a falsehood; he should not be trusted.

The tense silence was broken by the beep of Matthew's iPhone receiving a text. He raised his bushy eyebrows while I checked the message, the hint of a mischievous glint in eyes clearly visible above the same round specs on the end of his nose. It was from Shivani: 'Darling, I can't sleep. Longing for this evening. I want you so bad. Please don't let me down. Shivi. X'.

"She must be crazy for you to text at this hour. You've met my blind love: the ageing frump at my office." He chuckled. "But what should I expect?" Both of his hands were thrown high, briefly, in a pretence of self-mockery. "I think Matthew's lover is a more difficult temptation to resist?" It was as if he had read the screen himself.

I put the phone back in my pocket and met his smiling face. "It's obvious you must have known what was happening with Matthew, and I guess, somehow, you're watching me closely, checking everything I do?" No answer, his expression unchanged, just the same smile. "Well, you know about Shivani for sure; but I've told her nothing at all. I never will." I had no intention of putting another innocent life in danger.

"That's good." He still sounded so sincere, as if his only concern was my welfare. "It would be a grave mistake to confide in her. If you must go to this girl, be very careful and discreet. Remember your bail condition prohibiting contact with anyone at Dorrell's." This was reassuring, suggesting my instinct was right: no further harm to me was intended, at least not yet. He swivelled his chair slightly to one side and indicated the leather armchair beside the far wall. "Why don't you sit down? This will take some time and, I'm afraid, it will not be easy for you."

At last, was I really going to find out what had happened, what they had done to me? My chest tensed with anticipation. I eased into the comfortable armchair he had suggested, watching as he got up and walked round the desk to lean his stocky frame against it, closer to where I sat.

"Andrew Soulsby was unlucky," he began, his quiet words exuding calm authority. "He was in the wrong place at the wrong time.

"By now you will have read some papers on the Wilkinson case. There's a small group at that company engaged in secret research, and you, my friend, have become the first human experiment to test their theories – which makes you a rather precious commodity—"

"No doubt we're talking of Peter Cheung, Joe Peng and, I suspect, Jeremy Whicher as well?" I interrupted. "But why me?"

"Let me explain. Peter Cheung is an incredibly gifted man, a great talent. He has conceived and perfected a process of transferring total memory from one person to another." I don't think it hit me, at first, the implication of what he had just disclosed; what it meant for who I really am now, but I remembered that strange dream, floating, disembodied above an operating theatre, looking down on my body and another, like corpses in a morgue. "Only very few people," he was saying, "are engaged in the research with him, but the implications of it are immense, of course. Imagine it: every brilliant man or woman could, potentially, preserve their education and experience, their skills and knowledge, beyond death to revolutionise the speed of human progress. And nothing of this magnitude gets past the agency of the security service I represent. It has excited interest at the highest levels."

"You're a spy!" I had thought nothing else could shock me. "I can hardly believe it. Is this British Intelligence?"

"Yes. The Research Development Agency is ostensibly a small, independent charity promoting international research, but, in reality, it operates as cover for a section of the security service so secret that it does not officially exist. We work in close collaboration with similar agencies in a few friendly countries. And co-operation is sought when it's needed from others – the foreign aid budget provides scope to oil many wheels. We exist to do what has to be done covertly, outside the remit of national laws and democratic accountability.

"We intervened in order to monitor the path of Cheung's research and control how the results of it are eventually utilised. We ensure it remains top-secret, because if a whiff of it became public the massive ethical issues would, at best, delay for generations the chance to advance human progress exponentially. And," he added with such apparent sincerity and feeling that, I think, the hypocrisy was genuinely lost on him, "we also ensure that only the good guys have this knowledge."

"Well," I interrupted him, grimacing with bitterness, "it's such a relief to know that it's the good guys who have destroyed my life and family, and murdered innocents."

"You're bound to be angry and upset, but let me finish, please. Sometimes circumstances justify sacrifices being required for the greater good. The just wars of human history are full of examples of such individual heroism."

I suppressed inner fury, forcing myself to ignore such condescension and his patronising smile, since I still couldn't understand how or why I was in Matthew's body, and I needed to know what they proposed for my future.

"Matthew Campbell was also one of this group at Wilkinson's, and like all of them, he had invested heavily in the company. As you may have realised by now, he was bisexual and promiscuous. His private life became increasingly chaotic and, staring at professional disgrace and financial ruin, he contemplated suicide before deciding to volunteer as a human guinea pig, hoping to avoid the shame of bankruptcy and prison. Matthew gambled on Peter Cheung's bold claims that his discovery really represented the transplantation of the human soul, and Matthew had convinced himself that it would be him, his own self-awareness, that lived on in his chosen host if the experiment was successful.

"When he met Andrew Soulsby, the timing was perfect; he had found a suitable host: rather younger than him, physically fit, handsome and another lawyer to boot, with an attractive, sexy wife who was a barrister.

"We investigated before consenting to the live experiment and think it was your wife who unwittingly gave him the opportunity to target you. Matthew told us he met her at a Chamber's party when she let slip her stressed husband was suffering from headaches and worried about acting in the sale of her uncle's hotel in Leeds when a purchaser was found. Matthew had seen you at an earlier event in Chambers and liked what he remembered. So, he arranged for one of his companies to make an offer on the hotel. The transaction would never exchange contracts, but it gave him the chance to meet you and manufacture your introduction to Peter Cheung."

I felt uneasy, as though a forgotten memory had been partially revealed, a sense that there was more to it, something else that had happened, which was impossible, of course, since I hadn't been there. I must have been muddling recollections from previous Chamber's social events. I had been to a few of them with Cathy over the years but couldn't recall ever meeting Matthew Campbell.

"Are you listening, Andrew?" Michael Shapiro stared at me over his specs.

"Yes, I'm sorry. It's a lot to take in."

"Of course, I told you this is not going to be easy, but you need to concentrate. Okay?"

I nodded to confirm, and he continued: "Matthew and Peter Cheung were lovers and so Matthew found it easy to persuade him to carry out what would be the first live human trial. Although he was shocked at the extent of Matthew's problems and his impending fall from grace, for gay Peter Cheung, the prospect of not only testing his theories but also retaining his lover's affections and dominant, powerful personality clothed in the gorgeous body of such a fit and healthy younger man, proved too much for him to resist. We suspected that both of them were simplifying profound concepts, maybe confusing the idea of self – what might be described as the soul – with memory: the education and experiences of a lifetime, which would not alter the genes of the host, the capacity and abilities of its own brain. Matthew was blinded by desperation, though, and Cheung by hubris, and we decided to authorise their plan since it represented a unique opportunity.

"Matthew was to emerge from his anaesthetic clothed in Andrew's body, free from threats of bankruptcy and police investigation which would die with Matthew's corpse. He would be able to confirm for us the expected assimilation of his sense of self, all his memories and personality, within the host. Living Andrew's life, he could continue to monitor and report on the procedure's efficacy over the long term, particularly by testing Cheung's expectation that all of the host's memories died and would not revert over time."

"So, my body – Andrew's body – should have lived on with Matthew's consciousness knowing exactly what had been done... Just what went wrong, then?"

"In one sense their research is far from complete. The process is flawed to the extent that simultaneous transfers of both sets of life memories between two individuals are not yet possible, because the brain dies immediately in the donor party from whom memory is taken, and with it the potential to accept new memories. This means one body perishes – the donor – along with the life memories, the original soul, if you like, of the surviving body and brain which has received its new memories and consciousness."

"But somehow," I said, "rather than what they intended, I'm still alive in Matthew's body, rather than his consciousness being alive within Andrew, within the body I still think of as my own?" I shuddered at the enormity of what he was telling me, still struggling to take it all in.

"Yes, that's right." He beamed at me, shifting his weight up from where he was leaning against the desk, pushing with the palms of his hands behind his back, as though about to propel himself forward in my direction. "Peter Cheung reversed the planned transfer at the last minute without our permission. So instead of your body surviving with Matthew's memories in place of your own, it is your memories that live on in his body. What he did has caused us untold problems, not to mention the lives of two women. But he knew his importance to the programme meant we could not touch him; he gambled we would cover the fallout and damage limitation since he had still provided the first human test, albeit much trickier to monitor going forward. And he was right, of course. When we realised what he had done, it was too late, a fait accompli, and there was no going back. If only Joe Peng or Jeremy Whicher had told us of his change of plan, but he bullied them into it at the last, threatened them with no human trial at all if he did not get his way… And all of them are vital to us for this research."

"But why?" I asked, leaning forward, resting my hands on both knees. "Why did he do that?"

"Because Cheung was provoked into a crazy, jealous rage. He told us the whole thing quite openly afterwards. Matthew had promised him his love and fidelity, assured him his marriage had long been a sham since he was now certain of his own gay sexuality. But then, just before your planned operation, Cheung discovered Matthew was having a secret affair and cheating on him with a woman.

"Cheung had agreed their 'relationship' should remain secret until Matthew found the right time to tell his wife. Private time between them was always at Cheung's flat in St John's Wood, and he had given Matthew a set of keys. Matthew had been obliged to reciprocate with keys to his house – a token Cheung had insisted upon – but it was understood he would not go there unannounced in case Helen was home. In fact, Cheung never sought to visit Matthew's home until the Saturday before the planned operations. He had been having second thoughts and wanted to discuss it again with his lover, tell him he'd stand by him whatever scandal erupted and suggest they did not take risks with his life. He was going to confess he wasn't really certain that it would be Matthew's soul waking within Andrew Soulsby's body.

"When he couldn't reach Matthew on the phone he went straight to the house, knowing Helen would be busy with rehearsals at the

National Theatre. He let himself in, parking in the street a discrete distance away, and waited in the drawing room. He heard the car crunching gravel soon after and spied Matthew through the window with the smart young girl from his office. She was all over him. Cheung heard them laughing in the hall, going straight upstairs.

"It was bad luck. We know Matthew had never taken Shivani there previously. We believe they had used his private office or her flat in Palmers Green or, occasionally, the Covent Garden flat. But we suspect, since Helen was in town, he couldn't resist showing off the house for what he knew would be the last time with her.

"Matthew never knew Peter Cheung left the house quietly that Saturday afternoon, his eyes opened to his lover's true nature, his heart set in steel as he plotted revenge: the death of Matthew's soul, all memory of who he was vanished, consumed within another; a life extinguished. But the public humiliation would remain, with his cheating beau condemned to endure punishment for crimes he could neither remember nor defend, his promiscuity dashed in the fond memories of a family man denied the love and touch of the woman he would crave. Poor Andrew Soulsby, the man you feel yourself to be, was an unfortunate casualty."

"So, who am I; still Matthew, really?" It was an astonishing prospect.

"I know it will be hard to understand and accept, but in a way, you are neither Andrew nor Matthew but a kind of hybrid form of them both – indisputably Matthew's flesh and bones but with Andrew's memories, perhaps his soul?"

"What does soul mean?" I said with a disgusted shudder. "It is just his memories substituted for my own."

"It's not that simple, is it? Aristotle described memory as 'the scribe of the soul'. Think of it, Andrew: every memory and experience, a lifetime of learning and knowledge – your sense of self?"

The solemn chimes from the hall clock caught the silence that followed, and his eyes sparkled to challenge and prompt my understanding as I contemplated what he had said, what it truly meant for me. Did memory really equate with what religions and mystics call the soul, the very essence of individuality?

We all consider ourselves born unique and individual, aware of our self or soul quite separate and distinct from the physical body. If what he had suggested were true, it would mean the soul is something every sentient being creates from the raw material of body and brain: a work in progress built and developed from the first moments of life, formed and evolving through all life experiences and education; templates creating individual uniqueness only through those experiences and variables of nurture.

"What you've done interferes with the individuality of all life." He did not answer. "So, what happens to me now?" I asked him in dread of the possible answers, unsure who I was or what I wanted to hear.

"It depends on you. Co-operation will be easy and bring the promise of a decent life." He was the beguiling charmer, the Devil's advocate reaping my soul. "It's mainly about what you must not do. No attempts to persuade anyone else of what has happened to you. Strictly, not a word to any living person… ever. And we will need regular checks, some tests and counselling sessions to observe brain function, to analyse behaviour and memories, that sort of thing. It's particularly important we ensure the process is permanent, and that none of Matthew's own memories are revived. If they are, we will need to know."

He smiled, as ever reassuring when he noticed my frown. "Try not to worry. We understand you would hate everything about Matthew's nature and personality. The possibility of any of the host's memories reviving is considered remote by Peter Cheung."

Although I still felt I was Andrew Soulsby, a good man, the man I wanted to remain, I knew he must be wrong. They were there, supressed but not destroyed, remnants of his life lurking in my DNA: certainly, his body with its frailties and predilections; the woman raped in a dream that must really have happened in the bedroom of

Matthew's flat; the recognition of my office at Dorrell's last Monday – not déjà vu at all; the dream of a schoolboy, a young Matthew, I suspected. How many more would eventually resurface? And there were the subtle changes to my attitudes and perceptions – I didn't think that was imagined – the developing resilience, selfishness, really, which seemed to bother me less than it should.

I squirmed and shifted my position on the soft leather cushion but kept my own counsel about this for now, since instinct urged me to keep my doubts from Shapiro and his sinister agency. It was enough to cope with the revelation that I was the dishonest philanderer, the selfish man with his bent for Machiavellian cunning and intrigue, soon to be publicly humiliated as a common criminal. And yet I was not really that man; surely, he no longer existed? Shapiro had said I was a kind of hybrid of Andrew and Matthew.

To learn Matthew had been bisexual explained the frisson I felt when I saw that young man at the newspaper stand outside Leicester Square tube station, an obvious attraction that I had denied to myself as sexual in nature. Notwithstanding my liberal politics, I had found that difficult to accept; it did not seem right since it failed to accord with my personal experiences and the heterosexual orientation my memory told me was certain beyond doubt.

The truth was I had come to abhor Matthew as a cheat with his amoral, duplicitous personality – every aspect of the background, upbringing and education I felt was mine told me this – yet for all the power of that nurture, now I wasn't so sure, and the random image of Shivani which suddenly invaded my mind again caused no guilt, only an intense glow of pleasure. She was naked in a thunderous shower, soaping small breasts and erect nipples, laughing when I approached to join her. Was this another memory from Matthew's life or the fantasy of what I hoped for this evening? I struggled to dispel these thoughts as Michael Shapiro began speaking again.

"Providing we have your agreement, your full co-operation, we'll ensure you serve only one year in an open prison and keep you safe and comfortable. You will have the best medical attention throughout the rest of your life and sufficient money for your reasonable needs. We can also provide help to secure you modest employment, perhaps support work in a legal office. We should be able to get round any prohibitions imposed by the regulatory authorities.

"We anticipate you will always feel a close bond and affinity to those you view as your children, but you must never again acknowledge or have any contact with them. We have the necessary information – details of your estate and Cathy's, including the partnership life insurance monies owed by Peter Bright – and we can ensure it all passes to them. They would inherit a substantial amount and be left safe and financially secure."

"And if I don't agree to keep quiet and do what you want?"

Still his constant smile didn't falter, not even while he conveyed his chilling response: "That would certainly be unfortunate. If you talked, tried to convince others, it could place more lives at risk, even though the chance you would be taken seriously is remote. And complications may arise with that inheritance for your children… the law can sometimes be so unpredictable.

"As for you personally, at best a conviction for murdering Helen Campbell and Cathy Soulsby; at worst a decision to abort the experiment completely… I don't need to spell out what that would mean, do I?"

"Did I hear you right? I know your people are responsible for their deaths, not me. It's crazy to suggest I killed them." I put my head in my hands as the conspiracy of evil to either control or destroy me emerged.

"You need to remain calm," he said gently. "Helen's and Cathy's deaths were unfortunate – collateral damage, I'm afraid – but they knew too much, which meant there was no alternative for us. These last weeks have already taken a toll on you, and both of them were your wives in a sense, so after their deaths tonight, and with the criminal investigation ongoing, we feared your mental health may

269

suffer irreparable damage and so compromise the experiment. This is why the decision was made to tell you everything, explaining clearly to you the benefits of your co-operation and the consequences of your failure to do so. Hopefully, though, you can see now that it's going to be fine. Of course, you will need to comply, accept the new reality, and then, eventually, life will be good again... there will be fun." He sounded so laid back, so logical, it almost helped. "Have some water – take a few moments." He handed me the glass of water waiting on the desk, no doubt there in anticipation I would need it.

It was hard to believe that we were only minutes in a car from Chipping Barnet on the edge of the sprawling London conurbation. It was deathly quiet in the small hours of Friday morning in this leafy, prosperous suburb adjoining Hertfordshire fields. There were no noises from outside nor within the rambling house, just empty rooms and the sense of an unnatural peace.

I sipped the water, sitting up straight to do so, cradling the glass between my hands which were beginning to shake. Then I thought of what he had said – 'Life will be good again; there will be fun' – and more images flashed into my mind: the handsome young man at Leicester Square station; attractive women in summer clothes on the Underground; again, Shivani, her long, dark hair and brown eyes. They filled and calmed the voids of panic that had been building in my mind, reassured me as, eventually, I regained composure and perspective.

"So, you've framed me for both murders. But I thought Cathy's death was being passed off as suicide, and I presumed the police investigations of Helen's death would reveal no evidence of foul play, meaning the presumption of a tragic accident, or perhaps another suicide?"

He turned round and went back to sit in the chair behind my desk – was it really my desk? "Yes. Cathy's death will remain as a suicide," he told me, "Helen's the same or maybe an accident, unless the further evidence we have obtained as an insurance policy comes to light."

"How have you done that?" I was remarkably level-headed now, little more than curious. "How is it possible?"

"I'm not going into all the details, Andrew, but the agency does not deal in games of bluff. This is all very real."

"Even so, if I'm to treat your threats as credible, I need some idea of how it's been done."

That constant, almost smug smile faded at last, morphing into a frown while he considered, swivelling his chair towards the hall door, then slowly back to face me before he spoke. "A suicide verdict on Cathy could easily be overturned should later investigations reveal Matthew's unusual interest in her immediately after her husband's death, and his desire to meet with her, which Peter Bright would confirm was not welcomed."

His tone was sombre, a hint of concern as his face searched mine, uncertain, I suspect, whether I was capable of dealing with this. He paused, but I remained calm: he had no idea that I was contemplating a new future after finding Matthew's secret fortune – surely there must be one? – when there would be no imperative to work. And Shivani, the thought of her slender body, her passion, continued to lift my spirits, while the loss of Cathy and my family suddenly seemed distant, little more than background noise in my mind. But I knew never to admit any of this to him.

"Go on," I implored. "I'm okay; I want to know."

"There's much more unpleasant stuff we have on Matthew's history with women, and should this come to light, the post-mortem's finding – being supressed for now – that she had rough sex shortly before her death will become very significant, raising the spectre of rape. The DNA samples retained will, of course, turn out to match yours. Following the renewed investigation, a close neighbour will be found who saw you leaving the house at pretty much the same time the pathologist estimated death occurred. With such compelling new evidence, closer scrutiny will discredit the authenticity of the suicide note."

"I understand. And what about Helen?"

I think he was surprised and certainly encouraged by my outwardly calm acceptance of the conspiracy to entrap me. His further explanation came swiftly: "We could produce CCTV footage at Leicester Square tube station showing both of you engaged in animated conversation moments before she died. It would not be difficult for our experts to doctor images that follow on the crowded platform, to reveal you in close proximity just after she has inexplicably fallen onto the line in front of a train…" I shuddered at their callous disregard for life, the ruthless yet meticulous planning which must have been called for, as he continued: "A broken man on a killing spree with a history of violence towards women, and no shortage of witnesses to confirm what a tempestuous relationship he had had with Helen over many years…"

He fell silent with a shrug, his gaze still intent upon me, awaiting the inevitable capitulation to their will. It was a sinister and frightening revelation: I was the victim of not only Peter Cheung and his cronies at Wilkinson's, but, ultimately, a secret department of our own security service. They had fostered heinous human experimentation then resorted to murder and blackmail in order to cover it up.

"I have no alternative, do I? Not if I want the chance for some kind of life and future." Matthew's voice boomed from my lips, exuding a philosophical resignation towards the inevitable.

"More than some kind of life, Andrew." He became animated with what appeared, as always, to be genuine enthusiasm for my welfare. "After one year in open prison, a very good life: you'll have superb medical care and be free to live, pretty much, as you wish – the experiment would be flawed if there was any control over conduct beyond your silence and obligation to live for the world as Matthew – but, of course, there would be no further protection if you broke the law in any way, whether a mere speeding fine or a murder charge. You would be on your own then; you need to appreciate that."

The frisson of excitement I was beginning to feel for an uncertain future owed more to a growing confidence in my ability to eventually overcome their control than his false enthusiasm for my welfare, and although I had no real choice in the matter, I tried my luck, employing all the slow gravitas of Matthew's polished tones: "I do understand that, of course, and you will have my full co-operation for so long as your agency sticks to its side of the deal." His craggy face once more cracked a homely smile, and I let my words hang for just a moment, before adding, with a hint of intimidation, "Provided you make the nonsense of one year in prison disappear. The evidence of power and influence you've described to me suggests it will be easy to lean on the National Crime Agency to drop the investigation or, at least, arrange a deal that avoids prison. Give me that and we have an agreement."

His mask slipped into a scowl and, as he replied, I was reminded of the powerful voice that had boomed down the custody suite on Monday afternoon. "It's not possible, Andrew. Matthew's crimes are very serious and already known to many people. We would prefer to avoid the publicity of trial and prison, but there is a limit on what can be fixed." His elbows dropped on the desk, shrugged shoulders slumping forward, his angry eyes fixing mine. "You need to understand there is no option for you to bargain with us. You either accept what's on offer or endure the consequences. And should you fail to comply, strictly, with our arrangement, we will always find out, as sure as night follows day, and be in no doubt what would happen then, no doubt at all. Do you understand this, Andrew?"

"Yes, of course... I had to try." I attempted an unconvincing laugh. "I agree. I know I have to."

"Good." He rose from the chair, walking towards the open door leading into the hall, and I knew the meeting was about to end.

"There are still things I'd like to know," I said, standing up and moving to join him. "If only to satisfy my curiosity. I know the implications if I breathe a word."

"What things?"

"Is Matthew's consultant involved; did she help to synchronise the timing of both operations? She seemed so genuine when I spoke to her."

"You're too naïve, Andrew, not like the man whose shoes you stand in. But, as it happens, your instinct was correct. It was not that difficult to fix up Matthew's pending operation at very short notice. A vital case, unexpectedly coming to trial soon, requiring a pristine voice urgently, and Penny Simms agreed to make it happen. Money always talks. And she ran away on cue to our contrived emergency immediately after the throat surgery, before the anaesthetic had worn off. She was easy to play."

"Alex Grayling, the coroner, must be part of it, though? It was his dereliction of duty, failing to call for a post-mortem on my body."

"You'd already worked that out, hadn't you? He's a major investor in the company and a good friend of Cheung as well as Matthew.

"And I was being followed, watched most of the time, wasn't I? And always will be now, I guess?" I couldn't disguise the irritation in my voice, masking an anger too dangerous to reveal.

"Yes, followed and monitored, often with technology, but rarely by those you suspected. It will continue to ensure both your protection and your compliance… Try to forget it and live your new life."

I did not respond; what could I say since he had already made clear that I had no other options? My mind spun a medley of tangled thoughts, like the teeming words hiding in those legal tomes staring down at me from the bookshelves. I wondered if he appreciated how stupid his entreaty sounded, as though I could just forget that I was to be an experimental specimen, forced to 'live my new life' in a human goldfish bowl. He must have read the consternation on my face.

"It is necessary that you appreciate the level of scrutiny, the degree of supervision, you must accept, although most of the time you won't know it's happening. You will get used to it, Andrew, believe me."

"Have your agents been in this house, or have I imagined the invisible presence of strangers? I've felt it often. Once, I went out and left a *Guardian* newspaper in the hall. No one else was home, but when I got back later, I found *The Times* in its place. Were you responsible, or has my memory, Andrew's memory, been damaged by the transplant? I really need to know if I'm to have any chance."

He considered this, I think uncertain how to reply, if at all. He began to pace the red carpet covering most of the oak flooring in the study, stopping to gaze at his reflection through the French doors against the black void of night, as though this might inform his decision. The grandfather clock in the hall chimed to count another quarter-hour, a sign from the gods that appeared to settle his mind, and he turned to face me.

"I guess there's no harm in you being told now. The new gardener was one of our men. He lifted the housekeeper's keys for long enough to have another set cut, allowing us to come and go as we wanted. So, we've been able to watch and listen to everything in the house, and plant bugs on you. We also put surveillance equipment into the Cheltenham Avenue house. It means you've been observed and monitored like a baby in a pen twenty-four seven, Andrew." Then, he added as an afterthought, "Of course, in future this level of scrutiny should ease off a little, and there will be no medical or other tests without your knowledge." I suspected this was a lie to appease my sensibilities, as if such scant consolation – were it true – would make me feel better.

"What about the newspapers?" I asked.

"One of the things we have been checking on is memory function and, so far, you pass with flying colours. The newspaper test was part of this. They were swapped to check if you would notice and also to confirm your choice of Andrew's regular read had been no coincidence. Then there was the disabled alarm, used as another test, when you returned to an empty house after the funeral."

"And Cheung's missing details and telephone numbers – down to you?"

"They were removed from Matthew's phone records because it was important you had no contact or knowledge at first, to enable your conduct and reactions to be gauged and assessed. We needed to check on the initial success of the process, and it helped that both Peter Cheung and Joe Peng left to attend the annual conference of The Society for Neuroscience, only returning for the funeral… to observe your reactions.

"There will be investigations in greater depth soon with sessions of counselling and hypnotherapy to delve within your implanted memory and ensure it matches completely what our research has revealed of Andrew Soulsby's life. We want to check no strands of Matthew's memories remain to complicate your new existence and compromise the integrity of the project's potential."

This confirmed my earlier instincts; God knows what they would do to me if they found out some of his memories appeared to be coming through, not to mention the growing confidence of his personality. Unless, of course, the hypnosis had started already: the sense, last week, someone had been in my bedroom while I thought I was asleep; those fugue-like panic attacks that had devoured lost time from my life. If so, they might already suspect echoes of memory from Matthew's past – I struggled to accept it yet as my own real past – had been preserved. It was essential to conceal as best I could any evidence casting doubt on the complete success of their experiment: I think I had read somewhere that it is not difficult to resist hypnosis.

I asked him bluntly, "Have I been subjected to this already, without my knowledge?"

"Of course not," he said irritably, the mask of sympathetic understanding slipping momentarily again. "How could that happen? It would be impossible without your co-operation.

"Look, I know this is difficult." His voice reassumed its kindly tone, such hypocrisy. "So much to take in. I think, perhaps, we should leave it for now." He eased from the French doors behind the desk to stand beside me. I dwarfed his short, stocky frame but somehow still felt the menace of his presence invading my personal space, made all the more sinister by his guise of smiling concern.

His right hand moved to fish a thick wallet and small box from a pocket in his jeans. "Here, take these. Sleeping pills, some cash and a credit card. Two of the pills – no more – before bed. You may need them for a while. The card is in a false name, you'll see, but it will work up to a limit of five thousand pounds for now. Enough, with the cash, to keep you going. The pin is the year of your birth."

"What happens next?" I asked him, trying to conceal the strange mix of trepidation and excitement in my heart as I pocketed the pills and opened the wallet to scan, briefly, the card and wad of twenty-pound notes. Was it enough to disappear, move on frequently and lose their bugs, find Matthew's hidden fortune I felt sure existed? But at what risk and odds against their resources, particularly when I would have to use a credit card they could trace? And, anyway, I knew that the temptation of Shivani would prove irresistible.

"I suggest you leave here before 8am on Monday morning when the bailiffs are due. If you decide to take up with Shivani Kapoor," he said, reading my thoughts, "try to keep it low-key, and be very careful. Should the police find out, it becomes more difficult for us to keep you out of prison until the trial, whenever that comes, because of the breach in bail conditions – remember, no contact with anyone from Dorrell's. She'd be in trouble too, but she gets off on the illicit affair, so you ought to have no problem with her co-operation to keep it all secret."

"When will I see you again?"

"You will have the pleasure of my company again soon enough, when you're re-arrested – probably about two or three months from now, I would guess – at one of your weekly visits to the police station under the bail arrangements."

"Will I be kept in custody for long?" The thought of that small, solitary cell made my heart begin to race and my mouth run dry.

He placed a soft, chubby hand firmly on my shoulder for reassurance, and I had to resist the instinct to pull away from him.

"No. Nothing too onerous. If they charge you early enough, you could be bailed by the magistrates' court and out again on the same day. I expect DCI Doyle will time it to ensure you have to spend one night in a police cell – we have no control over her – but plenty of time out then before the trial, probably about nine months on remand.

"Just remember," he stared at me solemnly, "make absolutely no comments to them; silence; say nothing at all," he emphasised. "Whatever the provocation, unless and until I am with you. Okay?"

"Sure," I replied, feeling the physical relief when he removed his hand from my shoulder and turned to go, before stopping to face me after only a couple of paces.

"There's one more thing," he said, almost apologetically. "To the world you are Matthew Campbell, not Andrew Soulsby. You must get used to that in your mind. From now on I'll be calling you 'Matthew'; that's how it has got to work." He paused to let this sink in, but from what I had just learnt this was no more than recognition of a harsh, biological reality. In the silence engulfing us in that moment, I could almost hear the tectonic plates shifting in my brain, acknowledging a new emotional dawn; or perhaps they were merely reassuming their rightful position?

"Good luck, Matthew." He broke the spell, and before I could utter another word he strode out of the study, his footsteps echoing across the expanse of tiles in the hall until I heard the heavy front door clunk shut.

NOW

CHAPTER 36

We have not left the hotel suite since checking in at 10.30 yesterday morning. Great sex with Shivi and top-notch grub from room service with plenty of Champagne on ice, my first day of freedom lived up to expectations and then some.

We go 'home' tomorrow – Shivi's flat in Palmers Green. Today, she wants us to drive into Brighton, but I'm keen on more sex first; frankly, I can't get enough of her, she's such a lovely little thing.

When she emerges from the bathroom – at last – I take her in my arms and kiss her on the lips, but they remain clasped together, shut tight like a chastity belt. As my hands drift down her slender waist, wandering to enjoy the contours of her slim body, she pulls away, wriggling free with a playful laugh.

"I meant what I said, Matt." Her brown eyes are wide open, sparkling like fine gems. "We must hurry for breakfast to get the best of the day in Brighton. I need to dry my hair first though, and you have to get ready."

"Let's make time," I say. "It's still early, only just turned eight o'clock."

She frowns, crinkling her small nose delightfully. "No, Matt." Again, that insistent tone. "It's sunny and warm now but forecast for heavy rain later this afternoon. I want us to have plenty of time to walk along the promenade, and the pier, and the famous Lanes." She sounds animated, almost like an excited child. "So, you'll have to wait until this evening, Rambo!" She laughs, kissing my forehead, then flits across the lush, green carpet of the bedroom and takes out a hairdryer from her bedside cabinet.

I fight the urge to make her, since I've become fond of her. And I need to keep her sweet, not only for the certainty of regular sex but also to provide shelter for an ex-convict, currently of modest means. I don't want to rely on the Research Development Agency for help and support, so I amble off to the bathroom to shower, alone with my thoughts.

I convince myself a day in Brighton will be interesting. She believes I have only distant memories of one visit there nearly forty years ago, and, of course, she must never know the truth. But it should prove a good test of just how far I have come over the last two years; the extent to which I can discard emotions and sentimentality when experiencing another man's memories and pain, visiting his familiar haunts and special places. I will know it all, remember and feel the intense love and affection he had for his wife, revisiting the joys of their anniversaries. It might not be easy to appear calm and happy, keen to enjoy the experiences of a new city. And yet, I am confident: I'll be fine.

At first it had been so difficult, willing my conscious mind to ignore emotions calling from a past that had seemed anything but false. Too much alcohol helped to deaden the pain, and the affection from Shivi, not to mention the sex, was a comfort to me in the year before the trial. But it was really the time in prison that helped me come to terms with myself, to begin to understand who I am now, and feel a sense of purpose and hope for my future.

Perhaps it was the experience of deprivation and lost liberty, the hardships and strange combinations of human spite, greed and friendship. The shock had been extreme and forced me to confront the truth, to fashion a new persona, learning from basic human values so harshly exposed by prison life.

I now accept that I'm not Andrew Soulsby, not the person churning in my mind, still trying to infect my emotions with his grieving for a murdered wife and yearning for adult children who must never be acknowledged. This is false, not me, and yet as my moods swing, sometimes it still feels like a crushing burden that is so hard to suppress: another man's life masquerading in my head.

I need to dwell on my progress since Michael Shapiro told me the truth. I have come to recognise Andrew's extreme sense of loyalty is not normal. Most of the time I can control his over-blown conscience, impose what I feel sure must be my own personality, which only appeared distasteful to me before through the prism of Andrew's narrow outlook. When I am strong, I can keep his conscience at bay and see it for the fallacy it is, just an illusion afflicting the weak-minded: like the romantic love he believed in, conscience is a fantasy that restricts and inhibits careers and joie de vivre, contributing to mental illness and ruined lives.

I'm determined to reclaim my own soul and not let him spoil what chance I have of finding pleasure and happiness. I think of the way that pretty receptionist, Janice, with her thick, dark hair in a ponytail, reacted to me. I can charm women, they are attracted to me, and I intend to enjoy my new future with as many women as possible. Apart from Shivi while it suits me, why should I contemplate any emotional attachments?

There is no doubt that things are changing quickly for me now: since regaining my liberty yesterday, I can almost feel the evolution of my new-self happening with gathering pace. The agency must never know. To them I must remain Andrew in Matthew's body, their experiment a complete success. As long as they believe that, I think they will want to keep me safe. But I intend to research my history in secret, learn everything I can about my true self and the life and experiences this body has encountered. I hope to reclaim something from the destruction of my memories, to find the essence of my real personality. I often wonder whether Andrew Soulsby would have, eventually, sought to reclaim his history and life, his own destroyed memories, if the experiment had proceeded as planned?

I have spent long hours brooding on the agency's protection and encouragement of the cabal at Wilkinson's. Their sponsorship of sinister research has led to three callous murders and blown my mind, like a specimen eggshell, to be stuffed with a dead man's memory. Simmering resentment has fed a growing desire to expose them all, if only I can devise a scheme devoid of any risk to me.

But first I must break free, escape their clutches, and before it is too late. I'm not sure I can hide from them indefinitely what is happening to me. I am experiencing more flashbacks of what must be my own memories, although I can't claim to feel ownership of them yet. And in the last few days there has been something new: some of Andrew's childhood memories, things they expect me to know, are beginning to fade. I remember his primary-school friends were close, but I can no longer see them in my mind, nor recall their names.

Even in prison they insisted on continuing the three-monthly sessions to review my 'progress'. So far, they have always taken the form of an MRI brain scan (which can't be good for me, whatever they say), along with tests and questions relating, mostly, to Andrew's life and memories. The next one is due in less than two months. I want to be gone before then, which doesn't leave me long.

The key is to find Matthew's money, my money. I had received confirmation at my trial that substantial funds stolen from Dorrell's clients are still not accounted for, so I propose to discover, then access this hidden fortune, which is probably accruing interest for me now with various shell companies offshore. Such wealth should provide options, so long as I ensure the agency remain ignorant of my investigations: perhaps I might choose a completely fresh life with a new identity, free from surveillance in a secret location somewhere very distant and very warm. I believe I could persuade Shivi to come with me, run away with the man she adores. The fondness I feel for her must be a weakness inherited from Andrew, but the idea appeals to me.

Fresh from the shower, I emerge to find she is still drying her hair. I am compelled to stand behind her, entranced by her slender frame perched on a low stool at the dressing table, shaking back the cascading, black hair as she brushes out thick strands and whirls the dryer over them with such certainty of purpose. She must be aware of my face gazing upon her as our eyes meet through the looking glass, and I am tempted, once again, to fall upon her – just a few short strides from my grasp – rip the dress from that lithe, young body and insist on more sex. I take a step closer and the free-standing mirror vibrates gently, the reflection of her face quivering as though seen on the surface of a peaceful lake. It serves to emphasise her pale, gaunt expression and the need for me to remain patient, to wait at least until this evening.

I find myself thinking of Helen, who it turns out had been my real wife after all. If only I had known that my efforts to resist temptation were unnecessary, the call of loyalty to a dead man's love cruelly misplaced. On that Sunday, when I had confessed to Helen what I thought was an impossible truth, after we returned to the house late in the evening, I had sensed she wanted, even needed me, but I failed to respond, fighting what I perceived then as base instincts.

I often think of her, a fond memory from when I saw the world as Andrew Soulsby who had liked her very much; such an elegant, beautiful woman. I cannot begin to comprehend how or why I had allowed her to escape from the heart and bed of my former life. If only they had told me earlier, before I had confided my secrets with Helen and Cathy, both could have lived on in ignorance of the truth, and perhaps I might have been reconciled with Helen?

I still find it difficult to comprehend the degree of desperation I must have been suffering from, the level of depression that must have afflicted me, to seek my own sure death, merely in the hope of preserving the memories and knowledge of my life in the mind of another man. I can only be thankful for the twist of fate that caused Peter Cheung's vindictive change of plan. It saved my life, allowing me the chance to reclaim my own personality, uniquely enhanced by another man's perspective and experiences, and, free of a long prison sentence, I also have a chance to find that hidden fortune.

But for now, there is the day to enjoy with a young woman who adores me, and the delightful prospect of much more sex with her tonight. Life will be good again, just as Michael Shapiro predicted. I catch the glint of her eyes as she switches the dryer off at last and continues to pull the brush through her flowing hair.

I say, "I can't bear to let you out of my sight, sweetheart," and watch her lips purse a thin smile. I have such a way with women: she is besotted with me.

"Don't worry, Matt." Her soft, enticing voice is almost voluptuous in its intensity. "Now I have you back, my darling, I'm never letting you out of my sight again."

CHAPTER 37

It's 11.15am and I'm walking past the Royal Courts of Justice towards Fleet Street. I sense a strong familiarity with the place, this whole street scene, but I can't put my finger on it yet, claim definite ownership of it as belonging to me. It must, though, I know, because Andrew's memory tells me that he came here only once as a hapless articled clerk, embarrassed and anxious, trying to stamp legal documents. Having cocked it up, he stuck to the provinces and a routine career of mundane, non-contentious conveyancing.

We've been back from the hotel in Arundel for five days now, and I've made little progress in researching the history of my life, beyond confirmation that I am – more correctly was – a shit-hot City lawyer specialising in commercial litigation, first-class Oxford University degree and married to an accomplished actress (who liked to be called 'an actor', for Christ's sake), now deceased. All of which I pretty much already knew – although learning of the first from Oxford gave me a buzz. I've found nothing else useful online, apart from bucketloads of the salacious stuff about my trial, striking-off, bankruptcy and fall from grace. How we Brits love a good scandal; and yes, it hurts, more so as my sense of self has slowly fought to replace Andrew.

So, no 'eureka' moment yet, although earlier this week, when Shivi discussed some of the older cases I would have been dealing with, for the first time I felt something, not exactly remembering, more a nagging memory of a memory, the sense that I should have recalled some of it. She's been doing this for the last two years, particularly when I was on remand before the trial, trying to coax back my memory. There was no chance then, of course, when Andrew was still so strong. At the trial, retrograde amnesia was the basis of my mitigation, a contrivance pursued by Michael Shapiro. Strange to think that it was true, that my real memories were being suppressed by another man's. No one had really believed such an excuse, of course, except Shivi, blinded by love and knowing nothing of the conspiracy, always believing I was her 'Matty', genuinely plagued by amnesia.

She's been pleased with my progress this week, though. I've contributed usefully to our discussions – again a first – evidencing a detailed knowledge of commercial law and litigation procedure. Stuff Andrew would not know. It just comes naturally when Shivi prompts me. I think my legal brain is coming back, while the property law that was Andrew's bread and butter is becoming more difficult to recall. I still have a rough idea of that but not much more than the smattering I had always possessed. Andrew's expertise, if you can call it that, is definitely fading, all the boring conveyancing cases I could recall even a month ago, almost all gone now. There's little doubt what's happening to me signifies the failure of their first human trial, which is why it's so important to escape before the next session due with the agency's medics in less than seven weeks.

They'd informed me at the very first session, not long after Michael Shapiro had told me what they'd done, that I would only retain Matthew's physical characteristics, like his addiction to cigarettes, his brain power, high blood pressure and the skill I would apparently discover if I went on the golf course! They had explained it was my mind that had changed – a new memory of a 'kind' man's life, they had said – so all my attitudes and opinions, my temperament, were transformed, although the original sexual appetite and innate, physical things would remain. Of course, as I've felt my personality slowly returning, I've ensured to hide it from them at our sessions, always presenting them with the demure, reserved man, the timorous Andrew Soulsby they expect. But I'm not sure if I can keep it from them next time. It would come down to luck: how many more of Andrew's memories I lose in the meantime and, crucially, what questions they ask. Risks I don't want to take.

I'm due to meet Shivi when she leaves the office at about 6.30 this evening. We've got a table booked for dinner at Rules as it's the first Friday back in London since my release. Her treat, of course. I can live with it: what a gem she is! So, anyway, I decided to come up to town this morning, wander round for the day and hope something clicks here in Matthew's – my – backyard. It's a long shot, but what's to lose?

I realise that I've been standing on the pavement staring vacantly at the law courts, deep in thought for the last five minutes. I'm almost certainly on film. I need to go in there, run the gauntlet of security checks and look round, see what happens. But perhaps it would be sensible to leave that till later; right now, what I fancy is to sit down with a coffee and something sweet and comforting.

And then I see him, coming from the massive Gothic entrance of the Royal Courts of Justice, skipping smartly down the steps, not more than ten yards from me: the stooping, lean frame of Timothy Green QC, no doubt hot foot from a fat fee and still wearing his white tunic shirt with wing collar and studs under a pinstriped, black suit.

Andrew may have seen him at the odd function with Cathy – I can't be sure from his remaining memories in my head – but this recognition is immediate and strong. I know his voice before he speaks and notice the flicker of annoyance – or is it embarrassment? – as he looks up to find my bulky frame right in front of him, impossible to avoid.

"Matt, such a long time no see, old man." He is beaming at me now. "How are you?"

"Bearing up under the strain, Tim," I say as we shake hands. I have called him 'Tim' and, incredibly, it all comes to me: we're in the same Masonic Lodge; we have known each other since I first joined Dorrell's, over thirty-four years ago; and we've always had a good business relationship, meeting up socially quite often over the years. These are real memories prompted by seeing him here, and the first time I've been sure of Matthew's memories, felt them as my own.

"How is Hannah?" His wife's name has just popped into my head, and I remember the silly bitch: always plastered in make-up but plain with tree-trunks for legs, and a risible snob. We'd sneaked away once at a drunken party – his house in Dulwich, I think – and I'd only just managed it with her, a combination of copious booze and her lack of sex appeal. I recall she was so damn keen, though.

"Bleeding me dry as usual." He snorts a laugh down his pointed nose. "Between all the charity work, she still finds time to spend my money… But how are you, really?" He affects a concerned frown. "The wealthy City lawyer, 'bearing up under the strain', always raised a laugh, but now it's no joke. You've had a bad time of it, Matt."

"It's been an interesting couple of years," I say as he raises a quizzical eyebrow. "Look, have you got half an hour? I was about to get a coffee." I'm hoping to prolong our conversation, see if more memories will come.

"Well…" He glances at his watch, obviously wanting to be rid of the social embarrassment who no longer provides briefs helping to fund this QC's lavish lifestyle. "I have a bundle of documents to review, before another application over there this afternoon." He shrugs, nodding over his shoulder to indicate the Gothic pile behind him.

"Only a quick coffee. It would be good to catch up, even if it's only for ten minutes or so."

I think he is a tad curious, and certainly it would be awkward to refuse me, so we find a table in Soho Coffee, directly opposite, and both get a cappuccino. I'm buzzing with excitement, even before the caffeine. Parts of my life are coming back to me at last, not just those snippets I've previously experienced and still can't place as definitely belonging to me.

"So, I owe you an apology, Matt. I should have enquired after you, made time for a visit." I know he doesn't mean this, but I smile politely. "I've been so frantically busy, and it all became a little awkward, I suppose... You know how it is, old man?"

I do. Rats always desert the sinking ship, but I say what is expected: "Of course, think no more of it, Tim. There was nothing anyone could have done, and to be honest, I have only myself to blame."

"Well, you did always have expensive tastes" – pot, kettle, black, methinks – "and a certain reputation with the fair gender. It must have been a shock for you, though, when Helen died?"

"Yes," I say in my gravest voice, "a dreadful accident. She was such a lovely woman. I fear that I treated her very badly."

"Umm..." His bottom lip protrudes as his head nods almost imperceptibly. It's obvious that he heartily agrees with that assessment but doubts my sincerity. "And poor Cathy Soulsby from my Chambers. Another tragedy at the same time. You knew her as well." He says this definitively, no hint of conjecture.

"No, I don't recall meeting her." I can't yet fully suppress the pain and suffering of Andrew's memories when I think of Cathy. And her son and daughter. It still hits me sometimes, less frequently now, but when it does, I have to fight the urge to find out how those two youngsters are coping.

"Come on, Matt." He smirks. "I saw you both together at a Chamber's party, shortly before your life imploded, old man. No Helen with you, as per, and Cathy's husband had had to work late, she'd told me. Very cosy all evening. And I saw you both sneaking away. It had surprised me – that's why it's stuck in my memory – because I knew she was a strict Catholic who'd always seemed devoted to her husband. He's the chap you met just before you went AWOL for your operation. You told me at the time you were impressed and had decided to use him for some personal bits and pieces, routine conveyancing and such like. I remember thinking it was strange, and if I hadn't known you better, I'd have suspected a guilty conscience." He laughs, not really a friendly laugh. "Presumably you heard the poor chap died under the surgeon's knife? It was about the same time your throat was being snipped in readiness for the Wilkinson hearing, or so you fondly thought at the time."

"Yes," I respond, dumbstruck at the further memories flooding back. "I did hear about it." Of course. Suddenly I'm home. The George pub, the law courts, my offices near London Bridge: the backdrop to my professional life for nearly thirty-five years. And Pump Court; no coincidence that Andrew's Cathy was in the same Chambers as the lead counsel in Wilkinson. That's how I found my perfect host, although, as it turned out, I ended up hosting him!

I need a few moments alone, but I don't want him to leave yet. "Excuse me, Tim. I won't be two shakes." I smile, indicating the toilets with a turn of my head, as I scrape back the chair and walk smartly towards them before he has time to make his excuses and go.

I remember Cathy Soulsby from a wholly different perspective now, my own memory of her, no longer with Andrew's heartache and blinkered vision of perfection. The woman's face in my dream, beneath me on the bed, comes into focus at last: Cathy Soulsby!

It was after that Chamber's party. I recall she was rather drunk and fed up that her husband had been too busy at his office to accompany her. I had remembered Andrew from a previous Chamber's bash – that's right, I never did forget a face, did I, particularly pretty and handsome ones – and felt he would do just fine: a definite looker, rather younger than me and a lawyer to boot with a very serviceable wife. She was easy to play, and I relished the chance to charm her, then try her out that evening. She was on the plump side, but her buttocks and breasts were big in a voluptuous, sexy way that definitely turned me on, and she had a cute Yorkshire drawl.

I had let her ramble on about 'Andy'. He was working too hard and stressed, suffering from headaches. I'd given her my kindly, caring smiles – always helps to know when to be the attentive listener – although I'd turned off for most of it, concentrating only on the challenge of keeping eye contact and avoiding that great cleavage. But I picked up on his headaches, and then she let slip he was worrying about a commercial case, not in his comfort zone, acting for her uncle who was hoping to find a buyer soon for his hotel in Leeds.

Bingo! The meeting with Andrew was contrived pretty much as Michael Shapiro had explained. All I had had to do was put in a high offer for her uncle's ropey hotel through one of my shell companies, then arrange a meet with 'Andy' to waffle about technicalities when the conveyancing – which was never going to reach exchange – was underway. I'd sympathised (I remember, I'm really good at that): he didn't look well; such a worry about his headaches, he really should get them checked out. And kind, personable Matthew Campbell had the perfect recommend: Peter Cheung, who was nuts about me and putty in my hands. It was easy.

I thought nobody had seen us slope away early from the party that evening. Funny how things turn out, though, because if Tim hadn't clocked us there would have been no sarcastic revelation to me just now, and without that catalyst, when, if ever, would I have reclaimed this swathe of my life?

It hadn't gone so well back at the flat in Covent Garden, I recall. "Let's have a nightcap, and think how I can send you some briefs," I'd cajoled her, and she'd been up for it, arm in arm, laughing and giggling all the way along the Strand. It was way beyond flirting, and she knew as well as I did that my City commercial law practice would have no work for a junior criminal law barrister, however sexy she was.

When we got there, I'd given her another drink, then suggested a 'tour' of the flat, and she'd giggled some more, following me to the bedroom. She had responded well at first, happy for me to stick my tongue in her mouth, but then, when I'd pushed her down on the bed, it was all change: trying to get away from me, something about her kids and, as I might have expected, her boring husband. (If only she'd known how I had intended to liven him up for her!) Stupid cow.

Well, I couldn't accept that. I was too far gone not to have her then, one way or another. What the hell did she expect? I get it now, though, why she had been against Andrew taking up my recommendation to consult with Peter Cheung – how could she have told him the real reason she didn't trust me? – and it explains her reaction, the shocked look on her face, when, believing I was Andrew, I had turned up on her doorstep to offer my condolences.

***

When I get back from the toilet, Tim is still there. Good.

"Sorry about that; call of nature."

"Rumour has it that you are with Shivani Kapoor now, Matt?"

"Rumour is right. I'm very fond of her."

"Right." He smiles, clearly finding my professed fondness for Shivi hard to swallow. "She still briefs me, and George and Martin; plenty of work from her, in fact, since Wilkinson settled."

"Yes, I know. She talks of you all," I say, trying to remember 'George' and 'Martin'.

"She's clever. Double first from Oxford, wasn't it? It would be a shame to waste such talent. She could go far in my humble opinion." He always was a pompous bugger. I know what he's implying, though, and to be honest I can't feel any interest in her career. "Tell me, Matt, is it the intellect that attracts you, or the flowing, dark hair and pretty face?" No pretence of a smile, this is definitely an admonishment. Hypocritical bastard, he's only really bothered about her as a source of increasingly lucrative brief fees.

"Why not both?" I laugh.

"I need to be off." He eases from his chair. "It's been interesting to see you, Matt." He starts to leave, not offering to shake my hand this time, then turns back, his tall body leaning over the table towards me, like a sapling caught in a stiff breeze. "I almost forgot. Those confidential papers you gave to me. I still have them in my room in Chambers. Do you want them, or shall I bin them, given events?"

"I'll have them back, thanks," I tell him instinctively, but he must pick up from my expression that I have no idea what he is talking about.

"You've forgotten, haven't you? The large, fat envelope you gave me on the Friday before your throat surgery. You asked me to keep it safe and sealed to respect your privacy, but should you die 'under the knife', I was to give it to Andrew Soulsby and tell him his firm had a big new probate since you'd appointed him as your executor. I thought it was slightly melodramatic given you were only having a minor operation. But what a coincidence, Matt, that the poor fellow should be having his own operation around the same time and not survive it."

I remember now, such a vital memory to reclaim. "Yep, it was tragic. And perhaps not so anal of me to be cautious when you consider his fate." He doesn't look convinced. "I felt sorry for the guy," I lie, "thought it would be a profitable surprise for him in the event Penny Simms encountered fatal problems with my less than perfect heart. Who'd have thought it was his name on the surgeon's scalpel?" I smirk and see Tim wince – probably not the best of taste – but inside I'm jumping for joy. It has come to me, how I'd planned it all, written down the names, account numbers, pins and security details to access the fortune that *is* stashed offshore. No wonder I'd been suicidal at the thought I would have to spend years in prison, deprived of my retirement nest egg. That's why my desperate plan had been hatched, and Tim would have handed all the details to me, safe and sound, when I presented to the world –

and buxom, little Cathy, keen and enthusiastic then, no doubt – as Andrew Soulsby.

"I'll pop round with you now to collect them," I say, and as I get up, I also recall the false passport and ID documents within the envelope, the precaution that will have proved so prescient. Perfect.

CHAPTER 38

"Matt, it's so sunny, let's drive to Rock after lunch, then get the ferry into Padstow or walk round the sands to Daymer Bay." Shivani lays her paperback on the lawn beside the lounger and rests a hand on my arm. "This is a lovely place. Do you think we'll be able to come back to England, back here, for holidays?"

There's no chance, of course, but I look up from yesterday's *Sunday Telegraph Review* and pretend to consider this. "I don't see why not, if we're careful. We shall both have new identities, after all."

I told her my plans over dinner yesterday evening: a fresh start for both of us in India with new identities and access to the fortune stolen from wealthy clients over many years. We'll be very rich and, for me, no longer living with the stigma of bankruptcy and the disgrace of professional ruin. Everything is organised – tickets, false passports – ready to leave in a couple of weeks. I've been busy since the fortuitous meeting with Timothy Green just over two weeks ago. Not that she knows anything about that.

Involving Shivi represents a slight risk, of course, but I have become fond of her – can't seem to shake that feeling off yet – not to mention the great sex on tap; and then there's her invaluable knowledge of India and its languages from all the extended summer holidays she has spent there with her parents. My calculations were bang on, though: she bought into the scheme. When I explained about the funds offshore, what a very naughty boy I'd been, she was more excited than shocked, I think, and we had frenetic sex most of last night. The whole business really turns her on, just as I thought it would.

I wonder what she'd make of it if she knew the truth, and my need to escape the agency before the next assessment due in about a month's time. But I must never risk telling her. And she's already aware of the need for absolute discretion and secrecy, buzzing with the anticipation of helping me to spend so many millions of pounds. Which suits me for now. "Just think how far the money will go in India; we'll *never* be able to spend it all," she whispered to me last night as I moved within her.

"How about an early lunch?" I say, putting down the newspaper and making to get off my lounger. "We haven't eaten those fancy, wild boar sausage rolls you bought in the Wadebridge deli yesterday morning. Shall I get them now and rustle up a few sandwiches as well?" Hopefully she will take the hint and I can relax here a bit longer in the sun.

"Wait here, Matt." Excellent, just the job, Shivi. "There's something else I fancy before food." This gets better. "When I left you to finish the wine after dinner in Padstow last night, most of the shops were still open and I found some gorgeous, sexy underwear. Give me ten minutes, then come to the bedroom. Promise, it's worth the wait," she pouts, jumping up, and I settle on the lounger again, watching her sway across the lawn in a tiny, blue bikini, down steps to the sunken patio and beyond, through glass sliding doors into the lounge. As if I need sexy underwear, but I mustn't disappoint her... I know she enjoys that even more than me.

I light up a cigarette and inhale, looking round this large, enclosed garden. It's all so secluded, a luxury holiday cottage for two in its own private grounds, detached and solitary, yet only ten minutes in the car from Rock in North Cornwall. It was a good choice.

Everything has turned out well in the end. It's been worth all the trauma: bankruptcy; prison; the fight to regain my sense of self and personality from another man (and such a pompous wimp as well!), a process turbo-charged on leaving prison, particularly the catalyst of stumbling across Timothy Green in the Strand a fortnight ago. I'm still not one hundred per cent there yet, but I'm sure it's only a matter of time now.

I have remembered so much from my past, even my less-than-happy childhood. The image of the young boy in the conservatory was me, of course, the woman my cold mother. I felt nothing for her, and never saw her during the last twenty years of her joyless life. The bald man was my stepfather, and the prime mover, I suspect, of bundling me off to boarding school when I was eight. I have no recollection of my real father, beyond a vague sense of being informed he had been a dashing fighter pilot in the war who never settled to family life. Whether he died or deserted my mother and me is unclear.

I have strong memories, though, of dreading the school holidays, going 'home' to Wadebridge in Cornwall. I've not been back since childhood, but it was family, not the place, I hated, and something has called me here for one final visit before I leave the UK for good. And the beautiful surroundings of the Camel estuary have provided a perfect setting to reveal my plans to Shivi; she hasn't stopped going on about how romantic this part of Cornwall is.

She was due holiday, and the way she slaves for them, Dorrell's had no choice but to let her have a week at short notice. Picking this remote cottage up as a last-minute cancellation means that it's unlikely the agency could keep tabs on us here – even if they wanted to. They believe the experiment is still going well and there's no reason for them to be suspicious yet. Just to be on the safe side, though, I'd chosen last night's dinner venue at random as we strolled round the harbour in Padstow and gone for a buzzy, quay-side place with stunning views.

If I'm honest, Andrew is with me still, but only as a jumble of fast-fading memories. Although many parts of my own life remain outside the grasp of my consciousness, I've become confident they will all return eventually, and the important thing is that I have recovered my sense of self, my personality and unique outlook on life. Whether Andrew's old mother is still alive, I neither know nor care; his memories of her remain with me for now, but she means no more to me than any other stranger. And the same with his kids, Geoff and Lucy; I no longer feel tempted to find out how they're getting on.

What I do regret after this incredible experience is my treatment of Helen. If I could love, then I think I would have loved her. It may be Andrew's personality has left some lasting impressions on me, perhaps rekindled feelings for her I must have felt twenty-five years ago. Certainly, I've retained his view that she was a lovely woman in every respect. I should have been more discreet, more careful. I do not intend to make the same mistakes with Shivi. And, looking on the bright side, she's a much younger model.

I stub out the butt of my cigarette on the grass, treading on it for good measure as I get off the lounger. She's had long enough. Ready or not, here comes Matt!

CHAPTER 39

I discard my flip-flops on the patio and walk into the lounge, standing at the foot of the open tread stairs that rise towards the solitary, large bedroom and adjoining bathroom. I can't hear Shivi up there; in fact, the silence is only broken by a distant rumble that builds quickly into the roar of a tractor as it passes in the lane hugging the high garden hedge. I go back and close the patio doors to kill the sound of it fading into the distance.

I call up the stairs, "I'm on my way, Poppet. Dying to see the new outfit and do it justice." It's pathetic, I know, but she seems to like it when I call her 'Poppet', and nobody else will ever know. But there's no answer, which is strange. Normally, I'd expect a raunchy response, or at least to hear her giggling. But she is delightfully unpredictable, so perhaps she's changed her mind about the sexy gear and is silently waiting for me, prostrate and naked on the king-sized bed.

I climb the stairs, pausing halfway up to glance out the landing window which looks onto most of the front drive. The double gates are open to the lane which swings round from the rear garden to the front of the property. I thought I'd closed them when we got back last night. It was late, though, and I'd had plenty to drink. Easy mistake to make, I guess. Pushing my head closer to the glass, I check either side but can't see Shivi's Peugeot anywhere. She must have parked it daintily in the small recess at the other side of the cottage, rather than just leaving it at the front. She'd only had one glass of wine herself, although I'd assured her there was not much chance of encountering Her Majesty's Constabulary on these quiet Cornish roads at such a late hour.

I climb the remaining stairs, and at the top my eyes dart to the bed, keen to fall upon the smooth contours of my lover's body. But it is empty, made up, the coverlet neatly in place over the pillows at the headboard. Not at all like we'd left it this morning.

"Hello, Matthew."

I freeze and my heart jumps. It can't be, surely not. But there is no mistaking Michael Shapiro's mocking voice. I lurch towards the bed from where I can see his stocky frame consuming the Lloyd loom chair in a corner alcove to my left.

"It's you!" I gasp.

Overcome with a wave of nausea and feeling faint, I ease onto the end of the bed. My breathing has become heavy, racing my heart, and my chest is tight; it's such a terrible shock, and yet he looks so calm and relaxed as I stare at his grey beard and those straggling whiskers. I haven't seen him since our meeting in the cells immediately after I had been sentenced, just over a year ago, and I know from his odious grin that this reunion is no cause for celebration.

I feel the adrenaline pumping through my veins; I must try to get away. I stand up and glance around me, look back down the stairs.

"There's nowhere to run. Did you really think you could escape us, after everything I explained to you so carefully two years ago? ... You'd better sit down on the bed again."

Oh shit, suddenly I remember Shivi. "What have you bastards done with Shivani? I've told her nothing, as we agreed. I've kept my bargain, not said a word to anyone." My deep voice is wracked with panic, disjointed and shaking. And I feel cold, despite the warm weather; I'm trembling as I slump back onto the bed. "Has my liaison with Shivi caused the loss of another innocent life?"

"She is not so innocent as you might think." He smirks, and it is frightening to feel the menace emanating from him – where is my kindly protector now?

"More of the same: hypocritical self-justification for another murder?" I accuse him, my shrill voice full of anger, and I am surprised at the depth of feeling I seem to be experiencing for this young woman. I can't seem to fully rid myself of Andrew's naivety and sentimentality.

The fat man leans forward, his piercing eyes fixing me with a sardonic smile. "You have only ever been interested in one thing, Matthew. You're totally self-centred. What efforts have you made to get to know Shivani, consider her interests and what might be best for her?"

"And you, your people have, I suppose." I can't disguise the bitterness I feel towards him and the agency. Whatever I might be guilty of, I am not a murderer. All I had intended was for Andrew's body to live on with the benefit of all my experience and education. "Is she safe?" I ask him.

"Such touching concern." The bastard is openly mocking me. "If you're truly interested, then I can reassure you that Shivani is perfectly safe. In fact, she is already on her way to enjoy a well-earned holiday before she returns to concentrate on pursuing her stellar legal career."

"What do you mean?" He is making no sense.

"How do you suppose we know the experiment has failed, and that Matthew Campbell is back and scheming? …Imagine all that money you might have had, Matthew. A fortune to live like a king on the subcontinent. We'd been unable to trace it, but when you told Shivani your plans last night, to abscond with access to all that stolen money, that's when we knew for certain."

"No," I stammer, confused, "you're guessing, bluffing, but you're wrong. I am still Andrew," I lie. But how do they know about last night? I guess they've not stopped following me, but I've noticed nothing and I'm ever watchful. In the restaurant I was careful not to be overheard. There's hardly been time to force it from Shivi, has there? How long was I smoking that cigarette in the garden?

He is staring at me, his contempt obvious. "Ask me anything about my life," I say. "I can prove I am Andrew, like I did with Helen and Cathy. You *know*..." I implore him to believe my lie. I have to take the risk. After all, plenty of Andrew's memories still infect my head.

"Indeed, we know." He laughs. "Do you think an attractive young woman like Shivani Kapoor would look twice at an ageing, overweight lothario like you?"

What is he saying? Surely Shivi hasn't told them? She's crazy for me. I can't believe this.

"We've suspected for some time," he says, "well before your release from prison, that Matthew's memories were reverting, Andrew's slowly fading. But we couldn't be sure. Poor Peter Cheung was in denial.

"The irony is, if you'd been able to resist Shivani and just disappeared with your money and false identity, you might have got away with it. Unlike you, Matthew, not to see the risk of involving someone else. Maybe it's the remaining influence of a good man that's undone you. A kind of karma, don't you think?" The bastard is really enjoying himself.

My head is in my hands. And a strange thing happens. I start to cry. Big drops crawling down my cheeks. I can't remember ever crying before – apart from when the weakling Andrew Soulsby had control of me – not even as a child. I guess it's the sudden, visceral shock of betrayal, devastation at the prospect of a fine new life lost, and the fear of what is to come.

How could Shivi do this? How did she know? Her affection and desire, her infatuation with my wealth and power, her bad boy; it was all so real... surely? I still can't see her as a fraud and a traitor.

I look up at him, still smirking at me with sadistic pleasure. Suddenly, I feel tired and almost resigned to my fate. And I do feel genuine regret when it strikes me that I've always judged others by my own standards to justify taking advantage of them whenever I could. What if Andrew, the man who was in my head for so long, was not a freak exception to my rule of innate human greed and selfishness?

"Somehow, you've got to Shivi, and she's told you about the money. And you've drawn the wrong conclusions, because I'm still more Andrew than Matthew." There is no conviction in the lie, but the instinct for self-preservation has not yet wholly abandoned me, it seems. The possibility I am telling the truth might just help when they decide what to do with me.

"You don't get it, do you?" He is glowering at me. "She's always worked for us. Some of our agents are 'sleepers' we call on when needed. They occupy – or are destined to occupy – powerful positions in commerce, the professions and industry. And Shivani is destined for the highest echelons of the legal world.

"Although Peter Cheung's research had been progressing well, we became worried about your involvement, particularly when we found out about your affair with him. You represented a potential loose cannon. Shivani was instructed to instigate the 'secret affair' to keep you close. That's why she was transferred to your department at Dorrell's, and you couldn't believe your luck, could you?

"Secretly, she delved into your files, pored over the account ledgers and discovered your penchant for stealing clients' money. Later we were able to use this, instigate the firm's money laundering report and the police investigation. That would have put you out of harm's way for years, but your desperate plan was a surprise which suited us: you as the guinea pig for the first human experiment, until the shenanigans with Peter forced us to improvise."

He sounds proud of this duplicity, and in a crazy way it's helping me, reinforcing my life view of human nature. Of course, Andrew was an exception to the rule. But this is still a crushing blow: Shivi, another spy.

"I don't think I told her anything of consequence," I offer pathetically.

"You did well," he compliments me, and I think he means it. This man is not so unlike me. "There was no hint of the secret research at Wilkinson's, no suggestion of your illicit relationship with Peter. Even at the height of passion your mask as her only lover never slipped. She was impressed, I'll tell you, that the charm and fabricated falsehoods never faltered: you as a victim, the frustrated husband living in a sham marriage to an actress wife who had long since grown bored with him.

"If the memories haven't gone yet you may recall Shivani's attempts to get close to Andrew? We arranged for her to rent the flat in Palmers Green to try and cultivate him when your plan was first hatched. We needed to find out as much as we could of his character and personality. There was a 'chance' meeting in a coffee shop, but he refused to succumb to her flirting; an altogether stronger man." Again, the stare as he pauses, his accusation smacking of derision.

What nonsense. I know how weak Andrew was; frightened of his own shadow, and so serious. He was too scared of life to have fun and enjoy himself. But I remain silent.

"What a pity for you, Matthew," he continues after a moment, "that the experiment didn't work as Peter anticipated to extract his revenge on you. If it had – and we believed the signs to be good at the start – you would be a good man with a decent life left to live, atoning for the sins of a man you'd never really known, the man whose body you inhabited. As it is…" and he lets it hang, shifting nervously in his seat, crossing one leg on his knee. "I never enjoy this." For the first time he appears anxious, and he is not the sort of man who ever presents as anxious.

No longer remotely reconciled to my fate, now I'm frightened. "What do you mean? I'll co-operate fully, have all your tests and answer every question truthfully to help you find out what went wrong... Really, there is so much of Andrew left. Please, Michael." I appeal to him, but my normally powerful voice is shallow, my whole body shaking and I can't control it.

"I'm sorry, Matthew. We could never trust you again. And Peter needs to dissect that selfish, big brain of yours to find out exactly what's happening in there. It's the only way, apparently, and he is really looking forward to it. 'Hell, hath no fury', and his final revenge will be in the interests of medical research..."

Terrified, with sweat on my forehead and dripping from my armpits, my heart jumping like a firecracker, I stare open-eyed around me. Michael Shapiro is making no attempt to move, just sitting there. I look to the stairs again.

"No escape down there," he says, and for confirmation I hear muffled voices and what sounds like furniture being shifted below.

"Dear God, please don't do this. There must be another way. I can be useful to you alive." I know my appeals are useless, but I'm desperate, clutching at straws. "Please."

"I am not going to do anything." He smiles like the kindly uncle one more time. But it's obvious he intends no reprieve.

The bathroom. It's not more than six paces. I can lock myself in, maybe jump from the window onto the flat-roof extension of the kitchen below, then scramble to the drive and run for as long as my heart will last.

I leap up, rush for the bathroom door. Almost there, but before I reach the door it swings open, and a tall, hooded man – my executioner – stares at me through slits for his wide, red eyes. He raises a handgun with a long silencer pointing at my chest. I'm wetting myself, losing control of my bowels.

Shapiro's voice sounds like it's in the distance, telling me I have only myself to blame. I hear, "Goodbye," then a thud, like someone punching my chest...

Oblivion.

For writing and publishing news, or recommendations of new titles to read, sign up to the Book Guild newsletter: